WITCH'S CURSE

BY

SLOANE MURPHY

Witch's Curse
The Shadow Weaver #1
Part of The Seven Realms Saga

Published by Hudson Indie Ink
www.hudsonindieink.com

Witch's Curse/Sloane Murphy – 2nd ed.
ISBN-13 - 978-1-915118-04-2

And here you are... living despite it all

- RUPI KAUR

ONE

FALLON

SIX MONTHS AGO

Lying to your best friend for your entire life is the absolute fucking worst. It's even worse when she finds out the truth and her entire world spins off its axis. I'm trying to be there for her as much as I can. But I mean, I've known about our world since I was born. Keeping it from her, from them all until they aged into their awakening, has been an absolute nightmare.

You'd think I'd be relieved that the people closest to me all know the truth about who they are now. But Remy… well, there's more to it for her than the rest of us. I know that Mama has seen her path change a dozen times, which is one hell of a downside of being a Witch with a Mama who's a seer. Will she ever tell me my own path? Or will she just let things come to pass? She barely tells me what she's seen full stop, which means when my best friend tells me the shit she's going through, I kinda want to throw things because Mama probably saw it coming.

If only I'd gotten that trait. I've had my powers since birth, but my defining ability still hasn't emerged. I try not to be salty about it. All of my friends know their truths and powers now, and while they had to wait for it, at least they never knew that they were missing something. I've known my entire existence that something isn't there.

Even with my sigil of dominance around my neck—the sigil of my coven—my powers are still growing too slowly. I mean, I'm an heir. I'm not even close to hopeless, but the call for more power, more magic, is always there. It's a slippery slope. Many before me have fallen for the lure of more, but I've seen what happens.

Power destroys people. It ruins so many lives when it's in the wrong hands. Magic is no different. Too much in the wrong hands can have disastrous outcomes.

Though, I mean falling in love with your best friend's brother doesn't promise the best outcomes either. Not when he's a Hunter and Faction law is everything. The Hunters' Code is the one Colt lives by. He ignored it for a while.

After his awakening, we grew close. I was the only person other than his older brother, Bauer, that he could really talk to. And Bauer isn't exactly a talker.

But then, he left to keep the others safe. I get it, but that didn't make it any easier.

It didn't make it hurt less when he got back and told me that there was no future for us either. I'm a Witch. He's a Hunter. It's as simple as that if you ask him. Apparently, I'm not worth the risk of falling in love. I'm mortal, and he isn't. Well, not exactly. Those weren't his exact words, but that was the crux of it.

"Fuck!" I shout as I drop the vial of Dracul blood I've been working with and it smashes on the floor. My mama's shop keeps me busy while my friends are off living their lives, but I long for more. I was meant for more than this, and I know it. I'm careful to not cut myself as I pick up the shards. Dracul blood does terrible things to Witches. It isn't something I ever want to experience. I shudder even at the thought. I'm finishing with wiping the last of the mess up when the bell rings at the door.

My hand goes to my hip as I stand looking Colt Bennett over. Damn, why does the boy have to be so *hot?* Not that he wasn't good looking before he left, but now, with that extra swagger, the muscles, the tattoos, and piercings, I find myself trying not to drool. I should not be drooling. He made his thoughts and intentions more than clear, but damn, my lady boner don't seem to want to listen."Colt, what the hell do you want?"

"I was looking for you." He smiles and his dimples pop, and I swear to the holy mother, this boy was put on the Earth to test my willpower. I'm a sucker for those dimples.

"Don't you come here with that smile and try to sweet talk me, Colt Bennett. You had your chance, and you turned it down. Now, what do you want?" My sass-o-meter might be all the way up, but I think it might be the only way I teach myself to distance myself from him.

"I would never try to sweet talk you. Only a fool would let you go and then do that." I roll my eyes at him and move behind the counter. I need something between us, and on such short notice, this will have to do.

"Colt, you have ten seconds before I shimmy your ass straight out that door."

"It's a fine ass though," he says with a wink, and I grip the edges of the counter. Goddess help me. I narrow my eyes in his direction, and he offers me a sheepish smile. "Fine, fine. I need a favor."

"Of course you do." I sigh. "What do you want, Colt?"

"I need to know what's going on with my sister. Remy is being way too cagey, which isn't like her. Though she usually does up and disappear by this time when she awakens, but still. It's weird, and I'm worried."

"Colt, I'm not telling you one fucking thing about

Remy and what she's dealing with. If you want to know what's going on with her, ask her your damn self."

"You think I haven't tried? She won't tell me a damn thing."

"Then maybe keep your nose outta her business and focus on your own shit," I tell him as I cross my arms. "She's my best friend. I ain't telling you shit."

"Come on, Fallon. I'm worried about her," he says with a heavy sigh. I swear if it was anyone else, I'd say he was whining, but Colt doesn't whine. He usually gets his way because that's part of his charm, but not today, buddy.

"I said no, Colt. If there's nothing else, I need to clean all this shit up, and then I have a coven meeting. My life does not revolve around Hunter bullshit."

"Fine, I'm sorry. I thought that since we were close…"

I sigh and pinch the bridge of my nose before looking back up at him. The audacity of this guy. "Colt, we weren't close. I had a crush on you, we fucked it out a few times, and then you decided that being with a Witch was beneath you. Goddess forbid your daddy found out about you slumming it and not keeping the Hunter lines 'pure' or whatever bullshit it was you fed me. We're done."

"Don't be like that, Fallon. I came here because I was worried about my sister, not to hash this shit out again. I've tried to say I'm sorry a dozen times over. I was a jackass, but that doesn't make it any less true. There's a reason factions don't mix. I'm terrified that whatever has my sister this cagey will get her killed. If anything happens to her because she's not focused…"

"She'll be fine, Colt. She's a big girl. More than that, she's Remington Bennett. That girl would survive the apocalypse. You know it. I know it. Hell, our entire goddamn world knows it. Focus on not getting yourself killed, yeah? "

"If whatever she's hiding gets her into trouble…."

" I'll be on her side if they do," I spit, and Colt's eyes narrow in my direction. I cross my arms over my chest, staring him down. Remy's my best friend. If she's in the thick of it, I'm gonna be right there with her. "Maybe if you were a little less close-minded, she'd trust you enough to tell you what's going on with her, but it's not my place to tell you a goddamn thing. Now if that's all, I got shit to do."

"Fine, Fallon, but I think you need to remember that we can still be friends even though things ended badly between us," he says and turns to leave the store.

I sigh as my arms drop to my sides. Why the hell doesn't he get this? He turns back to face me, and I look him dead in the eye and give him the only truth I have. "We were never friends, Colt."

The moon is rising in the dark sky when we reach the clearing. Mama moves ahead of me, setting the wards and the ring of protection before we call the other covens to the meeting. Mama's the high priestess, which means things tend to work more on our time than the others. There's always been some resentment over the later meetings, but grumblings aren't anything new and nothing Marie Laveau can't handle.

It's been a month since we met with the covens, and even though this is our standard lunar cycle meeting, it feels like it's more urgent than that. Mama had a vision last night, and she's been on edge ever since, like this meeting couldn't come quickly enough. It makes me nervous. Mama usually isn't so easily shaken.

I join her, helping her set the circle by drawing each coven's sigil in blood at an even distance around it. Our sigil, the dominance sigil, is at the top of the circle.

"Are you ready?" she asks, and I nod before taking her hand. Our blood combines and drops to the ground at our feet.

"Vocamus matri et sorori vestrae Misericordiam adducere nos ut et in hac lunae iungere nobis. Inhabitare facit unius moris in unum sicut et nos venit. Sit dea."

I follow Mama's chant, bringing our coven sisters under the protection of our circle, while bringing them here to us. One by one, the covens join us and add their power to the call until everyone has arrived.

The power in the circle ripples over my skin, making me feel alive. It's hard to explain unless you're here, and in tune with the power of the Earth, but it's exhilarating.

"Welcome sisters, we wish you well," Mama says, her voice deepening and changing like it always does when we're here. It's like she's not Mama at all, but a powerhouse of a Witch who could literally rule the world. And well, I guess since she's the head of the world's Witches, she almost does.

Demetera, Angelina, Lizzie, Ilaria, Jodi, and Bree make up the rest of the Witches Council with Mama, and each of them have their heirs with them as is tradition. The heirs come to all meetings once we turn eighteen, to prepare us to take over when the time comes. It isn't something I like to think about, but then, I don't really like being an heir either. Sure, extra power comes with it, but so does a shit ton of extra responsibility.

"Before I begin, does anyone have anything they need to raise?" Mama asks the circle, and the heirs remain quiet. Seen but not heard is usually the tradition with us, though that doesn't always go as planned. I'm not super great at keeping my mouth shut all the time.

"I checked the cards, not two nights past," Ilaria says loudly. "Something is coming, something that will change the very foundation of who and what we are. We need to know more. We need to prepare." Murmurs go up around the group as people panic a little, but Mama raises her hand and quiet descends around us once more.

"Anything else?"

"There has been some desertion of coven members in a few covens. I know mine has suffered, as has Lizzie's," Angelina adds. "It usually wouldn't be much cause for concern, rogues are a well-known thing, but the rogue activity seems to have increased. As if they're forming their own coven."

"Thank you." Mama nods, as if she were already aware of it, and a pit forms in my stomach. She's not telling me something; I can feel it. Something *is* wrong.

When no one else speaks up, Mama continues, " I'm aware of some of this already. I had a vision last night, and something is definitely coming. It is much bigger than us. A change like we haven't seen since the War of the Fallen..." She pauses, letting her words sink in. Everyone just looks shocked, but the taste of fear coats my tongue. "But this is not our fight alone. Change is coming to the factions. If you'll please join hands, I will share the vision with you."

I take her hand in mine and clasp the other with Bree, the leader of our Australian coven. Once all hands are linked, I close my eyes and wait for Mama to show us.

Except I see nothing but darkness. I hear screams and

the gasps of those around us.

What the fuck is going on?

I keep my mouth shut, knowing this has to be Mama's doing. That or the vision has me in it. It's the only reason I wouldn't be able to see it. So I can't affect the outcome.

Why wouldn't she tell me? Why let me find out like this ?

She knows the others won't share it with me, so the only way I'm going to find out is from her.

The darkness ends, and I pull my hands out of theirs and fold my arms across my body. I might not say anything, but that doesn't mean I'm going to not react either.

"Is there anything we can do?" Bree asks, and it feels like everyone's looking at me. Though I'm sure that's my insecurity speaking, but I stand tall and try to not let it show.

"Not for now. If the heirs wouldn't mind giving us a moment, I have something else I would like to discuss with the coven leaders."

And like that, we're dismissed.

I leave the circle, the other heirs behind me, silent as can be as we walk toward the tree line of the clearing.

"Fallon…" Ella starts. She's Bree's daughter and heir, but I shake my head.

"Don't," I say quietly. I don't want Mama to overhear. It's not anyone's duty but hers to tell me things like this, and I don't want anyone in trouble on my behalf. "Don't worry about it. I get it. You guys really can't say anything. It sucks that Mama didn't warn me beforehand so I'd be a little more… I don't know, composed?"

"I get that," Charlotte, Lizzie's heir, says, looking at me with pity.

"It is what it is. Anyway, how's things for you guys? Any new gossip?"

"My life is dull. Mum only lets me study and practice," Charlotte sighs.

"Same," Daniella, Ilaria's heir, speaks up.

I suppose I have some things to be thankful for at least.

"What about you? Did you score that Hunter you've been simping over for forever?" Jacqui, Demetera's heir, asks, and I bristle at the sound of her snide voice.

"Leave her alone, Jacqui. Just because you haven't been touched by anything with a dick doesn't mean you get to take out your crazy on Fallon," Cassie, Jodi's heir, pipes up. I always knew I liked her.

Ella pulls me aside and away from the others. I've always been closest to her out of all the heirs. The others find it weird that I could be as close to a Hunter as I am to Remy, but they don't understand. And I kinda get that. I don't really expect them to understand it. Most people know who Remy was in her past lives, but they don't know her now. A Hunter reborn is different in each life, even when they get their memories back. The Remy in this life is far more bold and brazen, but she has more heart than ever before too.

"So come on, spill. You were practically glowing before," Ella gushes, and I laugh. So I fill her in on everything that's been going on here, with Remy finding out she was a Hunter, about Colt and Creek returning, and what happened between me and Colt.

"Holy crap," she gasps. "I knew he'd have a huge dick. I knew it. Colt Bennett is legendary in a whole different way from his sister."

"He's not like that, not really. Well, not in this life. I wish things could go back to how they were before."

ONE MONTH AGO

"Well, that wasn't quite what I expected," I laugh as I climb from Colt's truck.

"It was dinner," he shrugs with that cheeky smirk of his as he takes my hand and walks me to the door of his apartment building. This place is so freaking swanky, but it makes total sense for him. Colt couldn't move out and get a normal place like the rest of us. No, he had to have top of the line luxury. He's like a kid in a man's body.

"It was a fancy dinner," I joke as the elevator doors open and he pushes me inside of it.

"A pretty girl deserves a fancy dinner." His breath brushes against my ear as he stands behind me, and my entire body shivers in response. "Especially this pretty girl."

He reaches around me and pushes the button to the fifteenth floor as the doors close behind him. His lips touch my neck, and I swear my legs start to quiver while my heart beats so hard I think it might come out of my chest. We've been dancing around our attraction for months. Via FaceTime, text, calls while he was MIA, halfway across the world. I've had it bad for Colt Bennett for most of my life and now it's finally real.

Holy shit.

He pushes me up against the wall of the elevator and kisses me until I'm breathless. It isn't like I haven't been hoping for this moment. Hell, I wore this little black dress and scarlet lacy undies for a reason, but damn. I didn't wanna hope this much.

It's weird fantasizing about something for so long and then having it in your grasp.

I tense, my knuckles aching with the effort to keep my fingers wrapped around the waist-high rail that runs along all three panels of the elevator.

"Shh, relax. I won't bite." Colt leans down to come eye

to eye with me, his signature crooked grin making me feel marginally better. "Unless you beg me to, then all bets are off."

That gets a snort out of me, and I relax a little.

Placing his index finger at my chin and lifting my gaze to his, he takes my bottom lip between his teeth and bites down gently before whispering into my mouth, "I'm going to kiss you again."

I nod, but only barely. His stare is so damn mesmerizing that words escape me.

But when his mouth glides along my lips, his tongue soothing the small sting of pain from his teeth, my desire for him bursts into uncontrollable flames at my core. I can feel how wet he makes me as he gives me a preview with his mouth of what he's gonna do to my body. The bar in his tongue intensifies the entire experience, and I can't help but wonder how it would feel against my clit. My legs tremble with the thought.

We both jump at the sound of the ding announcing our arrival on his apartment floor. The steel doors slide open, and the opulence of his building slaps me in the face.

"Colt Bennett doesn't do anything in half measures, does he?" I laugh, and he grins at me again.

With speed that would make mere mortals envious, Colt bends and lifts me onto his shoulder in a fireman's carry, swatting my ass as he does so. I squeal at the sting, but it only makes me want him more.

"Where would be the fun in that? Going all the way is always the better choice."

I don't miss the double entendre of his phrase. If I had a doubt before then, he more than squashed it. It's clear as day that I'm about to get fucked. Quite literally. And I'm hoping I'm about to get fucked thoroughly.

I have a hard time making out anything about his apartment since my head is upside down. It doesn't help that I'm very busy slapping his ass and yelling at him to let me down either. If the floor is any indication, though, a lot of money has been dropped into this place.

We're somewhere in the middle of his living room when he slides me down his torso. Colt keeps his hands on me the whole time, stepping closer until he backs me against the couch. My knees bend against the cushions, forcing me to fall backward and sit.

My little black dress rides up my legs, and it doesn't escape Colt's notice. In fact, his eyes fixate on the bare skin of my tan thighs. If I had to guess, he can definitely see my red panties from his vantage point.

His nostrils flare, and his sea blue eyes shine with lust.

"Tell me, Fal," he drops to his knees and places his hands on my skin. The touch ignites a series of sparks that run from where his fingers dig into my flesh all the way down to my pussy and all the way up to my nipples. "When

you put those on tonight, were you hoping I'd take them off?"

His liquid blue gaze shoots to meet mine. He watches me, anticipating my answer, as though it's the most important thing he could possibly need to know.

"No." The disappointment on his face is palpable, so I put him out of his misery. "I was hoping you'd rip them off."

The sound that erupts from Colt is animalistic. He sounds more like a lion than a man. Reaching back, he bends his head to pull his t-shirt off his body, throwing it on the couch beside us. Damn, why is it so hot when guys do that?

My eyes immediately zero in on his nipple piercings, and it sends a jolt of lightning straight to my clit. What a fun little surprise.

"I've wanted this for so long, Fal. Too long. I want to take my time, and I want to devour you until you can't remember your own name."

Without a thought, my thighs spread to accommodate his hips and he takes the cue for what it is.

"How about you fuck me until I can't see, and then we'll go back for slow seconds? If you can go again, that is," I tease. Colt is nothing if not competitive. He can give me his carefree boyish charm all day long, but when it comes to a challenge, he's always ready to win. This is a

challenge I definitely want him to crush.

"Oh, Fal," he croons, his voice dripping with delicious warning, "remember you said that later when you're too sore to walk."

We laugh, the sound echoing throughout his immense apartment, but my laughter dies in my throat when he reaches beneath my little black dress and rips my panties into two pieces.

"Well, one fantasy down, a few more to go." His words barely register as my body shudders under his touch. He pulls me down by my thighs which makes my dress ride up to my waist, exposing my pussy to him completely.

I'm bare from the waist down, and he's naked from the waist up.

When his beautiful, full lips latch onto me, I whimper with pleasure. He's kissing me, his mouth moving like a lover. His tongue spears into me, the barbell reaching places I didn't know it possibly could. Licking and biting, he circles my clit before resuming his buffet.

I can't stop watching him as he eats me. It's addictive, and so fucking erotic, seeing exactly what he's doing to me. How much he's enjoying himself. It's almost enough to push me over the edge.

"Colt, oh Goddess, that's so..."

He spreads me wider, his hand moving to my ass and pulling me closer as though he can't get enough of me. It's a heady feeling, knowing my body is making someone like Colt mad with lust. It's empowering.

My hands go to his head, fingers digging into his scalp and curling around the smooth silk of his hair. My hips begin to thrust up, reaching for his mouth. Wanting more. Always more.

Colt's groan vibrates throughout my entire body, and it ignites a fire inside me that I can't stop. That I don't want to stop, ever.

And when he wraps his lips around my clit and pushes two fingers inside my pussy, I lose my ever-loving mind. I let out a cry, his name echoing between the four walls of his home. And still, he doesn't stop. I try to pull away, the sensation way too intense, but he doesn't loosen his grip, or stop his onslaught.

"Colt, oh my goddess, I can't..."

"Yes, you can."

He sends me over the edge and then he's back at it, devouring me like a starved man. His fingers curl inside me and reach a part of me that makes my hips jolt off the couch as I gasp for air.

My second orgasm hits me like a truck, the sensation so vivid and wild that I think I actually black out for a second. Because the next thing I know, Colt has his jeans off and my dress is no longer on my body.

Holy shit, his cock. It looked big through his jeans, but

holy Goddess of the Earth.

It's a monster.

We're both naked, and he's lying on top of me, his eyes searing a trail of fire everywhere they land. I'm so hot for him right now. He could ask anything of me, and I wouldn't even think twice.

Hell, I wouldn't think at all because I'm pretty sure my brain is fried from two back-to-back, earth-shattering orgasms.

"Fal?"

I can't really speak so I look at him, feeling the head of his cock sliding slowly through the juices of my pussy like he has all the time in the world.

"Hang on, baby. I'm about to rock your fucking world."

I don't have time to tell him that he already has. His dick slams inside of me until he's fully seated to the hilt, his balls slapping against me.

I'm so full, and he's so big, I'm not sure I'll be able to move or do anything.

But I'm so wrong.

Colt pulls back slowly, letting me feel every goddamn inch of his cock before he slams back into me again.

Over and over, he thrusts inside me like he has hours and could go all damn night.

It's torture. Slow, achingly pleasurable torture, and he knows it.

I reach behind him, nails digging into his back, urging him to give me more.

With one last crooked grin, he bends his head and kisses me like he kissed my pussy, and then he lets completely loose. His tongue fucks my mouth in rhythm with his cock, and the double assault is nearly overwhelming. As though he can feel that he's fucking me stupid, he takes total and complete control, holding me down and pistoning into me like a man on a mission. Every time his groin rubs up against my clit, my body shudders.

I come for a third time, but this time it's more intense, more beautiful. Colt comes right along with me, and I milk his cock. His seed spills so deep inside me, I can feel it against the walls of my core.

It's so fucking hot. Watching him throw his head back, eyes closed, mouth open, I hope to the goddess my body recovers because this is definitely something I want to do again.

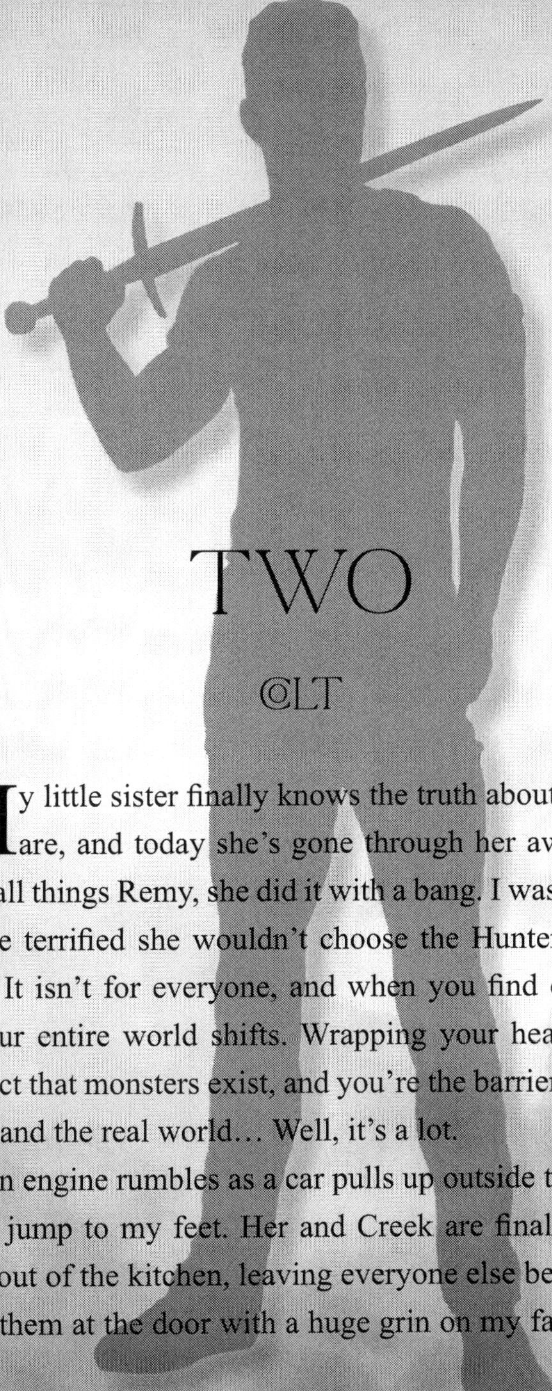

TWO

COLT

My little sister finally knows the truth about what we are, and today she's gone through her awakening. Like all things Remy, she did it with a bang. I was honestly a little terrified she wouldn't choose the Hunter life this time. It isn't for everyone, and when you find out about it, your entire world shifts. Wrapping your head around the fact that monsters exist, and you're the barrier between them and the real world… Well, it's a lot.

An engine rumbles as a car pulls up outside the house, and I jump to my feet. Her and Creek are finally here. I head out of the kitchen, leaving everyone else behind, and meet them at the door with a huge grin on my face. "Hey, little sister. Welcome to the clan for reals."

"You're such a goofball, Colt," she says, nudging me out of the way. I can't help but laugh as she walks through the house to the kitchen where everyone else is waiting. I follow behind her, laughing still.

"Yeah, but you wouldn't change me for the world!" The crowd in the kitchen is noticeably silent as we step inside.

"So, that was fun," she finally says, shrugging before taking a seat at the table and grabbing a donut. I stay standing, off to the side and watching her. This day will continue to be a lot for her. There's a lot to wrap your mind around as the memories start to filter back in.

"Remy," my dad starts, but Maddie, Creek's mom and our surrogate mom, interrupts him.

"Now then, her memories won't be back fully for the next few days, so no questions. From any of you." She pins each of us with a look that says she won't be taking shit from any of us, and Nate laughs next to her.

"My wife, badass, mother extraordinaire, and layer down of the law." He takes a sip from the mug in his hand, his eyes still dancing with laughter.

"Don't you start." She rolls her eyes at him, and I murmur in agreement. Their love is almost sickening. I mean, one day a love like that will be a life goal, but right now? Not so much.

"Remy is marked by Leviathan," Creek drops, and I swing to look at him before returning my gaze to my sister. Holy fucking shit. Bauer, our big brother, will lose his shit over this. He's such a nerd, he probably jacked off over his history books when he found out about our true past.

"Leviathan? That isn't possible," my dad says as Bauer leaves the room, practically running up the stairs in what I can only assume is in the direction of the library on the third floor. See, nerd. "Remy, will you show us your mark?"

"Sure, I showed Creek already, " she says, standing up and lifting her top. I move so I don't see my sister's tits and take in the sight of her mark. "I don't understand what the big deal is though?" It's fucking insane, I think it might be…

"Erm, Remy, it's still growing," Creek cuts me off, voicing my exact thought. I swear, we were close before the whole Hunter reveal thing. But when he joined me all those months ago after his awakening—to protect Remy from knowing the truth about what she was before she was ready—it's more like he's my brother from another mother. Literally.

"Growing?" Remy asks, and I understand the wariness in her tone. This is a whole new territory for all of us. None of us have ever been Angel marked. It's a fucking *huge* thing.

"Yes, sweetheart," Maddie says softly as she moves

closer to inspect the mark. "I've never seen anything like it, but it's beautiful. It's on the back of your neck, and from what I can tell, it's growing across your shoulder."

She pulls the back of Remy's t-shirt from her neck and hums. "Just as I thought. Your Hunter Mark is there, in the middle at the base of your neck, but it is surrounded by the mark of Leviathan. There's something extra that I don't recognize, though. It's like roots, or vines, with bursts of color and symbols. I imagine Bauer will want to start looking into this straight away."

"Will I not just remember what it means?" Remy asks, sounding as confused as I feel. What the actual fuck happened to her in her last life for *this* to happen? I keep my mouth shut. I know better than to try and weigh in on this stuff. The book smart thing isn't my bag. I'm the guy who storms the building *after* the book stuff. I know my strengths, and this isn't one of them, but I'll be here supporting my little sister no matter what.

"Not necessarily," Bauer says as he re-enters the room with a book bound in brown leather that looks older than anything I've ever seen. He sits across from Remy at the table and opens the book as everyone else sits back down.

"This is the mark of the Hunter," he says, showing her an image on a page, and I peek over her shoulder to get a look too. It's not like it's something I haven't seen before; I have my own mark on my hand. Though I keep it surrounded by other ink so it isn't so obvious.

"Is that Latin?" she asks, and Bauer nods.

"It is the old language," my dad says from across the room.

"Once your memories return, you'll be able to read it, write it, and speak it as well as the rest of us. And anything that's missing, Bauer can help you with," Nate tells her, as if trying to reassure her. She looks like she's about to drown, and my heart hurts in my chest for her. It's already a lot to take in. I can't imagine what all this Angel marked shit is doing to her too.

"Okay. Can I see that?" she asks Bauer who nods and spins the book so she can look at the image. She studies the Hunter's mark like her life depends on it. It's a circle wrapped in vines with a sword through the middle. The hilt is above the circle, as if the sword is piercing it.

"Every Hunter has one," Bauer says and lifts his arm to show her his wrist, surrounded by tattoos so that it's almost indiscernible. "We tend to disguise them when they're in an obvious place so it isn't like a beacon to the other factions. They appear in different places in each life, but your old mark will be represented by a constellation, which people assume are weird birthmarks like you always have. The more marks, the more respect a Hunter is given in the community. Unless they have been cast out as rogues for whatever reason."

"We can be cast out?" she asks, looking over to my dad, Nate, and Maddie. I stay quiet because it's not my place to answer. Plus, I'm shit with words, so I move back and cling to the wall with Creek to give her some space. I stay close enough for her to know that I'm still here if she needs me.

"We can," Nate says solemnly. "It is unusual though. If a Hunter breaks our laws—depending on the crime—there are two punishments. Banishment, which is being cast out of the community, or death. Upon rebirth, if killed, Hunters are usually not given the choice again until they have cycled at least twice as a human as part of their punishment."

"Holy shit. Nice of you all to have left out these wonderful snippets of information until there's no turning back." I wince at her words, but there's nothing I can do about it now. I was too excited about her remembering all the kick-ass times we had. I figured someone else covered the darker stuff.

"Remy, you have never been cast out or killed for breaking laws," my dad says, and Nate looks at him. There's something going on there, but why it's being brought up in the middle of this conversation I have no idea, so I tuck it away for later. "I'm sure you have nothing to worry about."

"What exactly are the laws?" She looks back to Bauer

who is scanning the book again. “And is there a picture of Leviathan’s mark in there, or am I going to have to do a weird mirror jig later?”

“I’ll find you a picture of Leviathan’s mark,” he tells her, “but your mark is more than that, hence the book. As for our laws, there are a lot, most will likely come back to you but the most important ones are: do not betray your faction, do not allow humans to become aware of any faction, and no mixing of the factions under any circumstances.”

“No mixing of the factions? What the…?”

“There have been Hunters in our history who thought the monsters were more than the filth that they are,” my dad says with disgust. If only he knew about my dalliances, but then, I’ve only ever fucked around with Witches. I’m sure he wouldn’t mind that so much. He’s talking about the Dracul and the Lycans, and those are beasts I wouldn’t put my dick near if you paid me to. “They thought they could be saved; that they were not so different to us. Fools.”

“Oooohhhhh.” She leans back in her chair and takes in thc looks of disdain on the faces of everyone sharing the room with us. I’m not the only one who agrees with Dad about the other factions.

“Exactly, but for now, try not to worry about all of this. You need to focus on staying rested and letting the memories come back to you.”

“Well, actually, I was thinking we could have some fun

and see how much is back subconsciously," I pipe up with a grin. "Throwing competition, anybody?"

Nate and my dad laugh as Bauer and Creek roll their eyes.

"Really, Colt? You just don't want Remy to beat you," Maddie sighs with a smile, and I scoff.

"Hey, I'll take what I can get for as long as I can. I'm all about playing the odds to my advantage." I laugh because I'm always up for a challenge, but my sister, being who she is, usually kicks my ass... Except when she's in these early stages of awakening, and I really will take any advantage I can get. It's all about strategy, baby.

"What do you mean, 'throwing competition'?"

"Knife throwing," Creek tells her with a grin that matches my own. "It might be a stupid competition, but it's fun as shit. Plus, you used to kick everyone's ass, almost every time, so it might be nice. You know, treat you to some humility in case everything comes back before you need to hone your skills."

"Is this a good idea? I've never thrown knives in my life, and if my inability to throw so much as a ball is anything to go by, this could be dangerous."

"You'll be fine, we're Hunters. We're made of tougher stuff," I tell her cockily, beating my chest with my fist, barely able to hold back a laugh at my own ridiculousness.

"Or at least we heal quickly," Creek offers with a shrug.

"Why not?" Nate shrugs, and my dad shakes his head.

"Fine, come on. Let's get the targets set up. Colt, your idea, your responsibility, so you get to help me and Nate haul everything out of the shed." He strides across the room, smiling at Remy as he does, and heads out the back door into the back yard. I follow him out with Nate and Creek in tow.

We get the targets set up, with the usual ribbing from my dad and Nate. Creek and I are beyond used to it at this point because everything about most of our training is made to be a competition. We're a competitive bunch, and if that's what it takes to make us the best Hunters we can be, I'm all for it.

We set up five targets, each one further back than the one before it, with the fifth one so far back that even with my enhanced eyesight, it's hard to see the center black dot on the last target. Remy joins us, huffing when she sees the target.

"This doesn't look impossible at all." We all chuckle as she rolls her eyes, so I saunter over to her with her old set of throwing knives.

"It'll be good practice. You can always have a few practice shots at the trees if you want. Seems fair," I tell her cockily.

"Hand me the stupid knives," she demands, putting her hand out to me. I hand over the five blades and watch as she tests the balance of the knives. The action is so familiar, like muscle memory. My sister is in there somewhere, that's for sure. I can't help but wonder which Remy she'll be this time. A new Remy, this Remy but way more badass, or the scary Remy. Scary Remy is a warrior who has a thirst for blood like I've never seen on anyone else. I'm hoping for the second option because I love my little sister just as she is.

We move to the targets and each of the guys take their throw, and then I step up to the plate. Everyone else is coming close to the black dot but still hitting the yellow ring, but I'm determined to win this shit. I take a deep breath and throw. When my knife rides the line between black and yellow, I can't help but cuss. I step back from the throwing line and wave for Remy to take over.

She steps up to the mark on the ground and palms the knife. This motherfucker will beat me, even as a baby Hunter. Motherfucker.

She throws the first knife and it hits the yellow ring. Relief swells toward the surface. She didn't beat me, but damn she was close.

"Beginner's luck," I grumble.

"Don't be sore, Colt," Nate chuckles as my dad makes a note of who came closest and we get points, one to five depending where we hit.

The second target goes much the same, yellow rings all

round, but this time Remy takes third, and Nate grumbles too about stupid girls and beginner's luck. I send a prayer up to the Angels because I want to fucking win. Remy's always been amazing at this shit—it comes so easy to her. Sometimes it's hard being the brother of a legend, but I swallow down the evil green monster.

"This is why you have the Archer's mark," Creek says to her, explaining things to her a little. It's a whisper, but with my senses turned all the way up, it's hard to miss the conversation.

"I have what?" she asks.

"The Archer's mark, it's one of your constellations. You've always been an excellent marksman. Your constellations represent parts of you from each life. Colt knows all this, so I don't know why he always thinks he'll beat you. But he always tries with each new life. I like watching him eat his words."

Asshole, selling me out like that.

"Your turn, Creek," Nate says. Creek steps away from her and to the mark for the third target and hits the red ring with a shrug. My dad and Nate's knives land in the yellow, my dad's closer than Nate's, but still no black dot.

I swagger forward, pissed about that little comment of Creek's, determined to fucking nail this shot. I throw, but I fumble the throw, and kick at the ground as my knife lands, riding the line of red and yellow. "For fuck's sake."

"It's okay, you might still beat me," Remy goads, and I give her the finger, which only makes her laugh. "It's all good fun, you big baby. Suck it up."

She steps forward, taking the spot I was standing in and releases the knife, and I swear to the Fates I hold my fucking breath. It lands, riding the line of the yellow ring and the black dot.

"Well hot damn!" my dad whoops, "she's still got it." I swear, he's only ever proud of her. Remy can do no wrong in his eyes, ever. Again, I love her, but damn.

"That's my girl," he says as she walks past him and gives her a high five.

"You showing them how it's done?" Maddie calls out from the back porch, protecting her eyes from the sun.

"She sure is," Nate shouts back, and she laughs.

"Lunch is nearly done, so don't take too much longer."

"Yes, ma'am," Nate tells her with a salute, and I chuckle as she blows him a kiss. I wonder if my parents would still be as happy as they were if Mom was still alive.

We each throw at the fourth target, but the yellow ring is still holding me captive. My teeth grind when Remy takes top place with her knife grazing the center dot again.

"Last chance, Colt. You're third, and your sister is winning. You think you can take her? There's only a point in it," my dad goads as I step up to the mark.

"Shut it, old man. I've got this." I roll my shoulders

and stretch out my neck.

"Get on with it, and stop delaying the inevitable," Nate calls out with a laugh. Apparently they don't mind losing as much as I do, but then I'm not surprised, they're all rooting for her anyway. She's the baby. She's new, so her winning is the best thing for her feeling at ease with what she's going through right now, but I'm not about to throw the game. Remy can win fair and square without my help.

I throw my last knife and yell as my knife hits the center of the target. "Hell fucking yes. You can go eat crow, old man."

Nate waves me off with a laugh and goes to retrieve the knife. "Only fair that we clear the board for everyone on this one."

The others take their turns, none coming as close to the bullseye dot, but none of them seem to mind. Remy steps up to the mark, and Creek steps up behind her. "You've got this. I've seen you make this hit without even thinking about it more times than I can count. Your mind is remembering, even if you can't tell. Don't think, just let go."

I watch in fascination as she takes a deep breath, focusing herself and then closes her fucking eyes before throwing.

She landed that shot, dead center, with her fucking eyes closed. I guess I know which Remy we're getting this life. "Holy shit."

"Woooooooo!" she cries out, and Creek laughs, lifting her up and spinning her around.

"I knew you could do it," he says as he puts her back down, and I groan. I'm happy for her, really. Damn, maybe next life.

"Come on, this is so unfair!" I whine playfully, and she laughs at me.

"Better luck next time?" Remy winks in my direction as dad and Nate laugh. "It was only one point. Who knows, maybe it was a fluke."

"Something like that," my dad says, shaking his head. "Colt, get this shit packed up, we'll meet you inside."

"Come on, man, I'll help you," Creek says to me as the others head inside.

It doesn't take long to get everything packed up, especially since Creek is all over my sister like flies on shit. I get that he remembers their past and she doesn't, but that doesn't make it easier to watch. She could still remember and feel differently. I don't want either of them getting hurt, but I keep my thoughts to myself and head back inside.

Everyone's already sitting at the table, and my stomach rumbles at the sight of the feast Maddie's put together for us. I take a seat, eying the goods loaded around the kitchen. The eggs, ham, cheeses, and pastries make my mouth water, and I practically groan as she adds potatoes and other meats to the table.

"Dig in!" she announces with a flourish of her arms, and in the blink of an eye, it's like feeding time at the zoo. Not that that puts me off, so I dive in with everyone else, enjoying the love and laughter around the table now that there aren't secrets between us anymore.

I eat more than I should, groaning when I've eaten so much I think I might be sick. Content sighs and groans ripple around the room as Maddie smiles from her seat.

"I'm glad that you all enjoyed it," she beams. It's so hard to try and imagine her out killing beasts and kicking ass, but that's our Mads.

I pat my stomach, enjoying the hubbub around the room as Remy and Bauer clear the table and load the dishwasher.

"You found the mark? What does it mean?" she asks him quietly, obviously not wanting to distract the others from their conversation, but I'm worried about her. I don't need to talk about tonight's patrol, so I eavesdrop. Sue me for being a protective asshole, but I'm not planning to change anytime soon.

"I did, but I don't know what it means yet. There isn't much information about it... or about being Angel blessed. At least, not that I could find yet. I'll keep looking, though."

"Thanks, Bauer, I appreciate it."

"Anything for you, Rem. You should probably rest. It

might not feel like it right now, but the ritual takes a lot out of you, and the next few days are going to suck."

THREE

FALLON

"Wait, wait, wait," I squeal as I perch on Remy's sofa. "You mean to tell me Creek kissed you, and you had memories about him telling you he loves you; but you haven't mentioned that to him yet? Mind blown, Remy. Mind. Blown. I need more details!"

She shrugs at my outburst, and I swear I want to slap her upside the head. Who shrugs at that?

"Can I ask you a really out of this world question ?" she asks, and I can't help but laugh.

"Out of this world is pretty much my specialty, so shoot." I grin at her, but she looks kinda terrified, which only makes me more excited.

“Are all of the monsters really as bad as my family makes them out to be? Or are there exceptions? Dracul who actually feel? Lycans who don’t want to dominate the world?” She wraps her arms around herself, and my heart twinges on her behalf as I try to think of the right way to put this. Hunters are so stunted in their world views, so I totally get why she’s asking me this, but shit.

“No, they’re not all that bad.” I sigh. I chew the inside of my cheek for a moment as I consider my words. “Don’t tell your dad I said so, though. Hunters are... Well, usually they’re pretty biased. Once upon a time all of our factions lived in relative peace. Hunters were created, essentially, to police the factions and to keep the rebels in line. At least that’s what I gathered from my ancestor’s journals.”

“Woah.” She leans back against the arm of the sofa, facing me. “Why don’t I know any of this?”

“Well, I mean, you might? Maybe you just don’t remember knowing. It’s most likely because it’s some closely guarded secret in the Hunter world, and if the Dracul or Lycans were to say something, no Hunter would believe them. Witches, well, we always ride the lines. Still, it would be thought of as some myth or some lie if a Dracul came up to you and said y’all were actually tight with each other. I’m only telling you because you asked, otherwise I’d keep my mouth shut. Goddess knows what kind of shit I could get into for telling you this.” I shake my head because my mama will tan my goddamn hide if she finds out about me telling Remy this stuff. While Mama agrees with me that love is love, the peace we have with the Hunters could be easily broken.

"Have you ever, you know..." she asks awkwardly, and I can't help but laugh. Remy isn't bashful, like ever, so I know exactly what she's asking me right now.

"Have I ever what? Fucked a monster? Yes, yes, I have. Like I say, they're not all bad. There's a reason you hunt rogues when you first start out. So that you see the worst their kinds have to offer, so when you come across someone different later, you think it's another lie—a deception to draw you in and get you killed. What makes you ask, anyway?"

I watch her closely because these questions are coming from somewhere, and while I'm happy to give her any information she wants, consequences be damned, Remy never asks stuff like this without reason.

"What happened?" I ask, and she shifts in her seat. She's always been shit at lying, and I can tell she's trying to work out how much to tell me right now.

She reaches around the sofa and lifts up a box before handing it over to me. "Open it."

I untie the bow on the box, holding my breath as I do. If this is some fucked up Dracul sex toy, I swear to the Goddess …

I lift the lid, and I'm pretty sure my heart stops.

My talisman. I didn't think I'd ever see this again after it was stolen.

"You got it back?" I ask as I run my finger over the edge of it. "But I don't understand... why the box? And why so big?"

"I didn't exactly get it back." She sighs, running a hand through her hair as she looks at just about everything in the room but me. What in the fresh hell?

"Girl, why are you so nervous? Your eye is practically twitching." I can't help but watch her intently, taking in every detail. "Tell me what happened."

"Well, I took Creek to the address you gave me to get your talisman. There were definitely Dracul there, but it was *not* some rogue nest. It was a whole-ass home, and a vampire clan lived there. There were families, with children and everything, but they discovered we were there."

"Oh shit." I lean back in the chair at her words. I didn't expect that. Like at fucking all. I would've never asked her to find it if I'd known.

"Something like that," she says, and she's shifting around all over again. She glances toward the door, chewing her lip before she continues, "but then someone helped us escape. He delivered that, or had it delivered here, this morning."

"What the ever-loving fuck! A Dracul helping a

Hunter..." My mind is officially blown. Like wide open. The Dracul and Lycans hate the Hunters as much as the Hunters hate them. I mean, I don't blame them. Centuries of being hunted will do that to people, but still. This is huge news.

"I know. I mean, I have no fucking idea about what's acutally happening here, but I know." She shrugs, and I go quiet, trying to think of what the hell to say.

"Who was it? Did you know him?" I watch her closely because that intuition I've always trusted, blessed by the Goddess, tells me that she's not telling me everything.

"Do you really want to know?" she asks, and despite the spike of fear that tears through me, I know I need to know.

"Oh, shut your face. I'm your best friend; if you're in a pile of shit, of course I'm gonna get right in there with you. Goddess only knows how your family might react, but me? I'm Switzerland, baby. I'm ain't gonna judge."

"Does the name Kain mean anything to you?" she asks, and I flat out stare at her, mouth gaping, eyes wide. Holy. Fucking. Shit.

"I... Kain... Surely not... Holy shit," I stutter through a whole mess of nonsense before climbing to my feet and pacing around the living room. This is huge. Like freaking gigantic.

She sits quietly while I pace, and I want to talk to her,

to reassure her that I'm not judging her because I would never. But holy, and I cannot emphasize this enough, *shit*. A Dracul named Kain can only be Kain Micheals. King of the Dracul. The monster that the other monsters are afraid of. And he was kind to her? He helped her escape? This makes zero sense. The man is known for hunting Hunters and absolutely decimating them. You don't become the King of the Dracul without being responsible for rivers of blood. I slide down the wall of her apartment, sitting on the floor with a heavy thump. Sushi, her cat, jumps on my lap and starts to purr while I stroke him, struggling to take the information in. It has to be a different Kain. Right? Because there's no fucking way it's the King of the Dracul.

"What did he look like? Because it can't be..." I trail off, staring at her with wide, unblinking eyes. This could change everything.

Everything.

"He was beautiful, though in a strange way. He had dark hair, longer on top, so it kind of fell in his eyes. Fal, they were the brightest blue I've ever seen, even with the amber ring around them," she rambles, a little breathless, and I blink hard a couple of times. Maybe I'm dreaming. That would definitely explain why the hell my best friend is reverently describing the King of the Dracul to me. "He was tall, definitely well over six foot, and broad, though not like Creek, but definitely lean beneath the black shirt and pants he wore. There was something about him. Like he had confidence in every word, in every action."

She glances back at me, and I know I'm struggling to close my damn mouth. But shit… This is a lot to take in.

"Did he have a ring? A silver ring with a black stone? Did you see any markings on his skin?" I ask quickly, but she shakes her head. My heart sinks a little, but then she speaks again.

"I didn't have time to look. The whole thing was so quick." Her words seem stilted, like she's still holding back, but I'm not going to push her anymore. She'll tell me when she's ready.

"Okay, well holy shit. I think that was Kain Michaels," I tell her.

"Who is he?" she asks, and my gaze snaps back to hers.

"Wow, your memories really aren't back yet. I'm surprised your brothers haven't given you the low down yet. You should really ask them for a history lesson because holy shit, girl." I run my hands through my hair, trying to disguise the fact that I'm almost shaking. "Kain Michaels is the last known living Dracul of the old times. Back when the factions were at peace, the Dracul were ruled by three royal families. Rumor has it the rest have been killed or are in hiding, but Kain, he's a man of legend.

" He fought in wars that are nothin' but myths now. He's destroyed entire empires and brought down kings and dictators. He's a force to be fucking reckoned with, Remy. The King of the Dracul is what they call him now. The last hope of the Dracul to bring peace back to their kind. To bring back the old ways, and supposedly let the other royals out of hiding.

" Legends say he was always the general of the Dracul; his father was a great mind, but even his father couldn't plan, strategize, and execute like Kain, and so he became the protector of the Dracul. The other royals looked after politics, keeping the relationships up with the other factions, keeping their people fed, and keeping them in line. Kain was the one who went to war with our factions, up against humans, alongside humans, to make the world a better place."

"Sounds like you like yourself a bit of Kain." She winks at me, and I can't help but bark out a laugh.

"The things I've read about him... It's hard to see him as the monster everyone wants to make him out to be. Then again, I've never met the guy. I've only got secondhand stories. Though knowing what I do about the Dracul and the Lycans—compared to the stories the Hunters tell—yeah, I kind of admire him a little. He gave up everything for his kind. Rumor has it that he had a love once and she was killed by the Hunters. That's what sparked the war between the two factions and what spiraled down to the world as we know it today. There's no firsthand stories of it in the journals, though, so it could be nothing more than a story. But the romantic in me likes to believe it's true." I shrug, starting to relax a little. If it was Kain, and he helped her, maybe it's a sign of things to come. Maybe the faction war is starting to ease outside of this guild.

"If it is him though, Remy, you have to be careful. I have no idea why he would help you. And I have even less of an idea why he would help you help me," I warn her. Even if I am hopeful, it still makes no damn sense in the long run.

"I will. It's not like I'm going to go out hunting for him. Well, I mean, you know what I mean, " she laughs, but it's stilted, so I brush it off for now. This was meant to be a lighthearted night.

"Well, that's a relief!" I say as I brace my hands against the wall and push away from it. "I think that's more than enough talk about magic and monsters. Let's get me something stronger than this soda, and then you need to dish about Creek!"

"Help yourself." She waves toward her kitchen, and I jut out my hip, placing my hands on them like a stroppy teenager.

"I know you're not gonna make me drink alone, Remington Bennett." I give her the side-eye, and she laughs. Mission "lighten-the-mood" accomplished. I head into the kitchen. She won't let me drink alone because that's just not who she is.

"Fine, but I'm only having one. I'm training with Bauer again tomorrow. Apparently getting my ass handed to me earlier this week means I need to step up my training."

Ouch, I do not envy her that. Bauer, her oldest brother, is a fucking stickler for the rules. He's also a real hard ass, not to mention way older than the rest of us. He's always been a bit reserved, almost like he keeps himself separate on purpose, but I've seen the guy fight. I would not want to be her right now. But she's a Hunter, and she needs to get her ass handed to her to help her stay alive.

"Uh, fucking duh! Can't have you out there getting your ass kicked in the real world, can we?" I ask as I pull open the door to her freezer. My hand hovers between two ice-cold bottles, so I turn to her and ask, "Whiskey or tequila?"

"Dealer's choice," she says with a small smile, and I shake my head with a small smile of my own. I reach for the tequila and work my way around her kitchen. This place could be my second home, hell if she had a second bedroom, and she hadn't been with Jack the Jackass, it probably would be.

I pour us both a drink over ice and make my way back to her on the sofa, handing her a glass before sitting opposite her again.

"Spill," I say with a wide grin. Goddess knows she's

gonna need the encouragement.

"So, we started off the same as always, except for me still being pissed at him for leaving all those months ago. I know he had a good reason now, but you tell that to my stupid-ass hormones. Anyway, things started to get better, and then there was this moment... I thought he was going to kiss me, but Colt happened."

"Fucking Colt," I grumble. I swear that boy will be the death of me. Or at least the reason I shut my legs and heart off to the rest of the world.

"Right, and don't think I'm not going to ask more about that, by the way." I wave her off because nope. Those are not details I'm going into with her. She loves her brother like he hung the damn moon, even if he did ghost her. I'm not gonna be the reason there's a wedge between them.

"Don't change the subject!" I insist, and she goes on to tell me everything again, from the beginning. I can't help but enjoy the down time with my best friend, pretending we're nothing more than two human women, and that man trouble is the biggest worry we have in the world.

My head pounds, and my phone won't stop buzzing. Tequila is the worst. I was out last night with Misty as Remy has been pretty MIA since the night she dished about what's going on with her. While she's kept in touch, it's been sporadic, which isn't really like her.

I hold my head in my hands and wish for a miracle. While Mama might have a tonic to sober you up from tipsy, a hangover is something she doesn't have a cure for. Which is why she laughed so loudly when she went to her store today to cover my shift. I haven't felt this lousy in forever.

And I swear, if my phone doesn't stop buzzing, I'm going to launch it across the damn room. I pull a pillow over my head, but my phone won't fucking stop, so I pick it up and groan when I see Colt's name across the screen.

What the ever-loving fuck does he want now?

"What?" I bark as I answer the phone. I'd feel bad if it was anyone other than Colt. Maybe. I don't like being pulled out of bed early when I feel like an actual dumpster.

"Fallon, we need you. Danny's hurt. We're on the way to your house now. We're about two minutes away." The line goes dead, and I stare at my phone, mouth hanging open in shock.

Well, fuck.

I didn't even know Danny was back in town, but if he's hurt and they're coming here, then it's gotta be bad. I jump out of bed and throw on some clothes, tying my hair back as I rush around. Thank the Goddess Rebel is at dance class this morning. She's too young to be seeing this shit just yet. As much as I might wish I could pass my heir status onto her, it doesn't work that way. Not unless I die, of course. I push the thought away and keep rushing through the house, trying to get as much shit ready as I can. I don't know what kind of shitstorm is heading my way, but I'm gonna try my best to be prepared for it.

By the time I'm ready, a pounding sounds at my front door. I run into the kitchen and clear off the table as Colt swings the door open. Danny is slung over his shoulder, blood pouring fucking everywhere, and I gulp.

I really hate blood. And I really hate that Witches are always cleaning up after Hunters and this stupid war of theirs, but it is what it is. For now, anyway.

"Put him on the table," I demand, trying to take stock of as much as possible in a few seconds as Colt moves toward the kitchen. Goddess, there's blood everywhere. "What the fuck happened?"

Colt shakes his head, shock apparent in the way he blinks at me slowly but doesn't manage to say even one word through his gaping mouth.

"Survived two tours in the desert and then a fucking fanger gets me." Danny coughs, and blood trickles from his mouth. At least a Dracul wound is reasonably easy to heal, as long as there's no venom.

Please don't let there be any venom. The thought all but disappears from my head as Danny blinks slowly, eyes going glassy in the moments before he passes out.

Colt jumps into action. "What do you need?" he asks as I move to the sink to wash my hands. Venom or not, dirty hands aren't gonna help anything.

"Go to Mama's kit and get me towels, scissors, and gauze. We need to stop the bleeding because I have to see the wound to actually heal it. If I go in blind, I'm gonna wipe myself out." I don't tell him that I'm already at half capacity because that won't help anything. He rushes from the kitchen, and I make my way toward the table, where Danny's bleeding generously all over the damn place.

I take a deep breath, quelling the shake from my hungover hands. I take a deep breath, steeling myself for the sight of whatever wound is waiting for me, but then Colt's back with the stuff I need. It's now or never, so I cut off Danny's t-shirt, stomach turning at the sight of the tears in his chest. Goddess, there's a whole chunk missing from his shoulder.

"Holy shit, a Dracul did this?"

"Babies. And fucking Rogues. There's so fucking many of them here. Danny shouldn't have even been there. You can't let him die, Fallon." Colt's distress bleeds out into the room, and I try not to let it get to me.

"I'm not going to let him die. For fuck's sake, Colt," I grumble through gritted teeth. I get that he's worried, but goddamn. "Nice way to not heap on the pressure, by the way. Help me clean him up, will you? We need to do his chest first since that seems to be the biggest issue."

We work together in near silence, only speaking when I instruct him on what I need from him to help his friend. It takes a while, but eventually I drop down into a chair, fucking exhausted. Danny is healed, at least. He's still passed out, but there was a whole hell of a lot of blood loss, so that's to be expected.

"We have blood packs in the fridge out back if you know his type. We can give him a transfusion and help him along," I tell Colt, who nods and heads to the back of the house.

It's freaking weird seeing him like this when things are so stunted between us. Especially after things got so damn intimate before. And I don't just mean the sex. Though, don't get me wrong, I miss that too. Because holy hells, I don't think I've ever come as much or as hard with anyone as I did with him. It was the other stuff, though, that I really miss.

Unfortunately, that was part of the problem. Colt only wanted some fun. It was stupid of me to think he might do something different with me. Some things are ingrained, and one of those things are his damn daddy's rules. Goddess forbid he go against his daddy.

He reappears and hooks his friend up to the blood bag before disappearing again without a word. The sound of the trickle of water against the tile lets me know he's jumping in the shower, and my toes curl. Goddamn, it isn't fair that I'm supposed to be pissed off at him right now. I miss him.

But I'm also a stubborn asshole. So until he apologizes, and does it right, I'm closed for business to him.

Unfortunately for me, that means I'm closed for business altogether because my stupid heart won't get over Colt Bennett. I knew the risk I was taking when we took it further, but I wasn't thinking clearly. I mean, he's Colt.

The flipside of that, of course, is that he's Colt. I should've known better. There was a reason I didn't say anything before he left. More fool me, I guess.

I listen as the sound of the water fades away and the door creaks open. A few seconds later, there's a slam as the door closes. I peek down the hallway and see that my bedroom door is shut.

Right, he has clothes in there. I let out a sigh and get to work cleaning up the space around Danny and then myself. When Colt reappears, his hair is still damp, with the floppy long top dropping down over his forehead. His eyebrow bar glints beneath it.

"I brought a t-shirt out for Danny too. As soon as he wakes up, we'll get him out of here. We have another big hunt coming up in a few days, so thank you for this."

"Yeah, I heard. The warehouse raid, right?" I ask, even though I already know the answer. Remy hasn't been around much, but when I have spoken to her, she's been worrying about what they're gonna find. I really need to check in with her again. The last time I really talked to her was last week when we talked about the whole Kain thing. Which, by the way, my mind is still blown about that little tidbit. Even with what she told me, it seems insane. Granted, that's Remington Bennett—the queen of the extraordinary and unexpected.

"Yeah, that's the one. We need to be in top form. Remy's coming too."

"Yeah, Mama and I will be there as well. Healing support and to take down the wards."

"Oh, yeah, right," he says, rubbing the back of his neck.

Goddess, this is so fucking awkward.

"Will you two fuck and get it over with already? You could cut the tension in here with a knife," Danny croaks as his eyes flicker open.

"And he's awake. That'll teach you for getting tagged, man," Colt jokes, dismissing Danny's accusation.

"Thank you for healing me up, little lady," Danny says as he sits up.

"Anytime, though, try to take better care of yourself in the future," I say with a small smile.

Danny offers me a tight smile as he pushes himself off of the table with a small grunt. I shuffle in place, glancing from the healed Hunter to Colt and then back again.

Seriously, this couldn't get any weirder if I actively tried.

"Okay, well, we'll get out of your hair. Thanks again, Fal," Colt says awkwardly.

"Bye, Colt," I say, hating how everything has played out with us.

Why can't that idiot pull his head out of his ass?

I pick up my phone as soon as I see Remy's name. It's been a weird week. I need some bestie conversation, stat.

"I need you. Can you come over and bring medical supplies?"

"Sure thing, I'll grab everything and head over now. What happened?"

"I'll explain once you get here," she says, and I can just make out a grunt in the background.

"Are you with Colt?" I ask despite the worry gnawing at my gut. My nerves might be up at the request for medical supplies, but I'm definitely not ready to see her brother right now.

"No, I'll explain everything when you get here," she says again, and I bite my lip. What the fuck has she got herself into this time?

"Okay, I won't be long."

"Thanks, Fal, you're the best."

"Oh, I know." I hang up the phone and start scrambling around my room, packing shit up and prepping to haul ass over to her place. I have no idea what the fuck is going on, but she's my girl, which means I'm gonna get to her in a heartbeat. I grab the pack with supplies and draw a portal to the alley beside her apartment.

I wait a minute, making sure no humans are around before I head out of the alley and breeze through the door. I smile at the people in the entryway like it's nothing more urgent than margaritas and gossip as I fight the urge to run for the elevator. By the time I reach her floor, my stomach is in knots, and I pound on her front door. I don't wait for her to answer, swinging the door open and storming into the room instead. "Girl, I don't know what you've landed yourself in this time, but you need to talk. I swear I only hear from you when you're broken."

"I'm sorry, and yes, we'll talk, but I'm still kinda bleeding. Can you help? I mean, it's probably basically healed by now, but I'll take all the help I can get." I wave her over to the sofa and close the door as she limps over.

"Pants down," I tell her, and she rolls her eyes at me before doing as she's told. I make her lie down so I can assess her injuries. The thigh looks the most worrying, so I check that first. "You're lucky it doesn't look like it's anything major. A few inches the other way, though, and this could have been real dangerous. What happened, and why did you call me for something that would've healed in a few hours anyhow?" I quirk a brow at her, and she rolls her eyes again.

I press my hands against the broken skin and watch as my magic fills the space, knitting it back together. She hisses and grits her teeth. "I was ambushed by a cluster of rogue Lycans. Twelve of them. They wrote off my goddamn Mustang. I want to kill them all over again for that."

"Holy mother of Fates. Twelve isn't a cluster, it's a goddamn rogue pack!" I suck my teeth and make a disapproving sound. "How the hell did you get out of that with only this and a few other cuts and bruises?"

"Are you sure you want to know? Because it's a whole thing that could very well get me killed," she tells me honestly, and I'm pretty sure my heart almost stops.

"How much trouble are you in?" I whisper.

"At the moment, not too much, but if people find out the truth, then a whole fucking shit pile." She sighs, and I remove my hands from her thigh. The wound is sealed, and everything is back as it should be.

"You can put your pants back on, you're all fixed up. I have a feeling we're gonna need pants and tequila for this conversation." I shake my head, still trying to process what little she's told me. She shimmies her pants back on, and I grab two shot glasses and the bottle before we settle back on to the sofa.

I pour us out a decent drink and throw mine back before offering her a tight smile and pouring myself another. “Okay, let’s go.”

“Honestly, I’m not sure where to begin, and I still don’t even know everything,” she says quietly, and I give her the look Mama gives me when she knows I’m holding back. We don’t have time for no more secrets; we’ve already had enough of those.

“So I told you about the whole thing with Creek already, which escalated this week, by the way. But there’s more… way, way more. Past Remy screwed me, Fallon, but I totally get it.” She takes a deep breath and looks me dead in the eye. “It turns out past me was as open and loving as I am now... and probably as open-minded as the Witches. I know that the Hunters’ stories, their ways, don’t make total sense… but now I know that Kain Michaels was my lover—no, he was my love in my first life and in many since then. I’ve always known the rocky truth, just not the whys or the whole story of why things are the way they are.”

“Holy shit! Kain Michaels... Damn girl, that Vampire is one fine piece of man meat.” My eyes go wide as I process her words. It really was him! Damn! “Keep going!”

“Well, it turns out that Kain wasn’t my only dalliance with other factions. I’m not sure which life it was, but in one of them, Roman Knight recognized me as his mate. I don't know how or why, or even much more than that yet, but that *is* how I got out alive tonight. He found me and tore the Lycans to pieces with two of his pack. That's why I called you. The overbearing asshole made me call you on the way back. He literally wouldn't put me down until he heard you agree to come over and patch me up."

I let out a whistle and fan my face because holy freaking hell. Only Remington Bennett could end up in this situation, and damn, I'm half jealous because I've seen pictures. Those guys are serious hotties.

"I don't know how it all fits together, but I know that Creek knew, in whichever life it was, that I was Roman's mate because he killed me."

"He did fucking what!" I screech, nearly dropping my glass. What the actual fuck?

"He didn't intend to; he was fighting Roman."

"And you barged in there like a woman possessed. Holy mother, Remy."

"I know, I know, but then there's Creek... And now they're all here. Together. In my goddamn city. In this one life. Each of them wanting a piece of me." She shrugs and shoots the tequila I poured for her, and I join her. "That's essentially it in a nutshell."

I sit there, silently blinking and trying to take it all in while pouring us both another drink. This is a lot to process. I mean, no judgement from me, though. I've messed around with the factions, but I'm a Witch not a Hunter. She was right earlier. If people find out about this, shit will hit the fucking fan.

"What are you gonna do?" I ask her as I sip at my drink. I need to know the plan because if she needs me, I'm there.

"I have absolutely no idea. I mean, what can I do? I can't ask my family for help, they'd probably kill me, literally. I can't be with all three of them, but I have no idea how I'll choose because my stupid heart belongs to each of them. But also, I have no idea what it is that's still missing from my stupid memories. I'm hoping that past me had a goddamn plan, or some way of working out where the hell she was going, because the path she's leading me down is murky at best. And at worst, it's the true death." She downs her glass, and I laugh.

"Girl, I say have some fun. Have a little harem, why the fuck not? The boys can learn to play nice... maybe even nicer than nice." I wink at her, and she finally laughs. But I definitely think she should do it. I've heard the stories. Remy has always lived for everyone else. Even as a human, she puts everyone else first. Look at her jackass of an ex, Jack. It's about time she did something for herself.

"Could you imagine the looks on their faces?" She giggles, and I laugh with her. I can't, but what I wouldn't give to see that pissing contest.

"I would pay to see it, sugar. Pay to see it!" I take her hands in mine and squeeze them, and it's then that I notice the black metal ring with a purple teardrop on her finger. "Uhm, excuse me, what's that on your finger?"

"It was a gift," she says coyly as I eye the ring on her index finger. It can't be… "Is that obsidian? Oh my freaking Fates, is this from Kain?"

She nods at me, and it takes everything in me not to squeal more and I fan my face again. "Girl, I need me a Dracul King. This is beautiful!"

"I mean, you can't have him, he's mine." She sticks her tongue out at me, and I can't help but laugh. It almost feels like we don't have this ridiculously huge secret.

"Territorial already, I see," I joke, and she sighs.

"Honestly, I don't know. When I'm here, like this, no not really. But when I'm with him, with any of them... I don't even really want to test the theory."

"I can imagine. But for real, if Creek knew once, maybe he'll be more open to helping you than you think? And Colt is more open-minded than people realize too," I tell her, hoping that I'm not completely wrong. I mean, he's an asshole, but he's happy to fuck around. Maybe this will be the eye-opener he needs.

"What on earth does that mean?" she asks. "It seems I'm not the only one who's been keeping secrets."

"It doesn't mean much," I sigh. "Honestly, I don't

know what any of it is, but when things make more sense, I swear I'll explain."

"Not in too much detail, please." She laughs, and I roll my eyes.

"With the amount of dick in your future, I can keep that to myself. Where are all of your many, many men anyway?"

"No idea. Roman left begrudgingly after he carried me here."

"He carried you here? Oh damn." I practically swoon at the thought of those giant arms wrapped around her, carrying her home like this is all something out of the fairy tales.

"Kain is holed up somewhere. He said he'd come for me when it was safe. Then there's Creek, and well... he's probably off with my brothers somewhere up to Fates only know what."

"Honestly, I don't know whether to be jealous of you or feel sorry for you." I smile sadly. "Whatever you choose, someone is likely to get hurt, and I know that's the last thing you want. Follow your heart, Remy. It hasn't steered you wrong yet. Jack being the exception of course."

"Jack would have been good for me if I was human. If I was human, my family probably wouldn't have disliked him as much either. Things would have been easier, that's for sure. And yet, as much as I want to throttle past Remy,

I can't find it in myself to regret my actions in my previous lives. My heart is so full, but I wish Mom were here. She'd know what to do and what to say."

I nod in agreement. "Yeah, your mama would have been on board and on your side, to the end. You could maybe talk to my mama? She's always felt the same as you, that love is love regardless of your faction. She hates the racism and bigoted nature of our kinds, and I'm pretty sure she plays with the other factions as a big fuck you to those who look down their nose sometimes. It's just the way she is. It's why I was always surprised her and your dad worked together so well, but I guess because she was so close to your mom, it makes sense."

"Thanks, but I don't think even Marie would be able to help me out of the mess I seem to have created for myself. One advantage to the swell of Lycans and Dracul, plus everything happening with my dad, is that people seem to have forgotten about my Leviathan mark."

"Small wins." I smile at her, trying to be as reassuring as I can, but this is definitely a situation. I'd forgotten about her mark in the thick of all this shit too.

"I've tried to keep it covered as much as I can. I think it's stopped growing now, but I still don't understand the symbols intertwined with it."

"Maybe ask one of your lovers. Creek obviously doesn't know much, otherwise he would have said something, but one of the others might." I shrug; if she's known them before, it makes sense one of them might have the answers she's looking for.

"Fallon, you're a genius."

"Oh, girl, I know. People underestimate me at every turn." I wink at her and finish my glass. " I better head on back. Mama will be waiting up for me. You'd think I was twelve, not twenty with the way she acts. If you need me, I'm here. For anything. Even facing off against your family."

"Thank you, Fal." She hugs me so tight it's almost hard to breathe. Goddamn Hunter strength. "You're the best."

"Don't you forget it," I say with a wink before releasing her. "You lock this door behind me. You might have a harem of protectors out there, but there's way too many beasties out there that you seem to be able to piss off or attract without even trying."

"I will. You going to be okay getting home?"

"Yeah, I'm catching an Uber. It'll be here any minute," I tell her because she still doesn't know about the portals. I hate Witch council rules sometimes, but there are some things a faction has to keep secret.

"Okay, stay safe, Fallon. Call me if you need me."

"Ditto, girl. Ditto."

FOUR

COLT

"I have no idea how I let you talk me into this," Remy huffs as I pull the chair out for her. "I can get my own chair."

"Come on, little bit. It's been forever since we hung out just the two of us. And after your birthday months ago was… well, it wasn't exactly a celebration, you know? Then there's everything that's happened since, so I wanted us to do something nice. Especially since I missed last year too." I smile that smile I know she can't say no to, and my grin widens as she caves.

"Fine, fine, I'll play nice." She laughs and takes a seat. I push her chair under the table before sitting down opposite her. "I don't even remember the last time I came here."

"Franco's is the best Italian on this side of the world, and I'll fight anyone who says otherwise." I grin, making her laugh at my antics. It's nice to see her smile. She's been so serious since everything happened, and I don't want her to lose herself in the madness that is our world.

"So you and Fallon, huh?" she asks, wagging her eyebrows at me, and I drop my head in my hands and groan.

"No, Remy." This is not a conversation I want to have with her. I knew taking it that step further with Fallon was a bad idea. My mind knew it, but my heart and my stupid dick didn't want to listen. They wanted her, so off we went like a puppy chasing a chicken. We had our fun, consequences be damned. And now she won't even talk to me.

"Oh, come *on*. She's been so tight lipped, but *I know* something is going on," she teases.

"Remy, please drop it. She's not a Hunter, so nothing can come of it." I smile, but I can feel how tight it is across my lips. I know there's no future there with Fallon. My father would go fucking nuclear if I started up something serious with her. And yeah, she kept me sane while I was gone, but no matter what I might feel for her, I don't want to put her through the craziness that is my life. Dating a Hunter isn't an easy life. It's the other reason we stick to our own factions. Others wouldn't understand the need to throw yourself into danger like we do.

"Does it matter that much to you?" she asks, and I shake my head. I knew she wouldn't understand. Remy wears her heart on her sleeve, and I love that about her, but it isn't as easy for me.

"It doesn't. But it isn't my opinion that matters. The Bennetts are a respected Hunter family. An affair with another faction, even with an ally, would devastate the people closest to us," I whisper so no one around us hears before picking up the menu.

"The people closest to us should love us regardless of who we're with," she argues, but I don't respond to it. She might be right, but that's not what would happen. Don't get me wrong, I know our dad loves us, but I also know that his beliefs are strong. When it comes down to it, he'll pick his beliefs every single time.

"You and Creek, though, that's a good match. That's exactly what people expect," I tell her with a forced smile because I don't want to push her, especially if she doesn't remember; but I desperately want a different conversation topic. "I'm happy for you."

"I hope you find happiness, Colt, no matter who it's with." She reaches over and squeezes my hand. My little sister, the hardass with a heart. I love her for wanting that, and for how open-minded she is, but being open-minded in our faction is dangerous.

"Thank you, now enough of this crap." I grin like an idiot, and she laughs at me at last. "Let's eat some good food, and then I'm thinking about some laser tag." Laser tag is something we used to do when we were kids, and we fucking loved it. I guess it was probably the Hunter DNA, but whatever caused it, it was always a fucking blast.

"I haven't been to laser tag in *forever*. Hell yes!" We order when the waiter approaches and shoot the shit. My steak is fucking beautiful, just like it always is here, and like always, I eat way more than I should.

"I have no idea how I'm going to run around laser tag right now." She puffs up her cheeks, and I can't help but snort a laugh at her.

"You look like a hamster," I say, rubbing my stomach. Honestly, I'm not sure how I'm going to run around at laser tag either, but I'm planning on kicking her ass either way. "But how about we walk there and burn off all those carbs? Plus, you can't back out. Creek and Bauer are on their way back from the airport—douchebag Archer was summoned home—thank the Goddess, so they're going to join us."

"You don't like him either?"

"Guy is so far up his own ass, I can see his eyes in his mouth. Thinks he's better than the rest of us, when he's a subpar Hunter at best. He's a damn good tracker, I'll give him that. It's why he was sent after Roman, but that's about all he's got going for him."

"I'm glad he's gone; Bauer was weird with him around."

"You noticed that too, huh?" I ask, leaving cash for the bill and standing.

She follows me out of the restaurant and out into the bright fall day before she finally answers. "It's hard not to notice. It's like he's harder, and just not Bauer."

"I think something happened a long time ago, and Bauer doesn't want to let his guard down, even if he says he can trust Archer with his life. He won't talk about it. He brushes me off, but yeah. It's weird."

Remy hums in the back of her throat, and we stroll in comfortable silence to the laser tag warehouse. The silence continues as we sit in the sun, waiting for Creek and Bauer to arrive. A few minutes later, Bauer's truck pulls into the lot, and they climb from it. Remy is practically drooling over Creek as he jumps from the truck and walks over to us.

"Down girl," I tease, and she shoves me, rolling her eyes.

We play-wrestle, and they reach us just as she manages to get me into a headlock. She releases me with a whoop and bounces around, celebrating her victory while I try not to be a sore loser. I totally let her win. Bauer bursts out laughing while Creek shakes his head. "You guys never change."

"I don't ever want to." She laughs, jumping back to me and hugging me tight. "You guys ready to be annihilated?"

We all laugh at her, shaking our heads. Inside, I'm excited as a kid in a candy store. We pay the woman at the counter and then gear up.

Creek finishes sorting himself out and heads over to Remy, and she practically swoons at his touch.

"I guess the love birds are teaming up." I laugh as she rolls her eyes at me, but Creek takes her hand.

"It's us four, versus the team already in there according to the guy who gave me the gear," Bauer says. He shakes his head as he sucks his teeth. "Poor fuckers."

"Yes!" I whoop, and Remy laughs at us both.

"Is that even fair?" she asks, and Bauer shrugs. Fuck fair. We're here to win.

"Nothing is fair in love and war. You'd do well to remember that, Remy," he says, looking at her with a flash of an odd expression, but whatever it was disappears, and he smiles. "Let's get this done."

He slaps the laser gun against his shoulder and heads into the dark room, and I bounce along behind him with my bestie and my sister behind me. This will be fucking epic.

FIVE

FALLON

Last night was the raid on the warehouse, and the entire night was a fucking horror show. Remy's secrets came out in the worst way, her dad threw her in a fucking dungeon jail cell while Creek stood by and watched. And her brothers? Yeah, they're both giant fucking bags of dicks.

I expected more from Colt.

I don't know why, though. Their bigoted ways are the entire reason Colt dropped me faster than a bad penny. Who cares if she sided with a Dracul and saved his life? The Hunters, her family, don't know the whole fucking story. My rage is real while I pace our sitting room like an irritated tiger. Mama is with Denny—Remy's dad—and the council. She has been since the first thing this morning, and she's pleading for leeway on Remy's behalf. But Denny is the leader of the asshole clan, and won't forgive Remy. The only thing she's done is fall in love with those they deem their enemy. They don't even know him. All she did was stop Bauer from trying to kill Kain. I don't care if he's the King of the Dracul and they have all sorts of sordid stories about what a monster he is. If Remy sees the good in him, then it has to be there.

If they knew everything… Goddess, I couldn't even imagine.

Creek surprised me the most, and not in a good way. I know he knows. He's known a long fucking time too. But he stood there and watched as her father deemed her less than for who she loves. I get that she told him to, but fucking hell. He did nothing. I've never been more ashamed or disappointed of the two of them before, but last night was a fucking mess.

The only problem with all my friends being Hunters is that I get swept up in all their fucking chaos. Witches have always typically been a neutral party in the faction war. We work with everyone. Except my family, while we've always worked with all factions, we've also been tied to the Bennett family for pretty much all of time. Again, thanks to my bestie Remy. In one of her earlier lives, she charmed one of my ancestors. Kismet they called it, and ever since, every life she's lived, my bloodline has been connected to her.

Do I have an issue with it? Not at fucking all. That girl is my soul sister. My ride or die. My loyalty is to her beyond all others. I know what she's done for my family throughout history, but more than that, she's been my friend, fierce and loyal, without even knowing what I was. She's been here for me through some of the worst times of my life—I would literally die for that girl.

So now that they've hauled her into Hunter jail, I want to blow some shit up. Mama wants to do the diplomatic thing first. Fuck knows how long that's going to take, so I'm stuck here, looking after Rebel and trying not to pull my hair out in frustration about my bestie.

My phone buzzes on the counter as I finish sorting out breakfast, and I groan when I see who it is.

Colt: Did you know?

Me: Does it matter?

Colt: Of course it fucking matters! How could you know and not say anything?

Me: Because it was no one's fucking business, Colt.

She's a grown-ass woman, of literally several lifetimes. I'm not going to judge one goddamn thing she does because you and I both know she would never judge us for our decisions. Hell, I could run off with a Demon and she'd tell me as long as I was loved, then to do what I was going to do.

Colt: That doesn't make it right. She protected the King of the fucking Dracul, Fallon. His kind killed our mom. It makes me sick.

Fallon: Ever wonder if you don't have the whole story? Stop being such a dick and pull your head out of your ass. And don't talk to me again until it's firmly dislodged.

I put my phone away and ignore the continued buzzing. That boy should be ashamed of himself. I'm not giving him any kind of time until he realizes how badly he's fucked up. Our world might be made up of monsters, but those monsters aren't all bad. He might be able to work that out if he took off the blinders his daddy gave him. The same way he'd realize that a Hunter and a Witch could work, but no. I'm not going to simp over some man child who doesn't think I'm good enough for him. Goddess forbid a Hunter be with someone outside of their faction.

I hope to fuck Remy gets through this bullshit and bashes some heads. If more Hunters were like her, our world would be a better place.

"Rebel, breakfast!" I shout over my shoulder, and I swear only a second passes before I hear her running down the hall. She comes rushing into the kitchen with the kind of joy only a child can really have and practically skids across the floor in her chair.

"Waffles! Yes!" She grins at me as she pours way too much syrup over them and the bacon. I start to say something to her, but bite my tongue. Who am I to take her joy?

"Remember to brush your teeth after breakfast, and then I'll drop you at Alexa's house while I go to the store, okay?"

"Yup! Can't forget to take my dolls, though! We're going to give them makeovers."

"Sure thing, sweet girl." I smile down at her and sip on my coffee while she jiggles around as she eats, dancing to the songs on her show on the TV that's just audible through the kitchen door.

The bell on the door rings to the store, and I glance over, finding two humans who have stumbled in here looking around wide-eyed. This happens a lot. They want love potions, their palms read, or their cards done. They have no idea that Witches are real. Some believe, but in that way that humans do where they think they believe, but if they actually knew the truth, they'd lose their shit. Why they think coming in here in the dead of night to do this is a good idea is beyond me, but there you go.

"How can I help you ladies?" I ask as I stand, the metal bracelets on my wrist jingling as I do. My maxi skirt sways around my legs as I move toward them, and they giggle, whispering to each other. I don't take it personally. The amount of times I've heard about how I look like Esmerelda from that Disney film, and the assumptions of me being Romani rather than what I am… I've lost count, but I don't let it bother me. People and their assumptions hurt them, not me.

"We were hoping to get our cards read," the redhead says, blushing as she does.

"Sure thing. Let me grab Misty to watch the store, and I can do that for you." I smile at them and head to the back room where I asked Misty to sort through labels earlier. After dropping more vials than I care to think about, I put her somewhere she couldn't possibly break anything else.

"Mist, we have two humans here for a reading. Are you okay to watch the counter?"

"Sure thing, Fallon." She smiles, jumping to her feet

and smacking her shin on the table. I wince as she holds her breath before smiling again.

"Are you okay?" I ask with a sigh. I swear I ain't ever met someone as accident prone as Misty.

"I'll be fine—it's nothing a little balm can't help."

I shake my head and leave the room, finding the girls looking over potion and tonic ingredients that look harmless if you don't know any better. "Come on, girls, the card table is back here."

Leading them through the store, their whispers and giggles grate on me. I'm stuck here with this when my best friend is locked in a fucking cell. I know Mama is doing everything she can, but it's honestly fucking ridiculous. And then you have these two clueless fucks, naive as shit and only able to be that way because of people like Remy.

I take a deep breath and try to center myself.

"Who wants to go first?" I ask as I sit down and pull my deck out of the drawer. I leave the others' decks in there. I only ever use mine, since shit tends to go weird otherwise. It's crazy, I know, but it is what it is.

"I do." The blonde puts her fucking hand up, practically jumping up and down before sitting in the chair opposite me. I take a deep breath and shuffle the deck while she gets comfortable.

"Pop your hand on top of the deck for me," I tell her, trying not to roll my eyes while she looks proud as punch about it. Human readings are always hit and miss, but I feel for her energy anyway.

"Thanks," I say with a smile and shuffle the deck again. "Can you shuffle cards?"

"Kind of?" she says with a shrug.

"Okay, I need you to shuffle the deck for me and think about what it is you're looking for answers to," I tell her, my smile pasted on my face as it always is with these readings. I hate giving them to humans because it seems so fake. Especially when I see something terrible, and I know they won't take it seriously. She hands me the cards back, and I ask the Goddess for strength to get me through the rest of the day. "Now, I need you to split them into three piles and then to put them back together. Don't even think about it, just put them back in any order."

I wait while she does it before cutting the deck with my left hand and laying down a simple five card spread face down for her. "Have you done tarot before?"

"No, never," she says, sounding almost afraid.

"Okay, so a five card draw is for illumination and clarity. The first card will tell you what is happening at the moment. The second tells you how you can weather it with grace. The third is the lesson, the fourth is what is leaving at this time, and your fifth and final card is what is arriving at this time," I tell her, trying to be soothing like Mama taught me, but she still looks terrified. Tarot is an art, not something to be afraid of, but I guess I can chalk the fear up to something else humans just don't know. "Are you ready?"

"No, I don't think I want to do this," she says, standing and shaking her head.

"Are you sure?"

"Yes, this was a bad idea. Lottie, we should go," she says, scrambling backward with her friend before rushing from the store.

Humans confound me. I put the cards back in the deck and shuffle it again before putting it away. At least it passed some time... Time where I don't sit around here and freak out about what's happening with Remy.

I check my phone for the umpteenth time and see a message from Creek.

Creek: They've made a decision.

What does that even mean? Why wouldn't he tell me more than that? For fuck's sake.

Men!

I head home once the store is closed up only to find Mama pacing the floor.

"They made a decision?" I ask her, hoping she'll clarify Creek's cryptic ass message, and she nods. Two weeks. It's been two fucking weeks of this diplomacy crapfest between Mama and the Elder Council.

"They're going to pass judgment tomorrow, but Fallon, I have a bad feeling." My heart sinks with her words.

"What can we do? We have to be able to do something! We can't just let them kill her or some shit. She fell in love! Where's the harm in that?" I pace the room, and she stills.

"There isn't anything we can do, Fal, this is Hunter business. If I try to intervene anymore… Well, let's say that things are strained right now." She sighs and sits on one of the stools. I head to the freezer and grab the bottle of tequila I keep in there and pour us both a shot. Usually Mama would turn it down, but she throws the shot back, and that worries me more than anything she could've said. So I sink mine too and then pour another.

"She's my best friend, Mama. My ride or die. I can't let anything happen to her. If only I had full access to my freaking powers, ugh!" I shout in frustration because I feel fucking useless.

"We've spoken about this, baby. Your powers will come when you're ready for them and not before. Your main gift will emerge and when it does, that's when the real work begins. The emergence of your true gift will feel like you're starting all over again. It might drive you crazy, it might mean you need to isolate yourself for a while until you get yourself under control, especially if you have power over an element. But what will be, will be. Trust in the Goddess."

"Mama, I've trusted in the Goddess my entire life, but the one time I truly need power because I need to actually help someone in need, I don't have much of anything that I can use to help."

"Fallon, you're an heir. You're going to need to learn the difference between what you can do and what you should do. One day you're going to take my place as the high priestess, and while I know it's been a while since we've spoken about it, that's not a small honor, Fallon. You will need to leave your other friendships behind, or at least not put them first. The Dominance Coven comes first, even before family. Then comes the covens as a group. And then everyone else."

"What if I don't want to be an heir? You have a second daughter. Rebel's already showing signs that she'll be more powerful than me. It's too much—all I want is to live my life, Mama. I don't want it dictated to me by the rules of others. I can't think of anything else worse than being captive to someone else's whims and wishes rather than being free to pick my own path."

She pales at my words, which makes my heart race wildly in my chest. I feel guilty for a second when she drops her head into her hands before looking back up at me.

"Fallon," she sighs, her shoulders sagging under the weight of my confession. "That's not how this works. Yes, Rebel would take your place in the event of your death, but she's not the true heir. Heavy lies the crown, and trust me, I know it well. Would you really wish this upon your sister?"

"No, I wouldn't. But still, I don't like it. I don't care if I sound like a petulant teenager, I was one not so long ago. This being second rate to Hunter bullshit pisses me off."

"And maybe when you're the high priestess you can do something about it. Especially with friends like Remington Bennett."

"If they don't kill her, you mean, " I mutter under my breath before throwing back another shot. She does the same, and I pour again.

"Yes, if they don't kill her. But still, you're friends with Colt and Creek. They both carry weight too. Try to be patient, I know being an heir isn't all it's cracked up to be."

"You still haven't told me about that vision either," I remind her, trying not to sound too salty but failing miserably.

"You know I can't." She shakes her head and does her shot. Mama pulls a face before swallowing around the taste in her mouth and shaking her head sharply. "And honestly,

I'm going to do everything in my power to prevent it if I can. So for now, I need you to keep on doing what you're doing. Patience is a virtue, Fallon, remember that."

"Easier said than done. "

"I know, baby, but for now, focus on what you can do. Maybe reach out to Colt and see if he knows anything," she offers with a small smile.

"That would work if I was talking to Colt. I might've told him to pull his head out of his ass after that night at the warehouse." I wince at the memory, not exactly feeling bad about it but not feeling great, either. Mama laughs, and I offer her a pained smile.

"Like mother, like daughter. I shouldn't be surprised. I said something similar to Denny."

"I hope she's okay, Mama."

"Me too, baby. Me too."

After all the worry and Hunter bullshit, my girl gets saved—well kidnapped, technically—by a goddamn Archangel. And I wasn't even there to see it! I had to hear about it afterwards from Creek. The man is terrible at telling a story, but damn, her being scooped up and saved by Leviathan? Goddess, it's enough to make a girl sweat.

Of course, now no one has any idea where she is.

Though, knowing Remy, it won't take her long to drive her winged friend to the brink of insanity. She'll definitely call. And if she doesn't? I'll kill her myself when her ass has the grace to show back up again.

So, I do what I do best, and I try to scry for her. Goddess knows she's spent enough time here, so I have enough stuff of hers. Unfortunately, whatever protections the Angel has in place are wicked strong because I can't pick up on her anywhere.

I'm not convinced she's still in this realm, but I know Remy; and if she wakes up too far from home, she'll lose her shit. It's times like this I wish my power would truly emerge. I truly don't care what it is because whatever it is comes with an upgrade. I literally power up. Yeah, watching comic show TV as a kid had me crying with laughter about their power ups. Though I always did love the yellow ranger more than any of the others, might be why it ended up being my favorite color, who knows.

Not having my power, and not knowing what's going on leaves me sitting here, twiddling my goddamn thumbs. Mama is off dealing with the fallout of Remy's kidnapping and all of the politics that go along with it. Creek and Colt are arguing, not that Colt and I are talking at the moment, but Creek has been utterly silent since it all went down. I don't know what's going through that boy's mind, but I half want to slap him out of it.

I pull out my phone and send Remy another text. I don't even know if she has her phone, but there's no way I'm running the risk of her having it and missing out on getting in touch with her. Hearing she's okay from others is one thing, but I need to talk to her before I'll believe it for myself.

"Fallon, is it breakfast time yet?" Rebel runs into my bedroom with a giant grin on her face. I swear all this kid does is eat. I try to remember if I was like this at her age. I know using our power takes a lot out of us, and she's still learning so much about hers. Add that to being a kid, and I guess it must be exhausting.

"Sure thing, sweet pea. Let me finish doing my face, and I'll be out," I tell her from my dressing table. She nods and runs from the room, back to the TV if I have to guess. I finish putting on my makeup, because my mama taught me that my face is as good an armor as anything else I can wear, and head out to sort out the rugrat.

It doesn't take long to get her ready, and her friend's mom picks her up for school, which leaves me clear to go to the store. I hope to the Goddess that Misty didn't fuck too much up last night. Fates, I adore that girl, but she's a hot mess.

SIX

FALLON

NOW

"Colt, I'm not doing this with you again." I hang up and throw my phone down on the bed, trying not to scream in frustration. That boy would drive a saint to despair, I swear it.

I lie back, and close my eyes, thankful that Mama and Rebel are staying with Aunt Celine tonight. Thank the Goddess for margarita night, even if it is a Thursday. A few minutes of peace is all I want. Between working at the restaurant during the day, covering the store at night, and still trying to maintain something of a life, I'm exhausted.

I'm hella glad Misty is covering the store tonight. I can't remember the last full night's sleep I had.

Pounding at the front door pulls me from a slumber I hadn't realized I'd fallen into. I stretch my arms over my head, muscles aching in that sweet post-nap sort of way as I push myself up. "I'm coming!" I shout, though it comes out a little scratchy.

I groan as I stand. A few more minutes sleep would have been awesome. I drag my feet as I head to the front of the house and sigh when I see who's at the door through the window.

"You can't keep ignoring me, Fallon." Colt's voice filters through the house, and I lean against the wall in the hall. I knew avoiding him and hanging up wouldn't last forever. He's as patient as a toddler waiting on ice-cream, but I'd hoped to keep it up for a bit longer.

I take a deep breath to steady myself then rip the front door open. "What do you want, Colt?"

"We need to talk," he says, his eyes pleading, but his crossed arms and blasé stance shout nothing but hostility.

"You already talked. You made yourself quite clear. So I'm making myself clear. Whatever it is that we were is done." I look him straight in the eyes so he knows I'm not fucking around.

"This isn't done. *We're* not done," he responds, and I roll my eyes.

"And like always, you don't take what I say seriously. You were right, this would never have worked." I run my fingers through my hair as he glares at me, wincing at the state of the rat's nest on top of my head. "Go home, Colt. I need to get some sleep."

"I was wrong." He steps toward the door, crowding my space, but I hold firm. "I was so wrong. I didn't even truly believe what I was saying but it's what I was taught. It's what I knew."

"It doesn't matter, Colt."

"It has to matter. Please, Fallon, hear me out," he pleads, and I huff. When the hell is this man-child going to take a hint? "Talk to me, Fal. Please."

"You've got fifteen minutes, but after that, you're gone, you hear?" I tell him, my tone firm as I open the door for him to step inside. I really do need to catch up on some sleep. Dealing with whatever the hell this shit is won't be conducive to that.

"I'll take whatever I can get."

I step back, allowing him to step inside fully. Closing the door behind him, I head toward the sitting room, sitting in the love seat with my legs tucked underneath me. Colt takes the chair nearest to me after hesitating long enough by the loveseat for me to fix him with a heavy lidded glare that more than screams, 'no.'

"Talk," I tell him curtly. I'm tired, and honestly at this

point, I've given the boy more than enough of my time and energy. I've had it thrown back in my face once already, I'm not going through that again.

"I was wrong, okay? I'm so sorry for what I said, but all I could hear was my dad and Bauer in my head talking about factions and duty. Then everything happened with Remy, and I realized two things. One, I wasn't alone, and two, I had no reason to be ashamed of what I was feeling. I know that sounds like complete horseshit, but it is what it is. It took me a minute to wrap my head around everything.

"I thought we were just having fun, you know? And then, all of a sudden, it wasn't fun, and we were creeping toward a place we couldn't come back from unchanged." He rubs the back of his neck. I can tell how hard he's trying to explain what he means, but man is he bad at it.

"Colt, you told me your kind and mine don't mix. That you need to keep your lines pure. That's a bit of a whopper to come back from with an *I'm sorry*," I tell him, tilting my head as I narrow my eyes. I truly can't believe he'd think that paltry apology would be enough.

"You made it sound like Witches are beneath you. Nothing more than rabble. Good enough to slum it with maybe, but that's all. I wasn't good enough to be with you, not because of *who* I am, but because of *what* I am," I seethe. I thought I'd moved past my anger over this, but apparently I was wrong.

"Obviously I'm a fucking idiot, Fallon. This isn't something new, honestly. Lifetimes I've gone around with my head up my ass, buying into the bullshit the Elder Council fed us, but you changed that. You made me doubt it. You made me want more. You made me more. Tell me how to make it up to you, and I'll do it," he pleads, kneeling in front of me.

"This isn't something I can tell you how to fix, Colt. This is something you need to figure out on your own," I tell him, crossing my arms. I need anything and everything available to me to put an extra barrier between us right now. I have to be strong because my body is screaming for him.

"Please, Fallon," he sighs, his mouth hanging open on my name. He takes a deep breath, and I try to prepare myself for whatever else it is he has to say. He swallows and shakes his head before begging, "Please."

"Your time is up, Colt. You gotta go. I need to sleep before I head back to the store tonight." He doesn't need to know that I don't actually have anywhere to go.

"Okay, I'll go. But I'm not giving up, Fallon. I'm in this, whether you are or not. And we both know I don't back down easily," he says as he stands. He waits for me to respond, but I have nothing else to say to him; so I sit and watch as he shakes his head before walking toward the front of the house. "It isn't over yet, Fallon. You'll see."

His words echo through the house before the door closes behind him, and I let out a deep sigh.

What the hell am I meant to do with that?

I pick up my phone to double check that Misty is still covering for me at the store tonight, and I'll cover for her next week since we're both in tomorrow. I'm going to need another drink to deal with everything Colt just dropped in my lap.

Men.

"Mama!" I walk through the house, looking for her. I really need to find her and then head back to the store. Rebel's dance recital is tonight, and there is no way Mama will miss it. I left Misty in charge while I popped home to get changed after yet another unfortunate accident with a potion and Misty's clumsy little brother.

"Mama! Are you here?" I call out again, but I don't see hide nor hair of her or Rebel, so I guess they've already left. I drop my keys on the counter in the kitchen and head to my room. It has its own entrance via the back of the house, but it doesn't get all that much use these days.

I throw my shirt into the laundry basket and grab another from my closet, ignoring the clink of the bracelets on my wrists. I check my reflection to make sure the bright colors don't clash and that my hair hasn't gone insane with this humidity. My black waves are still how I styled them earlier, though they've dropped a little, but my eyeliner has all but melted away because Mama refuses to keep the store less than like a hundred degrees. I touch it up, and the lines make my dark eyes seem bottomless. I paint another layer of red on my lips and head back out to the store.

It might be the evening, but that's one of our busiest times. Even humans want to believe in Witchcraft, so we walk a fine line between telling them the truth and making them believe we're only talking nonsense. Though, most of them desperately wish it were all true. Sometimes they just want a little potion or a card reading, or even an herb and root mixture. Without the right incantations, they're essentially useless, so I don't care to sell it to them. Nighttime is when most of our faction customers swing by too.

Since creating a portal isn't an option as humans are likely in the store, I climb back in my car and crank up the AC. I dance in the car the entire drive. The clouds are so dark, it looks like a storm might be rolling in. I pay it little attention as I pull into the spot out in front of the store. I hurry from the car, and get inside just as the heavens burst open, rain pouring like cats and dogs.

This time of year is a pain in the ass with the weather.

I check my phone and fire off a text to Remy. It's been

a few days since I've heard from her, but Goddess knows she has a lot going on right now. What, with all of the bullshit with Archer and adding that hottie of an Archangel to her ever growing harem. He kidnapped her, saved her life, and then stomped all over the Hunter Council so they couldn't hurt her. Can you say swoon? I don't expect to hear back from her anytime soon, so I silence my phone and pop it under the counter.

"Misty, girl. Where are you?" I call out. I don't see any customers, and the place really isn't big enough for her to hide.

"Back here. I thought I'd restock the tea leaves." Her head pops out of the back room, and the first thing I notice is that her hair is a frazzled mess. She trips as she tries to exit the room, sending bags of tea leaves flying across the store. I cringe as she hits the floor, palms first.

"Are you okay?" I ask and move to help her, but she jumps to her feet, her pale cheeks beet red, and waves me off.

"I'm fine, just tripping over air. If I didn't know better, I'd be convinced I was being haunted," she says as she scrambles to pick up the bags she dropped, and I watch closely to make sure she doesn't trip again. Either clumsiness runs in her family, or she really is haunted. That honestly wouldn't be the weirdest thing I've seen this week.

"Okay, well, you know how to cleanse yourself and your home of a ghost, right? Once you've put those out, you can head home; and please, take the bits to perform a cleanse with you. Better safe than sorry, sugar." I smile at her, and I swear it only serves to embarrass her more. Goddess give me strength to deal with this girl.

"Thanks, Fallon." The color on her cheeks deepens, and I wave her off. She's quiet as a mouse while she finishes up and manages to only drop three more bags while she stacks the shelves. I swallow my laughter. Goddess bless her soul, she's a mess.

I pitter around, making sure the usual night demands are available in the counter displays and straighten up in general. Goddess knows I love my mama, but she's like a hurricane. She sweeps through here and leaves chaos in her wake. This might be her store, but I'm in here more often than she is these days, so it's hard not to think of it as my own.

"Night, Fallon!" Misty calls out as she leaves, the bell over the door signaling the door closing behind her. I switch off the main lights—leaving on what Mama calls the mood lights. I like to call it a nighttime ambiance, especially with the dark storm clouds outside. It keeps it cozy in here.

Time passes quickly, and I read in the lulls of the evening, keeping my Kindle hidden near the register. A girl needs some form of escape, and since I've taken a self-imposed break from all types of penis, reading is my go-to relaxation tool.

My phone buzzes, so I pick it up and see a message from Mama letting me know that she and Rebel are home and that she'll see me in the morning. The woman is such an early bird, and I couldn't be any more different if I tried. I love the dead of night, which is how I ended up with the graveyard shift at the shop. Healers are needed at all hours, so someone has to be on hand pretty much constantly. It's that or we get woken up at the house, and that makes Mama spit feathers.

The grandfather clock in the corner chimes out and lets me know it's midnight, which is my cue to get up and lock the main doors. The shop is officially closed, but I'll stay around in case I'm needed. I walk around the place double checking I've locked everything up properly, both normal locks and magical ones, before I get settled on the sofa in the middle of the store by the books to take a quick nap. I might like the night, but I barely slept last night—for the last few weeks really—since that night at the warehouse.

It still makes me so mad that they did that to Remy, but I have to remember she's okay, that she's supposedly moved past it, and she isn't bottling it all up like usual. I push down the rising tide of power that follows my anger, since it really isn't the time to be getting worked up.

I get settled, laying down another layer of wards

because otherwise I know I'll never sleep, and then close my eyes.

Banging at the back door of the shop has me jumping up from my doze and scooting to the door to see what the hell is going on. I open the spyglass and find a bloodied Bauer being held up by his strange blond friend Archer on one side, and someone I don't recognize on the other.

Despite my feelings toward Bauer with everything he's put Remy through because of his ridiculously bigoted views on life, I open the door because Remy would never forgive me otherwise. Even if the guy doesn't deserve it, I could never do that to my best friend. I swear, he might be smart, but sometimes that boy is actually as dumb as a bag of rocks.

I wave them in, noting that Bauer is passed out between the other two. I'm guessing the nasty gash on his forehead that's pouring blood is why. "What the hell happened?"

The two with him carry him to the table we have set up for this exact purpose and lay him down on it. I wince as his head cracks down onto the table. Damn, I guess that's just another thing for me to fix.

"Help him," Archer snarls, and I roll my eyes. I've met him a handful of times, and he's always a total dick. I don't know why I expected anything different now as he's asking for my help. So I shoo those two out of my way and straighten Bauer up before assessing his injuries. The gash on his head is the most pressing, but there's a slew of other injuries to deal with too. I tick off a broken wrist, a couple of broken ribs, and a sprained ankle.

What the hell happened to him?

I shake my head and close my eyes, resting my hands over the head injury. The warmth that comes with healing fills me, like a welcoming comfort blanket, and spills from my hands. I hold the image of his injuries in my mind and focus on the one I'm healing, picturing it knitting back together.

It might not be how everyone does it, but my granny taught me this way, and it works.

It takes more than I thought it would to heal him properly, and I keep him unconscious throughout the entire process. Because even though he's healing, he's gonna be sore after all of that trauma.

"He's all fixed up," I tell them once I step away from Bauer. I lean on the counter behind me, feeling more than a little weak.

"Thank you, how much do we owe you?" Archer asks, walking toward me.

"The usual fee," I tell him. He nods and reaches into his back pocket and hands me a wad of cash.

"This should cover it."

"Thanks, I'll be right back, and then I'll help you get him out of here," I tell them, and turn my back on them to put the money in the register out front. They stay in the back, presumably with Bauer, but I can't help but feel on edge.

I test the wards on the store and find that the only one broken is at the back door where I let them in. No one else could possibly be in here, and yet, it feels like I'm being watched. I turn to head back to them and nearly jump out of my skin.

"For all things holy! Don't sneak up on a Witch like that." I scowl as Archer smirks at me.

"Apologies, I didn't mean to startle you," he says, holding his hands in the air.

"What's up?" I ask warily. The hair on the back of my neck stands on end, and I shudder in the seconds before a hand drops over my mouth and I feel a pinch in my neck.

"What the…" I ask, but my words slur as the edges of my vision go fuzzy.

"I'd say I'm sorry, but I'm really not," Archer snarls as I stumble forward. I try to think of a spell, any way to get out of here, but my brain is a jumbled mess, and I can barely focus on a thought.

"Get the girl, I'll grab Bauer, and then we can get going. Deacon will be expecting us soon," Archer tells the guy behind me who's already busy wrapping his arms around my waist. I try to fight him off, but it's like I'm submerged in water. My moves are sluggish, my mind is hazy, and my body just won't work properly.

"Time to get this party started."

SEVEN

COLT

"What the fuck do you mean Fallon's been taken?" I yell over the phone at my sister. What a way to start a fucking call. "Fuck this. I'm on my way."

I grab the keys to my truck and practically run from the house. I speed way faster than I should, reaching the manor in record time. I'm still reeling from having the weight of the world dropped on my shoulders after being named an Elder in the Hunter Council after the coup my sister led. I don't know if I'm strong enough to handle that and this as well. Fallon had better be okay. My hands shake around my tense grip on the steering wheel, so I take a deep breath before climbing from the truck. I try to calm myself, but it isn't fucking working. I slam the door to the manor open to find Remy and her guys already gathered in the main room.

"Break a few speed limits on your way here, big brother?" She smiles at me, but I'm not in the mood for fucking smiles. I want to know what exactly the hell she was going on about. Maybe I misheard her. Or maybe they're playing some dumbass prank on me and Fallon is going to pop out from around a corner at any moment, dragging my ass for not being the man she wanted again.

"Don't start with me, Remy. *Talk.* What the fuck is going on?" I demand before starting to pace because I can't keep fucking still. I reach a hand up and pull on my hair—a little pain to help keep my thoughts in line.

"Take a seat, Colt," Levi says calmly, his entire posture rigid as tension rolls from him. If he thinks I'm going to calm down, he has another thing coming. Archangel of War or not, this shit is too much to deal with.

"Bauer called me this morning telling me we needed to talk," Remy starts, and my eyes bug out. My heart slams in my chest, and I crash into the seat next to her, my leg bouncing. "He told me that Archer has been behind everything: the rogues joining together, the hybrids, all of it. Bauer's been trying to stop it all since Archer discovered he needed me to open the portal to the Shadow Realm."

She stops talking, and I lean back in the chair, my

mind officially blown. There's no way. Bauer wouldn't do that. But Bauer around Archer isn't the Bauer we know and love, so maybe he would. What the fuck is the world coming to when my brother takes and uses the girl I think I might be in love with to fuck with our sister? He's not this guy. There has to be something else going on... But I know Remy wouldn't lie to me, not about something like this. We've been through enough at this point that we don't keep secrets. Not anymore.

"Why does he need you?" I ask, looking around at them all.

"He needs me because before I was a Hunter, I was an Angel. A Shadow Walker. Which meant that I could pass between the realms with ease, and I'm the only one who can open the portal for more than a few minutes because my blood was used to seal the portal the last time it was opened."

"What the…" I can't even start to wrap my mind around this... She was an Angel? How is that even fucking possible.

"I know, it's been a day. I got back from talking to Bauer, explained everything to these guys, and then I got a call from Archer saying that he had Fallon, and that she's in the Shadow Realm. He insists we won't get her back unless I help him."

"You can't help that asshole," I grit out through my

clenched jaw, reeling from everything she's telling me. Bauer knew all of this? It's like I don't even know the guy.

"I don't intend to. But I *am* going into the Shadow Realm, and I *am* going to get her back. But I don't know how long that's going to take, which is why I called you. I need to make sure all hell doesn't break loose here when Archer discovers I've gone into the Shadow Realm rather than helping him."

"I don't… I mean… Holy fucking shit, Remy." I lean back in the chair and run my hands through my hair as I flick my tongue bar through my lips and mess with it, trying to give myself a minute to catch up.

"I know, Colt, but I don't see another way."

"Can you even do it? Since you're not actually an Angel, right? I mean, that's something we need to circle back around to because what the fuck, sis?"

"Yeah, it's a long story that I'll explain after this shit show is sorted out and Archer is dealt with. But whether I can do it or not, I'm going to find a way. There is no fucking way I'm letting her stay down there. Not when it's my fault she's there. I don't even want to think about—"

"It isn't your fault, *mon amour*," Kain says softly, looking at my sister like she hung the moon. Like he feels her pain. My heart pangs in my fucking chest again. "The fault is Archer's. And maybe a little of Bauer's."

"Maybe, maybe not. Regardless, we need to get her

back," she says to them before turning back to me a grim set to her features as she considers me. "You need to check in on Bauer. He was hurt when Archer called me. I don't care that he had a hand in this mess, he still tried to help us, and he warned me as best he could."

"I'll do more than check on him," I say through gritted teeth. I'm going to make him regret ever fucking messing with our family. The shit he gave Remy when he thought she'd betrayed us, and it turns out he's the biggest betrayer of all? Fuck. What does it say about me that I didn't see any of this as it was happening?

"We should call together the heads of the factions," Roman says. "Prepare and make sure that everyone is ready here before we leave."

"You're all going?" I ask, looking around the room at the determined looks on every single one of my sister's guys' faces.

"You didn't actually think we'd let her go alone?" Levi asks, eyebrow raised.

"But *you're* the faction leaders. Who will sort things out with the factions if you're not here?" I look at them all in disbelief. Surely they can't just up and leave. The world is a fucking mess right now.

"We have trusted people to help us. Just as the Hunters have their Elders, we have people we lean on. I have my Generals, Roman his Alphas. They will do as we ask while we are gone, for however long that may be," Kain says, and I scoff.

"This is insane."

"You'd rather we sent her to the Shadow Realm alone?" Roman asks, practically growling. His tone sets me on edge, making me instantly defensive, but I try to keep my shit under control because he's the Alpha of Alphas and one of my sister's boyfriends. It still feels weird thinking about it.

"Of course not," I mutter. I may not do a great job of proving it some days, but I'm not actually stupid. "But I know my sister. She'll get Fallon back with help or not. But what happens up here with her gone? You guys not being here could make an even bigger difference in everything that's going on."

"This is not up for discussion," Creek says as he enters the room. "If we can all go with her, then we all go with her. Our people here will be able to handle whatever shit Archer has up his sleeve, especially if we can get Bauer out of his grip. We'll hopefully finally have some idea of what's going on. Marie is gathering the Witch Council. She recommended we get our people here and meet in two days. She doesn't like leaving Fallon down there longer than she has to either, but she agrees that we need to make sure that Archer, and whatever he has planned, can be handled when we're gone."

"Okay, well, let's do that. You guys get in touch with whoever you need to. We'll have everyone meet here. It's the most secure place we have to gather that many leaders in one place." Remy looks at Levi, and he nods. "Will the Archangels help?"

"I don't know." He bows his head a little, and I can feel one of my eyebrows quirk as I watch the small smile that pulls Remy's lips up at the edges in response. "I will reach out to Serafina and see what I can do."

"Thank you," she says sincerely, and he offers her a grim smile of his own before leaving the room.

"I'll start contacting the Alphas," Roman says, and Kain nods, standing.

"And I'll contact the Generals. We don't have much time to get everyone here."

"Marie will open portals if needed," Creek tells them both, and they each nod, resolute in their directions. They move to leave the room, each kissing Remy on the cheek in turn as they go.

"I guess I should go and talk to Nasari and the rest of the Elders," I say wearily, standing.

"I'll come with you. The more people we have to explain what the hell's going on, the better," Creek says, standing with me. "We also still don't know which Hunters are working with Archer, so we need to tread carefully."

"I'll see what I can find out about the Shadow Realm.

Levi said my old journals are here, so I can only assume he means from all the way back." Remy shrugs, and my stupid-ass heart pangs one more time at the damn near broken look on her face. I need her to bring the old Remy back right the fuck now, otherwise I'll storm the Shadow Realm my fucking self. Consequences be damned.

Remy called this morning telling me she had an update. It's about fucking time. I've been losing my fucking mind. She asked me to swing by Fallon's and grab Marie and said that she'd explain more once we got there. She's been real fucking cagey recently, and while I get it, it frustrates the fuck out of me. Either way, I jumped in my truck, grabbed Marie from her place, and hauled ass over to the manor. When we got here, I came face to face with another motherfucking Angel, Nevin. I swear these fuckers are everywhere. At least this one is less terrifying than Leviathan. It could be the reedy build of him, or the nerd glasses, but he's not as imposing as the Archangel of War, who's apparently in love with my little sister.

I've met him a few times since he rescued her the day of her hearing, but he's always so fucking intimidating. He makes me feel like a scrawny kid, and I hate it. He loves my sister so fiercely that I've learned to deal with my weirdness about him... And the others.

"So, you think you'll be able to help us?" Remy asks Marie, and the rest of us shut up. She wants our help getting her to the Shadow Realm, where Fallon is being held. I've been losing my fucking mind worrying about her, but now Remy wants to head there to save her. I'm in two minds. One side screams hell yes, let's go get my girl, I was a fucking fool for thinking of her as anything else. The other side shouts that my little sister isn't going to walk through fire to jump through Archer Dotoro's fucking hoops. There has to be more to this than Bauer told us about. Granted, I'm still not over my brother's fucking betrayal, but right now, I have bigger things to worry about.

"I don't see why not. Your blood is still the conduit; I'm guiding the dormant magic in it. Fallon should be able to do the same for you from the other side to reopen it." Marie smiles tightly, the unsaid words hanging thick in the air. If she's still alive. "I brought you this."

She hands Remy a necklace with a pendant on the end. "Fallon's talisman?" she asks, and Marie nods.

"It should help guide you to her once you're down there since you still don't know where she is or who really has her." She looks pointedly at me, and I rub the back of my neck under the piercing stare, and I know instantly she blames me partially for this.

"We've tried to find Bauer, but Archer has gone to

ground. It seems that Bauer is with him. Willingly or not, we don't know, but I'd assume not at this point. Not considering that he came clean to Remy," I tell them as I pace the kitchen floor. "We've gone over every piece of information we've collected at least a dozen times. No one knows where they are."

"Could they have gone to the Shadow Realm as well?" Nevin asks.

"I don't think so. I mean, Archer obviously has someone opening temporary portals for him, but why risk possibly not being able to come back? He'd know I wasn't going to risk myself to bring him back, " Remy responds with a sigh

"It was just a thought," Nevin replies.

"It wasn't a bad one. Archer's too narcissistic for it," Levi adds. "I still think this is moving too quickly. We have too many unanswered questions."

" I'm not leaving Fallon down there a second longer than necessary, answers or not. We'll work it out when we get there. I can still go alone while you guys can stay and help keep the peace here."

"Not a chance, princess," Roman grumbles, and I silently agree. I can't lose anyone else, and I don't give a shit if that makes me selfish.

"Remy, you know I don't want Fallon left down there any longer than is necessary, but you need to be careful.

What if you can't get back? What if you don't have the power to bring the others back even if you can cross back?" Marie asks.

"Well actually," Nevin begins, "I think I have the answer to that. I kept reading after you went to bed last night since there were so many journals left to go through. I found some more stuff that I was going to mention before you left, but this is as good a time as any."

He takes a deep breath, and it takes everything in me not to scream at him to hurry the fuck up. Fate only knows what Fallon is going through in that hellscape. "After reading, what I managed to piece together is that Shadow Walkers could cross any realm portal without issue because of the magic in their blood. Amantara managed to take someone across and back with her, as long as her blood was close to their heart. She used a long necklace with a vial of her blood to do so. If we made something similar for everyone, there shouldn't be a problem with everyone getting back."

He takes a breath, as if waiting to see that we've all taken his bullshit on board. I'm yet to fully understand a goddamn word.

"We can send you with a spare for Fallon too. It's your blood that stabilizes the portal, so rather than having to spill blood to open and close it—which is what you'd need to do to carry people across usually—as long as they have your blood on them and the portal is to be opened by you, everyone should be able to pass without issue."

"Okay, then we need to get some vials," she says, like it's no big deal while I'm sitting here, mind blown all over a-fucking-gain. I am not the guy for this kind of shit. I'm the guy who comes in later and helps kill the assholes. My head hurts with all of this, but I'm going to stay here and fucking suck it up. For Fallon. Fuck knows she deserves better than me, but this has made me realize one thing. She's mine, and I'm going to do whatever it takes to get her the fuck back.

"Funnily, I have some in the car. I'm a Witch, so I have all sorts. Colt, come and help me," Marie says excitedly, latching her fingers around my arm and starting to drag me from the room.

"Well, I guess I better donate some blood," Remy sighs as we head for the door, and I shiver as I leave the room. Blood magic still creeps me out a little.

Marie and I walk out to my truck, and she points to the huge wooden trunk she got me to haul into the bed when I got her. I lift it again; motherfucking thing weighs as much as my fucking truck. I stagger back into the manor, dropping it on the kitchen floor and stretching out my hands because fucking ouch.

"Now then," Marie starts before bending down to open the trunk and pulling Goddess knows what out. "These should do the job nicely."

She stands back up and places a handful of small glass vials in metal housings on the table.

"That is one handy trunk," Nevin comments with a raised eyebrow.

"You shouldn't discuss a lady's trunk," Everly says, and I snort at how pink Nevin's cheeks go.

"I didn't mean…" he starts, getting flustered, but Marie laughs, ever the diplomat.

"She knows that," Marie reassures him, and I stifle the rest of my laughter.

"So what happens now?" Kain asks, having been mostly quiet and brooding this morning.

"Now, Remy needs to open a vein and fill the vials. Once you guys have your new amulets, if you will, I can use Remy as a conduit and open the portal for you all," Marie tells him, matter of factly.

"I guess I better open a vein then," Remy looks over at Kain with a furrowed eyebrow and a meaningful look, and I glance away. Bedroom eyes aren't something I need to see. While I've accepted my sister is dating a Dracul, the last thing I want to see is him feeding on her. I'm trying to come around, to more than paltry acceptance, but a few lifetimes of hatred is hard to get past.

"What happens after that?" Creek asks quietly.

"After that, Marie closes the portal, and the factions prepare themselves for the war that is no doubt coming,"

Levi says grimly.

"Does anyone have any idea of what we can expect once we go through the portal?" Roman asks, but the room stays silent.

"It doesn't matter. Whatever we find, we'll deal with it," Remy says confidently, but my stomach knots.

"Well, here's hoping it isn't the fiery pits the humans dreamt up."

"On that uplifting note, I should be getting back. I don't want to push my luck with Sef covering for me," Nevin says, drinking the last of the tea in front of him.

"Thanks for coming, man." Levi stands with him, and they hug it out.

"Thank you for all your help," Remy says to him, and I offer him a tight smile.

"No problem, but keep my name out of things if it all goes to hell… Oh look, I'm punny." It takes everything in me to keep the smile on my face and not punch him in his.

"Oh my fates. "

"Yep, I'm definitely out," he says, shaking his head. "Good luck all."

He waves and heads out of the glass doors in the kitchen and then his wings unfurl. I try not to gape at the sight. They're blue, well, a blue-black... they're so different from the nightshade black of Leviathan's. He stretches them out, shaking them once, and bends his knees before taking off into the skies.

"That is never going to not be weird," I say, wide-eyed, and Remy chuckles. Levi claps me on the shoulder, startling me and making me jump slightly.

"You'll get used to it eventually," he says before turning to my sister. "Okay, so Angel, I guess we better get these vials filled. Are you ready?"

"Ready as I'll ever be."

The vials are filled, and we're out in the backyard of the manor. I shake my hands out again because my palms are sweaty. This shit is in-fucking-sane

"Are you ready, Remy?" Marie asks, and she nods her head. My gut twists, but I keep my mouth shut. I have to just tell myself that everything's going to be okay. That Remy's going to find Fallon and they're all going to make it back safely.

"Sure, let's get this show on the road. Please look after yourselves while we're gone," Remy tells us, hugging us each in turn. "Be as safe as you can be, please. I wish there was some way we could stay in contact while we're gone."

"Don't sweat it, little bit. We have things covered up here. You go get our girl." I hug her tighter and offer her a small smile when I pull back. "I'll try to get our brother back amidst the chaos too."

"Thank you, Colt," she whispers, squeezing my hand. "Okay, let's go."

"Right, each of you take one another's hands. You have Remy's blood, so it may not be necessary, but being connected to the conduit can't hurt anything either. You should probably close your eyes too. And whatever you do, do not let go until you know you're there. Understand?" Marie asks, and I stand back further behind her. The others nod, and she continues, "Perfect, you bring my girl home, Remy. No matter who you have to kill to do so."

"I will, Marie. I swear it."

"Thank you," she says, and the same grim smile I've seen stretched over every other face at some point over the past few days pulls her lips tight. Marie shakes out her hands and offers a tight nod to my sister and her guys. "Right, here goes."

I watch as she closes her eyes and draws symbols in the air. The symbols glow and hover; and when each of them has a symbol behind them, they close their eyes and join hands. Just like that, they're gone.

EIGHT

COLT

Remy and the guys disappear in front of my eyes, and I shake my head. This shit is still a lot to wrap my head around. I've been a Hunter a while. This isn't my first life, but I've learned more about the other factions these last few months since my sister opened everyone's eyes than I have in all of my past lives put together.

"Right, we should clean up and head back. I have a dozen edgy Witches that want updates every ten minutes. We only have another day until Archer's deadline for Remy. It won't take him long to work out that she's not coming to help him," Marie tells me, resolute. I guess there's no fucking around when you're the High Priestess of the Witches. "You need to focus, Colt. I know you're worried about my daughter, but we have other roles to play in this. Remy will bring her back."

"I know, but I hate feeling like I'm on the sidelines," I tell her, rubbing the back of my neck.

"Once Archer finds out she betrayed him, it isn't going to feel like you're on the sidelines. You're going to be in the thick of it, so get your head in the game, you understand?" she scolds.

"Yes, ma'am." I nod before helping her pack up the few bits that she brought out here with her then head back inside to load up that godforsaken trunk. I don't know how she gets so much in it or how the hell she moves it without the help of a dozen people. It's rare that something makes me strain strength-wise these days, but fuck me that thing is *heavy*. I've lifted trucks lighter than that fucking trunk.

"Everything go okay?" Everly asks once we're inside and the trunk is all sorted out.

"As well as expected," Marie tells her. "I hope they're okay. Time moves differently in the Shadow Realm, but that's not the only thing that's different, their strength will be diminished down there too." She looks worried, and I try not to bug out. Why did no one mention this before?

"Do they know that?" I ask, and she shakes her head. Why the hell wouldn't she tell them that?

"Not as far as I know, but it doesn't make a difference

if they know or not. It'll take as long as it takes. They can't run through the levels of the Shadow Realm and magic Fallon to them. They're going to need help, serious help, especially if it's the Queen working with Archer. Though I can't imagine it," she tells us.

"You seem to know a lot about all of this."

"Read as many Witch grimoires as I have, and you'll pick things up too." She winks at me, and I try to keep my jaw from clenching. This doesn't feel like the time for cheekiness. Not when she's just told me that they're all likely to be a hell of a lot less effective than we all expected them to be. "The Queen isn't exactly a fan of humans or Hunters. So I don't see it being her, but stranger things have happened. Especially recently." She shrugs, picking up her purse in a clear dismissal of the subject. My gut churns. I have no idea how she can be so blasé about this.

"It was lovely seeing you again, Everly. Keep yourself safe, and set those wards the second we cross the property line, okay?" Marie tells her, and the other woman scoffs in return.

"I've been doing this a while."

"Things are a little different right now," I tell her, and she looks at me like she's going to scold me.

"You're not wrong," she finally says with a small shrug. "You both take care of yourselves, and I'll be here in this fortress if you need me, okay?"

They hug each other, and I offer her a wave. When she scoffs again, I open my arms, offering her a hug. "You're family, family doesn't wave," she says, patting my arm as she releases me.

"Understood," I say with a wink. I head out with Marie, carrying the godforsaken trunk out to her car. I drop it in the trunk of her car, and somehow, the suspension doesn't give way. If this car isn't spelled, I'd be amazed.

"Thank you, Colt," Marie says, patting my cheek. "Take care of yourself and get your guild ready. Now that Nasari and the others have left, it's on you to coordinate everyone here. I'll be around to help if you need it." She climbs into the car with a small smile before pulling away. I try not to take her comment personally; I'm sure she didn't mean to be as condescending as she was. She's got a lot going on.

Then again, leading a fucking guild isn't something I ever wanted *or* asked for, so maybe she's not completely wrong. Maybe I will fuck this up royally.

I climb into my truck, crank the music up as loud as it will go, and head back to my dad's place, trying not to think too much about the complete shitstorm I've found myself in the middle of. Needless to say, my dad is not taking any of this well. Everything with Remy, the new Hunter orders, or the Elder reshuffle.

It's been a lot to deal with.

Finding out Bauer was working with Archer and that it was likely Archer who attacked him with the Angel glass isn't making things any fucking better.

Yeah, living with him recently has been a fucking riot. I miss Bauer being around. Remy said Archer had him, and with as much as I have to deal with right now, getting him back is high on my priority list. Who knows how much information he might have or how much he could help tip the balance in our favor?

As I reach Salem's Bay, I decide not to head home. There's definitely someone in town who will help me with Bauer, but my dad isn't that guy.

I pull up out the front of a one-story house and chuckle to myself. Salem's Bay might not be the biggest of places, but I have more than enough Hunters staying here right now. With Bauer out of action and Creek off in the Shadow Realm, I'm down a dance partner. Fortunately, I know this guy is crazy enough to agree to help me.

"Colt Bennett. What the fuck are you doing here?" Elijah shouts at me through his screen door. I climb out of my truck and head up to meet him.

"Elijah, just the man I was hoping to find. How are you doing, you crazy son of a bitch?"

He opens the door and pulls me in for a bro hug.

"Fancy a beer?" he asks as we head inside. The hum from his AC unit fills the room on the unseasonably warm day.

"Sure thing." He heads to his fridge and pulls out two bottles, passing one to me before twisting the cap off of his. I twist the top and take a swig. Hello, sweet nectar.

"So what brings you by, mister boss man?" He laughs, and I shake my head. This Elder bullshit is for the birds.

"Don't start with that; it's fucking unreal. I'm here without the Elder title, if I'm being honest. I'm on a bit of a crusade mission, and I can't think of a better wingman," I tell him before taking another drink.

"What's the mission?" he asks, taking a seat and waving for me to sit too. I drop onto the couch opposite him and take a deep breath.

"I want to get my brother," I tell him straight. "Archer has him locked away somewhere, and despite everything the asshole has done, he at least tried to help, even if it was too little, too late. He'll know shit that can help us in the next few weeks."

I pause as I take another long pull from the beer. I take a deep breath before filling him in about Remy and Fallon.

"Holy shit, man. That's a lot. I got the gist of most of this from the gathering, but shit."

"Yeah man, there's a ton of shit going down, which

is why we need to get Bauer. He'll have invaluable information that we're not gonna get any other way. Numbers are down thanks to the Hunters that defected, but fuck them, they made their bed. We have enough people, especially with all the factions working together. I'm trying to minimize the collateral damage right now. You know that the humans are going to eventually figure out that something's up. If there's anything I can do to keep this fucking bullshit under their radar, then I'm going to do it."

"Makes sense. Fuck it, I'm in. Danny and the boys are back too, so I'll rope them in as well. Got to love the delta boys, running off to play in the human wars. Fortunately, they learned some new shit and got some new toys too. Might come in handy."

"Thanks, man, sounds good. I'm getting my shit in line today, and then tomorrow, we hunt."

"Count us in. Let me know when and where," he says, and I stand, draining the last of my beer.

"I'll drop you a message later tonight after I've gathered some intel," I tell him. He stands as I head out the door and to my truck. He waves me off with his beer bottle as I pull out of his drive.

One thing down, only another fucking shit ton to get sorted out.

When I get hold of Bauer, I'm going to knock him the

fuck out for putting us in this situation. I've met Archer, he might've been the one driving this crazy train, but my brother is definitely the strategic mind behind it all. There's no doubt in my mind that without Bauer, Archer would still be sitting, dick in hand, wondering where the fuck to start his stupid world domination quest.

I drive through Salem's Bay back to my dad's place, finding a few cars in the drive. I guess Nate and some of the others are already here. Good. That means I don't have to deal with my dad's bitching on my own. I love the man, but fuck me, I can't deal with his shitty moods for much longer. He either needs to get on board, or shut the fuck up. He has to see how twisted everything was when he allowed what happened to Remy to go down without fighting back. I clench my jaw as I try to swallow the rage that still burns in my gut about it. What kind of father does that? I've never done the kid thing in any of my lives, but you bet your ass if I did, I'd never let someone else dictate the life of my kid.

Fuck.

I punch the steering wheel and take a deep breath to calm myself back down. I'm supposed to be an Elder now. It's stupidest fucking decision I ever made, accepting that title. There are so many other things I want to focus on right now, and instead, I'm attending Elder meetings and dealing with people's petty little problems.

I decide right then that I'm naming Nate my right hand. He can deal with the petty squabbles while I focus on the bigger stuff.

Like Bauer.

Like Fallon.

Like Archer.

Fuck.

There's so much going on right now.

There's nothing quite like a divided focus to really fuck things up. I climb out of the truck and head inside, and laughter reaches me as I put my hand on the door handle. Good. Laughter means there's no whining going on. I follow the sounds to find everyone in the kitchen.

"Colt!" Maddie calls out as I enter the room, and she rushes to give me a hug. I haven't seen her since accepting the Elder position, so I wait it out and let her fuss. Fates knows it's been nice having her around since Mom passed away. No one could ever replace Mom, but it's nice to feel that kind of motherly love sometimes.

"Hey, Mads." I hug her back and wave to the guys in the room. Dad and Nate are sipping on whiskey, no real shock there, and a few of their other Hunter buddies are drinking a beer.

"What did I miss?" I ask, grabbing a bottle for myself from the fridge and sitting at the bottom of the table, opposite my dad. He's still upset that he didn't get the Elder seat. I'm not stupid. I know Remy was offered it first, but the clever bitch turned it down. I'm almost positive my dad would've revolted if she'd taken it.

"Not much here," Nate says. "How was everything on your end?"

I fill them in about everything that's happened the last few days, but I don't mention anything about going to get Bauer. These guys are skilled Hunters, but there's a little too much with the politics that have to balance with this. My dad would probably have Bauer killed for his betrayal, but I'm not that guy. Bauer tried to redeem himself, and if we get to him and he helps us, I don't see why the punishment can't be minimal. I'm not naive enough to assume he'd get off scot-free—he has the whole council to answer to—and I'm sure between Rem and I, we could swing it. I'm just not sure what's going on with her right now, though, so Fates knows what she'll be like when she comes back from that hellish place.

I suppress my shudder and take another drink after I finish filling them all in on everything. "I'm going to crash. It's been a long day."

I stand and drop my bottle in the trash, give Mads a goodnight hug, and head upstairs.

I crash onto my bed fully dressed and kick off my shoes but end up staring at the ceiling as the moonlight filters in through the window, wondering how the fuck we're going to get through all of this.

I've spent the entire fucking day tracking down that twat bag Archer, but with the help of a trusted friend who has some mad genius hacking skills, we finally managed to find him and my brother. Thank the Goddess for our big-brother government having cameras every-fucking-where these days.

I scrub a hand down my face, trying to wipe away the exhaustion that's starting to settle in, and make another pot of coffee. Fuck knows I'm going to need it to get through tonight. I gulp down a shot of espresso while I wait for the coffee to finish brewing and drop a message to Elijah, letting the boys know we're on for tonight. Could I wait and plan some more? Fuck yes I could, but I'm not going to.

Archer needs to be set off balance, and he's expecting to hear from Remy tomorrow. I want Bauer out of there before that bomb goes off. Fates only knows how Archer's going to retaliate, but I want us free and clear beforehand so we have enough people in place to deal with whatever comes from the fallout. And maybe Bauer can give us an insight into the crazy that is Archer.

I pour myself a mug of coffee and load it up with sugar

and cream before gulping it down. I grab a cold slice of pizza from the severely lacking fridge and chew it down, despite how gross it is. I need enough sustenance to get me through, not a five-star meal. Though, I'm definitely going to beg Maddie to make a pot roast the next chance I get. I miss home cooked food.

Car doors slam, announcing that Elijah and the guys are here. They make their way into the house as I pour another mug of coffee. "Anyone?" I ask, holding out the pot as the four of them filter into the room.

"Not for me," Elijah says, but a few of the others accept so I pour out the cups before putting another pot on. "What do we know?" he asks impatiently.

"We know where they are. There aren't any eyes inside, unsurprisingly, but I have it on good authority that their watch changes over at midnight. It's when they're the least prepared, so that's when we'll hit," I tell them.

"Do we know numbers?" Danny asks, and I shake my head.

"No, we're blind in that respect. Like I said, no eyes inside, so beyond the blueprints I managed to get my hands on, I have no idea what's happening inside those four walls." I wave to the blueprints of the warehouse I had my friend pull and let them pore over them. I've stared at them enough today. I could draw them in my damn sleep.

"Looks like a pretty standard layout," Elijah mumbles,

and I nod. He studies the blueprints for another quiet moment before he starts directing on which points are the weakest and easiest to infiltrate. I let him get on with it. I know my strengths and weaknesses, so there's a reason I went to him for help. Between him and Danny, I'm positive they could literally overthrow countries, so leaving the planning of this to them is a no-brainer.

"Sounds good to me, man, let's gear up," I say, and laugh as I notice the new kevlar the guys have on already.

"I have some for you in here." Elijah points to the duffel at his feet.

"Good looking out, man," I say with a short nod before heading to the weapons cache in the sitting room. Some people have bookshelves. We have fake shelves that open into a gun cabinet, crammed full of all sorts of goodies.

"Damn, man, you upgraded." Danny claps me on the shoulder with a smile as he peers in behind me. "But I brought you some new toys too." I grab my sawed-off shotgun and slip a Glock in my thigh holster before following him back to the kitchen.

The duffels are open on the table, and Elijah hands me a vest. It's lighter, thinner than usual, but if these guys have it, it's probably some new, not yet seen, military grade shit that isn't available anywhere else. I take off my t-shirt and slip the vest on before shrugging back into my t-shirt, making sure I have enough ammo to sink a goddamn ship before I'm ready to head out.

"Are you boys good to go?" I ask, and nods around the room greet me.

"Then let's head out."

NINE

FALLON

Two stinking weeks I've been in this stupid 'comfortable' cell. Or at least I think it's been two weeks. I'm only going on the meal rotation... if you can even call what they give me a meal. Wherever we are, my magic is nullified, so I can't even get myself out of this Goddess forsaken hellhole. I've never felt so goddamn helpless, and I hate it.

The only thing I'm thankful for is that the place is pretty clean, and they're intent on ignoring me other than when absolutely necessary. I'm being kept in what could pretty much be called a hotel suite. I haven't seen anything other than the inside of this room, and it's the same place I woke up after that asshole Archer drugged me. Fuck, he is such a dick.

I scream in frustration for the umpteenth time, but still no one comes. I'm sure the people back home know I'm gone by now, but why would anyone suspect Archer? Goddess knows I didn't. I let him waltz in without so much as a second thought. Look where that got me.

The lock turns on the metal door—which is the only sign that this room isn't what it's made out to be—and I scramble to my feet. It opens, and I come face-to-face with the same dark-haired guy who's been bringing me my 'food' all week. He looks human, but I know better than that. He wheels in a cart with a covered plate, a flower, and a glass of water.

Okay, so apparently today will be a little different.

"I spoke to the boss man and told him you might be trapped here, but you don't deserve to be treated like a prisoner," he says with a cheeky smile.

"But I am a prisoner," I remind him, crossing my arms.

"Maybe, but you don't have to eat like one. Come on." He winks as he rolls the cart over to the table on the other side of the room, and places the contents onto it, flower and all. He lifts the metal cover from the plate, and the scents hit me in an instant.

"Is that…?" I start, mouth watering, and he laughs.

"Country-fried steak, mashed potatoes, and collard greens with gravy," he says, and I eye him warily.

"Why are you being nice to me?" I ask.

"We're all trying to survive here. Casualties of war aren't really my thing. I don't buy into all their madness, you know. I'm actually happy here."

"Where exactly is here?"

"The Shadow Realm. Level six to be exact: greed."

"That makes total sense, and somehow none at all," I say, raising my eyebrows.

"Come on, eat. You have to be hungry after the abysmal food they've been giving you." His smile makes me want to trust him. He hasn't been cruel or anything when he's come in here; but if we are in the Shadow Realm, that means he's a Demon, which doesn't exactly inspire trust.

"I swear it isn't poisoned," he says, holding up a hand and placing the other on his chest.

"Of course you'd say that!" I roll my eyes, but my traitorous stomach growls without my permission. "Traitor," I whisper, looking down at my stomach, and he laughs.

"Okay, how about we start fresh? My name is Deacon, and I'm a lowly servant to the higher Demon who looks after this level of the realm. I also occasionally wolf out a little when my inner Demon gets a bit ragey," he tells me, sitting at the table, crossing one leg over the top of the other. "Come on, let's talk and eat."

"You're a werewolf?" I ask, moving toward him

hesitantly.

"No, Lycans, werewolves—they could only ever wish they were like me." He winks. "I wolf out, but I'm not a slave to it. I think the name for what I am is lost to humans, though they get their information wrong about us anyway. I have extra nifty little tricks too." He waves his hand in the air, and a circle of fire appears. Through it, I see Remy and her guys in some weird cave.

What the hell?

"I can show you what you most want to see," he says, and I wonder why it showed me what it did in that moment. Unless Remy is my way out... because right now, that's all I fucking want. To escape from here. I fight to keep the hope that blooms in my chest from reflecting on my face. I knew she'd figure it out. My bestie is a badass.

"Can you see it?" I ask, and he shakes his head.

"Nope, stupid balance. Only you can see that which you wish to see. Come on, eat before it goes cold." He motions for me to sit, and I hesitate for a moment. Fuck it, I'm hungry.

I sit and pick up a fork, taking a bite of the steak and gravy, trying not to groan. Fuck me, that tastes good.

"Good right?" he questions and leans back in his chair like he has nowhere else to be and nothing else to do. He's completely at ease, which sets me on edge.

"It is," I tell him, careful not to thank him. I don't

know much about Demons, but I know not to thank them. Selling my soul is so not on my to do list while I'm stuck here. I try to eat slowly, but my gurgling stomach tells me to forget my manners, and I practically inhale the food. Deacon doesn't interrupt me while I eat. Instead, he sits there watching me, which is creepy as fuck, but I'm too hungry to care.

"That was amazing," I say as I wipe my mouth on the napkin when I'm done.

"I'm glad. Now, any more questions before I head back to work? It's nice here, and the company isn't bad either, so I'm happy to bunk off." He winks at me, and I roll my eyes.

"How long have I been here?" I ask, trying to get a bearing on everything that might help me later.

"Today is day twelve, though time moves differently here to what it does on Earth. Your friends probably think it's only been a few days," he tells me openly.

"Who's your boss?" I ask, leaning forward with my eagerness to get more information.

"My boss is Greed himself. He's the guy in charge on this level of the Shadow Realm."

"Why do you need me?"

"We don't really, but the Hunter needs your friend to do something for him, and he thought you'd be the best way to encourage her. No one wants your pretty little head to roll." He smiles, taking a strand of my hair and tugging on it gently.

"I'd rather keep my head where it is," I snark as I pull back enough for him to drop my hair. "What does he want Remy to do?"

"He wants her to open a portal, and he needs her blood to build a bridge between our worlds. He wants dominion in both," he replies, and I try not to gape at him.

"How the fuck would she do that?"

"She's a Shadow Walker. Her blood is a very powerful thing." He shrugs as if what he's saying is common knowledge. The hell was I supposed to know Remy's a Shadow Walker? Is there no end to all of the amazing things my bestie is capable of? "It's amazing what's possible with the right ingredients, though you'd know all about that wouldn't you?"

"Remy would never—" I start, but he stops me.

"Even to save her best friend? I think she might." He smiles smugly, and his blue-green eyes practically fucking sparkle with glee. "She had better anyway because time is running out."

"What does that mean?" I ask, but he stands, brushing me off.

"You'll see," he says ominously as he gathers the dishes from the table and heads for the door. I try to stand, but I'm paralyzed. My eyes widen and flick to him. "Can't have you try to escape now, can we? You're still needed for the moment."

He pushes the cart out, and the sound of the lock echoes through the room. Once it's sealed, I can move again.

Dammit, he seemed so nice too. What a dick bag.

At least he gave me some answers.

Demons are assholes.

Since Deacon left Goddess knows how long ago, the door hasn't opened. It's as if the visit earlier was a test that I failed, and I have no idea how.

Fucking Demons.

I tried to summon my magic after he left, since magic of some form obviously works here, but I only made myself pass out while trying. I've never not been in touch with my magic, so it feels like a part of me has been cut out. I'm trying not to focus on it, but what else is there to think about?

I take a deep breath and try to meditate, hoping to completely zone out, but the thoughts in my head are way too loud.

The lock turns in the door again, but this time I don't cower. This time I'm pissed off.

"I come bearing gifts," Deacon's voice rings out as he

walks in, and the door shuts quickly behind him. I ignore him, staying cross-legged on the floor with my hands in my lap, staring at him with a raised eyebrow.

"What's up, little Witch? Didn't you sleep?" he asks, eyes wide and obviously thrown off by my hostility.

"Why can't I feel my magic?" I ask, not answering his question.

"Your magic doesn't exist here. It's tied to the elements of your realm. Of Earth," he explains openly, stealing a little of my ire.

"Oh."

"So, did you not sleep?" he asks again, and I shrug.

"It's hard to know when it's night and day in here, so no. I didn't sleep."

"You should really sleep. You seem cranky," he teases, and I try my best not to let out a frustrated scream. Cranky? This stupid Demon has no fucking idea.

"This isn't cranky. You wouldn't like me cranky."

"Maybe not on Earth. But here, you're essentially mundane. You don't have anything special to attack me with here," he tells me. "Now then, would you like some breakfast? If you don't want to nap after, I can take you for a little stroll and show you more of your temporary home."

I don't really care about seeing this place, but I jump on the opportunity. A chance to get out of here and maybe find a way to escape? There's no way in hell I'm turning that down.

"Sure thing." I move to the table where he's waiting for me with yet another cart.

He removes the cover from the plate, placing a glass of orange juice next to the plate of steak and eggs. I eye the knife, trying to think of a way to hide it once I've finished eating. I smile sweetly at him and take a seat. I don't have a plan, and even if Remy is coming for me, Deacon said there's a time frame. I'm not the sort of girl to sit and wait to be saved. Not now that I have an opening.

He smiles, pouring two mugs of coffee and handing one to me before putting the sugar and cream on the table. "This looks great," I tell him and dig in. Goddess knows I need the protein after twelve days of bread and cheese.

I'm not sure I'll ever look at a cheese sandwich the same way again.

Again, he sits and watches intently while I eat. "Do you want some?"

"I don't eat. Well, not that anyway." He smiles, and it's so dark a shudder runs down my spine. I don't ask any other questions; I don't think I want the answers anyway. Nope. This guy might seem nice enough, but that smile was all predator.

I eat slowly, trying to drag out the time before we leave, regretting that I agreed to it. At the same time, I can't wait to get out of this place. I don't feel like myself here.

At this point, I'd rather deal with Colt and all of his drama than deal with this Demon and his unreadable intentions.

What I want most, though, is to feel my magic and not feel so fucking useless.

"Come on, eat up. Don't worry, we won't go far." He grins again, and I chew the steak, barely tasting it. I should probably tell him he's grinning like a psychopath, but I'm not sure he'd take the offense intended.

"I'm not that hungry," I tell him, pushing the half-eaten food away.

"Okay, then let's go. By the way, when you're back, you should probably shower and change." He looks at me all judgy, eyebrows raised, and I scowl.

"If I had a bathroom, I would," I snark. I found the toilet, but there's nothing more than a sink in there.

"You have a bathroom." He looks at me, and I can tell he's trying not to laugh at me.

"No, I don't!" I say through gritted teeth. I don't exactly want to fight with the only person being nice to me. Not to mention he's a Demon, and I'm stuck here without my magic. The odds aren't exactly in my favor.

"Sure you do, just like you have a closet full of clothes."

"Funny, I haven't seen any," I tell him snarkily, my patience wearing thin. He waves his hand and two doors appear on the other side of the room.

Fucking Demons.

"Why were they hidden?" I ask, trying not to snap at him. I fail spectacularly.

"I guess someone was having fun with you." He winks. I clench my fists and take a deep breath. Punching the Demon isn't going to help me right now. I've also never actually punched anyone in my life, so I'm pretty sure I don't even know how.

"I guess so," I tell him, trying to calm myself down.

"Shall we go then?" he asks, standing and tucking his chair back under the table. I slip the knife up the sleeve of my hoodie when he turns, hoping he doesn't notice.

"Sure, why not? Actually, can I shower first?" I ask as nicely as I can muster.

"I don't see why not," he says, and I head over to the two new doors that appeared. "It's the one on the left."

I open the one on the right, just in case. But he wasn't lying, so I grab some clothes, as if that was always my intention, and head into the bathroom, locking the door behind me.

Oh my Goddess, there's toothpaste! Yes!

I don't even want to think about my breath right now.

I turn on the shower and strip out of my clothes, bundling the knife up with them to keep it hidden since there isn't anywhere in here I can actually hide it. There's a sink, a bathtub, and a shower. Not that you'll find me complaining about any of those things, but they're not conducive to concealing a stolen weapon.

I turn on the water, only giving it a short moment before I jump under the stream, moaning as the hot water cascades over my skin. It feels so damn good. As much as I'd like to spend the rest of the day under here, I wash quickly, scrubbing the grime from my hair and body, before grabbing a towel from the rail.

I tie my wet hair in a ponytail and dry myself off before dressing quickly. I don't want to keep the Demon waiting, especially since he seems intent on being nice to me.

"Right, I'm ready," I say as I open the door, steam billowing out around me.

"Change of plans, sweetheart." The voice stops me in my tracks, and my heart pounds in my chest. I take a deep, warbling breath, and try to keep my cool.

Archer fucking Dotoro.

"What the fuck do you want?" I hiss, wanting to launch across the room and tear his eyes out. I might never have trained to fight, but anger is a powerful thing.

"Now then," he says with a cheery smile, "is that any way to speak to the man who holds your freedom, your very life, in his hands?"

"Eat a dick, Dotoro," I spit at him, while Deacon edges closer to me slowly as if he's afraid.

"I see my Demon friends have been doing their job and

taming you," Archer says, glaring at Deacon. He grits his teeth in a sneer and turns back to me with narrowed eyes. "It doesn't matter, I always did like my lovers with a little fire."

"Ha!" I shout. "You couldn't handle me if you tried."

In a blink, he's in front of me, his hand on my throat, squeezing tightly. "Listen here, you little bitch, you are only alive because you're useful to me. Push me too far, and you won't be useful anymore."

His fingers grip tighter, cutting off my air before he throws me backward. I crash into the wall, my legs barely keeping me upright as I gasp in a deep breath.

What an asshole.

"What do you want?" I ask with a weak cough, my voice hoarse.

"That's as simple as it is complicated." He grins, his arms going behind his back as he stands tall. " I want to come out of the shadows. I want to rule, to raise the Hunters above the humans and into our rightful place in the hierarchy. Why should we follow their laws? Bow to them? They have no idea, but they will."

"You're insane," I tell him, and I try not to watch as Deacon edges even closer to me. He almost looks concerned, but I'm not a fool. He's a Demon; his only concern is for himself.

"How about we take this down a notch," Deacon says,

easing himself between us, and blocking me from Archer's line of sight. I roll my eyes, but fine, whatever. The Demon wants to de-escalate, who would've thought it? Though if either of them thinks I'm falling for this good cop, bad cop thing they have going on, they can think the fuck again.

"You're right, where are my manners?" Archer asks with a smirk. "I thought I'd drop in and make sure you're being treated well before I meet with your bestie. She's going to be helping me out a little, all for little ol' you. Aren't you a lucky Witch to have such loyal friends?"

I don't bother responding because he's not really engaging. He's painting pretty words as a tactic to delay, and that only serves to make me curious.

"What are you really doing here, Archer?" I ask with a sigh, forcing more exasperation into my tone than I truly feel.

"Well, that would be telling wouldn't it," he says, moving forward and booping me on the nose. I clench my fists and try not to growl at him. I'm not an animal, and this dickhead is getting on my last nerve.

"I could make you tell me, you know, if you weren't so afraid of me that you banished me to the one place I can't access my magic." His eyes go a little wild at the accusation, and he moves closer again before seemingly getting a hold of himself and taking a deep breath.

"Silly little Witch. Taunt me all you like, but the only

way you're getting out of here alive is if your friend does exactly as I say. Otherwise, Deacon here will snap that pretty little neck of yours." He bares his teeth at me, and I grin. I'm not scared of Archer Dotoro, not even now.

I'm so fucking angry.

And an angry Witch isn't a Witch you want to cross.

How dare he use me to get to Remy? How dare he kill so many good people in his ridiculous quest for world domination? Could he seriously be any more cliché?

"Why now?" I ask, tilting my head, trying to figure it out. What's different now ? Why this lifetime?

"Why not? Especially with Remy thinking she's so clever, re-aligning the Elder Council, making everyone believe the monsters are no less than us. Filth is what they are. They should be serving us, not working alongside us."

"Wow, it's like you opened your mouth and Bennett Senior's words fell out. Brainwashed much?" I laugh, trying to rattle him. Guys like him don't usually spill their guts unless they think they're winning or if they're angry. It's like their feeble sense of reason disappears completely if they experience any minute form of emotion at all.

" I'm tired of this. Deacon, let's go and discuss the details of everything with Azriel, shall we?" Archer asks with a sigh.

"Yes, let's," Deacon says, bowing his head slightly.

What the fuck does Archer hold over the Demons?

Or is Decon bowing to him because Archer is working with his boss? Archer leads the way out of the room, with Deacon on his heels.

"I'm sorry," he mouths back to me, and I shake my head. I don't believe him, but I can't focus on that. Not now, not when Archer Dotoro is here diatribing his world domination plan to anyone who will listen.

What the fuck is going on?

I don't know how much time has passed since they left, but I've slept and eaten several times. I even ran myself a bubble bath. Now that I have the opportunity, you bet the fuck I'm making the most of it. I might be trapped here, but they can only make me miserable if I let them. And if they need Remy's help, I'm guessing that Archer is shit out of luck. Based on what Deacon showed me, I know it's only a matter of time till I'm either saved or I die.

While I'm not exactly ecstatic about the possibility of dying, if that is my path, then I'll go back to the Mother, and watch on, cheering my friends on from the other side. Wherever that may be, but knowing what I know, I know that this is not all there is to life.

Even if I'm 'just a Witch'... one of the only true mortals among the supernaturals that roam the Earth. But being mortal makes every day that much more special, which is why I'm enjoying the shit out of my current bubble bath.

Apparently being a prisoner isn't so bad right now. Even if the gnawing feeling inside of me grows each day that I'm out of touch with my magic. It feels as if my soul is being eaten piece by piece with every hour that I'm away from home.

The door slams open to the bedroom, and I jump. A little water sloshes over the side of the tub, but I settle, knowing that the door to the bathroom is locked.

A sharp crack rings out, and the door flies open. Deacon stares at me, his eyes frantic. "What the fuck was that earlier!" he screeches as I rearrange the bubbles to make sure I'm covered, trying to keep my cool about the fact that he stormed in here while I'm naked.

"The fuck are you doing storming in here while I'm naked?" I ask pointedly. I might be a prisoner, and really, he doesn't have to be as nice as he has, but I'm hoping he keeps it up.

"Fuck that, Fallon. He wants you to be tortured. Fucking tortured! There are some sick assholes down here, especially on this level, that would do anything for a little extra of whatever it is they want that day." He paces the bathroom, and I try not to let my fear push to the surface. Torture is so not on the list of things I want from today.

"You're going to torture me?" I ask him quietly.

"Of course I'm not going to fucking torture you. Just because I'm a Demon, doesn't mean I'm a fucking monster! He's lost his damn mind. All that power will go to his head." He runs his hand through his hair and side-eyes me.

"What power?" I ask cautiously. Hunters don't have power.

"The power he bargained for. For the blood of the Shadow Walker," he tells me almost despondently. "Get dressed, I need to make the room more secure. I can't do that with you naked."

He turns and leaves the room, pulling the door closed behind him, and I rub my temples. I'm so goddamn confused by all of this.

The blood of the Shadow Walker? So maybe Archer doesn't actually want world domination? Every time I get a semblance of an answer, I end up with even more fucking questions.

Remy better hurry her ass up and get here before Archer figures out she's not coming to meet him back on Earth, otherwise all hell might quite literally break loose. I'm not sure any of us would be able to survive that.

I pull myself out of the tub and dry off before slipping into the clothes I'd brought in here with me. The harem pants and crop top aren't my usual style, but they looked fun, and it isn't like anyone will make fun of me down here. I'm, quite literally, in Hell. The Shadow Realm is seriously no fucking joke. I dry my hair, wrapping it to keep it out of the way, and head out to my room, or prison cell, whatever you want to call it.

Deacon is waiting for me in the room, but he's not alone. He looks tense as fuck, and his jaw looks so clenched I'm afraid he might crack a tooth.

"Who are you?" I ask, eying the dark-haired man with a jaw that could cut steel who stands in front of Deacon.

"Me? I'm your worst fucking nightmare. You can call me Azriel." He grins at me, revealing all four fucking rows of his sharp teeth.

Well shit.

"Well, Azriel, my mama told me never to let strange boys in my bedroom, so I'm going to have to ask you to leave," I say to him, my hands on my hips, hoping to any goddess listening that my sass might get me out of this shit because it's all I have.

"Oh, little Witch, I'm going to have so much fun with you." The fire in Azriel's dark eyes glows, and he smirks. "It's going to be fun to see how many ways I can break you."

The glee radiating from him sends shivers through my entire body. His pale skin practically glows, and I notice his pointed ears as he sweeps his hair backward as he runs his hand through it.

"Nope, not today. I have plans with Deacon," I tell him, trying to keep the fire inside of me burning. Anger is better than fear. That's what I have to tell myself. "You can try to break me some other time."

I move to walk away from him, but he appears in front of me, wisps of black smoke coming from him as he reappears. "I don't think so, sweetheart."

"Az," Deacon starts, but the Demon pins him with a look that makes me want to curl up and rock in a corner. Deacon shuts up and throws me one last desperate look before disappearing from the room.

Azriel grabs my arms, and blackness surrounds me. I'm still conscious, and I can feel his grip on me, but all I can see is a never-ending pool of inky darkness. I try to breathe, but the air whips past us so quickly that it stings my face and steals my breath.

When we stop, the jolt is so abrupt I swear I get whiplash. It takes me a second to truly take in my surroundings. The dark and damp room is tiny, and there's a single wooden chair in the middle. Azriel's grin makes my skin crawl, and I take a step away from him. He grabs me, faster than I've ever seen a creature move in my entire life, and throws me backward. I crash into the brick wall, my head bouncing off it so hard I have spots in my vision and I struggle to stay conscious. I feel myself losing the fight as Azriel crouches down in front of me, lifting a lock of the hair that has fallen from my wrap. He leans in, so close I can feel his breath on my skin. He takes in a deep breath, and I can practically feel his smile.

"Oh yes, little Witch. We are going to have a lot of fun."

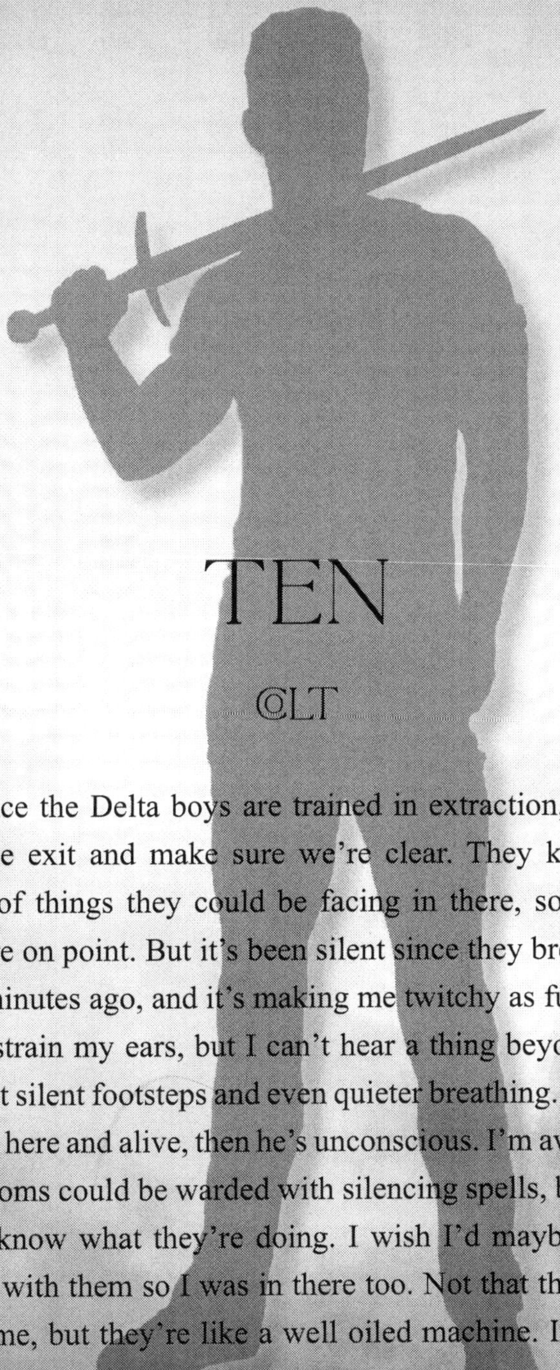

TEN

COLT

Since the Delta boys are trained in extraction, I cover the exit and make sure we're clear. They know the sorts of things they could be facing in there, so I know they're on point. But it's been silent since they breached a few minutes ago, and it's making me twitchy as fuck.

I strain my ears, but I can't hear a thing beyond their almost silent footsteps and even quieter breathing. If Bauer is still here and alive, then he's unconscious. I'm aware that the rooms could be warded with silencing spells, but these guys know what they're doing. I wish I'd maybe joined Delta with them so I was in there too. Not that they don't trust me, but they're like a well oiled machine. I'd likely get in their way, and I'd honestly rather this be stealthy.

Don't get me wrong, if I thought I could get to Archer and take him out of the equation, that would be my first move. I'm not foolish enough to think he doesn't have a contingency in place, or that he's foolish enough to stay in one place for long now that everyone knows he's target number one.

Gunfire pops from inside the building, and I go on high alert, watching for anyone trying to escape or enter the warehouse. I crouch, gun aimed, breath steady.

"Colt, be ready!" I hear Elijah shout, and seconds later the five of them are running at me, Bauer slung over Elijah's shoulder in a fireman's carry. "Move your ass!" he shouts as he runs past me, and I take up the rear, keeping my gun high. No one else comes out of the warehouse.

We run a few miles through the woodland to where we left the trucks and pile in. Bauer is slung in the trunk since he's still unconscious, and then we peel out of there before anyone can hope to find a trace of us.

I barely breathe until we've been on the road a while, driving around in circles to lose anyone who might've caught our tail. It's the dead of night, so we're not exactly weaving through traffic, but unsurprisingly there's still enough traffic around that we blend in easily enough.

Elijah slows the car, making the last loop before we head back to my dad's place. I let out a deep breath when we pull into the drive, even though Bauer is still unconscious. Elijah has barely said a word but jumps out of the truck once he parks. Danny pulls the other truck in next to us as I help Elijah with Bauer. My breath comes easier once we let everyone back inside. My dad's still not around, though I'm not completely surprised. He said something about staying with Nate and Maddie for a while... something about family betrayal and all that, but I wasn't really listening. He's bitching and moaning so much at the moment that I've started tuning him out entirely.

We get Bauer in the house, and Elijah lays him on the sofa while I grab some glasses and a bottle.

"Well, that was more fun than I expected," Danny says, laughing. His friends join in, and they sit and talk war stories with Elijah while I half listen. My focus is mainly on Bauer, though.

He needs to wake the fuck up already.

Doesn't he realize how much we need his help?

How much I need his help?

Fates knows we're wading through the biggest pile of shit I ever remember us facing. It was easy before, in other lives I've lived. There hasn't ever been anything like this before. Sure, there was the war against the factions, but that was nothing like this.

And I wasn't the one in charge.

Remy's life wasn't in danger.

I wasn't in love with Fallon.

Everything seems so much more intense, extreme, and overall fucking insane this time around. It makes me wish for the quieter times, but then, I wouldn't give up feeling the way I feel about Fallon for a quieter life. Do I wish she wasn't in danger? Hell yes, but then again, we're always in danger with the lives we live. We always have been.

I run a hand through my hair, which desperately needs to be cut. I'm going to start looking like that bastard Creek if I'm not careful.

"Right, well, we should probably head out," Elijah says after more than a few quiet minutes on my part. He polishes off his drink as he stands.

"That's cool, man," I say as I push myself out of my chair as well. "Thank you all for your help tonight. Sorry I'm spaced out, I've got a thousand and one things I'm trying to work out right now."

"It's cool, we get it," Danny says with a nod. The rest of them stand and head to grab their guns from where they dropped them in the kitchen.

"If you need me, you know where to find me. Let me know if you run into any issues with him," Elijah says, nodding toward Bauer.

"I will, thanks. I really appreciate it, man. Keep the phone nearby. Archer is likely to retaliate, probably tomorrow since my sister was meant to meet him today. Instead of meeting Remy, he lost Bauer, so fuck only knows what's about to go off, but it definitely isn't going to be pretty."

"I don't doubt it. I won't go far, and the boys are crashing with me through all the madness, so we'll be able to move quickly if you need us."

"Thanks, man, I'll be in touch." I give him a bro hug and see them all out, calling out thanks to the others as they jump in their truck and leave.

I close the door and lock it. If Dad wants back in, he'll have his key. My body sags with exhaustion as I secure the rest of the house. Fuck knows it's designed to practically be a fortress if shit gets too real.

Once everything is locked up, I head back to check on my brother. I have no idea what they knocked him out with, but he's still out cold. He looks okay otherwise. Maybe a little banged up, but better than I expected, considering. I still have no idea why he sided with Archer in the first place, and it's pissing me off. The Bauer I've always known would never side against family. Not for anything. Family always comes first, and it always has.

We've pulled each other out of some serious shit in the past, but he never talked to me about any of this, so I don't know how long it's been going on. I try to pinpoint the time in our lives when things changed, for any clue of when something changed with him. But he's lived a few lives without me, so it could've easily happened then. I truly have no fucking clue.

This Hunter life is seriously twisted sometimes.

I ended up crashing on the other couch while I waited for Bauer to wake up, but I get up, shower, and make coffee, and the fucker is still out cold, so I call Marie. Knowing my luck, Bauer's probably knocked out by one of Archer's crazy-ass Witches, and that's why he's not waking up.

I refuse to believe it's anything worse than that until Marie either confirms or denies my suspicions. She said she'd be here soon, so now it's just a waiting game.

And waiting really isn't my strong suit.

"Where is he?" I hear Marie before I see her, but then she and that huge trunk of hers float in the door.

"You can float that thing?" I ask incredulously. I fucking hauled that thing and nearly pulled a few things.

"I can, but it was nice of you to carry it." She winks at me, and I can't help but laugh. Leave it to Marie to lighten the mood with a little humor. "Now, where is your brother?"

"He's in the sitting room, knocked out on the sofa. He's been that way all night, " I tell her as I follow her and the floating trunk into the main room. She moves to where his head is resting on the arm of the sofa and places her fingertips on his temples.

"You were right to call me," she says, eyes closed. "The magic keeping him down is dark. Archer obviously didn't want his secrets given away too easily. It's going to take me some time, but I'll be able to wake him."

"Thank you, Marie. I didn't know who else to call."

"You're family, Colt. I'll always help if I can. Your brother's family too, even if he is a fool." She opens her eyes and moves over to her trunk that settles on the floor. "You should give us some space, this probably isn't going to be pretty."

She shoos me from the room, so I head to the kitchen and pour her a mug of coffee, leaving it on the unit inside the sitting room before retreating again. When a Witch tells you to get out, you get the fuck out.

Except all that leaves me to do is wait again.

Wait for Bauer to wake up.

Wait for Archer to make his move.

Wait for any word at all about Remy and Fallon.

I hate waiting.

I chug down another mug of coffee, for something to do, while I try not to pace. Pacing will only make time move slower.

My phone starts to ring on the counter, but I hesitate

when I see the display.

Unknown Caller.

This isn't going to be good. I can feel it.

"Hello?"

"You shouldn't have done that, Colt," Archer practically hisses down the line. "You shouldn't take what is mine. Especially when your sister already didn't come through for me. Now, her pretty little Witch friend will pay. Doubly so since you took Bauer."

"Fuck off, Archer. You won't hurt her. You know Remy or I will rip you limb from limb if you do. That's if the Witches don't beat us to it."

"I'm not scared of you! Any of you! I have more power than you can possibly imagine in my corner."

"It all sounds like words to me, Archer. I don't think you have anything in your corner but threats and lies. Without my brother or my sister, you're nothing. You can't act out your master plan, and Bauer can't help you come up with another one."

"You're half right. Except, I don't need either of them to bring hell down on you and your precious humans. Maybe you should turn on the news, Colt," he says before disconnecting the call.

"Shit," I say before storming into the sitting room and turning on the TV. Marie glares at me, but I flick over to the news channel. The screams hit me instantly.

"No one is sure what exactly is happening here, David. There was an explosion at the high school, and it seems the students and teachers are trapped inside. No one has been able to get inside yet, but the screams and gunfire has been almost constant," the woman on the news channel says with the image of the school ablaze behind her. My stomach sinks all the way to my feet.

What a fucking asshole.

I turn the TV off. I can't watch anymore. If the school is sealed, we need Witches. I shoot a message off to Elijah telling him to gear up and look at Marie. "My brother will have to wait."

We pull my truck up on the far side of the school, away from the fire trucks, the cops, and the news crews. This isn't exactly something we want broadcasted to the entire country. Marie whispers under her breath, and a portal opens beside my truck. Five Witches walk through as Elijah, Danny, and the boys pull up.

"What a fucking mess," Elijah growls as he jumps out of his truck. I climb out and walk around to where the others are standing. "What's the plan?"

"We need to unseal the doors," Marie tells him before turning to the Witches. "We need to circle the school. Move around, so we're equal distance apart. Once the circle is complete, we'll begin."

"Once the seal is off, we can go in and deal with whatever the fuck is in there," I tell them.

"What about the humans? What if they've seen the factions?" Elijah asks, his voice hard.

"We'll deal with that if we have to, but Marie and the ladies can make them forget if necessary," I say, and Marie nods a confirmation of my words. "Okay, let's do this."

The Witches head to their places in the circle, and all we can do is wait for Marie to give us the go ahead to get inside. Screams ring through the air, and my anger multiplies tenfold.

"Why the fuck would he attack a high school?" I hiss, fury burning through my veins.

"Because he knows we're ready for him to attack *us*," Danny says. I get it, but for fuck's sake. They're kids. Kids are off limits. Always. Humans are meant to be off limits too. It's part of the Hunter fucking Decree.

I clench my fists and then release, trying to work out some of the rage in any way possible. Nothing is working. I want to wring Archer's fucking neck.

I mean, I'd really like to torture him slowly, but I'll settle for anything right now.

Marie starts to chant, and I feel the power of the circle in the air.

Thank fuck we have Witches on our side.

I drop a text to Luc and Tobias, the proxy leaders of the other factions, since Remy told me to keep them up to speed with anything happening here. It would be nice to have some extra supernatural backup since I have no idea what's happening inside, but I also don't want to show our hand too early. I tell them we have it under control and to stand down unless I say otherwise.

I hear the pop in the air, and then I feel the whip of power as Marie and the Witches break the seal on the school. "Let's go."

"We'll keep the path clear for you," Marie tells us as we check our weapons.

I head toward the back entrance of the school with Elijah, Danny, and the guys at my back. Time to see if the Witches' spell worked.

I reach for the door and rip it open.

Good.

We work our way in, moving down the hall, entering classrooms full of kids and teachers, telling them how to get out and to stay quiet.

"They're in the gym," a teacher tells me, showing me her phone. A message from another teacher, I assume.

"Thank you," I tell her, and usher her from the room while the guys do the same with other classrooms. We try to empty the school as much as we can before we reach the gym. I'm not sure why the cops aren't trying to get in, but I'm thankful for whatever it is Marie is doing to keep them occupied.

We work our way toward the gym as silently as we can, but every scream just makes me that much angrier.

Elijah moves to the doors and looks in through the small glass window.

"Fuck," he hisses quietly. "That's a whole lot of fucking bullshit in there. There's at least a dozen Dracul and Lycans. No Witches that I can see, but they have at least half of the fucking school in there. There's already a ton of bodies scattered across the floor, and there's blood fucking everywhere."

"Well, then I guess it's time we saved the day," Danny says with a grin. "I hate this shit, but man do I also love this shit."

I pull my gun and take a deep breath. I don't want to go in there guns blazing, but what other choice do we have? I check the ammo tucked in my belt, making sure it's secure before shit hits the fan.

"You guys take the Lycans, and Elijah and I will handle the Dracul," I tell him, and they nod, reloading their ammo to ensure they have the right bullets. I hope the humans stay the fuck out of the way, and that we can get a Witch in here to take away their memories before the cops get here.

"Let's do this," Danny says with a huge grin and kicks

the doors open.

"Party's here boys," I say cockily with a smile on my face. I lift my gun. I stop thinking and let my body do its thing, not stopping to think about the humans or think twice about taking the lives of the Dracul here. I know the guys have my back and will handle the Lycans while Elijah and I focus on the Dracul. Considering how fast they can move, they're not very clever.

Then again, if they're following Archer, how clever can they be? I shoot and reload, ears ringing from the screams and the gunshots around us, but I don't stop until every Dracul is down. Elijah grins at me as he finishes off the last one standing. "Bet I killed more than you."

"Oh, fuck off." I laugh quickly, making sure the Lycans are down too. I'm covered in blood, but I feel good. I feel more useful than I have since all of this started. This, right here? This is what I'm good at.

"I assume it's my turn?" Marie says from the door and looks around the room disdainfully. She walks to the middle of the gym, her heels clicking on the floor. "You boys should probably make yourself scarce looking like that."

"Yes, ma'am," Danny says with a grin, still riding the death high. We follow him out and back to the trucks.

"Thank you, boys, for coming to join the party," I tell them as they climb into their truck.

"Glad we didn't miss it," Elijah says, grinning. "Make sure to invite us again next time."

I pat the hood of the truck, and they peel out while I strip out of my t-shirt and wipe the blood from my face and arms. I grab a spare shirt I have in the back and shrug it on. There's not much I can do about my jeans and boots, but at least they're black. I lean against the hood and wait for Marie to reappear, all the while trying not to think too hard about what Archer's game plan is.

This is obviously just the beginning, and as devastating as it is, it's too small to be his master plan. And without Remy, he won't unleash the Demons any time soon. Still, I have no doubt he has something up his sleeve.

We really need to wake my fucking brother up.

I watch on as Marie and her Witchy friends try to wake my brother. I chew the inside of my cheek and try not to let my frustration show. It was only hours ago we were at the school dealing with Archer's retaliation for taking Bauer from him. I don't want to think how he's going to react when he realizes that Remy is in the Shadow Realm, but I try not to focus on that. Now definitely isn't the time

I hate feeling so useless. Like a spare part.

I've already done everything I can do. All Hunters are

on high alert, and the other factions too. I've spoken to the council and told them what happened and what our next steps are here, but now all I can do is wait.

Wait for Archer's next move.

Wait for my brother to wake up.

Wait for any word at all from the Shadow Realm.

It's driving me fucking insane. Patience is not a virtue of mine.

I head out to the back yard to take out some of my frustration on the equipment my dad keeps out here. But I hear my dad's voice, and my stomach drops. I look up as he comes out onto the porch.

If he's here to see me, this probably isn't going to be a barrel of laughs.

I've barely spoken to him since I accepted the position with the Elders since that conversation itself was brief and tense. And that's saying something considering that things were already tense after I ripped into him for his treatment of Remy. Was I a dick to her? Yes, but I also tried to fight the council's decision while he did absolutely nothing before they brought Remy into that chamber. Did I forgive her at the time? Hell no, but I didn't want to see her dead.

And when I started to get a better understanding of everything after that conversation with Remy and her Angel about how she couldn't be cast out, things between Dad and I got heated. It just took all of that for it to dawn on me how much of a hypocritical asshole I was being.

"What's up, Dad?" I call out, lowering my bow. He glares at me from the porch, obviously expecting me to go to him, but if he wants to talk, then he can come and talk to me. I'm sick of dropping everything when he calls. He might be my dad, but that doesn't give him the right to be a complete asshole to me.

He grumbles as he crosses the yard to where I'm standing, stopping and watching me. Exasperated, I sigh. "Can I help you? Or are you going to stand and scowl at me all day?"

He still doesn't say anything, so I turn my back and nock my arrow. "Don't you turn your back on me, boy."

I roll my eyes at his growl but pull the bow back and release it, hoping to send some of my growing frustration with it. I take another deep breath before turning back to face him. "What do you want, Dad?"

"I came to get an update on your brother," he says, and I cross my arms. It's more to make sure I don't lash out at him at this point.

"Of course you did, " I say with a heavy sigh. "You could have asked Marie."

"Marie was busy," he grunts, and I roll my eyes.

"That's because she's the one working on Bauer. I don't have anything new to tell you. So unless you're here to apologize, you might as well leave."

"I have nothing to apologize for. You're the one who needs to apologize," he shouts, his facing turning red. Here we go.

"No, Dad, I don't. I forgave my sister for loving whoever she wants because I get it. I fell in love with a Witch. I accepted a position offered to me by the Council. I don't have to apologize for any of that." I run a hand down my face as he grows redder around the face and neck. Honestly, I don't think he'll ever get it.

"Your sister is a traitor! She always has been. I thought we'd managed to knock that nonsense out of her, but no, she's been lying to us all along. And now, the council, *your* council, is making her way of life the *right way.* Those monsters are nothing but filthy animals that deserve to be put down."

"Dad, you're nothing but a backward-minded bigot. I honestly have no room in my life for such narrow-mindedness, so if you can't get on board, get the fuck out," I snap, trying to keep my temper in check. I'm on the verge of failing, and I'm certain it's going to get ugly.

"How fucking dare you," he shouts, rushing toward me. I brace myself for the impact I know is coming and grunt when his fist connects with my face.

I spit out the blood I can taste in my mouth and wipe the blood trickling from my nose. I grit my teeth, tempering my breathing before saying, "That's the only fucking one you get for free, Dad. You hit me again, and I'm going to show you exactly why I was voted to be an Elder." He rages before me, but we both know that he's old, and I'll knock him on his ass in a heartbeat. He doesn't want that blow to his ego—I know it, he knows it, and chances are the Witches inside my house know it too.

"You are a disgrace." He spits at my feet and turns, storming from the yard. He slams the door as he enters the house. I know the only reason he hasn't kicked us out of here yet is because technically, this is my house. I bought it three life cycles ago, and we've all lived here since. I'm not sure even Bauer and Remy know that, but he'd rather live elsewhere than admit he's been living in my house. Especially now.

I unstring the bow and put it away with the quiver of arrows, locking up the armory before heading back inside.

I head to the stairs so I can clean up in the bathroom, and I kick off my boots. This might be my house, but I know my mom would scream at me from the beyond if I trod mud up the stairs. I'm just grabbing the bannister when I hear Marie call my name.

I turn back around with a heavy sigh and head back toward the sitting room. Marie's face looks grave as I walk in, and my heart sinks. I'm not sure if she wants to talk about me or about Bauer, but either way, I'd honestly rather not right now.

"Are you okay?" she asks softly, and I nod.

"I'll be fine. How's Bauer?" I ask, nervous because I really need the information inside his head.

"We undid the spell that's keeping him under, but I can't tell you what sort of things he was going through while he was trapped inside himself. When he wakes up, he might not be the Bauer you're hoping for."

Shit.

I swear, if I get my hands on Archer fucking Dotoro, I'm gonna tear his head clean from his body. What a fucking dickhead. All for what? I can't think of anything so important that I'd betray everything I knew and everyone I loved.

Though I could say the same for Bauer—I still have no idea why he did what he did. Why did he work with Archer? It's completely beyond me. At the end of the day, I hope I get my brother back, and I get the chance to find out.

"It's going to take time for him to wake fully, but there's nothing more we can do. I'm leaving some herbs for tea. When he wakes, make sure he drinks it. It will help him settle back into this world and help him adjust. Prepare yourself, though."

She smiles at me sadly, and my heart sinks. This isn't the news I was hoping for. "Thank you, Marie. I appreciate it. If there's anything I can do for you, let me know."

"Hush, child. I watched you boys grow up alongside Fallon and Remy. You're family. No payment is needed."

She pulls me in for a hug and practically crushes me, but it's everything I didn't know I needed. I've gone from being a carefree guy with no worries, to having the weight of the world on my shoulders at warp speed. She's as much of a surrogate mom as Maddie has been, and I really needed this hug. "You call me if he wakes and the herbs don't help."

"I will," I tell her, and she releases me from her grip. Marie and her circle gather up their things and head out, leaving me in this big house alone once again, waiting for my brother to wake up.

I take a seat in the chair opposite the sofa where Bauer is lying and close my eyes. It's been a long few fucking days, and I'm beyond exhausted.

"Colt?"

My eyes fly open to see Bauer trying to sit up, his entire body trembling with the effort.

"Hey, big brother," I say softly, standing and crossing the room to him slowly.

"How did I get here? Is this real?" he asks, his voice still shaking.

"It's real. Had to kill a few people and get some Witchy woo-woo to break you free from whatever he did to you, but you're back." I sit on the coffee table in front of the sofa, keeping a reasonable distance between us, just in case.

"I'm so sorry, Colt." His voice catches as he speaks, and it shatters my heart. I can count on one hand the times I've seen Bauer break, and that's exactly what's happening. "I can't tell you how sorry I am."

"It'll be fine, big brother. I'm not saying I forgive you because fucking hell, Bauer. But right now, we have bigger shit to deal with," I say, not really knowing what to do. Remy usually helps when this shit happens, but she's not here. It's just me.

"What happened while I was out? What happened to your face?" he asks, and I shake my head. I just manage to stop myself from reaching up to touch the throbbing spot on my jaw.

"There's time for that later. Let's get some food in you and then get some real sleep." As much as I want to bombard him with questions, he looks like shit. I'm not sure which one of us is actually more exhausted. "Marie left some tea for you too. To help with whatever might still be going on with you."

"Okay," he sighs, his eyes sad and tired. I help him stand, but his legs give out under him, so I sit him back down.

"You wait here, and I'll get some food. We can talk later," I tell him, trying not to worry. I don't know how long he's been under like that. It could've been ever since he warned Remy, and that was weeks ago. A Hunter can survive without food and drink for a while, but it fucks us up royally.

"Yeah, okay, man." I jog into the kitchen and pull one of the many Tupperware containers Maddie made for Dad and chuck one of them in the microwave to get warm while I heat some water for the tea Marie left for him.

In the few minutes it takes to put it together, Bauer is silent, and I try not to think too hard about what sort of punishment Archer dealt to him, trapped inside his own mind. Fates knows we have enough demons to deal with normally.

I steep the tea and take a sip. Fuck me, that's bitter, but at least it isn't scalding. I grab a fork for the pasta and take it through to where Bauer is sitting right where I left him, staring at a wall.

"Here you go, man," I say, popping it all down on the coffee table in front of him and sitting in the chair again, giving him some space. He seems like himself, but Marie wouldn't have warned me without reason, so I'll be cautious until I know for certain that my brother is back and himself. I flick the TV on and leave the football game on in the background while he slowly eats. That alone is enough to tell me he's not okay, but I wait and give him the chance to eat and get his head back to where he needs it to be.

He drains the tea in one go, wincing as the bitterness hits him, but he swallows before closing his eyes and leaning back on the sofa.

"I saw it over and over again," he says, his voice so quiet I barely hear him. "You, Remy, Dad. All of you, dying, at my hands. Your blood covering every inch of me. It didn't matter what I did, no matter how hard I tried to change it, I killed you. All of you. Again and again."

"It wasn't real," I say, trying to reassure him, but he looks at me, eyes haunted, and he's so broken I know my words don't matter.

"It was real to me. I can't even count how many times I killed you or led you to your death, Colt. Over and over." He takes in a shaky breath before meeting my eyes. "How long was I out?"

"When did he do this to you?" I ask and he winces.

"After I spoke to Remy," he says quietly, looking down at the floor.

"About three weeks," I tell him softly, and his shoulders droop.

"It felt like about six months, maybe longer. I don't know. I lost count."

"Why did you do it, Bauer?" I ask. I know I said I'd let him rest, but I can't wrap my head around it. Family is everything to him. I imagine that's why Archer tortured him the way he did, and it's exactly why I can't fathom a reason behind his stunt.

"I loved him, or at least I thought I did," he says, his eyes pleading with me to understand, to not judge him. Shock hits me because in all our lives, I'd never suspected it. He never even hinted…

"But as time went on, he started getting more and more out of touch with why he first started his search. Then this thing with the Demons happened, and I knew he wasn't the man he used to be. I realized too late that I was in too deep. I tried to do what I could, to warn Remy, but then Dad got hurt, and I didn't know what to do. It was a warning to me, really. He could tell I was growing hesitant and that I was pulling back from him." He takes in a deep breath, and I try to process everything he's telling me.

"I don't know what to say to that," I tell him honestly. "It has nothing to do with you loving him, though I mean, us Bennetts really seem to know how to pick 'em." I laugh dryly. "I don't know. It's done and in the past. We need your help; Archer is out of control. He took Fallon."

"He did what?" he gasps before his head droops, signaling his defeat. "I'm so sorry, Colt."

"Yeah, he has her trapped in the Shadow Realm. Remy is there now trying to get her back."

"She went there willingly?" He looks alarmed, and my heart races.

"She went to get Fallon, rather than meeting Archer to open a portal for him," I tell him.

"Fucking hell, this is so fucked up. That's exactly what he wanted. Fallon's powers don't work down there, and I'm guessing that was their escape plan. He never wanted her to open the portal, at least not from here. I don't understand the magic of it all, but it can be closed from here if it's opened here. If Remy opens it in the Shadow Realm—she can only close it from that side unless she has help—she'll be trapped there."

ELEVEN

COLT

"What the fuck do you mean she'll be trapped there?!" I try to keep my anger in check, but I'm failing. Epically.

Bauer flinches at my words, but I can't find it in me to care right now. He was a part of this, and because of it all, our baby sister is risking everything. And now he's telling me she might not ever be able to come back? *Bullshit.*

"I don't know everything, Colt. Archer is so paranoid he never tells anyone the entire story. I know what I heard," Bauer says, regret obvious in his tone. A lot of fucking good his regret does us now.

"We need to call Marie. There has to be a way to fix

this," I say, standing and grabbing my phone from my pocket.

"Without help from the Shadow Realm, I doubt there's much that can be done. And it's unlikely anyone over there will help her," he says sadly.

"I swear to the Fates, Bauer, if she doesn't come back—if any of them don't come back—I will never forgive you." I fire off a message to Marie explaining everything Bauer told me while he sits there with his shoulders slumped and head hung.

"What else do you know?" I press. I can feel his shame, and yet it isn't enough to stop my biting tone. He made his bed, I saved his ass from it, but now he has to live with what he did.

"I have names. Witches that are helping him create hybrids. Helping him create the momentary tears into the Shadow Realm. And I know locations. Where he's keeping his armory, where the people he's gathered are training," he says, looking at me hopefully. This change in our roles is enough to make my head spin, but *goddamn,* he fucked up. This, at least, is good news.

"Awesome, I'm going to call Elijah, so you can give him and Danny the locations. They can do with it what they will. You'll forgive me for not including you in our plans quite yet."

"I get it. I need to earn yours, as well as everyone else's, trust back. I know I fucked up, Colt. I know. I have a lot of people to explain myself to, but I'll do whatever it takes." I believe him, I don't want to, but I do. As much as I hate to admit it, my big brother hurt me more than I thought possible. What Remy did was one thing, but at least no one got hurt. What he did… So many lives have been lost already, and his actions have left Remy and Fallon in the Shadow Realm, suffering through Fates knows what.

"The council is aware of your role in everything that has happened too, so hopefully this will go some way toward making their ruling regarding your status less harsh, but I can't guarantee anything. Elder or not," I tell him as I sit back down, scrubbing my hand down my face.

"I understand," he says softly and leans back on the sofa, staring at the ceiling.

What a fucking mess this all is.

I send off a quick message to Dad, Nate, and Maddie to let them know that he's back and talking. I have no doubt they'll all want to see him. Even if Dad still isn't talking to me.

"Where is Dad?" Bauer asks softly. Speak of the fucking devil.

"Staying with Maddie and Nate. After the reshuffle of the Elders, and the new laws regarding hunting, he was... Well, he was pissed. He's barely spoken to me since I accepted the position."

“I’m sorry, man.”

“It is what it is. He was already pissed at me anyway since I sided with Remy against the two of you and your bigotry.” He shakes his head and sighs.

“I didn’t mean to be such an asshole to her about everything. I was angry because she’d lied for so long. It’s hypocritical, I know, but it put her in more danger, and I couldn’t force myself to look past that. But trust me, these last few weeks have shown me that the shades of gray are more prominent than I ever thought. It’s hard to overcome hundreds of years of conditioning, and while working with Archer, those prejudices were working for us, for him. But I’m trying to get better. I am.”

“Well, that’s something at least, I guess,” I say as my phone starts to buzz on the coffee table. Messages flood in from Elijah, Dad, and Nate. Well, today’s gonna be a fucking barrel of laughs.

“Dad and Nate are heading over. Prepare yourself because it isn’t likely to be pretty. Though Dad will probably forgive you more easily than the others. He won’t talk to me or Remy, so maybe it’s a good thing.” I sigh, flicking my tongue bar against my teeth. It’s a terrible habit, but I can’t seem to stop when I’m stressed. “Then Elijah, Danny, and the boys are coming back over later. Maybe we can hurt Archer just enough that he focuses on us, rather than on trying to find Remy or fuck with Fallon too much."

"Whatever I can do to help," he says helplessly, eyes vacant as he shrugs. I'm not sure if it's shock or shame ruling him right now, but I'm struggling to care either way. Again, he made his bed, and I'm going to let him fucking wallow in it. "I'm going to go grab a shower and freshen up before everyone heads over. I've been in this shit for weeks."

"It's your home as much as it is mine."

"Thank you, Colt. For not leaving me to rot," he says softly as he stands.

"You're family," I tell him. Because that's the long and short of it. My family is everything to me.

I've never been one to hide from confrontation. Hell, normally I fucking revel in it.

But confronting my dad, after everything he said to me, the way he spoke about Remy… I'm done. It might have taken me a minute to get over what my sister had hidden from us all, but considering everything that happened between Fallon and I, I got on board pretty fucking fast. And if I have to hear my dad talk about my sister like that ever again, I'm likely to lay him the fuck out. Family or not.

He might be my dad, but my sister has been there for me, no matter what, through everything. Even at a cost to herself. She's selfless to a fucking fault, and as much as it hurt me when I found out that she hadn't trusted me enough to tell me the hidden parts of herself, I at least understood.

I've been an asshole my entire existence. I've taken what I've wanted, done what I've wanted, and said fuck all to the consequences. Except once all of this rolled around, I realized that I can't just fall back on being a dick any more. No matter how much it's in my nature. I'm an Elder now, and people are looking to me for guidance, for leadership, and for everything my sister has fought for. I need to step the fuck up.

Even Bauer is owning his fuck-ups.

It's time for me to own mine.

Which is exactly why I took this stupid fucking title. I've never wanted anything less in any of my lives, but if this is what the guild wants, I can sacrifice for my people the way my sister always has. It's something to be schooled and have your ass handed to you by your little sister, let me tell you that.

So because of all of this bullshit, I'm hiding in the garden while my dad and Nate talk to Bauer. I can hear them, if I want to, but I'm shutting it out. I can't deal with any more useless rage today. My hand still tremors a little if I let myself think about everything too deeply.

I pull the string of the bow back, line the arrow up, and hold my breath before letting the arrow fly toward the target at the other end of the yard. I nock another in quick succession. It isn't quite punching Archer in the face, but imagining his face on my target is doing all sorts of good things for my inner happiness right now.

I wish there was a way to get in touch with my sister. To see if she's found Fallon. Hell, to make sure she's still alive. Granted, if anyone was going to go into the Shadow Realm and come out victorious, it would be Remy.

"Colt!" I look up to see Rebel running toward me with Marie entering the yard from the house right behind her. I crouch right before she reaches me, her arms open wide. Rebel hugs me tight, clinging to me desperately, as tears run down her face.

"What's wrong, my little warrior?" I ask.

"I dreamt of my sister. What they were doing to her," she sobs. I hug her back fiercely.

"It was a dream, sweetheart," I say, running a hand down her back. "She's going to be fine. Remy will make sure of it, I promise."

Marie looks at me with tears in her eyes, and it occurs to me that Rebel's dream might not have been only a dream. Her mom is a seer after all.

Well, shit.

"I tell you what, how about you come train with me

today, and we'll make sure that you can protect yourself and your mom against any of the things that go bump in the night?" I ask softly, trying to soothe the sobbing little girl in my arms. There's such a big age gap between her and her sister, but I know Rebel thinks that Fallon hung the moon.

She nods, her tears subsiding. "Yes, please."

"Awesome, we have a deal. Now, why don't you go inside and splash some water on your face while I talk to your mom?"

"Okay," she says softly and runs toward the house. "Mama! I'm going to train with Colt!" she shouts as she runs past her.

"Oh, baby, that'll be nice." Marie gives her a watery smile as Rebel runs past her.

"You holding up okay?" I ask Marie as I reach her on the porch.

"I'll be fine," she says, wiping away the last of her tears. "You have enough to worry about without this old woman's nonsense."

"Marie," I start, but she holds up a hand, stopping me.

"Pssh. I'm having a moment. Hearing Rebel's dream with everything that's going on? It got to me for a minute," she says, clearing her throat. "Don't think for a second, boy, that I'm losing my edge."

"I would never." I grin.

"What's going on in there?" she asks, pointing to the house.

"Dad and Nate came to talk to Bauer. I decided to stay out of the way," I tell her, and she frowns.

"You shouldn't avoid your father, Colt. He's the one who needs to apologize." I snort at her words.

"Yes, because my dad is the kind of person who apologizes." I roll my eyes. "I have more chances of beating Leviathan in a fight than I have of getting any sort of apology from my old man." She tuts, and I shake my head. Seriously, the Angel would beat my ass to a pulp, and I'd still be waiting an eternity for an apology from Denny Bennett.

"It's fine. Like you said, I have a lot going on. There's too much going on to worry about that right now. As long as he follows orders when it counts, that's all I care about right now. Archer has gone quiet, which has me a little worried. The school, while ruthless, feels like a diversion rather than the main event. And obviously, Bauer's little nugget about Remy being trapped has been fucking eye opening."

"Worry about what is in your control for now," she says, squeezing my shoulder. "Trust that your sister will do what she must to ensure the safe return of everyone, including herself. She's stronger than any of us realize."

After everyone left after catching up with Bauer, and Maddie had cooked enough food for an army and shoved it in my fridge so I could stay fed, I turn on the oven to heat the lasagna Maddie made for me earlier. It came with a threat that I better eat, and feed the riff raff that she somehow knew would be here tonight. Which is exactly when I message Elijah and Danny.

I've been trying to keep myself busy, occupied enough so I don't lose my shit about Fallon. About how badly I let her down. Trying to convince myself it wasn't my fault she was taken isn't fucking easy at all. There's no way I could've possibly known, but in quiet times, like right now when the house is silent save for the low murmur from the TV in the sitting room where Bauer is resting, it's all I can think about. Times like this is when it takes over, and I struggle to fucking breathe through it all.

I sent my sister into the fucking Shadow Realm for fuck's sake. I have no doubt she would've gone regardless, but I didn't do anything to stop her. I didn't even try to dissuade her. Because if anything happens to Fallon, I'll never fucking forgive myself. I feel sick even at the thought.

My stomach turns at the memory of all the things I said, and all the things I didn't say too.

If anything happens to her, and Fallon doesn't make it back…

I shake my head, trying to dislodge the thought because I can't think like that. I wasted so much time being an ass to her and letting my dad and my guild tell me what I wanted was wrong. How I felt was wrong. I know now that if I get her back, if she forgives me for having my head up my ass, I'll never make her regret it. I'll spend our entire existence making it up to her.

Some might think I'm a fool to love a mortal, especially when I will be reborn and she won't. Those people can fuck right off.

Three loud, short bangs on the door breaks the silence.

"I've got it!" Bauer calls out, and I hear his footsteps on the creaky floors as he heads to the door. The voices get louder as Elijah and Danny come into the house.

"Oh, Colt, baby, you cooked for me. You shouldn't have," Elijah coos as he swaggers into the kitchen with a laugh.

"What can I say, I'm a domestic fucking goddess," I say, greeting him with a slap on the back. "Seriously though, if I don't feed you guys, Maddie will have my hide."

"That woman terrifies me." Elijah shudders, and Danny laughs at him.

"I could eat," Danny agrees, and Bauer grabs plates and cutlery while I pull the lasagna from the oven and take it over to the table. Elijah heads to the fridge and grabs some beers before sitting down with the rest of us.

"Fates bless Maddie and her cooking," Danny says as he cuts at least a quarter of the lasagna and drops it onto his plate. I laugh at him, and he flips me the bird. "Do you have any idea how long it's been since I've had a decent home-cooked meal? You're lucky I'm leaving you any at all."

"Help yourself, man. You should see my fridge." I laugh with a shrug, taking a swig of my beer while the others dish themselves up some food.

"I'm moving in," Danny groans around a mouthful of lasagna.

"It's not like there isn't space, " Bauer says with a small smile. He's not wrong. This house is huge, and it's way too big for the two of us. I don't see Dad coming home anytime soon either.

We shoot the shit while we eat, and I enjoy the company, pretending like the weight of the world isn't resting on my shoulders. I know that after whatever Bauer tells us tonight, I'm going to have to call an Elder meeting. Thank Fates for younger Elders and Skype, though, because all the travelling isn't feasible right now.

Bauer clears the table when everyone's done and grabs another round of beers, handing them to each of us before taking his seat again.

"So I guess I need to thank you guys for saving my ass," he says before taking a long draw from his bottle. "So thank you for saving my traitorous ass. I'll do my best to make it up to you."

"You're Colt's family, and that means you're our family. We don't leave our own behind," Elijah says, and Danny nods his agreement. Bauer launches into telling them what they need to know regarding locations and security systems at each of the sites that he knows Archer has acquired. He also details any wards that might be in place, and the numbers of potential bodies at each site.

I sit and listen, stomach churning as it hits me how involved he was in all of this. Bauer is a strategic guy, and logic is his lifeblood. It's evident that he picked these locations and helped Archer build this entire army against us. Bauer's the one who helped him plan where to hit us, and told him what our weaknesses would be. Bauer taught him how to cripple us in the worst of ways, detailing what would cause us the most damage, not necessarily in terms of numbers, but in morale instead.

"You told him to take Fallon," I say, glaring at him across the table. His eyes go wide at my words, and then he nods, the movement small, but it's enough.

"You motherfucker!" I shout slamming my bottle down onto the table.

"I didn't know," he tells me sadly. "I knew she was

Remy's friend, and Remy is Remy. She would sacrifice herself for her friends. I didn't know about you."

"That doesn't fucking matter, Bauer!"

"Colt," Elijah says firmly, drawing my attention to him. "You boys can settle this later, but for now we need to think this through and be smart about this. Hitting Archer where it hurts and make him feel the pain you feel."

"His brother," Bauer says softly. "If you want to make him hurt, you need to take his brother."

"I didn't even know he had a brother," I say, the bite of my tone still very much present.

"It isn't something that's all that well known since his mom died in childbirth. Everyone thought the kid died too, and Archer saw to that, considering their dad had been killed by a Lycan. He thought it was the only way to keep him safe. He's not of age yet. He's away at school, being kept very much out of everything. But if you want to hurt Archer, you need his brother, Dylan."

"Which school?" I ask him.

"The same school as Nirvana," he says softly. "Where better than a place we'd never even think to bring trouble to."

"Fuck my life." I flick my tongue bar between my lips while I try to think of a way to keep Nirvana out of this if I drag this kid into our war.

"We keep the kids out of it," I say finally. It's hard to

give up what little collateral we might have, but I have to draw a line in the sand. I won't stoop to Archer's level, even if it would give me an advantage. "Kids are off limits."

"But—" Bauer starts, and I shake my head with resolute certainty.

"End of discussion. I will not stoop to his level. We'll find something else," I tell them all, and Elijah and Danny nod while Bauer looks at me like he's sorry for even bringing it up.

"When do we start hitting these sites?" Elijah asks with a grin.

"As soon as fucking possible."

My phone rings on the table, and Marie's name flashes on the screen. I pick up straight away because she never calls this late.

"Colt! They took her, they took my baby!"

"Marie, calm down. What happened? "

"I will not calm down, Colt Bennett, they took Rebel! I went to check on her, to make sure she was asleep, and I saw them disappear in front of my eyes!"

"Marie—" Panic claws at my throat but I swallow it down. Now is not the time. I need a clear head.

"Don't you 'Marie' me, boy! Get my babies back, and bring me that asshole's head. I'll make sure he suffers for eternity if he harms my girls." The line disconnects, and I flinch.

“Fuck,” I sigh, and the others watch me closely as I drop my phone on the table.

“Looks like Archer doesn’t care about kids being off of the table. They took Rebel.”

TWELVE

FALLON

I wake, my neck stiff from where it hangs down to my chest. As I become more aware, more and more pain filters into my conscious state, and it takes everything in me not to cry out.

Azriel is the cruelest being I've ever come across in my life.

I lift my head slowly, one of my eyes is swollen shut, and I can feel dried blood crusted on my face and hands.

Hours.

He tortured me for hours. Asking questions he knew I didn't have answers to. Taking such joy from each scream he pulled from me, no matter how hard I tried to resist.

He captured my tears in a vial before licking my face to taste what was left.

He's the most vile creature in existence.

Once I get my magic back, I'm going to tear the skin from his body slowly, making sure he stays conscious the entire fucking time.

I try to move, pulling at the restraints keeping me in this stupid fucking chair. Between the exhaustion, the pain, and the blood loss, I'm so weak I can barely keep my head up.

Fuck him for making me feel so powerless.

I close my eyes and send a prayer to the Fates that Remy finds me soon. I'd much rather have my magic, but with my options limited, I know Remy is pretty much my only hope.

There was a moment where I almost thought that Deacon might let me go, but when he left, leaving me with Azriel, my hope left with him. Any remnants that might have clung with his departure left with each hit or tear of my skin.

"Oh goodie, you're awake." I flinch at the sound of Azriel's voice, and he laughs. It pisses me off, but it's all I can do not to let my tears of frustration fall. I will not cry for him again.

"Fuck you," I spit, and he laughs again.

"Oh, breaking you will be such a sweet joy. Such fire

from someone so breakable." He grins at me, and I close my eyes.

My good eye flies open as he grips my jaw so hard my eyes water. "You will watch every second of me breaking you, little Witch. And after, when I rebuild you, you will thank me for making you mine."

I try to pull from his grip, trying not to panic at his words, but it's useless. I can't break free from him, but I don't let that stop me from trying. I won't let him break me.

He lets go of my jaw and pushes my head back. It cracks against the back of the chair, but I find relief in the fact that I didn't let him win. Not yet. Not ever, if I have my way.

"I will never be yours. You're going to regret ever making a deal with Archer Dotoro," I hiss through the pain, and he smirks at me.

"Oh, little Witch, are you hoping your little Shadow Walker will save you?" he whispers, crouching down in front of me. "I have a little secret for you. Even if she doesn't help Dotoro, if she tries to reach you here, I'll tear her apart just like I'm tearing you apart. I'll make you both mine. There are more nightmares on this level of the Shadow Realm than you could ever dream up."

"Which level are we even on?" I ask, not expecting him to answer. I want to know if he'll tell me the truth.

"Level six. Greed." His eyes light up. "This is my level, and I do so love to collect people."

I try not to react to his words, but I'm surprised he gave me the same answer as Deacon. Unfortunately, it isn't like I can get word to Remy. The light inside me flickers, but I bite down on my resolve. No, he will not break me.

"What do you even want with me?"

"Oh, little Witch, you were a nice little topper on the deal. I never expected to get a Laveau Witch out of my bargain with the Hunter. He isn't even who I answer to. This was just a good little side deal, but it was a very welcome little surprise. He doesn't know I have no intention of giving you back, but then, he didn't mention that he even wanted you back when he handed you over. All he asked was that I keep you hidden. Foolish Hunter, not watching his words. Tip of the day—mind your words when dealing with Demons."

"I'll keep that in mind." I roll my eyes, and he sighs.

"Well, it's no fun breaking you in this state, now is it?" he asks with a frown. He flicks his hand, and all of the aches and pains in my body recede. I feel the swelling in my eye go down, and then I can see properly again. Once I feel a little more back to myself, he grins down at me. "Much better."

He moves toward me again, and it takes every ounce of strength I have not to flinch and plead with him not to hurt me again.

"We're going to have so much fun down here until the Hunter finds a way to open his portal. And then, then I'll keep you when we head to Earth too. You can be my personal little plaything," he says, running a finger down my cheek. I try to pull away from him, but the restraints keep me held firmly in place.

I let out a growl of frustration, and he laughs at me again.

"Oh, little Witch, I'll keep breaking you and this pretty little face and putting you back together until you see things my way. You should give in. Things will be so much better once you're with me. You'll see. Now, where is your Shadow Walker friend, little Witch?" Azriel asks me again, and I shake my head, my face already stained with my tears again. I didn't want to cry, but I couldn't stop them from falling.

"I don't know," I say, my voice hoarse from the screams he's already pulled from me. I'm not even lying, but after Archer appeared again a few hours ago, screaming and shouting about Remy betraying him, betraying me, the question has been on repeat. The pain has increased each time I tell him I don't know anything.

I want the pain to stop almost more than anything, but I can't tell him what I don't know.

But he doesn't believe me.

"Maybe our friend Deacon can help?" Azriel smirks and steps back from me. I let out a sob, but catch myself before I start fully crying again. The sheer relief of him stepping back is enough to make me want to cry until I pass out.

Not that he'll let me pass out. Each time the pain got to be too much and I passed out, he'd bring me back to consciousness. I've lived each and every second of his joy over my pain.

The door opens behind him, and I see Deacon. His face is taut as he takes me in, but he doesn't show even a hint of actual concern for me.

"You called for me, Az?" Deacon asks, looking away from me. I can't help the pang in my heart at the sight. I know we aren't friends or anything, but goddamn. I thought maybe he might be a little more willing to help with how he was acting earlier.

"I want you to get her to tell me where her Shadow Walker friend is. I know you know how." Azriel winks at him before leaning in to kiss my cheek, and my stomach churns. It takes everything in me not to empty the contents of my stomach all over him. He moves to leave the room, but stops and turns back to me. With a wave of his hand, my pain disappears again, and I suck in a breath, taking the small relief for the short time I'll have it. He smiles again and leaves the room, closing the door behind him.

"Please get me out of here," I whisper to Deacon, but he looks unaffected by my plea.

"Where is your friend?" he asks, and my heart sinks. It was foolish to think he was anything more than a Demon. Of course he's not going to help me.

"I already told him, I don't know," I say, voice shaking as he moves toward me, his hands raised. It takes every measure of strength I have not to flinch as his hands move to my temples.

"This is probably going to hurt," he says softly, so softly I almost think he might be sorry for what's happening, but my thoughts are ripped away and pain unlike anything I've ever encountered rips through me. My screams fill the air around us.

I curl in on myself in the corner of the room, having been freed from the restraints once I was passed out. I'm not sure which of them did it, but as Deacon tore into my mind, I know he saw what I'd seen when he showed me the ring of fire days before. At least I think it was days. I've lost track of time completely. My meals have gone back to nothing more than bread and water, another of Azriel's ways to break me I assume, but he has no idea how stubborn I can be. I will never willingly give him what he wants.

Though, if Deacon can tear into my mind the way he did, I might not have a choice. I can still feel his claws at the edges of my mind. My body shakes as I sit, watching the door through the darkness of the room. The only light is from the bottom of the door, where it doesn't quite meet the floor.

I close my eyes and try to slow my breathing, to try to stop the shaking. It takes a while, but finally I still, and my mind is calmer, though fear still grips me. What Deacon did was worse than anything Azriel did. Hurting my body is something I can survive, but breaking into my mind... That violation is greater and much harder to recover from. While I'm grateful my body doesn't hurt right now, I'd rather take the pain to my body over my mind every single time.

I have no idea what else he managed to get from my thoughts. I tried to shield myself against the onslaught, but even with every shield practice I've ever done with Mama, nothing has ever torn through me the way he did.

I shudder at the thought of it.

I never want to deal with that again.

Footsteps approach my door, and I go rigid in an instant. I hold my breath and send a prayer to the Goddess to protect me. I don't know if she can reach me here, or if she can even hear me, but I cling to it. The footsteps stop at my door, the light broken by the feet of whoever is out there.

"I'm sorry." I hear the words said so faintly, I wonder if I imagined them before the person moves away from the door. The footsteps grow quieter the further away they get. I let out the breath I was holding slowly, trying to hold on to my sanity while telling myself I didn't imagine it.

I move so I'm lying on the ground. It's hard and cold, but it's still better than being trapped in that chair, and I try to get comfortable. Closing my eyes, I try to drift off to sleep.

I feel myself falling when I hear a scream, and my eyes spring open.

Who the fuck was that?

I scramble to my feet and move to the door as the screams get louder.

"Please, please, let me go," the voice cries, and my heart screeches to a halt in my frantic chest.

That can't be Rebel.

I won't believe it.

There is no way Mama would have left her alone after I was taken. Colt wouldn't have let them get her. I pound my fist on the door and shout for Azriel, Deacon, anyone, but no one comes. Her screams go on, filling my ears, breaking my heart, and breaking me.

Azriel might not have managed to break me before, but I'd happily give myself over for my sister.

"Stop it!" I scream, pounding on the door again when I hear that insufferable chuckle on the other side.

"Hello, little Witch, are you ready to give in yet?" Azriel's voice filters through the door, and my knees almost give out.

"Let me see her," I plead.

"Only once you agree to be mine," he says, and I can hear his smile.

"Please, let me see her, and then I'll do whatever you want," I beg, hating every word as they tumble through my lips, but I'd give anything for my sister.

"As you wish," he says, and the screams stop. I hear shuffling and my door starts to open. Azriel strides into the room and stands in front of me, looking more human than I've seen him before. His skin isn't quite so pale, his ears are no longer pointed, and he only has one row of teeth. His jaw is just as sharp though, and his hair and eyes are both so dark they look black. I guess he saves the terrifying form for when he wants to extract my screams. "Make one move, and I'll cut her throat. Slowly. Do you understand?"

I nod my head, and he grins again. "Don't look so glum, little Witch. You're going to enjoy life at my side. I'll make you immortal, and you'll be mine forever."

He moves to the side, and I can finally see Rebel, being held up by two Demons. Their pale skin glows against her darker skin, and the moment I see blood dripping from her fingers, I clench my fists. “Send her home.”

“Once you’re mine. For now, she can stay where I can keep an eye on her,” Azriel says. With a wave of his hand, the two Demons walk away and I hear them put her in a room down the hall from me.

“How do I know you won’t harm her anymore?” I glare at him. I might be willing to make this deal for her, but I’m not going to make it pleasant for him.

“It’s all in the wording sweetheart. Pick your terms carefully.”

I take a deep breath, and prepare myself to sell my soul.

“So you wish for your sister to be free and to have power beyond what you would have had in your previous life. Any other demands, love?” His voice makes my teeth grind, but it’s taken me long enough to word that little in such a way that there are no loopholes to my requests that I don’t feel like I have the time for the rest. There are many other things that I wish for, but I fear they’re nothing more than children’s dreams at this point. Azriel brought me to this small, dark room after I agreed to bind myself to him, and it’s just the two of us sitting at opposite ends of what looks like a formal dining table. It’s silent, save the crackling fire that warms the room. He keeps smiling at me, and I swear it makes me want to punch him in his pretty face. How fucking dare he smile at me like that after everything he's put me through?

I wish to go home, I wish my friends to be left alone, that no harm comes to them, I want my mama and sister to be left alone, to live their lives without sadness in their hearts at the fact that I'm stuck here. I know in my heart that these are things he cannot grant. At least not fully.

"I want you to leave my friends alone. I want no harm to come to them from you and yours," I tell him, jutting out my chin a little, and he grins again.

"Okay, sweetheart, your friends will suffer no harm from my hand or any of those that serve me, so long as they do not attack me first. I have some demands in this bond of ours too, since I'm giving up your sister. That alone will be more than a bit of a headache for me."

I nod, unable to speak, mainly for fear that if I open my big mouth, I'll rail on him and this goodwill of his will disappear. I need Rebel to be free of this place, and for that, I can clamp down my jaw and keep my words to myself. While I might be a victim in all of this, I refuse to play the part. I'm a fucking survivor. What I'm doing is simply another tool to ensure my survival.

"Come closer, and we will start the bond," he says, beckoning me with a curled finger. I begrudgingly stand from my seat and move closer to him, sitting in the chair beside him when he beckons for it. It takes a lot out of me to not flinch when he reaches for my hand, but I try to school my features so that the mix of fear and utter hatred isn't as easy to read on my face as it usually might be.

With a click of his fingers, a black chalice with rubies appears on the table between us, and he begins to speak in a language that grates against my ears. It's an old language, probably older than even he is. Something inside of me recognizes that much, but I don't understand a fucking iota of what he's actually saying. What I do understand is the build of power in the room. It builds to be so much that it pushes against my chest, and I feel as if I can barely breathe.

His hand shifts, black claws appearing in place of where his fingers were moments before, and he takes my hand. He uses one of his claws to cut our entwined hands, spilling the blood into the chalice. He presses his hand against mine, our blood mingling together in the open wounds. I feel it, the power in his blood. It's like the kind of thing that you desire to touch so badly that it burns, but you know that touching it would be the worst thing you could possibly do.

His hand shifts back, and he lifts the chalice to his lips, taking a sip. I shudder when he places it against my lips, tipping it up until the blood spills inside my mouth. I want to spit it out, but I swallow, the warning in his eyes is clear.

Once I swallow, he continues to speak before he stands, letting go of my hand and throwing the rest of the blood into the fire.

"It is done, we are bound. Tied to each other in every possible way." I gulp at his words because that sounds like more than I signed up for, but there is little I can do about it now.

"What were your terms?" I ask, knowing it's too late to do anything, but I also know he wouldn't have made the bond without them regardless.

"That you are mine. No other shall touch you, shall captivate your mind, be a part of you so long as my soul exists. I made you mine, wholly, and I do not share what is mine. Remember that, Fallon." His words are so at odds with how he is usually, I feel like I have emotional whiplash. He watches me intently before sighing, then turns and leaves the room, leaving me in darkness with nothing but the fire for warmth.

My prison cell has been upgraded. It turns out selling your soul to a Demon will do that, and now I'm back in the room I was in when I first woke up here. I watch Rebel sleeping on my bed, unable to rest myself as I guard the room from the assholes that wait outside. I can't do much against them, and Azriel swore no further harm would come to either of us, but something is wrong with Rebel. She doesn't seem like herself, and the guilt of it eats at me.

It's my fault she was taken. My fault that she's here.

It might be Archer's fault overall, but I couldn't protect her from these monsters. Not when I couldn't even protect myself.

And now I'm going to be trapped here forever.

But it was all part of my bargain. I saved my sister's life, and in return, sacrificed my own. I try not to dwell on everything I'll be giving up, including my own fucking sanity.

Though deep down, I'm still hoping that Remy comes up with a way to beat Archer, and in turn, free me from my deal. Don't get me wrong, I would sacrifice myself for my sister happily, but without that shred of hope...

I don't even really want to think about it.

"Fallon?" My heart races at the sound of Rebel's murmurs as she wakes. She's too young to be here, to have gone through what she's gone through. The shadows I see in her eyes as she takes in our surroundings serve as a reminder that no matter what I've given up, it was worth it.

"I'm here, Rebel," I say softly from my corner of the shadows. "You should go back to sleep, sweetheart. It's the middle of the night."

"Okay," she says, still half asleep, and lies back down.

I let out a deep breath as her breathing evens out again, and she leaves this horror for her sleeping world.

"Fallon?" The whisper reaches me as the door to the room cracks open, and I see Deacon standing in the sliver of light. I glare at him, but I guess he can't see me when he opens the door wider to find me in the darkness.

"What do you want?" I hiss.

"I wanted to say I'm sorry," he says softly, his head hung. "Much like you, I'm a prisoner here. Azriel is the higher Demon of this level. If I go against his wishes..." He shudders and waves for me to join him outside of the room when he notices Rebel sleeping on the bed. He frowns at her, but shakes his head and opens the door wider for me, inviting me outside of the room.

I sigh and stand because really, what other choice do I have other than to wake Rebel with his blathering?

"You can be sorry all you like, Deacon. You still did what you did. I won't ever forgive that," I tell him straight. "I'm here against my will, and I made the deal I made to save my sister from a similar fate. Beyond that one choice, I have no agency. I'm a prisoner here, and I've bent to Azriel's will at a cost, and it's probably greater than I ever thought I would have to pay."

"If I could save you from it, I would. Is your sister okay?" he asks, and I glare at him.

"No thanks to you, but she'll be fine," I hiss. "I need

to get her back to my mama. She's gotta be losing her goddamn mind."

"I will see what I can do," he tells me softly. "I truly am sorry. I have never had family, so I do not know what it is to sacrifice for them, to love someone in that way, but I can see how hurt you are. I can see how her being here haunts you, and so I will do what I can to help get her back to your realm."

He doesn't wait for me to respond, turning and leaving me in the brightly lit hallway instead. I look around, taking in the space around me, and realize this is the first time I've seen it. I guess since I'm bound to this place now, they don't have any fear that I'll attempt to escape.

The hall is little more than a mezzanine, looking down to another hall below. We're on the fourth and top floor, and the hall is a horseshoe in shape. It seems as if each level is laid out in a similar way. There are so many doors on each level, but I can't imagine that they're all bedrooms. I shudder to think what they might be. At the curve of the horseshoe is a giant white staircase that seems to link each level, descending to the ground floor, which is full of tables.

This place looks like nothing more than a fucking library. I roll my eyes and head back into my room. I move the dresser as quietly as I can in front of the door. I'm not stupid enough to think that it'll stop a Demon from trying to come in, but it makes me feel a little better anyway.

Exhaustion pulls on me as I settle onto the bed next to Rebel, who's thankfully still fast asleep. There might be thirteen years between us, and I might have resented having so much responsibility when it came to her before, but now I know I'm probably going to miss out on watching her grow up, and my heart aches. I'm grateful to have this little chunk of time with her, even if she is still trapped here. I close my eyes to try to shut out my racing thoughts and get some sleep before whatever fresh hell tomorrow brings.

THIRTEEN

COLT

"She's back?" I ask, voice pitching at the end of the question. I'm positive I sound as confused as I feel.

"She appeared in the kitchen while I was making coffee this morning," Marie says, her voice thick with emotion. "I have no idea how."

"Is she okay? Did she say anything?"

"She doesn't seem hurt, and she says she wasn't. She said that she went to see Fallon in a big fancy castle. She said Fallon says she loves me, but that she can't come home right now, but she'll try to come home soon." Her voice catches, and I know she's losing the fight to keep her emotions locked down.

"Holy shit." I let out a rush of air, not sure what else to say. "Did she see Remy?"

"No, she didn't mention Remy. I'm sorry."

"No, don't be sorry. She's back, and she's not hurt. That's what matters right now. I'm glad she's back, Marie."

"He's still going to pay for this," she says, her voice sharp with anger.

"He will. Elijah and Danny have a light show set up for him tonight. I have a feeling we'll be hearing from Archer Dotoro in the next twenty-four hours, whether we want to or not."

"I don't want to know what you have planned, but make it hurt."

"I plan to." I smile down the phone; she can't see it, and I'm kind of glad.

"I'll talk to you soon, Colt."

"Hug Rebel for me."

"I will," she says, disconnecting the line. I drop the phone on the table in front of me and look back up to the room of people facing me. Both on Skype and in the room.

"Rebel is home," I tell them, and the entire room lets out a sigh of relief.

"That's good news," Nasari says over the Skype call.

"Now let's fuck Archer's shit up enough that he'll think twice about fucking with the kids again," I say with a slightly manic grin. "First, has everyone pulled their kids home and made sure they're safe?"

Everyone nods, and some weight lifts from my shoulders. I wasn't wrong when I said no kids would be hurt if I could help it. I'm not sure how I ended up being tapped as the leader of the Elders, though it probably has something to do with Remy. Either way, here we are, and I'm glad. Someone has to make sure that line is toed.

"Okay, good. Are everyone's teams ready to go on our signal?" I ask, and a murmur of agreements reach me.

"Awesome. We'll reconvene in seven hours. Get ready for some fireworks!" I clap my hands together as everyone says goodbye and the Skype calls shut down, leaving me with the people in the room. Elijah, Danny, Nate, Maddie, Bauer, and Dad. I didn't necessarily want everyone here, and fuck knows Dad argued enough about coming, but at the end of the day he needs to get in fucking line. The others were more than happy to be here and to play their part.

"I assume Nirvana is on her way home?" I ask, looking at Maddie. She grins.

"No, she's going to stay with a friend. I want her with someone so far removed from all of this bullshit, that no one will even think to look there," she tells me, her eyes hard. After Rebel was taken, I sent word out to pull in everyone not yet of age to make sure they were safe. I wasn't about to risk any more lives than necessary.

"Yeah, that makes sense," I say with a nod before glancing around the group. "Is everyone okay with what they have going on tonight?"

"We've got enough explosives to bring down a small country. With the Witches' help bringing down the wards, we shouldn't have a problem. Danny and I have our teams ready to go," Elijah says with a grin. He fucking lives for this shit.

"Awesome, I'll let you guys go and rest. We need to be on top form for tonight. The smallest fuck up could cost us greatly," I tell them all, not looking to where my father sits actively avoiding looking at me.

"Thank you, Colt, for being so thorough and involving us all," Maddie says, patting my arm.

"You're family," I tell her with a smile. "We don't leave family behind."

"That's right," she says with a smile before glaring at my dad. "It's about time we all remembered that."

"Maddie..." Nate warns, but I shake my head.

"Maddie, it's fine," I say wearily, flicking my tongue bar around my lips.

"It is not fine," she says harshly, but I shake my head, and she thankfully relents. This is not the time to try and pick a fight with my dad. He has his own role tonight. I made sure that he was included. The only one who would stay behind with me is Bauer. As an Elder, I can't go into the fray tonight, which pisses me off, but it is what it is. Bauer, however, I want at my side. It isn't that I don't trust him...

Okay, it is a little bit that I don't trust him. I just don't want anything to go wrong tonight, and he's the only real wild card on the board. If I can see him, I know that if anything goes wrong, it wasn't because of him. Unless the information he gave us was bogus. But that's a bridge I'll cross if we come to it.

"Well, we'll be off then. Take care of yourself tonight, boys."

"We always do." I wink at her, and she scoffs at me before pulling me in for a hug. "I'll call you guys when you're getting into position so we can hit everywhere at once, okay?"

"We've got it. You did good, Colt."

"Thanks, Maddie." I smile at her, saying goodbye to Nate as the two of them leave. My dad leaves with them without a word to me, just a grab of Bauer's shoulder. How he can forgive Bauer, but not Remy or I, blows my fucking mind. There's nothing I can do about it, and at this point, I have bigger fucking things to worry about than my dad's approval.

Like stopping this stupid fucking war before it gets a chance to start.

Today passed in the blink of an eye, and now I'm sitting at my kitchen table, which has turned into a base camp for all things war. I have three screens, split into nine each. Each mini screen is linked to a different unit at a different location, who are all ready to blow some shit up. I have an earpiece and a mic linking me to all of them. This has to be the most tech shit I've ever used in my life. Thank the Fates for Elijah and Danny sorting everyone out and getting the tech to the other groups across the world as quickly as they did. This way I can monitor every fucking thing happening.

Witches were the first to head in, breaking the wards on the various sites we're targeting. I'm sure this isn't everything, but it's as much as Bauer could remember off the top of his head, and Archer's too fucking full of ego to think we'd attack him on such a grand scale, especially after last time.

Especially without my sister and her band of merry men.

Which is exactly why I can't wait to fuck his shit up. Archer Dotoro can eat my ass with his ego.

"Unit in position," Elijah's voice crackles through, and the other team leaders confirm that they're ready to go too. I look at the time on my phone, and as the minute rolls over onto the hour, I give them the signal.

"Light it up."

The words are barely out before explosions rock the screens, and whoops cry out from our teams. When each site is up in flames, I reach back out to the teams. Bauer looks uneasy at all of it, but I can't tell if that's simply because it's happening or because it's happening to Archer because of him.

"Job well done everyone. Now get the hell out of there."

Confirmations come through from everyone, advising they got the order, and the cameras shut down on the screens before me. Once everyone's disconnected but the Elders, I say my goodbyes with a confirmation that we'll catch up again in the morning to debrief and assess what our next steps are. Hopefully, we'll have heard from Archer by then. Though hopefully he was in one of the places we blew to kingdom come, and this shit is over. At least, the shit here. I'm trying not to think too hard about everything going on in the Shadow Realm since it's out of my control.

I have enough to focus on here as it is.

"I did a thing," Bauer says quietly, and I look up to meet his gaze. I already know I'm not going to like whatever the fuck it is he's about to tell me.

"What. Did. You. Do?" I grind out.

"I had a friend check on Dylan," he says, almost

looking afraid.

"You did fucking *what*!" I roar. "Are you fucking insane? I told you *not* to touch the kid!"

"Yeah, but he took Rebel. And I didn't touch him. My friend checked in with him, with a message for Archer. Just enough for him to know that we know where his brother is," he says softly. I hate how much I wish I'd thought of that, but I'm beyond pissed that he did it without saying anything.

"If anything happens because of this, Bauer..."

"I will take full responsibility. I acted on my own, but I knew if I said something, you'd shut it down because of everything I already did. It was a good idea, Colt. It will knock him off course. I know him, Colt. I know every weakness he has. Including me," he says it quietly but firmly, and I realize that he's right.

Fuck.

I fucking hate being schooled. Especially by my big brother. Especially with everything that's happened so far.

"It's also easier to ask for forgiveness than for permission," I say begrudgingly.

"Pretty much," he says with a shrug. "I'm not sorry. Between everything tonight and reaching out to Dylan, Archer will start spiraling. He'll act brashly, and that's when he'll slip up."

"It's done. We'll deal with any fallout," I say succinctly,

and he nods.

"I really am sorry about all of it. Especially about Fallon. I didn't know, but I should have," he says, but I shake my head. Now is definitely not the time.

"Like how we should've known about Remy and her guys? You had no more way to know about Fallon and me than either of us did about her."

"It doesn't matter, you and I have always been closer. Remy has always been, well, Remy. She was there, and when she was, she was like our missing link. But when she was off running around the world, racking up allies and lovers, it was you and me. Always. And I missed this because I was too wrapped up in my own bullshit."

"I could say the same about you and Archer," I say softly, sitting back down at the table. He heads to the fridge and grabs two beers, walking back over and handing me one before sitting down.

"That's not something you could have ever known. We hid it, and we hid it fucking well. Same as Remy, I guess. What a fucking group we Bennetts are."

"Right," I say, lifting my bottle to him, and he clinks his against it.

"So, you and Dad?" Bauer asks, and I shake my head as I swallow the amber nectar. That's another fucking thing I don't want to talk about right now. Not after a successful mission.

"Nope. Not something I want to talk about."

"He's being a dick," Bauer says, and I nod.

"Not going to disagree with you there!" I laugh. "But there's not a fucking thing I can say or do to make him be less of an asshole."

"I could talk to him?" he offers, and I shake my head again. I'm doing a lot of that tonight, it seems.

"Nah, man. If he wants to be a dick, let him. I have enough to deal with at the moment."

"If you're sure."

"More than sure. As long as he toes the line, that's all I give a fuck about."

"Okay, man. I'm going to head up to bed. If you need me, you know where I am."

"Thanks. Night."

"Night, Colt."

A whole day passed with no sort of retaliation, or even word from Archer, and it's making me antsy. There is no way that he's not up to something. Even Bauer is shocked, and it's making me edgy as hell. I hate waiting.

"Still nothing?" Bauer asks as he enters the kitchen.

"Nope," I tell him as I nurse the mug of coffee in front of me.

"Are you hungry?"

"Nah." I shake my head and lift up my mug. "I'm good with this, thanks."

He shrugs and starts banging around the kitchen, making himself some big breakfast. Bauer always was the cook out of us all. I can just about burn beans.

My phone buzzes on the table as Bauer's pings in his pocket. A sense of dread fills me, and I know. I know that it's Archer. I pick up my phone as Bauer watches me, pulling his out too. A message from an unknown number with a video clip attached.

I swallow as I hit play and Archer's face comes into frame.

"You Bennetts, you think you're so smart. Hitting my sites, like I didn't have others just in case Bauer turned on me." He laughs manically, and it's hard to watch as the camera flips and refocuses. The view makes me want to throw up, but I keep it down. "Their screams were like music to my ears. A special song for me. This was on you Bennett brothers. You have to know that your sister and her little Witch will pay for this too." The bodies are still smoking, blackened from the fire that burned them. I can't tell who they are, but I know the building behind them. The Elder Tower. They're behind it, in the background. How the fuck did he get in there?

The video ends with more laughter, and I drop my

phone, running to the sink and spitting up my coffee.

"Colt," I lift up a finger to stop my brother from speaking while my stomach rolls again.

"There were kids in that pile, Bauer," I say, spitting into the sink before rinsing my mouth.

"This is my fault," he says, hanging his head.

"No, this is his fault. All of it is his fucking fault," I seethe, gripping the counter until my knuckles turn white.

"If I hadn't taunted him with Dylan..."

"Then he'd have retaliated for our move last night anyway. He knows how to hurt us. Our people are what we value the most. Hurting them hurts us. He knows that." I sigh, my anger and guilt rolling around inside of me and fighting for dominance. I made the call to attack his buildings. The weight of this is on me. No one else.

"We need to stop him, Bauer. For good."

"I know," he sighs, clasping my shoulder. "We'll stop him."

"First, we need to find him," I say quietly. "But before that, I need to call the other Elders and tell them what's happened."

I sigh and leave the room, knowing that the calls I'm about to make will be some of the hardest I've ever made.

FOURTEEN

FALLON

“Can you give me my powers back?” I ask skeptically as Azriel grins at me. He invited us down for breakfast in his private quarters, and we’ve all eaten in silence. But then he dropped that little bomb on me.

“Well, I can gift you power,” he says, smirking as he leans back in his chair. “It won’t be the same power you’re used to, though; it will be more. But I’ll give you a little at a time. You’re going to have to earn it as well as my trust. I can’t have my newest plaything using that power against me, now can we?” He winks, and I force myself to smile at him. Of course there’s a catch, he’s a Demon. There’s always a catch.

"And how exactly would you like me to prove myself?" I ask him, trying to keep the rage from my face. I'm madder than a nest of hornets, but I can't let him see that.

"Well, I think that's best discussed when small ears aren't at the table, don't you?" I swallow the bile that rises at his words. There isn't a chance in hell I'll do that for him, not for all the power in the world.

"If you say so," I say back, not wanting to let him know he got to me, though Deacon balks at my answer. Tough shit. He don't get to judge, especially when he has no idea who I really am. A plan starts forming in my mind, but I keep the glee from my face. These Demons might've bitten off more than they can chew, especially if Remy is on her way here. I intend to have enough power by the time she gets here to turn these assholes to nothing but dust.

I pop a mini bagel with salmon and cream cheese in my mouth, groaning as I chew. These guys might be assholes, but the food here is fucking divine. Rebel is oblivious to it all as she tucks into her pancake stack, and I'm glad that the resilience of her youth is benefitting her right now. I'm damn near envious.

I sit quietly, pretending not to be interested as Azriel discusses his next steps with Deacon. Deacon's eyes keep darting in my direction, most likely trying to assess what game I'm playing, but I shrug when I catch him staring. I'm gonna be the best damn prisoner they ever had, and then I'm gonna be the worst fucking nightmare they never could've imagined haunting them. I'll raze this entire fucking realm if that's what it takes.

I try not to think about home too much, though. Thinking of Mama, Colt, and everything back home makes my heart fracture a little more with each wayward thought. That's everything and everyone I might never see again if everything doesn't go my way or Remy never makes it here, which is a possibility I haven't accepted just yet.

"Yes, I think that's an adequate move," Azriel says, pulling my focus back to the table. "Fallon, you should say goodbye to your sister. Deacon's touching plea on your behalf won me over. What can I say, I'm in a good mood. He'll be delivering her back to the mortal realm after breakfast." He smiles at me, and my eyes dart to my sister before meeting Deacon's. If he hurts her, I'll make sure he dies first. Slowly.

"I appreciate it. You have my gratitude," I say. I might have sold my soul to this asshole, but I'm never gonna say 'thank you', not down here. I've sold my soul, not my mind. I ain't stupid enough to give myself over to him fully.

"I'll let you all finish up, I have some matters that require my attention. Come and find me once they leave," he says to me with a wink before disappearing from sight. He's gone before he can see the shudder that runs through my body.

"How could you agree to his terms?" Deacon hisses, eyes darting to Rebel before coming back to me.

"I didn't have much choice, did I?" I ask with a narrow-eyed glance back. This motherfucker.

"I could have found a way," he sighs, shaking his head.

"There's nothing you could've done, you said that much yourself last night."

"So you'll let him own you, all of you?"

"He might own my body, but he ain't ever gonna own my mind or my heart. Those I'll keep for myself."

"He will try to take all of it if he grants you power," Deacon says, damn near pleading with me.

"Don't sit there all high and mighty and act like you care," I hiss at him. "You kept me here long before he found me. You don't know me, you don't know what I'd do to keep the ones I love safe."

"If you betray him, he will kill you and everyone you love," he says sadly. "Rebel, come on, sweetheart. Let's take you back to your mom."

Rebel squeals in delight as she jumps from that table. I'm not sure how she tuned out from that delightful exchange, but I'm glad as hell she did.

"Are you coming too, Fallon?" she asks, hugging me tightly.

"No sweetheart, I need to stay here. But you tell Mama

I love her, okay?" I boop her nose gently, and she giggles.

"I love you, Fallon. Come home soon okay?"

"I'll try, baby girl. I love you too."

Rebel left with Deacon, and I haven't seen him since. That was hours ago, and I've taken the opportunity to explore my new prison since Azriel hasn't popped up again either. Whatever's keeping him busy, I hope it keeps him for a long time because I'd be more than happy never to see his smug-ass face again. Why are the pretty ones always epic fucking assholes?

I continue to walk through the gallery I discovered about half an hour ago. The artwork hanging on the walls is like nothing I've seen before. There's a lot of pain mixed in with so much hope. The bright colors are broken by the dark, sweeping brush strokes. Something about it holds me in thrall.

"I didn't expect to find you here," Azriel's voice breaks my peace, and I try not to sigh.

"Well, you sure don't know me very well, do you?" I ask without looking at him. I stroll to the next painting while he chuckles beside me.

"There is plenty of time for that, love. I'm glad you found a place that brings you some fragments of happiness."

“Or merely a distraction.”

“Oh no, love, I know that look. The wistfulness as you fall into the story before you. This art speaks to you on a deeper level than you’ll ever admit to me. I almost find it amusing.”

“And why’s that?” I snap at him, and his grin widens.

“Well, because, sweetheart, this is my personal gallery. For my work.”

My eyes go wide, and I falter. “You painted these?” I ask, almost breathless. There’s no fucking way.

“Each and every one. Immortality has its downsides, you know? No better way to pass the time than explore how color and emotion merge on the canvas.” His grin is wide as I look back to the artwork, still not fully believing someone like him is capable of work like this.

“I should head back to my room,” I finally say, stepping away from him and putting distance between us.

“Is that an invitation, love?” he leers, looking me over from head to toe. The hairs on the back of my neck rise at the unwanted attention.

“It is not, nor will it ever be,” I tell him succinctly.

“If you say so.” His voice washes over me as I walk away, and I feel dirty. “I will find you later, love. We have work to do.”

I keep my head high as I stride quickly from the gallery, and I try to realign my thoughts about the monster I know and the man who created such beautiful art. Is it possible I misjudged him? I shake my head to dispel the thought.

Not a chance.

Right? Right.

Trying to navigate my way back to my room is harder than I thought it would be even if I stumbled upon this place by accident. I'm sure I'll end up going in circles for a while, but finally I find the hall with the sweeping staircase and climb it as quickly as I can.

I'm beyond breathless by the time I reach the fourth floor.

Why the fuck are there so many fucking stairs?

I curse whoever built this place as I walk at a slower pace to my room, trying to catch my breath. By the time I've walked the long hall, my lungs don't feel like they're burning anymore, and I push the door to my room open. My jaw clenches when I see Deacon sitting on my bed.

"Az said you were coming here. When you weren't already here, I figured I'd wait. I hope that's okay," he says softly as I close the door behind me.

"What do you want, Deacon?" I ask with a sigh. I don't have the mental capacity to spar with him on top of all the other shit that's going down right now.

"I wanted to let you know that she got home safely. I wiped her memory of anything that was done to her. She thinks she came here to see you."

"That was kind of you," I offer warily. Does he want a fucking award or something? "Why bother being so nice?"

"Because she's a child. Children should never be used as pawns in war. Azriel agreed. He only used her upon Archer's insistence in the first place. He never would have touched your sister otherwise."

"So I'm meant to believe that Demons have some moral code they play by?"

"You don't have to believe a thing I say, but you should know that not everything is what it seems. Not always," he says passionately. "I will leave you alone, but if you need anything, push the button by the door. Someone will be able to bring you anything you want or need."

He waves his hand and a console appears on the wall next to the door. "You live here now. While you are tied to this place, Azriel wants it to be your home."

"He only wants that so I'll give him what he wants," I hiss.

"That may be the case, but do not scoff at what he offers. It could be much worse. He could have taken everything he wanted against your will. Be glad for small mercies. He obviously sees something in you that he likes, otherwise he would not have been so kind." He closes the door after him, the last of his words barely out before he disappears from sight and leaves me wondering what the hell is going on in this place.

Everything's confusing as hell, and it's hard to tell who's a friend and who isn't. Deep down I know everyone here's my enemy. I'm not here by choice, but I can't help the small part of me that wants to believe there's good in both Azriel and Deacon. I'm pretty sure that part of me only exists to keep me from losing my mind while I try to find a way to get out of this place. Planning an escape that probably ain't gonna happen might just be a way to keep me distracted long enough for Remy and her guys to find me here.

Either way it ain't gonna save them from my wrath when I'm done here.

It's surreal being here like this. I'm free, but at the same time, I'm not really. I think that's why I keep finding myself back in the gallery. Art has always called to me, and there's freedom here. I can almost forget where I am and the circumstances of it all while losing myself in the beauty. Even the darkest, saddest of paintings leads me down a path to someplace that isn't here.

And yet, I know that Azriel created this place. I know that this part of him is different from the side I saw so frequently when I first got here. I know that I'm here with him, quite literally, for eternity.

So I'm trying, and mostly failing, to soothe my angry and hate-filled heart.

"I find you here once again, love." Azriel's voice is soft, lilting, and as full of charm as ever. "I like that my escape calls to you too."

"Well, it's the only escape I'll ever have." I sigh. "Unless you up and decide to let me go, of course."

"I couldn't, even if I wanted to. You are not the only one bound, love." I look over at him, and I swear there's a sadness about him. "I might be your monster, but that doesn't make me a monster."

I swore to myself that I wouldn't give in to the words of his bond, but when he's like this and I know that I'm likely the only one to have ever seen him like this, it's hard not to soften a little. Though the war that rages inside of me when it comes to him is fierce, he chips away at me a little each time we talk openly.

"It still makes you my monster."

"Yes, love, I know, but even the villain deserves a happily ever after sometimes. Sometimes the villain isn't even a villain, just a guy caught between a rock and a hard place with a knife at his throat." His gaze doesn't waver from mine, and for a second, I swear I see a glimmer of regret. It's gone so quick I doubt whether I really saw it at all. It's his words that truly make me think. Are we both victims of circumstance? Him, of whatever he speaks of, and me, the friend of one of the most powerful Hunters of all time.

Not that I blame Remy. She didn't ask for any of this. All she wanted was equality between the factions, which is long overdue.

"Sometimes," I start. "Sometimes the villain becomes the villain because he loses himself to what he thinks he must do rather than what is actually needed. You can't possibly stand there and tell me you're not a monster after what you did to me. After you brought my sister here."

"That was not my choice," he argues, but I shake my head.

"Maybe it wasn't, but you didn't have to use her against me. But you did. You used her to bind me to you."

"And if I tell you that wasn't my choice either, I wonder if you would believe me," he says, looking back at the dark painting before us.

I ponder his words, but the part of me that rages, that hates everything I've been through, that writhes like shadows brought to life within me, refuses to believe even a hint of that possibility. I won't survive this if I don't hate him. He looks back to me, and I know he sees my thoughts written all over my face by the tight smile he gives me. He squares his shoulders.

"I will leave you to your escape," he says tautly before turning and walking away, leaving me to watch his retreating form, as the war inside of me rages once more.

I've lost track of how long I've been stuck here since Rebel went home. Nothing much changes here. Azriel flirts, Deacon tries to pretend he doesn't care about it, and I'm trying to cozy up to Azriel so I can get more power quickly so that I can get the fuck outta here.

Though, as much as I hate it, the lines with Azriel have started to blur the more time I spend with him. He walked me through the gallery again, explaining the pieces to me from his perspective. We've eaten together and talked, and he's one charming son of a bitch. It's hard to not forget that he's my captor, and that I'm still held here against my will. Until the evenings.

Or moments like this, when he calls me to the main hall and he grins at me like the villain I know he is. He's practically giddy by the time I reach him.

"You summoned me?" I try not to roll my eyes, but that's essentially what this was.

"I have a surprise for you, sweetheart," he says, barely able to keep still with his excitement. "It seems your rescue party made something of a faux pas, and Deacon here caught them. They're in the cells as we speak!"

I look over to Deacon who nods subtly. I thought maybe

we were building a friendship... Did he really betray me so much that he would bring them here? I look away from him—I can't bear to see the truth of it from him—and look back to Azriel.

"Would you like to see them?" he asks eagerly. I can't tell if this is some sort of trick, so I cross my arms and tilt my head upwards to look at him properly.

"Am I allowed to see them?" It kills me to ask, but I know that the wrong answer could end in a whole world of pain, and I've already suffered enough. If I can avoid pissing him off, you can bet your ass I'm going to.

"Of course, I wouldn't have asked otherwise."

"Then yes, please. I'd like to see them all," I tell him, and he nods, disappearing from sight and leaving me alone with Deacon. This place has ears everywhere so I don't dare ask him what the hell Azriel's playing at. All I can hope is that my friends have done what I had begun to think impossible.

I might be a Witch, but even my faith has its limits.

My footsteps echo off of the hard floor while I pace, waiting for Azriel to return. Goddess only knows what the hell he's doing to them that's taking him so long. I can't help but bite at the skin by my thumbnail. It's a horrid nervous habit I've had my entire life. I thought I'd managed to get it under control, but the circumstances of late have pushed me too far apparently.

Azriel reappears with Remy in his grasp, and I swear my heart stops momentarily before my feet move without thought and I'm running at her. She catches me in a hug, and I absolutely fucking lose it. Sobs rack my body, and there's nothing I can do to stop them. "I knew you'd come," I tell her through my tears. "But it's too late, and he has you too."

"He doesn't have shit," she tells me with a cocky smile.

"Oh, is that right, sweetheart?" Azriel coos at her. "If you ask me, I have pretty much all the cards in the deck. I have your Witch, and I have your lovers. Hell, I even have your brothers, they just don't know it yet."

She rolls her eyes at him, and I can't help but smile. Whatever she's been through, my friend is still herself. "You know what they say about those who sit themselves too high," she says to him, smiling. "They hit the ground, hard and fast."

"Oh, I like you," he says with a smile, and my skin crawls. There's the villain, back at the forefront again. "Maybe I'll break my bargain with Archer and make a new one with you. Would you like that, little Hunter? I wonder what it is you'd give up to protect the ones you love. To protect your beloved Earth and all its ridiculous humans. I could kill Archer for you and call all the Demons back. It could be so simple. You wouldn't have to lose anyone else." He pauses, and I feel my eyes go wide at his words.

"I could probably even give you the soul of the human Archer killed. It has not been long. It isn't likely her soul will have moved on yet," he taunts her, but he sounds so genuine, and based on what I've learned, he probably is. I might not have been here very long, but I know him. He wouldn't offer if he didn't mean it.

"What human?" I ask, my hand on my throat, trying to keep myself steady.

"Everly," Remy whispers as her eyes fill with tears.

"You let him kill her?" I shout at Azriel, and he winces.

"I didn't let him do a thing, my little Witch. I had no idea about his plans. But if you want, I could gift you her soul," he offers, and I scream at him in frustration and rush forward with raised fists. I have little strength next to him, but he lets me beat my hands against his chest before he wraps his arms around me to stop me.

"Fallon, stop." Remy pulls me away from him. I'm not sure if it was for me or if she got a glimpse of tenderness he has when he touches me. There's no way in hell she'd be comfortable with that.

"I will never forgive you for this!" I shout at him, ignoring the hurt in his eyes.

"You have my offer," he says to Remy. "Think about it. I'll give you an hour with your Witch before I'll return and demand an answer. Do not disappoint me, Hunter."

Azriel disappears from sight, and I look to Remy with

tears in my eyes. I know her, and I know how much she loved Everly. "What is going on in your mind?" I ask, my eyebrow raised. "I know you're not here and not fighting him without some ulterior motive."

"I... we had a plan, but his offer—" she starts, but I cut her off.

"Don't do it, Remy. It was worth it for me, but you'd be giving up so much more than I did. I don't have epic love or a whole world of people relying on me. They need you," I plead, unable to stop the pain from what I've been through from coming through.

"But what if it was only temporary? Wouldn't it be worth it then?"

"Trust me, nothing is worth what this bond does to you. I'm pretty sure my soul was shredded the moment I agreed to it. I'm not the person I was before I came here. Please don't do this to yourself, Remy."

Remy sighs at my words and sinks to the floor. I sit down with her, and Deacon disappears from the room. We spend the time catching up, and I give her a very brief and condensed version of everything that's happened since I was taken. Her smile is tight, but it's so nice to be here with her. Even if our time is limited.

It's not long before Azriel reappears, more composed than he was when he left. He won't look at me, which immediately sets my teeth to grinding. Deacon is with him, but they're both focused on Remy. I'm not really surprised, though. She has something about her that really draws people in.

Azriel smiles at her, and I recognize the same smile he offered me when he gave me my deal. "Have you decided to take me up on my offer?"

"I've thought about it, and I have a counteroffer," she says, nodding as she stands. Deacon disappears again, and the part of me that's more in tune with Remy than it should be goes off like a fog horn. She's working with Deacon. What the fuck?

"How about you do everything you offered, and I don't kill you?" She smiles at him, baring her teeth as she moves to stand in front of me. I step back as she reaches down and pulls a blade from her boot. My heart all but stops. Azriel's eyes go wide when he sees it, and in a heartbeat, more Demons than I care to count are at his back.

A small part of me doesn't want him to get hurt. I fucking hate that that part of me even exists.

The bigger part of me hopes to the Goddess that Remy has a good fucking plan to get us out of here.

"If you think that's enough to stop me, you've underestimated me." She laughs before slicing the blade across her palm, and her blood drips onto the ground before us.

"Oh little Hunter, your blood doesn't scare me."

"No, but they might," she says as four men I've never seen before appear in the room with Remy's guys and Deacon. A woman appears beside Remy. The power coming from her and the four I don't recognize is enough to nearly knock me off my feet. It's as if the whole room holds its breath for a second, and then Azriel reanimates.

"Betrayer!" Azriel shouts to Deacon, anger painting his face as his true form reappears, sharp rows of teeth and all. Deacon sneers in response, and all hell breaks loose.

In the blink of an eye, Remy is in front of me, trying to protect me as more Demons storm the hall. We move backward until we reach the dais at the far end of the room with the creepy-ass thrones.

"I need you to stay here," she says, pushing me behind one of the thrones. "Do not try to be a hero!"

I nod because I trust her with my life, quite literally, and I'm not equipped for this fight. All I'd do is get in the way. I still barely have any power and hand-to-hand combat isn't exactly my strongest skill. Though if we survive this, you can bet your ass that's gonna change. I can't put myself in situations this dire without a way to protect myself ever fucking again.

She dives back into the madness, and I hate that all I can do is sit and cower, watching from the sidelines. It's yet another thing this place has taken from me. My agency and ability to protect myself. I grit my teeth against my sneer.

It's hard to keep up with everything going on. The mass of bodies and smell of blood is hella overwhelming, but I try to track my friends and the people they brought here with them. Remy slices through Demons like it's nothing. The five strangers she brought with her are absolutely fucking terrifying, moving with practiced ease and leaving destruction in their wake. I try not to watch them too much, but I can't help but be held captive when the woman takes the head of a Demon without even blinking.

"Remy! No!" I cry out as I see a Demon coming at her from behind, but she doesn't hear me in time. I watch as his claws tear through her back, and a scream rips from my throat. He says something to her with a grin on his face, but she refuses to bow down. She lifts her sword and takes the Demon's head.

My eyes pull away from Remy in time to spot Azriel across the room. His claws rip through Creek's chest, and it's like my entire world tilts on its axis. In my periphery, I can just make out Remy falling to her knees as one of the strangers rushes to Creek, so I try to move toward Remy.

Levi appears behind Azriel with one of the strangers as I rush across the room. They each grab one of his arms as the woman shoves her hand into his chest and rips his heart out. His body crumples, falling to the floor as the few remaining Demons disappear from sight.

I clasp a hand over my mouth to stop from crying out. I know I shouldn't be sad or hurt that he's gone, but I can't help that I am. It's no good, the pain of it all, of all the death necessary to save me is too much and I can't stop the scream that rips from my body.

Deacon appears beside me, and I feel the rush of power draw to him from where Azriel lies slain.

I guess he didn't do it for me after all.

My last thought is of my friends, hoping that someone here is strong enough to save them all as the darkness takes me.

FIFTEEN

I wake in the room that has been my prison cell for longer than I want to think about, and I start to cry.

"Fallon, what's wrong?" Deacon's voice shocks me, and my tears stop in an instant. I sit up, swiping at my cheeks, to find him on the sofa, disheveled and half asleep.

"I had a really good dream, and I wanted it to be real," I tell him softly, embarrassed by my tears. I need to be stronger if I'm going to survive with him and Azriel. He gets up and walks over to the bed, sitting on the edge as he watches me closely.

"It wasn't a dream," he says, and my heart skips a beat. "It was real. Your friends were here. They came for you. Azriel is gone, and the bond you made to him now belongs to me. We plan on breaking it."

I sit in silence, blinking at his words. It can't be real. I take a deep breath, and I realize it's true. I can feel the bond between us, the same way I could feel it with Azriel. Remy came for me.

"Wait, but Creek, Remy…"

"They will both be okay. Morganna will ensure it."

"She's the woman who was with Remy yesterday?"

"I forget that you don't actually live here. Yes, Morganna is the Queen of the Shadow Realm, and the men with her, they're the Four Horsemen. They're all very good friends with Remy. You definitely have some powerful allies."

"Holy shit," I gasp, leaning back on the head rest. Remy is friends with the Queen of the Shadow Realm and the Four Horsemen. Why am I not actually shocked ? I mean, I'm totally shocked, and yet not at the same time. I have no idea how it's possible, but with that girl, I guess anything is.

"Something like that. When I went to Caleb, or Conquest, your friends were already there with them, trying to find you. We decided to work together to get you free from Az while also fucking with Dotoro's plans. It seemed like a win all around."

"Thank you," I say softly. "It doesn't seem like enough, but the words are all I have. So thank you, thank you for risking everything and going to them in the first place." I know I shouldn't say thank you. I was so sure I wouldn't ever say it to a Demon, but I'm already trapped here. He might think he can save me, but I'm not so sure. I can feel the bond's grip even now.

"I don't need any thanks from you, Fallon. Forgiveness maybe, but definitely no thanks. I owe you this and a thousand times over for what you endured here at my hand."

"I don't blame you," I tell him, trying to be as firm as I can. "What else could you have done? Azriel was more powerful, and you did what you could, when you could." He hangs his head, even as I say the words, and I can tell he doesn't believe me. Pride sure is a pain in the ass. I get it, he hates what he did to me. I fucking hate what he did too, but I know that Archer and Azriel were the real force behind it. Azriel saw that I was trying to find a glimmer of hope here, and Deacon was the only being it could have been. He tried to crush that.

So while I hate it, I don't blame Deacon. Some little, very fucked up part of me doesn't even blame Azriel or his jealousy. He always seemed angry whenever Deacon spoke to me or was near me. Which in itself was insane because he was the one who made Deacon watch me.

I shake my head. I'm not even going to try and unravel it yet. "Can I see my friends?"

"Remy and Creek haven't woken yet, but as soon as they do, I've asked Caleb to let us know so that you can. I assume they're the two you mean from what you've told me before."

"Yeah, I meant those two. How are the others?" I ask because I know if Remy survives and one of them doesn't, she'll go nuclear.

"The Lycan and the Dracul are out cold, but the Archangel is fine. I'm pretty sure everyone will be okay, the Queen's power..." He shudders a little as he looks away from me. "Her power is unfathomable. But until they are up and about, we'll work on breaking the bond so that you can leave here. In the meantime, no more locks and no more guards. Do as you wish. You are a guest here."

It's been nearly a week, and there's still been no news about Remy or the others. I'm about to lose my freaking mind. I head down to the breakfast room, which happens to be the room where I originally made the bond with Azriel. The same pang hits me every time I enter the room, but I dismiss it because there is no way I'm actually sad that he's dead.

His death means I'm free. I can go back to my old life on Earth.

I don't know if I'll fit in my old life anymore. I'm not the same girl I was before all of this. While it isn't a bad thing and I'm definitely stronger, I'm also still very broken. Facing down everything that comes with that is a little terrifying.

Deacon is already here, eating and reading, which is the same way I find him most mornings. As soon as I sit, a woman appears with my breakfast, just the same way she does every day. How they know what I want each day is beyond me, but they've yet to get it wrong. I put it down to some weird part of the bond that Deacon now holds and try not to think on it too hard because it creeps me the fuck out when I do.

I might have spent my whole life around magic, but it works differently here. Now that I know I have a way out, I don't have to learn to live with it.

"How are you feeling today? Did you sleep better?" Deacon asks with a warm smile. "No nightmares?"

"I'm okay, I'm really looking forward to this bond being broken... And yes, nightmares still," I tell him honestly. We've been working on breaking the bond the entire week, but it's taking a lot out of us both. It's mostly because I don't know the exact wording Azriel used for the bond, so it's almost like trying to do a puzzle blindfolded. We've only got bits of the information to try and piece it all together. Plus there's the whole risk of shredding my soul thing—since Azriel mentioned that to me, I told Deacon about it. The cursing that followed was enough to make anyone blush. It's gonna take time, that much is pretty clear.

"It will get better," he tells me confidently. "And word came this morning that Remy is awake. Caleb requested your presence at the Shadow Palace. So eat up, we've got a trip to make." His words are begrudging, and he seems more tense than I've seen him in the entire time I've known him. What is it about going to the Shadow Palace that puts him so on edge?

He doesn't talk much about the Queen and her Horsemen, so I have very little information, which makes me more than a little wary. But he did say they're close with Remy, so I have to believe that they can't be as bad as Deacon implies with his unwillingness to talk about them.

We eat in silence, and my nerves only build with the prospect of seeing Remy. I assume since there was no word about the others, they're still out cold, and the thought that they were hurt trying to save me… What if she blames me?

I mean, I know she wouldn't since that's just not how she is, but still. Fear isn't a logical response, though, and I'm not exactly the most logical person in the world.

I finish eating, glad I put a little effort in when I dressed this morning. I feel nervous, which I know is ridiculous, but it is what it is.

"Are you ready?" Deacon asks, and I nod, unable to speak. "Let's go." He stands up, putting down his book and offering me a hand. "Hold on tight."

I barely hear his words before I'm wrapped in darkness and the feeling of falling overwhelms me. In less than a blink, the darkness clears, and I find myself outside what I assume is the Shadow Palace.

The huge, beautiful building is cut out of the black rock halfway up what seems to be a mountain. A river of lava sits at its base. Spires reach up as far as the eye can see, and gold glitters across the palace at different doors and window frames.

A winding path leads from where we stand at the foot of the mountain, and a gate of gold, carved with the most beautiful artwork of vines, flowers, and thorns sits in front of us. It's framed by a wall of black stone that seems to run the entire length of the palace.

We're silent as we walk down the path toward the enormous gates. They open, revealing a bridge made of the same black stone as the palace walls, with rushing water below. We follow its path, and I realize it moves toward a waterfall, which leads straight to the lava below. Holy crap. Shadow Palace indeed.

Once we reach the other side of the bridge, the dark, ornate doors to the palace shimmer as we pass through them, reacting to our presence and allowing us entry.

I gasp at the difference between the inside and outside of the palace. It's such a stark difference that it takes a moment for my eyes to adjust. Here, the walls and ceiling are all white, and the curved ceilings make dozens of arches. The pillars dotting the entryway are stone men, reaching up and holding up the ceiling. This room branches off into three different directions, and it seems as if there's a hall to the left and right of us. The last one is straight ahead, leading into what I'm assuming is the heart of the palace. One of the men from the other day waits for us here.

"Deacon, glad you're both okay," the guy says, though the lack of smile on his face makes me apprehensive. The menace that comes from him is staggering. He's all dark and broody, with nothing but sharp edges. I don't know that I've ever described someone that way before, but it's truly the only thing that fits. "Fallon, it is nice to finally meet you. My name is Malik."

"You're one of the Horsemen?" I ask, and he almost smiles. But only almost.

"Yes, Plague." I try to stop the shiver that works its way down my spine and fail, but he doesn't seem to take offense. "Caleb and Remy are in the atrium. I can take you there if you'd like. "

I look between him and Deacon, who nods and disappears from my side.

"I guess that's a yes," I say, trying not to sound bitter about Deacon abandoning me here with this crazy powerful guy who could probably end me with nothing more than a thought.

"Don't mind him, he has his own issues with this place. I promise I won't harm you. Any friend of Mara's is a friend of ours."

"Mara?" I ask, and Malik chuckles lowly.

"Remy," he says without offering any explanation, but I don't bother to ask either. How very strange it is here. We walk for a while through the maze that is the Shadow Palace before he pulls to a stop in front of a door. "They're in there waiting for you, so I'll take my leave. It was nice to finally meet you, Shadow Weaver."

I blink as he leaves, wondering what the fuck a Shadow Weaver is. I shake the thought away. I have way more to worry about right now. My nerves are trying to get the best of me, but I flat out refuse to be afraid of my lifelong friend, so I take a deep breath and open the door into what looks like a world full of plants. Light shines down through the glass ceiling and the chirp of birds fills the room.

I spot Remy across the room with, who I assume from Malik's words earlier, is Caleb. Between us sits a small table with two chairs, a tray complete with a tea pot, cups, and an assortment of cakes. I look past it to Remy, who gasps when she finally sees me.

"Fallon!" She rushes at me and engulfs me in a hug, and I cry again because the embrace damn near feels like home. I hug her back fiercely, trying to get the tears under control.

"I'll see you ladies later," Caleb calls out, but I barely notice him move past us and leave. I know I should feel rude, but my emotions are so fucking all over the place right now, I can't make myself care. I manage to get myself basically back under control and pull out of the hug.

"Remy, I'm so glad you're okay. I thought you were dead. How's Creek? How are the others?" I ask through my tears, and she pulls me back in and hugs me tighter. Okay, maybe I'm not actually completely under control just yet.

"I'm fine, but more importantly, how are you? I'm so, so sorry it took us so long to find you, Fallon." She holds me even tighter, and it's like a freaking vise grip. I'm not even mad that I can barely breathe through her iron embrace.

"Remy, can't breathe," I sputter with a laugh, and she lets me go.

"Sorry. Come on, let's sit. I'm sure there's so much to catch up on."

Hours pass while we catch up about everything that's happened back home since I was taken. I glaze over what happened to me since I'm not really ready to go through it properly, but because she's Remy, she understands. She doesn't judge as I laugh or cry, or do both at the same time. She tells me about everything that they've been through trying to find me, and my heart feels heavy with guilt. At the same time, I feel so loved that she would go through that for me. She finishes telling me one of her stories before eying me cautiously.

"And well, I mean, I died," she tells me with a small shrug, and I swear my heart stops as I choke on the tea I'd just taken a sip of.

"What do you mean, you died? You're here," I shout, my voice way higher than usual, but what the actual fuck? She can't just drop something like that on me!

"I mean that being down here unlocked something inside of me, some sort of power. Morgan did something before we came to get you to make sure that if I died, I wouldn't actually die. Well not really."

"Remy, I'm so confused."

"I'm an Angel now," she tells me, and I feel my eyes go wide as I lean back in the chair, trying to put my mind back together from where she just blew it fucking apart. Holy crap. How is that even possible?

"You're a… I mean… you can't be… can you?" The words barely make sense, but the fragments are all I can get out as my mind whirrs around the new, unexpected information.

"Apparently, I can be, and I am. My mortal self died, and I was out for a few days. When I woke up, I was like this." She waves her hand in front of her face, and I notice for the first time the slight glow to her skin. Her features are a little sharper, and her hair is a little shinier. I thought it was this place, but apparently not.

"Holy fuck, you're an Angel. Oh my Goddess, do you have wings?"

"Levi says so. I haven't gotten that far, though. Apparently I'll get all of my memories back eventually too. Like alllllll the way back."

"Wow."

"I know." She sighs as she sits back in her chair, and her eyes glass over. "Oh my fates," she gasps before tears start running down her face. I have no idea what is happening, so I reach forward, covering her hand with mine.

"Everly is dead," she croaks, and it hits me as hard as it did the first time she told me.

"I know, I wish I could change it," I say, but it's as if she doesn't hear me.

"Archer... he killed her."

"He's such a motherfucker!" I curse, but she doesn't even blink. I don't think she can hear me.

"They killed her when we were here and there was nothing I could do about it," she says, and then her eyes cloud over again. She screams, and I'm not sure she even knows she's doing it. I squeeze her hand and cry with her. Goddess knows we've both lost so much. Too much.

" I'm so sorry, Remy."

"There's more," she starts, and it looks like someone knocked the wind out of her. "It's Creek. He's dying. Caleb is keeping him in stasis, but without extreme measures, he'll actually die."

"What the fuck are extreme measures?" I ask, my world spinning out of control as I try not to focus on the fact that Everly is dead because of me... Or that Creek could die because of me.

"Morgan offered to give him her blood. It will heal him."

"Why is it even a question then?" I ask, incredulous.

"Because if she does that, she transfers some of her power to him and he will become half Demon."

"Holy fucking shit." I can't quite wrap my mind around it all. We sit quietly while we both try to digest everything, but I eventually ask, "So what are you going to do?"

"I have no idea, but I have to make a decision today." She sighs. "I don't want to lose him, Fal. But I don't want to turn him into something he'll hold against me for the rest of our lives."

"Which is gonna be insanely long now!" I can't help but laugh, but it sounds harsher than it should. Everything is changing, it's all so fucked up, and I can't help but feel responsible. The laughter probably isn't appropriate, but it's all I got right now.

"Something like that. Providing no more insanity rains

down on us at least."

"You really shouldn't tempt the fates like that, Remy." I roll my eyes at her because why would she even put that out there? I still pat her hand, offering what small comfort I'm capable of considering my extreme self-loathing at the moment.

"But I get it. Honestly, I wouldn't know what to do if I was you either. If you let him die, it could be another fifty to a hundred years until you get to see him again. Which for an immortal is a drop in the bucket, but at the same time, your mind isn't that of an immortal yet. Fifty years is still a long time. I don't know that he'd want to be gone from you for so long knowing that you were still alive. Especially since the others will all still be around."

"This, right here, is the exact the dilemma I'm having. I'm seriously considering asking Morgan if I let him die… once he cycles back to us, if she'll give him the option then. I don't want to be the person making this decision. It shouldn't be mine to make. It'll suck not having him around, but like you said, fifty or so years is a drop in the bucket to an immortal right?" She leans forward onto the table and props her head in her hands. "Talk about first world problems, but fuck my life, Fallon."

"I get it. The thought of going back home, after everything that's happened here... I don't feel like myself anymore," I say quietly. It's one thing to admit it to myself, but to say it out loud? Ugh, it feels so real.

"I know. Morgan said something about that, but she's going to help."

"I still can't believe that the Queen of the Shadow Realm and her Four Horsemen are good friends of yours. So weird, and yet, totally believable. It's unreal." I laugh.

"Has Deacon unbound you yet?" she asks cautiously, and I almost jerk back from the abrupt change of subject.

I take a deep breath and consider my words before carefully saying, "Nearly. Apparently, it takes time so that he doesn't shred my soul completely or something. Honestly, I'm not even sure I'm ready to go home yet, so I don't mind. Don't get me wrong, I miss Mama, Rebel, and everyone else so freaking much, but I don't feel like I really belong there anymore."

"Oh, Fal, I'm so sorry they did this to you. Once we're ready and Deacon pulls back his Demons, I'm going to tear Archer to pieces just for you. Fuck everything else. No one fucks with my bestie like this. I wish I could fix it all for you." I laugh wryly at her words. I wish she could fix it all too, but I think I might be beyond fixing.

"Hopefully Morgan can help. But, I'm not gonna lie, I'd still like to see him as fish food as long as you let me help." I wink at her, slapping on the mask I know she needs right now. The silly-ass comment makes her laugh, exactly like I thought it would.

"Whatever you need."

"Thanks." I smile tightly at her, and she offers a small smile back before staring off into the distance. Pain like I haven't experienced since Azriel's torture chamber pierces my mind suddenly, and I bite my tongue to keep from crying out. Remy's lost in her thoughts and doesn't seem to notice, so I close my eyes and clench my fists, trying to ride it out, but Goddess, it fucking hurts.

The pain starts to subside, and I let out the breath I've been holding.

Hello, love, Azriel's voice whispers in my mind, and panic floods me. What the fuck?

You didn't think you'd be rid of me quite that easily, did you?

I run from the atrium without a word as fast as my feet can carry me. I don't have a destination in mind, but I collide with Malik, who catches me and keeps me from falling. He takes one look at the panic on my face and brings me back to my room in Azriel's… Wait, no, Deacon's palace, and then disappears again.

The pain in my mind is gone, and Azriel's voice hasn't appeared again. Maybe I panicked for nothing. Maybe the stress created a hallucination of sorts.

That's all it was.

Right?

I try to calm my breathing back down to something close to normal and try to swallow down the fear that grips me.

Fuck, I feel like I'm gonna be sick.

Though, that's more than the Azriel thing. Guilt crashes down on me like a tsunami. Everly is dead because Remy was trying to save me instead of being home. Creek might die because they came for me. Rebel got pulled to the Shadow Realm because of me. My throat feels like it's closing, and I try to suck in air, but my panic grows.

Why wasn't I stronger?

Why couldn't I fight off Archer and his goons? If I'd been stronger, more powerful, none of this would be happening right now. People wouldn't be dead because of me.

"Fallon, what's wrong?" Deacon's voice filters through my panic, but it feels like he's so very far away.

I feel him grasp my arms, and he spins me around to face him. He looks fucking terrified, and I have no idea why. He hugs me, pulling me so tight I think I might pass out, but the panic ebbs away the longer he holds me.

Once the panic dies down, sobs rack my body, and he tucks my head under his chin. Deacon contines holding me, letting me get it all out. He strokes my hair and whispers words that I can barely make out, but they soothes me nonetheless. I cling to him like he's my very last lifeline.

Then guilt floods me all over again because he was my captor, and I shouldn't find comfort in his embrace. Yes, he helped save me, but he also hurt me. A lot.

I pull back from his embrace and smile at him, half ashamed of crying all over him, and half angry at myself for everything else. I shouldn't feel this conflicted about him. I should never have been conflicted about Azriel either.

I don't even dare think of Colt because that's a whole other sort of guilt I can't even begin to cope with right now.

"Are you okay?" he asks, and I nod, unable to speak. "Okay," he pauses, running his hand through his hair.

"I," I croak, but I really can't find the right words. I needed him and he was there, but whatever this could have been, if we were different people in entirely different circumstances, isn't something that can ever actually be anything.

"Don't worry, Fallon. I know," he says sadly. "I'm glad you're alright. I'll be around if you need me, okay?"

I nod and he leaves the room, turning back to look at me one last time before he closes the door. The regret and longing on his face are more than I can handle right now, so I curl up on my bed and wish for sleep to take me away to a place much simpler than this.

SIXTEEN

I've been hiding in my room for two days, having food brought here while I try to get my shit together. I know I've been through a lot and can accept that I have some trauma to deal with, but that doesn't stop me from feeling like I'm being a whiny freaking drama queen. Deacon came in for an hour or so yesterday and made another attempt to break the bond, but he barely spoke to or looked at me while we did it. So that was another fun thing to add to my list of reasons to wallow in bed for the rest of eternity.

See, whiny drama queen.

I made a decision when I woke up today, though. I'm going to be a better friend to Remy. She needs me, and I ran off like a crazy person without a word before disappearing. Again. That is not the friend I have ever been, and I have no intention of becoming that person just because I'm fucking sad.

So I throw on some clothes, make myself somewhat normal looking, and head down for breakfast. I find Deacon there already, and before my ass hits the seat, he shakes his head without even looking at me. I stop mid stride. "Don't sit. You're back off to the palace today. Killian will be here for you shortly."

"Another Horseman?" I ask, feeling awkward as fuck right now. I don't know what's going through his head. He's as readable as a blank sheet of fucking paper, and I honestly can't figure out how to act around him.

"Yes. Are you feeling better?"

"Yes, thank you," I say, but the conversation feels so stunted, and I know that's my fault. I don't know how to fix it, and I'm not sure if I even want to. I stand there awkwardly, not wanting to sit down since he so obviously dismissed me. It only takes a moment before my anger shows its stupid face. I'm pissed as hell that he's being so dismissive, which makes absolutely zero sense.

I'm just opening my mouth to lay into him when a light-haired guy appears in the room, startling me enough to make me jump. His eyes sweep around the room until his gaze falls on me. "You must be Fallon."

"That's me. I'm guessing you're Killian?"

"The one and only." He smiles warmly, and I let out

a sigh of relief. Okay, finally someone here who isn't absolutely fucking terrifying at first glance. "Let's get this show on the road, yeah ? I'm hungry enough to eat a horse."

He holds out his arm with an incline of his head, and I take it, threading mine through his as I did previously with the other Horsemen, and then the darkness wraps around us.

We land back in the palace, outside another stunning ornate, gold door. In fact, everything about this place is stunning and not at all what I would expect from a place called the Shadow Palace. "Head on in. Mara is in there waiting for you," he says before opening the door. I walk in, and once Remy waves at him, he disappears from sight. I guess he's not joining us for breakfast.

"Sorry I left so abruptly the other day," I say as I sweep across the room, finding Remy sitting in front of a table full of more food than I think I've ever seen in my life. There's a bounce in my step from my new resolution to not be so whiny, and since Azriel's voice hasn't made another appearance, I feel lighter. It could also be that the bond is nearly destroyed. There are things to be grateful for, and I intend on trying to focus on those.

"It's totally fine. I can't believe that was only two days ago. The last two days have felt like forever, and I slept through most of yesterday."

"What did you decide about Creek?" I ask hesitantly as I sit at the dining table and pour myself a glass of orange juice.

"I did it," she says quietly and stuffs a piece of bacon in her mouth, as if looking for an excuse not to talk about it more. I can't help the questions flooding my mind. She really did it. I mean, I expected as much. I couldn't let the love of my life die if there was another option either, but it doesn't feel real.

"You really did it?" I ask. I'm not the type to hold in my thoughts, and I'm beyond flabbergasted. She nods at me, and I lean back in my chair, processing it all. Yeah, I'm shocked, but I really do get it. Once it all settles in my mind, I relax. "It's for the best, I guess. At least you'll have another powerhouse on your side. Not that you need any more, but you know what I mean. This way, he doesn't need to leave you, and he won't age when you don't."

"There is that, I guess. I had this dream, and it felt so real. I saw him, and he told me to do it. I don't actually believe it was close to being real, but I can't say it didn't play a part in my decision. I can't lose him, Fallon."

"You'll never lose him. Even if he wouldn't have picked this particular path, though knowing him, he would've…

He'd still never leave you. I believe that in every part of my soul." I take her hand and squeeze it. I can't give her much, but this is a small comfort I can offer.

"How did our lives get so complicated? I miss the days when our biggest problem was how much of a jackass Jack was." I laugh before I notice the weird look on her face. My stomach fills with trepidation.

"So Jack's a Demon, and he's a friend of Archer's," she spits out, and I damn near drop my fucking glass.

"I'm sorry, what?! How did you miss sharing that bit?" I screech, and she has the gall to shrug.

"I guess, with everything else I dumped on you, I forgot to add that part." She laughs, and I lash out at her playfully.

"How the fuck do you miss that, girl? Holy fucking fuck. Jack is a Demon? No wonder your family hated him! Explains his grade A douchebag status too." I let out a bewildered laugh, and she shakes her head.

"I don't know how I could've been so blind." She sighs, and I shake my head.

"Oh no, girl. That is not on you. You had no idea about this whole world then. Man, I can't wait to cut off Archer's dick and stomp on it." I grin a little maniacally, the thought filling me with more joy than it probably should, and she laughs.

"So," she starts, teasing as she picks up another piece of bacon. "You and Deacon…"

"There is no me and Deacon," I tell her, rolling my eyes and hating that anything between us is apparently that obvious. "He helped me when he got the chance, and I'm sure he shielded me plenty too, but there is no me and him. Honestly, I was on the cusp of something with Colt, but after all this…"

"Colt loves you," she tells me, and I bark out a laugh. "He might not have said it, but it's in everything he does. You should have seen him after you were taken. If he didn't know it before, he knows it now. I'm not going to tell you to pick him because he's my brother. All I want is for you to be happy. If that's with Colt, awesome. If it's with a Demon, then so be it."

"Honestly, right now, I need to find myself before I do anything else," I tell her, wrapping my arms around myself. I hate how vulnerable I feel, but it's Remy, so I know it's okay to open up to her.

"Now *that* I understand."

"I bet you do. Here's me complaining when you have all this shit going on," I sigh apologetically, but she waves me off.

"Don't even. Your problems are just as important as mine."

"Nobody's life or death weighs on my problems, Remy. I'm pretty sure yours are a teensy bit more important, but thank you. It means a lot that you came here for me. I didn't say it before since there was so much going on, but thank you. You guys risked a lot. Everything really, for me. I'm not sure what I did to deserve a friend like you, Remy, but I'm so fucking thankful that I have you. You're my person. My ride or die, even if you can't really die anymore," I tell her laughing.

I steadfastly try to ignore her eyes turning glassy as she tries to blink back tears. That wasn't my intention at all. I just need her to know how much she means to me. My emotions are causing a riot inside of me on any given day, and I'm never sure how I'm going to be feeling. It feels ultra important to make sure the people who mean the most to me know what they mean to me right now.

"I love you, Fallon. There is no way in hell I wasn't going to come for you. Even with everything that happened, even if I'd known it was going to happen as a result, I'd still have come. I might have left the guys at home, but I'd still have come. You're my ride or die too. If I had the power to make you immortal, I would in a fucking heartbeat."

"Thanks, but no thanks." I laugh, suppressing a shudder. Immortality isn't for everyone. "I like the idea of only having a limited time. It makes things that much more precious because there's only a limited time to experience them. Plus, an immortal Witch? Can you imagine the outcry with the covens?"

She laughs. Remy's met the covens, so I know she

understands what I mean. They would squawk and squawk. The drama of it all would be goddamn neverending.

"How's my mama?" I ask quietly. I haven't dared ask before now because I miss her so much it hurts.

"She's your mom. She's worried as fuck but staying strong for everyone else, the same as always. I left her and Colt in charge of making sure everything runs smoothly at home, and I'm positive they've had Archer running in circles."

"I can't believe how long I've been gone."

"Yeah, but time moves differently down here," she tells me, and my mind whirs. How is that even possible? "It's faster here than home, so you haven't been gone that long to them back home. It feels longer than it is there."

"Well, shit. I guess that explains why it took so long for you to find me. Well, on top of the Demon assholes and all that."

"They weren't all assholes," she reminds me, and I think she's probably talking about her friends more than anything considering she barely knows Deacon. And despite his softer side, there's no way she'd think that about Azriel.

"No, I suppose not. I'm still kind of reeling from how nice the Four Horsemen of the freaking Apocalypse are. They definitely ain't what I imagined. And a Queen of Hell, or the Shadow Realm, or whatever. Also not at all what I pictured. No horns, y'know?"

"I guess that's the thing about our world. Nothing is ever really what it seems. Well, most things at least."

"At least it's not boring?" I ask with a laugh, and she nods and laughs along with me. It's crazy, but my life has actually always been boring. Even with the magic. Unfortunately, nothing about our lives is boring anymore.

After coming back to the sixth level of the Shadow Realm, Deacon was so quiet it was as if he wasn't even sitting in the same room as me eating dinner. I've already had enough hallucinations running through my head, surely I'm not imaging him now too.

It occurs to me that this could all be a figment of my imagination. Maybe Azriel really has pushed me over the edge during one of his torture sessions, and I finally broke. Maybe everything since then has been one long, hellish hallucination.

Except I'm pretty sure if that was true, I wouldn't be able to think it.

I can't help but let my mind drift to home, back to before everything got so fucked up. Back to when Colt first came home, and we reconnected—and by that, I mean that we finally hooked up after a year of FaceTiming and one hell of a slow burning buildup. Then everything went to shit with him because of the Hunters' ass backward ways, and I retreated. Honestly, I'd give pretty much anything to go back to when the worst thing I'd been through was bigoted bullshit that kept from being with the guy I wanted.

Things seemed so messed up then, but now I really would give anything for that to be my biggest problem, and the worst thing I was dealing with.

If only I'd known.

I get lost in my own pit of darkness and despair until Deacon stands up, the scrape of his chair legs on the stone flooring pulling me from my pity party. He looks at me, and he almost looks torn.

"We'll finish breaking your bond soon. We'll do another session tonight; and after that, it shouldn't need much more before Morgan can sever it completely." He looks down at me, and it feels as if he barely sees me.

"Thank you," I say softly. I recognize the tortured look on his face. I see it in myself when I dare to look in a mirror. I know how much he hates what I went through here and what he did to me. What they all did to me.

The thought of someone touching me makes my skin crawl. It's another thing to add to the list of ways I'm not going to be the same once I go back home. I've always been very tactile, but other than the odd hug with Remy, I tend to keep my hands and my body to myself.

Some scars will likely never heal.

At least not the mental ones.

"When?" I ask, and he continues to stare at me.

"Now? Later? Whenever you want." I watch him; he's as unmoving as a statue.

"Is something wrong?"

"What could possibly be wrong? My friend, who was more my boss than friend, and was also a giant asshole is dead, and I have to live here and clean up his messes. I have to live with the things that asshole made me do. And you're about to leave, likely to never return, which I obviously don't blame you for. What could possibly be wrong, Fallon?" His chest heaves as he finishes speaking, and he leaves the room before I can utter another word. I hate how much all of this has broken him, even if he is part of the reason I'm broken too.

I should hate him, but I don't. I can't. And maybe that's another part of me that's broken. Maybe it's a twisted form of Stockholm Syndrome, but I can't hate him. If anything, he's my savior as much as Remy is. Remy and the others seem to like him… not that they know everything, but still. I know she's teased me more than once about him, and it's easy to see why. Somehow I'm comfortable with him. I'm at ease. Maybe because of what he did, or maybe in spite of it, but either way, we're both still here.

He hurt you, love. In inexplicable ways.

I swear I want to scream at that voice in my head, but I ignore it. If I don't ignore it, it gets louder. Only Azriel could haunt me from beyond the grave.

Maybe Deacon knows, maybe that's why he's being so aloof. So distant. I heard what he said to me before he walked away, but there has to be more to it. He was willing to risk everything to save me. He knew the costs. That has to be worth something.

Right?

I sigh and drop my chin in my hand as I finish eating the tasteless meal. I know it isn't the food because the food was the only good thing about this place for a while. I give him time to cool off before I go after him. I know where I'll find him.

As much as I want to go back to my room and crawl right back into bed, I know that's not the answer. I need to be free of this bond. He wasn't wrong about that. He wasn't wrong about me likely never coming back, either.

I'm not ruling it out completely, though. Remy has some strong ties here, and I can almost see the charm of it when we're at the palace with her friends, but it's different for me. I don't know what she went through for those people to love her as fiercely as they so obviously do, but I do know that my strength is less than Remy's. It's at least different.

I sigh before standing and heading toward the cells

where I was held. It's where I found Deacon the last time I searched for him. It's his own personal form of torture, reliving what happened in those rooms.

Maybe, one day, I'll be strong enough to free him from his own demons too.

SEVENTEEN

"We need to go see your friends," Deacon says as he walks into my room without even knocking. I mean, not that it matters, I've barely left my bed for the last few days.

I've sat up to work on breaking the bond some, but the voice inside of my mind will not leave me alone and has monopolized most of my attention. I'm sure it's the manifestation of all of my guilt and trauma about everything that's happened, but I know better than to dismiss it as nothing. Azriel spoke of binding our souls, and though his body was destroyed, I have this horrific niggling feeling that while I'm sure the voice is nothing, I might be trying to downplay it because I'm sick to fucking death of shit happening to me.

"What do you mean we need to go see my friends? You're the master of the realm, or the level or whatever this place is. You go see them. I can stay here."

"Fallon, you cannot hide here like a petulant child. That isn't going to change or fix a damn thing. Right now, Demons are running fucking riot all over your home realm, I thought that considering who is back there, you might want to be involved."

He's right, love, probably something you should get out of bed for. I'm not here to make your life worse. I couldn't bear to be separated from you, and so, here I am, the voice in your mind. For now, anyway.

I roll my eyes, ignoring the addition of Azriel's voice constantly in my mind. I tell myself that the words are probably just a manifestation of my deepest fears from my subconscious, but the churning in my stomach picks up again.

"Fine, I'm up," I tell him, flinging off the covers. Really, I've had enough of wallowing. I'm not usually the woe is me type, but fucking shit, I have had a *rough* few months. I'm allowed some woe is me, 'pity party for one' time.

"Don't take too long. I imagine we're interrupting them eating, and I really don't want to piss off Caleb and the others more than I need to."

"Yeah, stopping Remy from eating isn't exactly a

pretty sight, especially not if we're coming with bad news anyway. What exactly is going on back home?"

"I'll tell you when I tell them, it'll save time," he says, eying me warily.

He doesn't want you to crumble before he gets you to the palace, love. He doesn't think you're strong enough to handle it. He's wrong though, you're one of the strongest creatures I've ever met.

Will you shut up! I scream back internally, and I hear a chuckle before I'm met with blessed silence. I don't care if it's all a figment of my imagination, I honestly can't take it right now. I climb all the way out of bed, then shower and dress quickly. It might've added time, but the shower was needed. Did I mention my pity party for one in bed for a few days already?

Once I'm presentable, I find Deacon waiting outside my door. He looks me over before looking up to the ceiling. I'm not sure exactly what is going on with him right now, but his back and forth is giving me whiplash. I can't even begin to deal with it.

"Let's go," I say, and he nods without saying a thing.

I try to not take it personally. I'm not the only one going through a lot right now. I know he hated Azriel, but I also saw how they were together. I genuinely think they were actually friends underneath it all. He takes my hand and that darkness wraps around us once more. I'm finally getting used to it, but it's still a little off-putting. Whispering he calls it. It feels like a strange name for it, but it also kinda makes sense in a weird kind of way. It is a very quiet way to travel.

We appear outside the doors of the throne room at the palace, and Deacon pales. I really wish I knew what he has against this place because he's so fucking weird when we come here, and for a while before and after too. Though, considering this is a literal palace of horrors underneath the beauty—at least that's what I've gathered from the rumors I've heard from Demons on our level—it isn't entirely surprising he has such a visceral reaction to it. Not that he lets them see it, of course. If I hadn't spent so much time with him, I'm sure I'd put it down to him being a dick, but I can see the truth behind his behavior here.

He takes a deep breath and pushes the door open. We find Remy, her guys, the Queen, and three of her Horsemen all sitting around a dining table, eating, laughing, and joking. It's so surreal to see, especially considering the ever-changing wheel of emotions churning away inside of me. Remy is right at home here, just like she is litearlly fucking everywhere. I'm not jealous of her adaptability, she's had literally thousands of years to build that sort of thing, but I guess I'm a little jealous of her ability to deal with things as easily as she seems to be able to.

"Sorry to interrupt," Deacon says, clearing his throat,

trying not to seem as uncomfortable as I know he is. "But shit is happening, and I think we need to call back the Demons running riot on Earth."

"What's happening?" Remy asks with a sigh, pinching the bridge of her nose. I feel bad that we have to bring this to her since she's already been through so much. She doesn't seem to ever get a break. It doesn't matter whether she can handle it or not, it still doesn't seem fair.

"Archer used the Demons in an attack, but I don't know much more than that. I do know that can't keep waiting, especially if we want to keep casualties at a minimum. I think they know about Az," Deacon tells them, and I try to keep the shock from my face. I can't help but hope Mama and Colt are okay, trying to ignore the pang of longing in my heart for home.

"Will they even come back that easily?" Remy asks, looking back to Morgan, and she nods. I stay quiet because I'm essentially still useless here.

You're never useless, love.

"They likely do know about Azriel, which is why Archer has lashed out. But if Deacon pulls the leash, they'll come back. And then maybe Archer will stand down," Morgan advises her, and I can't help but speak up.

"What if Archer isn't leading all of this?" I ask quietly, hoping they can't see how worn out I am. This room is full of powerhouses, and then there's me, useless in my current state. The longing for my powers should scare me, but I'm tired of being weak and useless.

You tell them, love. You know I'm more than the monster I let everyone see. I knew you'd catch on when we were talking. See, you're far from useless.

"What do you mean?" Morgan asks me, her eyes calculating, and it makes the butterflies in my stomach transform into goddamn eagles. She's kind of terrifying. I take a deep breath and try to tell her what I know.

"Azriel said something when we were together about how he wasn't answering to Archer, that it was an added benefit of his deal instead." I look over to Remy, and I can see the fear in her eyes. It isn't there for long, but I've known her long enough to recognize it, and I hate that I put it there.

"Did he say anything else?" Levi asks me as he takes Remy's hand.

"No."

I could tell you more if you'd let me in fully, love.

I shake my head again to try to clear my head of his voice, hoping like hell no one noticed the difference.

"He was probably talking out of his ass," Killian says, rolling his eyes.

"But what if he wasn't?" Roman questions, and the tension in the room ratchets up about a thousand degrees. I know no one wants to think that the problem is even bigger than it is. But if Archer isn't pulling the strings, then it really could be much bigger than anyone ever thought.

"Then that's something to worry about after we deal with everything else that's already on our plates. Right now, we know what the situation is, and how we can fix it, so we'll do that first," Morgan says matter of factly.

No one argues, though Caleb does frown in her direction. Ultimately, he stays quiet, so I do the same. Goddess knows in this room I'm definitely not the one to be making insane decisions. I want my bond broken, this voice out of my head, and to go home. It might make me weak, but after everything that's gone down, I think I have the right to be weak for a moment. Once I get back home and get back to being me, get in touch with my powers again, then I'll be strong. But right now, it 's not the time.

"What do we need to do?" Remy asks, looking at the Queen expectantly.

Morgan inclines her head with a kind smile. It's odd thinking of a Demon Queen as kind, but weirder shit has been happening lately. She heaves a heavy sigh before saying, with a tone of resolute surety, "You don't need to do anything. This is a Demon problem. Though if you want to lend us a little power, I'll never turn that down."

"Can we do that?" Remy asks, her gaze bouncing between the Queen and Levi. The rest of us stay quiet, waiting for more information.

“It isn’t something we can all do, and usually it’s rare that it happens at all,” Levi tells her, and I tuck that little nugget away for future use. I have no doubt it’s information the grimoires would be thankful for if nothing else. “But you and I have done it before, and I’m pretty sure that’s how you and Morgan sealed the portal before.”

Morgan nods at his words, and Remy lets out a deep breath. I wrap my arms around my middle, silently standing beside Deacon, wondering what our place in all of this will be.

“Okay, well count me in. How do we do this?” Remy asks.

“Is this really a good idea?” Kain counters, and she fixes him with a raised eyebrow as some of the Horsemen exchange glances.

“It is a little risky,” Caleb finally admits, “but I think it’s also necessary. We can do it without you, Mara, though we’ll still need your blood for the portal to bring that many Demons from your realm at once. But an extra show of power, especially considering they’re going to fight the tether, wouldn’t hurt.” I remember I need to still ask her about the whole Mara thing, but it’s another thing I tuck away for later.

“Okay, then I’m in,” she says, and it’s as if the whole mood of the room changes. I gulp, knowing that whatever is coming can’t be good.

With a wave of the Queen's hand, the table and chairs disappear from the room after everyone stands. Caleb and the Queen bicker quietly between themselves, but I keep to the edges of the room, not really wanting a part in any of this. I feel a bit like a spare part and half wish that Deacon had left me in bed.

On the other hand, witnessing the level of power in this room at work, working together, excites me in a way it probably shouldn't. Deacon moves away from me and over to the Queen, who then waves Remy over to them. I inch closer so I can at least understand what the fuck is about to happen.

"So, what exactly do you need me to do?" Remy asks cautiously, as all of her guys gather around her, looking like they're going to explode at any second. It's hard to not notice Creek's absence. He's always been the calm in the storm that is their family. I have no idea what's going on with him since Remy agreed to Morgan's offer, but I hope he's okay. Guilt pools in my stomach for how little I've thought about my friend, but I give myself a little grace because *shit,* there's been a lot going on.

"You need to let me in like normal, and I'll do the rest. You should probably keep your eyes open if you can, since, you know... Demons," the Queen tells her, and Remy smiles confidently. That's just how she is. If there's a problem she's going to face it head on with grim determination.

"What is the plan once they're here?" Levi asks tersely.

"They will be dealt with," Caleb tells him, leading him and the others behind the thrones where Killian and Malik are already sitting. Caleb takes his seat and nods at Morgan, prompting her to take Remy's hand. Deacon moves to stand at her other side and drags his extended nail down his forearm, blood rushing from his vein as he starts speaking in the harsh Demon language that makes my skin itch all over again. Morgan spills her own blood followed by Remy's.

I've never been one to avoid blood and gore, but this is a lot. I move to the corner behind the thrones to a place where I can still see and hear everything but can stay the fuck out of the way while the insanity continues.

Morgan joins in the chant as beads of sweat roll down Deacon's face, and I gasp when I see the portal opening before us. It's so very different to the portals we open with Earth magic. It's a pulsing, angry red that's rimmed in black. Demons start to fill the room, shouts growing louder as Caleb and the other Horsemen demand their complete compliance.

I feel myself go pale as more and more of them fill the giant room. So many Demons. So much power in one room. It's enough to make me feel dizzy.

That's because of our connection. You need to take a deep breath, sweetheart. Do not show these assholes any weakness. They'll use it against you.

I take another deep breath because holy hell. There really are so many of them... and they were all out there running riot on Earth. Just causing absolute fucking chaos.

I glance over at Deacon, and it occurs to me that he didn't really explain what happened, and my stomach twists. Why wouldn't he explain it?

Deacon and Morgan go quiet, and the shouts from Demons in the room only grow louder. Scuffles break out as the portal closes.

"Kneel!" Morgan shouts, and the power from her command makes me tremble as I fall to my knees along with the Demons in the room, despite the rest of them managing to stay standing. It's just another testament to how very different from them I am. "Traitors, you have broken one of the very few rules I enforce, and for that you will bleed."

Screams ring out around the room, and I feel the wash of the power, spinning around in an instant, hoping to miss the sight of viscera and gore. It's impossible to not hear as blood pours from the Demons and splashes over the obsidian colored floor. Screams fill the cavernous room as they fall to the floor. The crunch of bones is impossible to miss. It's enough to make me gag. Once upon a time, I could handle this, but after everything I've been through since I got here? I curse Deacon again for not leaving me the fuck in bed. I did not need to witness this punishment. While I want my own vengeance, it's mine to take when I'm ready. This feels way too soon. I haven't even begun trying to process my trauma. I'm definitely not at whatever step this is on the ladder.

"Silence!" the Queen shouts, and it's as if she stole their tongues. Not so much as a whimper sounds out in the throne room. I turn to face Remy and the others on the dais, keeping my eyes high to not watch the Demons writhing in pain. They more than likely deserve every ounce of the pain they're getting, but my stomach can't handle this vengeance shit right now.

"Who among you wants to gain my mercy?" Her voice rings out against the silence as she watches the masses to see if anyone volunteers themselves. Nothing but silence and the odd whimper fills the room. Kain mees my eyes over the crowd, a frown creasing his lips as his eyes narrow, and I realize I'm trembling. He moves toward me, standing with me and holding my hand while Morgan stares with cold challenge at the mass of Demons in front of her. It's so obvious why Remy loves him. He's the quiet strength of her group, and I'm beyond grateful that he's offering me some of his support right now.

"So be it," she says, shaking her head. "Your betrayal will cost you the ultimate price. You will not volunteer for my mercy, so you lose all access to it. Your lives are forfeit." I gasp, but Kain wraps me in his arms and holds me tight, shielding me from it all while I try to stop the shaking that seems out of my control.

Seconds pass in utter silence before the Queen's words break the silence. "You wish to speak?" I look back at her, though Kain still has a grip on me, and I see her talking to a lone man standing in the crowd. He nods, and her eyes flicker across the room and the vast amount of Demons crammed in the space.

"So be it. The rest of you I shall leave to Deacon." Deacon looks at her and nods, resolute.

"To the cells?" she asks him, and he nods again, as if speaking might break him. Though I suppose her power could have extended to him. I really haven't learned that much about what she can actually do in my time here.

"So be it," Morgan says almost sadly, and with a clap of her hands, her power extends through the room and then recedes. Kain releases me, and I see a lone man standing where there was a crowd a moment ago.

"I forgot how much of a punch your power packs," Deacon says to her, rubbing his jaw.

"I didn't mean to get you in it," she says frowning, but he waves her off.

"Can I leave him with you guys? I'm going to have a hard few days' work with what looked like a few hundred Demons. And I still need to break the final tether with

Fallon," he says to them, speaking of me, but not even glancing my way.

"Of course, I'm sure Malik and Killian can get the information we need from him." Her gleeful smile sends a shiver down my spine. "And leave Fallon here while you handle the others. These guys will be heading home in a day or so. I'll call for you when we need you for the final tether so I can capture her soul."

I look at Remy, but she's watching the Queen, not me. They're talking about me as if I'm a child to be handled, and it rankles me. But Deacon nods at her before glancing at me and disappearing from sight without so much as a word to me.

My anger is unreasonable, but it's there. He left me here with Demons I don't know without so much as a single fucking word.

He doesn't care for you, love. He's very good at deceiving people. It's why he was my second.

The voice in my head doesn't help my mood. I guess I'm staying at the palace then. Maybe I can get some more fucking answers here.

It doesn't take long for the guys to leave the room, leaving me alone with Remy and the Queen.

"I'll leave you two alone. I want to drop in on the sixth level and make sure no one thinks about trying to save their friends. Demons are typically pretty loyal, especially to their kin. They're also so goddamn greedy on that level," the Queen says with a dainty wave of her fingers before disappearing too.

"She is… woah," I say as I sag, a mix of relief and well, exhaustion.

"I know, right!" Remy smiles before pulling me in for a hug. "Sorry, that was a lot, even for me. I can't even imagine how that was for you, especially with everything you've been through lately."

"It's fine, I'll be fine," I tell her because I can't even fully untangle the crazy that's going on in my mind right now, so I'm not about to ask her to try. I'm also not gonna mention the Azriel thing because I don't want to seem even crazier than I feel.

You're not crazy, love.

I strain to stop myself rolling my eyes. I don't want to give Remy the chance to question me too much. My feelings about him being with me, while also technically being dead, are conflicting enough on their own without giving further voice to it.

"Are you sure?" she asks. "You look tired again."

"It's been a lot to deal with. Undoing the tether is a lot, Rem. It's draining, like way more than creating the damn thing was. Maybe it's because it was Azriel's bond, and he's not undoing it, but it's hard. But at least it's nearly done," I tell her, trying to not sound as tired or as sad as I feel.

"Well, from what Morgan said, I guess we'll be going home in a few days once she works her magic on you. Hopefully that helps."

"Seeing Mama and Rebel again will help. It feels like we've been gone for a year." I smile at her, but it must miss the mark because she hugs me again.

"Is everything else okay? I know we haven't spoken much about Azriel or Deacon," she says, a gentleness to her tone that I'm not used to hearing, and I freeze. Has she seen something? Could she know? Do they all know? I think about saying something, but then stop myself. She's prying—there's no way they could know about the Demon soul trapped in my mind. I think. I need to get home and look at the grimoires. There has to be an expulsion somewhere, and if that doesn't work, I'll know I'm actually losing my damn mind.

"I'll be fine. I need to get away from here and never come back," I tell her, hoping that it'll be enough. But a niggle in my gut tells me that I'm not done with this place. "It's been different since Az… but I'm still in the same room, still wandering the same halls, the gallery. I really need to get home."

“I get that. I miss home too. Except going home means facing everything that’s happened since we left, and I’m not sure I’m totally ready for that, either.”

“I know that feeling well. The thought of Mama’s face when Rebel was taken because of me haunts me whether I’m awake or asleep.” I give her a nugget of the truth, just a slither of the guilt that threatens to swallow me whole each day.

“You can’t think she actually blames you, Fallon. You were being held prisoner!”

“I don’t really know how I feel about anything right now,” I tell her as I move to sit on the edge of the dais. Maybe telling her the truth won’t be so bad. Maybe it’ll help me work out some of the twisted shit in my mind. “It’s so strange because I know Az was an asshole. He held me prisoner and bound me to him for fuck’s sake, but there was also another side of him. And it’s hard to align all of that inside myself, especially since he’s gone now.” Especially since he still literally haunts me. I take a deep breath and continue.

“Then there’s everything else, what I endured, Deacon, Colt, going home, facing everyone... I know Morgan will fix me or whatever, but I’m different, Remy. I feel fundamentally different, so how am I supposed to face everyone back home who’s gonna expect me to be the same person?”

"Be yourself. Broken parts and all. You let the people who love you help you heal," she says softly. It's a lot easier said than done, though. I know she understands that, but she still doesn't know everything that happened.

"Yeah, I guess," I tell her, dropping my head as she moves to sit beside me.

"Is there anything I can do, Fallon?" she asks, resting her shoulder against mine. Just like we used to when we were younger and the world wasn't this complicated. Back when we were teenagers and our biggest problems were boys, and that was the end of the world.

"You're already doing it. Just being here is everything I need right now. Not pushing me to talk or to feel. Just letting me be."

"I can keep doing that. You know I'll only push if I can see that you need me to."

"I know, and I love you for it." I rest my head on her shoulder, trying to keep the swirling emotions inside of me from rising up and spilling out. Everything is so overwhelming. I don't know that I've even processed everything fully yet.

"I love you too, Fallon."

"Ride or die," I whisper, as the tears I lost the battle against fall onto her skin.

"Ride or die."

I spent the rest of yesterday exploring the palace and its grounds. This place is one hundred percent terrifying, but I had to get some time to myself. Remy seemed eager enough to go back to her guys, which left me alone with my thoughts.

Unfortunately, it also left me alone with the voice inside my head. Except, for a change, rather than taunting me, he almost seemed sorry to have given me another burden on top of everything else. Which leaves me as conflicted as ever.

I tried to clear my mind. I even sat and tried to meditate, but hours passed, and I found no peace despite my efforts. My thoughts bounced from everything that's happened since I came here, to my mama and Rebel, to Colt, Deacon, and the potential mess I've made of everything by having such a fickle fucking heart. So today I'm trying something new.

No boy drama.

Goddess knows I have enough other shit to work through. This bond, the trauma that I've pushed all the way down, which I'm hoping doesn't manifest anytime in the future, and home. Or at least, my upcoming homecoming.

Archer hasn't been dealt with, not truly. Which means this isn't the end of it all. I said as much to Remy and

Creek at lunch earlier, and they shared an ominous sort of look with each other before trying to reassure me that everything would work out. Azriel's voice was incessant during the whole exchange, so they probably thought I was on the edge of a breakdown if they gave me any more bad news.

It was nice to see Creek again though, even if pain recognizes pain. I can see he's still struggling a little to be okay with being part-Demon. We both have a new darkness in us. But he did pull me aside to tell me that I'm not alone in my struggle, and I hadn't realized how much I needed that. I know Remy will try to protect me from anything and everything, it's part of who she is as a person. But Creek isn't like that. He'll tell me the truth of it, even the darkest, scariest, most gut-wrenching parts. Don't get me wrong, he'll shield Remy from it because he's loved her since she was born, even if he didn't know it. He doesn't love me in the same way. He doesn't want to lose me, but it won't shatter his world if I'm gone. No need to protect something that it wouldn't break you to lose.

I stare up at the ceiling in the room that Malik gave me in the palace and wonder where the hell it is we go from here.

Oh, love, at least I'll always be with you to help you.

Unless I expel you, I think, smiling to myself.

You wouldn't do that to me would you now? I thought

you were a good Witch.

“Even a good Witch has her limits. And you are mine,” I utter and close my eyes. Closing my eyes makes it like he’s in the room with me, and my breath catches in my throat at the realization.

Now then, you know I never wanted to hurt you. I had a task to follow. I told you once before, sometimes a villain is just a guy in a shitty position with his own monsters.

“I will never forgive you, so if that’s the game you’re trying to play, you might as well give up now.”

Oh, love, I thought you knew me better than that. I will never give up.

EIGHTEEN

Today's the day.

It's the day we break the final strings of the bond, the day Azriel's voice disappears from my mind for good. Above everything else, it's the day I get to go home. Staying at the palace has been good for me the last few days. It's helped me heal more than I thought it would.

Maybe it's being around Remy, her guys, and her friends. Maybe it's seeing another side of this place. A place that isn't as full of darkness as I originally thought. Or at least it isn't a place that constantly reminds me of my darkest memories.

But today isn't about darkness or the memories that haunt me. Today is about getting to see my mama and my sister. It's about seeing Colt, though my stomach still ties in knots when I think about seeing him. It's a mixture of excitement and guilt. I know that, but I have no idea which one will win when I finally get to see him.

I shake off the negative thoughts because they'll only breed a downward spiral and climb out of bed. I don't know how these guys do it, but all of the clothes in the room fit me perfectly. It isn't something I'm gonna complain about, but Demon power definitely seems to trump Witch power. But then, this isn't Earth magic. All earth magic comes with a cost. There needs to be balance. It's the rules for the power they wield here.

I pull myself from yet another rabbit hole, apparently distraction is gonna be enemy number one today, and shower quickly before dressing. I take in my reflection as I sit to do my hair. My dark hair isn't as glossy, my skin doesn't glow as much as it once did, but I can tell it's my eyes that look the most different. I half wish that breaking the bond fixes that, but I don't hold much hope. Not for my eyes anyway. No magic will take away the shadows in my mind.

Thanks to the spell Killian showed me yesterday on the way up to my room, I can get around the palace without one of them present. I cast it with the little power I have that Azriel gifted me, and I follow the gold glitter trail to the throne room where everyone is meeting for breakfast before going home. I don't have any idea how long I've been gone in terms of time back home, no one seems to have an exact science for it, but I hope it hasn't been too long. I know time passes quicker here than home, but the thought of Mama and Rebel makes me wanna get back even faster.

I reach the throne room and find a long table full of food, but Creek is the only one here already.

"Hey," he says with a brief wave from the table. He doesn't come and hug me, but after me recoiling the last time he tried, it isn't that surprising. I'm kind of glad he doesn't try again. "How are you feeling?"

"I'm looking forward to getting this bond finally severed and going home," I tell him truthfully as I take a seat, taking in the spread on the table before me.

There is so much food here, but between the eight guys, I'm still not sure it will be enough. I pour myself a glass of juice and put a few different things on my plate. Not that I feel like I can eat, but trying not to eat around this group means a mega hassle, so I chew slowly. We eat in relatively comfortable silence. I know he has a lot of shadows of his own to deal with, just like he knows I do.

It isn't long until Levi, Roman, Killian, and Caleb join us. The guys are loud and rowdy enough that my silence isn't really noticed, which I'm thankful for. Today is sad for pretty much everyone here. Us all going home isn't as joyous for them. I get it, Remy and the guys are their friends. They have a similar relationship dynamic, which I'll admit I'm a little jealous of, but in our world, not everyone is so casual about the poly thing. I mean, I have no issues or judgements about it, and no one would dare say anything to Remy or any of her guys about it because well, it's Remy and her guys.

Anyone else though—me for instance—I'd never hear the freaking end of it.

It's not much longer until the only ones missing from breakfast are Remy and Kain. Even Deacon is here, sitting beside me, though having barely spoken to me since he arrived. Two guesses why they're late, I laugh internally. The chatter is relaxed around the table, and it's almost fun to watch how everyone acts with each other.

Everyone finishes eating, and with a flick of the Queen's wrist, the table clears. I know everyone else here calls her Morgan, but that seems a little over friendly considering I've barely spoken to her.

Just as the table clears, the door to the throne room opens, and Remy and Kain join us. She smiles sadly as she looks at the people around the table, and Malik jumps up and heads over to her.

"Don't look so sad, Mara. We'll miss you too," Malik says, hugging her. Kain moves over to the table as everyone else starts to stand. I stay planted in my seat, watching them all closely. As much as I hope I don't see these guys again, they're obviously close with Remy, so it's pretty likely I will. "Take care of yourself, and if your Demon gets out of hand or everything gets too much, come and find us now that you know how," Malik tells her softly.

"Are you ready to break the bond?" the Queen asks me, pulling my attention away from Remy and her goodbyes. I glance up at her to find Deacon standing beside her.

"I am," I say softly, not quite able to meet her eyes fully.

"And you've severed the bond?" the Queen asks Deacon, who nods.

"Yes, at least for the most part, the final strings are still there, but I know that is part of what you'll do when you end it for good."

Malik appears by the Queen's side, and she smiles at him. It's a soft look that almost doesn't suit her, but it shows just how much she loves him.

I look back over at Remy and see Killian speaking to her. "It was good to see you again, Mara. Hopefully next time isn't quite so fraught and dramatic."

"I hope so too," she tells him.

"Come on, K, you've been talking for an age, my turn," Caleb says with a laugh, and I can't help but join in. I haven't seen much of Caleb, but he kind of reminds me of a Labrador. Full of bounce and energy. I'm sure he's absolutely fucking terrifying underneath it all, he wouldn't be a Horseman otherwise, but still. Total Labrador.

Killian rolls his eyes at him. "I'm done with my lengthy goodbye, hell forbid you don't get to say a thing." He walks away still chuckling as Caleb wraps Remy in a bear bug, lifting her from the ground and spinning her around.

"Don't stay away so long this time, okay, Mara? A guy would think you've forgotten about him."

"Forget about you? Only dying could make it so," she tells him, and I know I ain't the only one in the room holding their breath.

He puts her down and smiles sadly. "Little too real there, Mara. But I'm not kidding, don't stay away so long. Morgan misses you, even if she doesn't say it. I know it. If we could come to you, we would but…"

"But visiting me would literally be the end of the world as we know it," she laughs as he nods.

"Yeah, not exactly a stellar way to leave the Earth just to see a friend," he says casually, and a thought takes root in my mind. Maybe I can find a way for them to come to Earth without wreaking havoc and destruction. It's a perfect kind of thank you for everything everyone here has done for me. Remy's voice pulls me from my train of thought, and I focus on her again.

"I understand, friend. I'll make sure to come back, but you have to remember time moves faster here. Before I forget in the whirlwind… What are we doing about the major amounts of Angel glass back on Earth?"

"Bryce already dealt with it. He had a trusted friend go and relieve Archer of all of his supplies. Didn't want to send you back and leave you vulnerable."

"Thank you, Caleb. Really."

"Anytime, Mara."

He squeezes her again before strutting over to our little group, leaving her with the last Horseman, Bryce. I haven't really spent any time with him at all, but he seems dark and mysterious. The dark to Caleb's light.

I can't hear what she says to him, but I see him shake his head and put his hands in his pockets. Their words are obviously for just the two of them.

"Are you ready?" the Queen asks, holding out a hand for me. I take it and stand. I have absolutely no idea what's coming, but I trust that she knows what the hell she's doing. Deacon takes my other hand and closes the circle, and I feel the rush of power instantly. It like standing in the middle of a train track and staring down a fucking freight train. I have a brief moment where I wonder if I'm gonna survive the impact.

The two of them start to murmur in what I've decided is an old Demon language because I really have no fucking clue what it is. I don't really want to know, either, I decide. It's hard to focus as their words continue and the power increases, pulsing through me in electric currents.

It pushes and pushes until I feel like I'm going to burst, and then I feel it expel from me. I start to droop, and I'm caught in the seconds before I would've hit the floor like a sack of potatoes.

"I've got you," Caleb whispers as he helps me stand. The Queen takes my other hand from Deacon, and I feel her power flood through me. I close my eyes at the rush of it because it's really almost too much. Waves of warmth crash over me, though, and I start to feel lighter. It lasts for a few moments, washing over me until I can finally stand again. It keeps coming, though, and I damn near feel like I'm floating, anchored by Caleb's touch alone.

"How's that?" the Queen asks after a few more intense moments, and I open my eyes. I feel almost good as new. Holy shit. I think I feel better than new.

"Thank you, I—" I pause, my voice breaking with the thick emotion clogging my throat. I didn't think I'd ever get to feel whole again. I practically jump on her with a hug, unable to stop myself. "Thank you so much."

"You are more than welcome, Witchling. Do not be a stranger," she says as she pulls out of the hug, but she catches my arms and watches me closely. "I have a feeling your path will lead you here again. Do not fear this realm. You have my protection now. You won't come to harm in my realm again."

I blink at her, unable to say a word, so I nod. How

could she possibly know?

That's when I realize Azriel's voice is gone. Usually he'd be incessant about the Queen. He's finally gone. Relief makes me sag, but a pang of something I don't want to name fills my heart.

"Are you ready?" Morgan asks softly, walking toward Remy who smiles sadly at her and nods.

"It doesn't matter if I am, we have things that need to be finished."

"You know where we are if you need me, and we are always here for you, Mara. Always." She takes Remy's hand and squeezes it as Levi steps away giving them some space.

"That works both ways, you know," Remy says softly. I'm sad that she's so sad, but I'm so freaking excited to get home. To finally feel more like myself again. Or at least, as much myself as I ever dreamed possible.

"What?" Morgan asks as Remy shakes her head.

"I'm thinking about my brother, Colt. He's never going to believe this. Honestly you should've seen him the first time he met Levi. I think him meeting you and the Horsemen…" They start laughing again, and I chuckle a little myself. Colt will lose his shit when he hears all about this. Demons have always been a weird thing for him.

"Any friend of yours is welcome in my home, Mara. I'd like to meet him one day maybe."

"You can count on it," Remy tells them all, her eyes going glassy.

The Queen leans in and their whispers aren't audible to my ears, but they hug and I can just barely hear Remy again.

"Okay, thank you. For everything, Morgan."

"Shall we get this portal sealed once and for all?" the Queen asks with a clap of her hands, and my heart races.

Remy's gaze flicks to me and she smiles before looking back at the Queen. "Let's."

I watch in gross fascination as Remy pulls necklaces with vials of blood from the bag she brought in with her, briefly explaining that the blood is hers and we need it to get home safely. She hands one to each of her guys and then one to me.

"Please don't expect me to keep this," I say, pulling a face at her. I love her, but this is a bit much. She laughs at me and shakes her head.

"You'd be amazed how many people would pay a hefty amount of money for the blood of a Shadow Walker, but those vials aren't necessary when you travel on a portal opened with Mara's blood." Caleb winks at me, and I roll my eyes at him.

"You and Colt would have the best of bromances," I chuckle, and Remy joins in, though Caleb looks all kind of confused which only makes me laugh harder.

"I have one request," Bryce says quietly, and we all turn to face him. "Please keep our friendship known to only those who need to know. We have enemies everywhere. I would hate for you to be used as a pawn to get to us."

"We can do that," Levi says, shaking his hand. "I'm not sure how many would believe us anyway."

"Well then, let's get you guys home, shall we!" the Queen says, clapping her hands. "Mara, if you help me open the portal, then it will be easier for us to complete the seal."

Remy looks back at me as she walks toward the Queen, and I hate the pity I see on her face. I'm sure she doesn't mean to let it show, but I'm still pretty much powerless here.

"Let's get this show on the road," Remy says as her guys move to stand behind me.

The Queen slices her arm and draws a circle on the floor of the throne room with her blood before motioning for Remy, who offers her arm. The Queen slices it with a sharpened talon. "Lay your blood over mine."

Remy walks the circle as instructed, holding the cut open to keep the blood flowing. Once Remy comes back to the Queen's side again, she grimaces at me before slicing

Remy's arm once more and doing the same to herself again. She dips her fingers in Remy's streaming blood and draws runes on the floor. The runes call to me, the power of them feels dark, but it whispers my name like it's searching for me. Like it belongs to me. I find it hard to focus on anything but those whispers until the Queen speaks again.

"Everyone that is going back needs to be inside the circle, but do not disturb the markings," she says softly before rejoining Remy and slicing their arms again so a stream of their blood joins at their feet.

"Picture where you want the portal to open," she says quietly to Remy who closes her eyes. My heart races at the thought of home, but those whispers call to me even louder. They don't want me to leave. The power in the room intensifies until I can feel it crawling over every inch of my skin.

"You guys can start going through now. Mara will come through last so we can seal the portal behind you."

"Thank you, all of you, for everything," Kain says proudly before stepping into the portal. Roman waves before stepping into the portal behind him.

"I'll see you guys soon," Creek says with a smile, taking my hand and walking through with me. He almost has to tug me away from the whispers and into the pulsing black portal. As we step through, Azriel's face flashes in my mind, but then in an instant, we're back, and I can't think about him.

I stumble as we leave the portal, but Creek keeps me standing as my power rushes back to me. It's enough to steal my breath and make my knees weak. It takes a minute, but everything eventually settles and I can breathe again. I suck in giant lungfuls of air and try not to cry.

Another heartbeat later, Remy and Levi appear through the portal, and she nearly stumbles too, which makes me smile. We've always been too alike that way. Kain catches her while she continues to bleed on the ground by the portal, then uncorks a bottle of blood and pours it on the ground to mix with her own blood.

"Et clausum sigillum. Semper et in saecula saeculorum. Tantum aperiatur nulla voluntas et cogitatio nostra porta patet," she murmurs while the blood soaks into the ground. After a moment, the portal shuts.

Once it's closed, it's like the world comes back into focus. The darkening sky, the cold breeze, the chirping birds.

"Is it done?" Kain asks softly.

"It is," Remy tells him, taking a deep breath. "We're home."

"We are," Roman says, his chest rumbling. "I need to run. I'll shift and clear the perimeter, just to make sure we're clear out here before I go."

He looks like he's about to crawl out of his skin. I

wonder why he didn't shift more in the Shadow Realm. Remy nods at him and says, "Okay. Go run. We can catch you up with anything once you're back."

He nods at her and takes off for the tree line.

"I'll check the house," Kain says and flashes away from us.

"I need to call Mama," I say as my emotions start to get the best of me.

"Come on, I need to call Colt too," she says, taking my hand and turning toward the house. We pause as she looks back at Levi. That's when it hits me. Everly isn't here.

My heart breaks for them both. I can't even imagine. I didn't know her that well, but my throat clogs at the thought of her not being here. Goddess only knows how they feel right now.

"Come on," Creek says softly, stepping up on my other side when Kain reappears in front of us.

"It's safe. Let's go in together," Kain murmurs, and Remy nods, turning to Levi who has been silent this entire time.

"Levi," she starts, but he shakes his head. His wings unfurl, and he shoots up into the sky without a word.

We walk toward the house quietly, Remy's hand clasping mine like she might break if she lets go. But it's okay because I hold hers just as tight.

Kain opens the glass doors for us, and Remy stills by

the door. She lets go of my hand as her eyes go glassy, and she moves forward alone.

"Come on, let's go get my phone," Creek says and leads me toward his room. My hands start to shake the closer we get. The thought of talking to Mama, hoping she doesn't blame me for what happened to Rebel, makes my stomach churn.

Creek opens the door to his room and motions for me to enter. The lights flicker on as he follows behind me, and he grabs his phone from his bedside table.

"Two secs," he says, plugging it into the charger. "It's almost dead, but that should be fine to call your mom."

"I could portal home," I say softly, scared to touch the phone.

"I think you should give yourself a day or so to let your magic settle again. You don't want to end up hurting yourself." He looks so fucking sad as he says the words, his eyes flashing with something a little indiscernible. My heart hurts just about as bad for him as it does for me.

"Are you okay, Creek?" I ask, avoiding the phone for a minute. My nerves are winning out for the time being.

"I will be," he says, scrubbing a hand down the back of his neck. "I mean, I'm fine with what happened. It's an adjustment, but I know Remy loves me regardless. I'm more worried about my mom and pops and about the Hunters in general. As you've seen, they're not the most open-minded bunch most of the time."

"Well, tell them in your own time then. Physically, there's nothing different about you, so they won't be able to guess. I get it, though. Sometimes talking about what happened really doesn't make it better. You have to deal with it yourself first." He nods at my words and sighs.

"Do you want to call Colt too?" he asks, and I shake my head.

"I know that Remy said he was going crazy while I was gone, but I'm not ready to see him just yet."

"I get it," he says softly with a comforting smile. "You should call your mom, though, she'd want to know you're here. I'll call Colt after."

"Thank you," I say to him and pick up the phone. My hands shake as I dial Mama's number, and I hold my breath as it rings.

"Creek?" Her voice filters through the speaker, and I start to cry in an instant.

"Mama," I blubber, and I hear her cry out.

"Oh, my baby, you're back. I will be there as soon as I can. I love you, Fallon. Are you okay? Let me get your sister sorted out, and I'll be right there."

"I'm okay, Mama. I really missed you. I love you too. Is Rebel okay?"

"Rebel is fine. And we'll talk all about how okay you are. I'll be there soon, baby, okay?"

“Okay, Mama, see you soon.”

I can’t believe the date.

It’s only been three weeks here since Archer and his cronies kidnapped me.

But in my mind, I’ve been gone for so, so much longer than that.

I’m sitting on Remy’s sofa, sipping a cup of coffee, trying to calm my nerves. Colt texts Creek to say that he was getting Mama and they’re coming over together. The thought makes me excited and want to throw up all at the same time.

I’m not ready to face Colt yet. Not with the insanity that are my dumb feelings for Deacon and Azriel swirling around inside of me still. Colt wanted to fix things with me before I was taken. Maybe if I had tried, if I hadn’t been so stubborn and listened to him, he’d have been with me that night, and none of this would’ve ever happened.

I take a deep breath and let it out slowly when I hear a knock at the front door. Kain stands and moves far faster than I ever could to it. I stand, and in a flash Mama is right in front of me. I can’t help the squeal that comes from my mouth as I dive at her, and she starts to cry as she cradles me close.

"Why don't we get you two some place where you can have some privacy and some time to talk?" Kain offers, and I nod, pulling back from Mama a little and wiping away my own tears. Maybe it makes me a coward, running before Colt even gets in the house, but right now, all I want is some time with my mama.

He takes us to the library, and quickly takes his leave, giving us some privacy. Once the door closes, Mama pulls me in tight again, and I can't help the sobs as they rip from my chest. I really didn't think I'd ever get to see her again.

She rocks me until my tears dry up before leading me to one of the many tables here. She forces me to sit before circling to the other side of the small table and sitting herself. She grabs my hands in hers, running a soothing thumb over my knuckles as she stares at me, tears swimming in her eyes still.

"Are you okay, baby?" She looks at me with such fierce love. But there's also so much fear there that it physically hurts me. I fight the urge to pull my hands away from her and rub them over my aching chest. I can't lie to her, but I don't want to hurt her either.

"I'm not ready to talk about it yet, Mama. But when I am, I will. Trust that I'm okay though. I'm better already at home, being here with y'all."

"Do you want to show me? Would that be easier? I can't help you if I don't know," she says, dropping my hands and leaning over the table to cup my face. I suck in a sharp breath. "Show me what we're fighting against. I couldn't see you when you were down there, and I've never been more afraid in my life."

"Mama, I don't know," I start. I mean, It's not like this isn't something we've done before. Goddess knows it's how we catch each other up on coven business, but showing her this feels different, way more intimate.

"I can't help you heal if I don't know what you're healing from," she says softly, and I crumble a little. I don't want her to see how broken I got or just how helpless I felt as I gave up. But she's right. I'm gonna need her. I'm gonna need space and time, but I'm gonna need her more. Especially since I'm kind of scared of using my magic again.

Scared that it could awaken something more.

Scared that Azriel's voice isn't really gone, and that I'm more broken than I think.

Not that she'll see those parts, but still.

"Okay," I whisper, a shudder going down my spine. "I'll show you." She closes her eyes, and I place my hands on either side of her neck.

"Ostende," I utter and feel the rush of my power. I bite down on my lip and close my eyes to try and control the magic. Control how much she gets to see. My heart races as sweat trickles down my face and neck from the tenuous

hold over my control.

I can't hold it for too long, though.

I tear my hands away from her, knowing that she saw what she needed to and no more before shutting my power down and pushing it away. I wanted nothing more than to get it back, and now I have one more reason to hate Azriel and Archer. I shouldn't be scared of such an important part of myself.

"Oh, baby, my poor sweet baby," Mama cries before moving around the table to wrap me up in another hug. My whole body trembles, and all I can hope she thinks is that it's from showing her. If she knew the truth… I don't even want to think about it. A Witch should never be afraid of their power. It only ever leads to dark places.

"Let's get you home. Do you want to say goodbye? Talk to Colt?" she asks, letting me go from her embrace.

"No, Mama, I don't think I'm ready to see him yet."

"I understand that," she says softly, her gaze flicking over me, silently ensuring herself that I'm definitely all healed. "I'll open a portal, and we'll get you home. I have just the thing brewing to help you sleep properly."

"Thanks, Mama." I smile and take her hand, walking with her through the portal she opens. All I can do is hope the potion fixes more than my fear of sleep.

NINETEEN

"Fallon." The pounding at the door to my room makes me jump, and I want to hide when I realize it's Colt calling my name. I guess Mama didn't really think that avoidance was the best solution for my problems. "Fal, I know you're in there. I need to see you. Please."

It's the please that breaks me. Colt is a nice guy, but he usually gets what he wants. Please isn't something he says too often. So I crawl from bed looking like I've been hit by a dump truck and unlock the door before scurrying back under the covers. It might make me a coward, but fuck it, I need all the barriers between us that I can get.

"Thank you," he says softly as he enters the room and closes the door behind him, leaning back against it. He looks me over, and I can see the concern etched clearly on his face. He looks older than he did when I was taken. I guess these last few weeks have been as hard on him as they were on me.

Well, maybe.

"You disappeared last night…" he trails off, watching me, and I feel a pang of guilt jolt through my entire body. It's just one more thing to add to the overwhelming pit of guilt already consuming me, I guess.

"I'm sorry, I— "

"You don't have to be sorry, Fal. I was worried. It's all I've been since you were taken. Worried. Terrified. Pissed off. I'm so sorry this all happened to you because of Bauer." He hangs his head, but I still reel with shock. Because of Bauer? What the fuck?

"Bauer?" I ask, and his head snaps back up. He's so pale he looks like a ghost.

"Remy didn't tell you?" he asks, and I shake my head.

"We had a lot going on. We didn't catch up beyond the surface shit," I tell him, blinking and struggling to take in the fact that Bauer's one of the bad guys. There's gotta be more to it than that. Life ain't ever as black and white as all that.

"Bauer and Archer… They've been, I don't know? A thing for a while, it seems. Bauer was helping him because he loved him. But he came clean to Remy when it all started spinning out of control. He never meant for you to be taken." I pull the duvet up higher as I try to process his words. Bauer was always distant, the eldest brother who hid away in his books. It's hard to believe, but it's not the kinda thing Colt would lie about. He used to think his brother hung the moon.

"Where is he now?" I ask, trying to stomp down the fear that pools in my stomach, making me want to heave.

"He's not going to hurt you again. I won't let it happen." He strides over to the bed and sits in front of me, taking my hand. I pull away from him, trying to not let the hurt in his eyes reflect in my gut. I have too much guilt swirling around already. I can't add this to it. "I should have been there. I should've been looking after you and protecting you."

"You couldn't have known, Colt. No one could've known. Hell, I should've been able to protect myself."

"I can help with that if you'll let me?" he asks, his eyes searching my face.

"Colt," I sigh, trying to think of the right words to tell him everything that happened. I can't find them.

"Fallon, you don't have to tell me what happened while you were gone. You don't have to relive it. All I want is to help you get over it. I know I fucked up before, and if I hadn't, maybe none of this would've happened. I know I was an ass. I also know that I was so wrong. You are the best thing to have happened to me in all of my lives. I was scared before, but I've never been as scared as I was when I thought I'd never see you again." He cups my face with his hand and I sigh, leaning into it. Okay, this isn't so bad, right?

After all, this is all I wanted before my life was completely turned upside down.

"Colt, there's stuff I need to deal with before I can even think about anything like this."

"I get that, and I'm not rushing or trying to pressure you. I just had to tell you. I'm not going anywhere, and I will end this bullshit so you never have to go through something like this again. Even if it costs me everything else, it will be worth it to know that you're safe." Tears fill my eyes at his words, and I can't help but feel like I betrayed him in the Shadow Realm. I didn't think I'd ever see him again, so I locked away the part of my heart that held him, and in the insanity of it, let myself try to find the best in Deacon and Azriel. I never imagined in doing so that I'd feel anything for them, but as twisted as it is, I did.

And now I'm back and everything is so fucking mixed up.

"You need to rest and recover. Remy told me they healed you, but some things can't be fixed with magic. I'll be here so you can sleep," he says, leaning forward and kissing my forehead. "I'll make sure the house, you, your mom, and Rebel are safe. And then when you're ready, I'll teach you how to protect yourself with more than magic."

"Thank you, Colt." I sigh. "Thank you for everything." He moves and tucks me in once I lie back down.

"Sleep," he murmurs, stroking my hair. "I won't let anything happen to you."

Colt has barely left my side since he showed up at my house two days ago. I mean, he's still been doing all of his Hunter crap, but it's been nice having him with me. It's been a bit of comfort amongst the terror of trying to get myself back to normal.

Apparently getting back to myself means him dragging us to the manor. I left him outside with Mama when I came into the house because I wanted to see Remy alone. I know I'm going through some bullshit, but I also know I'm not alone in that. She lost Everly, and I imagine that's like losing her mom all over again. I don't want to be a shit friend. Not after we've been through so much, so even with the fear that fills me at the thought of coming here, and the ever-mounting possibility of attack, I'm here. For her.

I take a deep breath and knock at her door. She opens it, and the look of shock on her face at my being here isn't lost on me.

"Hey," I say softly, entering the room and shutting the door behind me before walking over to her bed with her. "How are you feeling?"

"Honestly? I don't know. I feel like I've cried so much. It feels like there's a lead weight sitting on my heart, and the guilt from what happened to Everly is eating at me. It's like I can't escape it. And yet, at other times, it's as if I forget that she's gone, and I think about her as if she's coming back. But when I sleep, I see it again and again, but every time I still fail to save her," she says, and my heart breaks for her. Grief is something I understand. It's weird and twisted. At least her grief is to be expected, but my heart hurts for her feelings of guilt. It isn't her fault at all. It's mine. I was taken, and she came to rescue me. So much shit happened because of that.

"I get it," I tell her sadly as I sit next to her. "Grief is a weird thing, and it hits us in different ways. It's brutal." Goddess knows I've been going through my own weird sense of grief about Azriel, which is absurd.

"It's worse because I didn't really know her that long, not really, and it feels like I'm being greedy with my grief. Olivia and Astrid are handling it way better than I am."

"Maybe they are, but then again, maybe they aren't. Either way, they didn't witness it, Remy. That's gonna be a score on anyone's soul. You feel everything so deeply, I'm not at all surprised that it's haunting you. You're allowed to grieve however you need to."

"I guess." She frowns. "I don't want to be a big mess tonight."

"Feel whatever you need to feel."

"Enough about me," she says, squeezing my hand, and I avert my gaze, looking down at the floor instead of at my best friend. "How are you?"

"I'm getting there." I paste on a tight smile and glance up, hoping she doesn't see through it too much. "It's gonna take time, but I refuse to let them take away all the good parts of me. Whatever Morgan did helped, so I at least feel less broken." I give her some semblance of the truth because it's better than telling her everything. I can't imagine how she'd react to knowing that I think I'm scared of doing magic alone ever again. And did I mention I've been hearing Azriel's voice in my mind since you guys killed him? I really think it's gone now, but I'm scared shitless it's gonna come back.

"If there's anything I can do, let me know."

"I promise I will, but you have enough to worry about already. Don't spend too much time on me. I'm working it out." I squeeze her hand before standing. "Now then, come on. We don't want to hide away all night and miss out."

"I know," she sighs before standing and flattening her skirt with her hands.

I lead her through the house to the sitting room and out

the doors to the back yard. The moon shines down around us, helping light the space as we descend from the back porch. Lit candles form a pathway across the lawn, so we follow it to the tree line. We follow the path silently until we come to a clearing that's completely lit with candles. There's a low wooden pyre in the middle with Everly's body laid across it. Her eyes are closed, coins on both of them With her arms crossed over her chest, she looks at peace. Mama has done a beautiful job with her.

I can almost feel Remy's swell of emotion as she takes in the candles and flowers lining the base of the pyre. Olivia and Astrid, Everly's daughter and granddaughter, walk toward us, and Olivia places a crown of flowers on mine and Remy's heads. They match the flowers at the base of the pyre, and my throat clogs with emotion at the realization. She hands us each a candle and ushers us over to where Remy's guys are waiting for her.

We stand with them, and the grief in the air is suffocating. Everly was so, so loved, and though I only spent a little time with her, it is easy to see why so many people are here for her.

Colt and Mama move to where Olivia and Astrid are waiting, and I step away from my friend to go stand with them. Remy has all the support she needs. I glance over my shoulder to see her guys huddling around her as I cross the open space. Mama will need some support, she knew

Everly too. For longer than I realized.

Levi moves from Remy's side to stand beside the pyre, and it's so quiet, you could hear a pin drop.

"Tonight, we say goodbye to an old friend. A mother, a daughter, a sister, a nana," Levi says, as he smiles down at Astrid sadly who is starting to cry softly. "Everly was more than just a friend, she was one of the brightest souls I have encountered in a millennia. She was taken from us far too soon, but I know that she's still with us. In our hearts, in our memories, watching down on us.

"I remember the first time I met Everly. She was a young woman and headstrong, especially for her time. She loved passionately and was fiercely loyal. She called me out on our first interaction, and I think I loved her a little right then. I knew she would be a dear friend.

"I remember when she met the love of her life, and how her own mother fretted about a love that could burn so bright, her fear it would die out quickly, but Everly knew better. And oh how right she was. Her life was not without its dark moments, but she taught me to see the light in things. Not to dwell on those low moments, to look forward to when the light would re-enter our lives and lead us out of the shadows.

"If it wasn't for her, I might have been lost a while ago. She kept my feet firmly planted and I will miss her deeply. Until we meet again my friend. Until Avalon."

"Until Avalon," I murmur in time with everyone else. Power hums in the air, prickling across my skin. It's almost too much, but I refuse to let it win. Levi moves to stand back a little, and Olivia steps forward.

"My mother was a proud woman. But she was also full of light and laughter. She always had a kind word when you needed it, or a stern one if that's what you needed instead." Olivia laughs a little as a tear falls. She swipes it away before continuing, "She loved like no other, and I can only hope to be half the person, the mother, that she was, but if I manage that, I still know that she'll be proud of me. She always was. No matter how many times you fall down, it's getting back up that matters. That's what she'd tell me.

"I miss you, Mom. I wish we had more time together, but I know that you're still with us, and I'll make sure that Astrid remembers how amazing you were. That she has a real childhood, even among everything life throws at us. I love you." She picks up Astrid and kisses her head, trying to keep her tears under control as she stands on the other side of Colt.

Mama joins Levi standing over Everly's body, and they bless the body, wrapping her in the white sheet that was laid over the pyre. Once they step back, Levi waves, beckoning everyone to move closer to the pyre.

"We send this soul to Avalon, and may she watch down

upon us in eternal happiness." Levi's words are thick, and he clears his throat before leaning down and placing his candle at the base of the pyre. We each follow suit with a few softly spoken words, and then Mama spreads the flames until they engulf the pyre and Everly's body.

I ache with the sorrow seeping through the clearing. Feeling everyone else's emotions is something new for me, but it's like I can't turn it off. I look over to Mama, hoping she can't see my panic. Colt takes my hand, as if he could sense my panic, and it's like the world goes quiet and I can breathe again.

"Let's give everyone some space, shall we?" he asks softly against my ear, and I nod. We move back toward Mama and leave the clearing, giving Everly's family time to mourn.

Colt drove us all home, we dropped Mama off, and then he took me to his house. Bauer isn't here right now apparently, which makes me feel a little better because I'm not sure I'll be able to not just flay his ass on sight. I'm pretty sure that's not what Colt had in mind when he said about doing things to help me heal.

Though after having said a final goodbye to Everly, I'm not the only one with emotions running high. If I was

Bauer, I'd be hiding from us all right now too.

The entire time since I've been home has been a bit of a daze, and I swear the more I try to focus, the harder it is. It's like I'm still not quite myself, like something is missing, or is off. So I'm sitting here, in the library, a place I've always felt at home, sipping on hot cocoa because Colt knows me well enough to know that it's one of my favorite forms of comfort. I mean, besides tequila, but the last thing I need at the moment is alcohol clouding my mind any more than it already is.

"You look lost in thought.." Colt smiles at me as he stands in the doorway, hands on the doorjamb as he leans into the room. His t-shirt rides up, showing a glimpse of his inked-up abs. I've always been a sucker for his style of charm, the boyish, carefree way he carries himself with a dash of the swagger that comes from someone who knows themself inside and out. That's Colt in a nutshell. He knows who he is, and he isn't sorry about it. Despite the fact he seems to have grown up a lot since he became a Hunter Elder, I'm glad he hasn't lost that bit of himself.

"Now then, Ms. Laveau, are you checking me out?" he teases, and I can't help but roll my eyes.

"So what if I was? You wanted me to look, otherwise you wouldn't be peacocking over there," I tease him right back, and he barks out a laugh.

"Can't blame a guy for trying to get your attention."

He chuckles as he comes to sit opposite me. "Pretty girl, sitting with her head in the clouds. You know I'm a sucker for a girl surrounded by books."

I try not to blush, thinking back to the first time we were together. It was here in this library, back before Remy knew what she was and the world turned upside down. Things were easier then. It was fun, and hot, and damn if my thighs don't clench together remembering just what he's capable of. But that was a different time.

"Maybe this pretty girl isn't a sucker for the cocky guy covered in ink and piercings anymore," I say, raising an eyebrow as I take another sip of my drink. This back and forth makes me feel normal. Human, even. Or at least as human as I've ever been.

"Oh, I remember how much this pretty girl enjoyed my piercings," he teases, and I blush again.

"You always were a tease," I joke, and he grins wider.

"Anything to make you smile," he answers, and my heart does that weird flip flop thing all over again. Right now, it's almost easy to forget everything that's happened. But then a pang of guilt hits me, and I see it reflected back at me when the light in his eyes dims a little.

"Colt, I'm gonna need some time."

"I wasn't trying to rush you," he says, red creeping up his inked neck as he runs a hand through the mess of hair on top of his head.

“I don’t want you to think it’s because of you. What happened to me when I was gone…” I trail off, and he takes my hand from across the table.

“You don’t need to tell me, Fallon. But if you want to, I’ll listen,” he says softly, the warmth from his hand comforting me.

And so I tell him. Not everything, but some of it anyway. What I survived, about Azriel and Deacon. I leave out the part about the voices in my head, but I lay most of it out for him. I try not to take it personally when he clenches his jaw or the way his hands ball into fists and those icy blue eyes of his are practically glacial as I talk.

Once I’m finished, he stands, pacing the floor. He turns as if to speak to me, but then continues to pace instead. I wait patiently because I know I threw a lot at him. I know if it was the other way round, I’d have likely lost my shit. Even before we were messing around, we were friends. We have been our entire lives. That sort of bond is the kind that makes you want to raze countries when the other person gets hurt. So I get it, but it doesn’t stop the butterflies from tangoing in my stomach or the little voice in my head telling me that he’s pissed at me.

“Colt,” I start, and he turns to face me.

“ I’m so fucking sorry, Fallon. I swear if Azriel wasn’t dead already I’d cut him open and dance on his fucking innards.” I wince at the visual. “I don’t understand how you could feel anything but contempt for him, but I also didn't go through what you did, so I'm not going to judge. Same goes for Deacon."

I shiver at the venom in his tone when he says the name. "It's fucked up, I know," I say, hanging my head.

He strides over to me and crouches down, lifting my chin so I'm looking him in the eye. "You have absolutely nothing to be sorry or ashamed about, Fallon. Nobody, even me, gets to tell you what is right or wrong to feel because nobody else went through it. You made it through. That's what matters, and if you need reminding of that every goddamn day, then that's what I'm going to do."

A tear slips down my cheek, and he stands, lifting me as he does and wrapping me up in the biggest hug. He holds me until the tears are gone and I'm weak from the emotion.

It's almost funny how I wanted to avoid the one person who somehow has all the right words to make me feel almost whole again.

TWENTY

My phone buzzes on my bedside table. I contemplate not looking at it, but when the buzzing continues, I groan and give in. Though when I see Colt's name on the screen, I half wish I'd rolled over and gone back to sleep.

"Hello," I say groggily.

"Fal, it's me."

"No shit, Sherlock. I have caller ID," I grumble and snuggle back under the duvet as he chuckles down the line.

"Sorry, I didn't think you'd be asleep. You've always been a night owl like me, and I kinda lost track of time with the meeting tonight."

"Oh yeah, I forgot. Sorry," I mutter, remembering he has a house full of Hunters. He hosted the Elder meeting tonight, which was super secret because Archer seems to have a mole within the Hunter ranks and it's causing chaos. "How was it?"

"It went about as well as expected," he sighs, and I swear I can feel his frustration even though he's nowhere near me. I really need to talk to Mama about it. It can't be right. I file it away for another time as he keeps talking. "I wondered if you wanted to come over and talk some more. There's a ton of people here, so there's no pressure. I miss you, Fallon."

I can hear the loneliness in his voice. I get it. It's easy to be surrounded by people and still feel alone. Colt's lost a lot of trust in people recently with everything he's learned about his family and everything that's been going on with Remy, and Creek.

"Sure, I'll be over soon," I tell him with a small smile. I know he can't see it, but I think he knows anyway. I sit up, ready to get out of bed and get dressed when he speaks again.

"Thanks, Fal, do you need a lift?" he asks warily. I haven't mentioned that I'm not using my magic to him, but I can't imagine it's hard for him to work out considering the amount of time he's been with me since I got back. Which is yet another thing for me to feel guilty about.

"No, I'm good. I'll get myself there. I won't be long."

"See you soon." The line goes dead, and I flop back down onto my pillows. This is probably a really bad idea.

I don't want to lead him on when I have no idea what's going on in my own head, but I also know that when I'm near him, when I touch him, everything else goes quiet. It's hard not to crave that, but I don't want to use him either.

I try not to think too hard while I throw on a pair of jeans, a white tank top, and a dark shirt that makes my skin seem to glow. I fluff my hair, my naturally loose curls still holding despite me having rolled around in bed for most of the day. I grab my phone and keys and quietly head out to the main part of the house, trying not to wake Mama or Rebel. It might only be half past ten at night, but they're both usually out cold by this time of night.

I grab my heels from the back door and tiptoe through to the front.

"Where are you sneaking off to?" Mama's voice calls out in the silence, and I damn near squeal.

"Mama, are you trying to kill me?" I bark and then shake my head. "Sorry. I'm extra jumpy these days."

"I know, sorry," she says, smiling, though I know she's not all that sorry at all. Mama always says what doesn't kill you makes you stronger. She's not usually wrong. "But still, where are you sneaking off to? "

"I'm going to see Colt," I tell her, looking down at my bare feet.

"Mmmmmmm." I look back up and see her sipping at her tea. "Do you think that's a good idea?"

"I don't see why it wouldn't be." I shrug.

"Fallon, you went through a lot. Maybe you should focus on yourself rather than on a boy," she says, raising an eyebrow and giving me that 'mom' look she does so well.

"Maybe I should, but I also need to get out of my own head. I can do that with Colt. He makes the world quiet," I tell her softly, and I can feel her watching me. It's as if she sees straight down to my very soul.

"Hmmmm," is all she says. "I'll create a portal for you, so you don't have to drive."

"Thanks, Mama," I say, wringing my hands. I hate that I'm still too scared of myself to use my magic.

"Just until you feel more up to it. But this can't last forever, baby. Your magic is as much a part of you as the blood that runs through your veins." She moves over to me and cups my cheek with her hand, lifting my face so I'm looking into her eyes. "You are stronger than the worst things you've survived."

She doesn't say anything else, opening a portal for me instead. I kiss her cheek and slip my heels on before stepping through.

If only she knew the truth of it.

I wake up in Colt's bed, wrapped up in his smell, and I

smile. Just for a minute, I forget everything that's happened. I'm living life from six months ago, back when everything was still simple. Easy. It only lasts a few moments, but I cherish those moments before reality crashes down and pulls me back to the shit show that is my life.

Colt's inked-up arm is draped over me, and it's so freaking heavy I swear I'm going to go full pins and needles if I don't move soon. I wriggle away from him, but his hand grips my hip and drags me back against him. "Where do you think you're going?"

His voice is low, husky, and full of sleep, and my heart races in my chest. A second later he releases me and sits up, dragging a hand down his face. "Sorry."

"It's fine," I tell him, but he's facing away from me. We're both still fully dressed, which makes me laugh a little. "We obviously passed out talking. It happens."

Voices float through the door, and I sigh. When he said his house was full last night, he wasn't joking. Most of the Elders left in the dead of night, no one would have any idea they were even here, let alone that they left. But some of Colt's Hunter friends stayed here, along with a ton of other Hunters, Bauer, and Denny. A house full doesn't quite cover it.

"We should go down," I start, pulling the duvet off.

"You can use the shower if you want. I'm pretty sure Remy still has some clothes in her old room if you want them. Not that you need them, you look amazing, I just mean…" He rubs the back of his neck as red paints his cheeks, and I laugh.

"Colt, it's fine. I'll grab a quick shower, get changed, and then see you downstairs. Please save me some food because I'm starving." I smile at him and dash from the room.

I knock on the bathroom door just in case, but when there's no answer I slip in and lock the door. Somehow, even with three guys living here, there's always clean, fresh towels, and it doesn't smell too much like boy. I grab a quick shower, keeping my hair dry because this mop isn't something I need to deal with this morning. I pop it in a messy bun on the top of my head, and run from the bathroom to Remy's old room. The thought that it would be occupied didn't cross my mind, but I'm glad it's empty when I get there, though it's obvious someone slept in here.

I dress as quickly as I can, and thankfully, despite her being a bit taller than my tiny ass, we're similar in size. I end up in a pair of shorts and a tank top, pulling a shirt on over the top, and I'm done. I check myself in the mirror and leave the messy bun. I won't be here for too long today, so I'm gonna let it be.

The smells from the kitchen waft up through the house, and my stomach grumbles. That's what I get for not eating properly since I've been home. I lost some weight while

I was in the Shadow Realm, and I'm missing some of my curves, so I know I need to start taking better care of myself. It's not the easiest thing to do when it feels like my mind is like looking into a kaleidoscope.

It's a mess there, and it makes me nauseous every time I try to get introspective or whatever.

I push the thought back and head downstairs, finding the kitchen overflowing with a literal penis parade. It is such a goddamn sausage fest here that I almost feel like I shouldn't even be here.

"Hey, Fallon," Creek's voice makes me jump, and I spin around to find him walking toward me from the front door.

"Hey, what are you doing here?" I ask, trying to not let my guilt eat me alive at how uneasy he looks. My appetite disappears in an instant.

"Colt dropped me a message and said people were hanging out for breakfast. I see that, same as always, he undersold the amount of people here." He laughs, and I join him before the laugh cuts off abruptly in the wake of yet another surge of guilt.

"I—" I start, but he holds up a hand and shakes his head, interrupting me.

"Fallon, I need you to know that I don't blame you. For any of it. I'd do it all again in a heartbeat. Adjusting is hard, but I can see how uncomfortable you are. Guilt isn't going to help anyone. You went through enough already. Give yourself a break." I pause, considering his words. He looks genuine, but that doesn't stop the churning in my stomach.

"Thank you," I say softly, and he closes the distance between us, pulling me in for a tight hug. I sink into it. I've missed my friend, but guilt is a funny thing.

"Now, let's go get some food before these vultures eat it all." I follow him into the kitchen, and a round of cheers go up at his arrival. Danny and the other Delta boys are sitting at the table, there are other Hunters spilling out onto the back deck, taking advantage of the early sun, and I even notice more through the hall, spilling into the sitting room.

"How many people are here exactly?" I chuckle as I find Colt, and he grins back at me.

"What can I say, people love me." He shrugs before stirring the eggs in the pan. All I can do is laugh at him again. I guess since he's been on his own more, he's finally learning how to cook.

"That they do. Can I do anything to help?"

"You can sit your pretty ass down and let me feed you," he says, motioning to one of the empty stools at the island. It doesn't happen often, but I do as he says and sit down, letting him fix me a plate as I sit back and enjoy the banter that floats around the room. I don't see Bauer or Denny, but I'm sure Colt's brother and dad are skulking around here somewhere. I try not to think too much about it and enjoy being part of Colt's world for the morning.

We're all sitting, laughing, and joking when Colt goes tense. He's looking down at his phone with a tight frown pulling his lips down.

"What's wrong?" Creek asks, stealing the words from my mouth. The entire room goes silent, waiting for him to speak.

"Archer," is all he says, but it's all he needs to say. Archer Dotoro is enemy number one to every single person in this room. Though, I can't help that niggle in my mind at the memory of Azriel telling me that Archer wasn't the guy behind all of this, that he was a pawn in a much bigger game.

That doesn't stop the room turning to ice at his name.

Colt taps his phone, and Archer's voice fills the room.

"Good morning, Bennett family. Once again, you couldn't do what I asked. I thought you'd learn your lesson. Are enough of your loved ones not dead yet? Do you really need me to prove that you will do what I need before I leave you alone? Of course you do, so more people will have to die because you can't leave well enough alone can you? You couldn't even do one little thing right. I tried to tell you. I even tried to show you. But you've forced my hand. I'm not a bad guy. You can't do any fucking thing right can you. So now this is your fault. The blood that spills will be on your hands."

His voice goes quiet before the line goes dead, and it feels like like the room is frozen in time for half a second.

"What a fucking jackass!" Colt shouts. A heartbeat later an explosion sounds, so loudly my ears ring and the whole house shakes. People are on their feet and moving in the blink of an eye.

"The cars, they blew up the fucking cars!" someone shouts, and in the next second, gunfire sounds. Everyone hits the deck.

"Danny, you and your boys get to the armory in the library. If anyone else brought guns, grab them. We've got a showdown on our hands, boys!" Colt orders, and everyone else moves, without a hint of second guessing. He crouches down in front of me and wipes some blood from beneath my ear.

"I need you to get upstairs. If anything happens to you…"

"I'll be okay," I tell him. I stand and quickly glance out of the window and gasp. My stomach drops all the way to the fucking floor. "Colt…"

There are so many people outside, and all of them are

armed to the teeth. There's no way we have enough people here to fight this. He follows my sight line and shouts his frustration.

"Fuck!" He grabs his phone and dials. I hear Remy's voice through the line as gunfire starts up again and more people flood in the front door. They're waving at us, so I assume they're Colt's friends.

"Colt? What the fuck is going on? Where is Creek?" Remy shouts.

"It was an ambush. We need you, Remy. Now. At the house." He doesn't waste any more words."I need to get to higher ground and get a weapon," he says as wood shatters around us from more gunfire.

"Bobby is hit!" I hear from the sitting room.

"You do what you need to do. I'm going to help as many people as I can," I tell him, my hands shaking at the thought of using my powers again, but there's no way in hell I'm letting Archer take any more people from us if I can.

"Fallon," Colt starts. I can clearly see his concern for me, but I know he's torn. No one wants to lose more of their people.

"Don't fight me on this, Colt. Go do what you have to do. I've got this." He pauses for a second before kissing me with so much heat my toes curl. I push at his chest. Now isn't the time.

"Do not get yourself hurt," is all he says before he takes off up the stairs. I touch my lips and then hit the floor as more gunfire rips through the room. I'm not sure how much longer the house can withstand this sort of punishment, so I climb to my feet and haul ass into the sitting room, preparing myself as best I can to use the gifts the earth blessed me with.

Mama arrives a few minutes after I send her a quick text. I can't keep up with all of the wounds on my own. I'm half drained and still fucking terrified. I need her, and she portals into the room and starts a makeshift triage space in an instant. I'm more than happy to let her take charge.

It feels like forever before I hear Remy's voice above the screams and gunfire. I'm amazed I can even still hear.

"Colt!" she shouts from outside. Someone flicks the lock on the front door and then heads back upstairs. The door bursts open, and I see her face go even paler as she takes in the sight before her. Colt and the guys managed to get people to fall back so the kitchen is a safe zone again. Mama's in there working on someone while I'm in here. Colt appears from the kitchen as Remy enters the house.

"What the fuck is going on?" she hisses, and Colt scrubs a hand over his face.

"The Elders met here last night. We've only been communicating virtually up until now, but information has been leaking somehow, so we wanted to meet face-to-face in case the video feed was being hacked. The communication must have been intercepted because at sunrise, there was an explosion out the front, and then all fucking hell broke loose. Fallon's in the sitting room trying to heal people, but she's still not doing great. Creek is out the front, trying to slow people down, but he was freaking out about using his powers, in case he hurt people he didn't mean to. I don't know what to do, little sister. I have no idea where Dad is, but I saw him slip out before the chaos began. I haven't seen him since."

"You don't think he…" She shakes her head, and I try not to eavesdrop too much. My stomach sinks at the realization that I haven't seen any of them.

"I don't know anymore," Colt answers her, and he looks as drained as I feel. I turn my focus back on the bleeding bullet wound beneath my hands and push my magic into the empty space, watching it knit back together. Luckily it's through and through, so there's no bullet to extract. That shit takes longer. I lose track of Remy and Colt's conversation until I'm done.

"I'm heading back out there," Remy tells Colt. "Get people upstairs, keep down here clear. I'm going to fucking finish this." She grips her sword tighter and heads back out the front. Goddess help anyone who gets in her path.

"You heard her," Colt shouts. "Let's get everyone onto the second floor. We have plenty of space. Let's clear this floor, just in case."

Bodies appear from upstairs and help us carry the injured back up the stairs where I continue to work, barely even paying attention anymore. My hands are slick with blood, and my shirt is crusted with it, so I've given up on trying to keep them clean at this point.

"Fallon," I hear Mama's voice and spin around. "We're good for the moment. The factions have arrived, and Remy and Creek have cleared the front. Take a breather and go clean up." She speaks softly, like I'm a deer caught in headlights that might bolt at any second. I don't blame her. My hands haven't stopped shaking all morning. I don't usually deal with the gunshots, the explosions, or any of this stuff. I usually clean up the aftermath.

This is something else entirely.

I move robotically to the bathroom, and as the blood runs from my hands in the warm water, I can't help but flash back to the last fight I saw. The one where Azriel lost his head. When Creek and Remy nearly died. My breath picks up, and it suddenly feels like I can't breathe at all. I scramble back and curl into a ball in the corner.

I'm not sure how much time passes before the door crashes open and Colt barrels in. He picks me up and sits with me in his lap, holding me close to him.

"You're okay. I've got you," he murmurs to me, over and over again, until I feel like I can breathe again.

Once I calm down, Colt leads me downstairs. The panic only starts to build again when Kain walks in the front door with Colt's dad over his shoulder. Roman is behind him with Archer over his.

"Shit!" Colt swears, and I hear Bauer call out for Remy as they all move into the kitchen. I follow Colt behind them all, where I find Maddie, Nate, and Mama, along with Remy's mom and Creek gathered around the island.

Holy fucking shit. She has wings.

Remy's mom is an Angel.

Colt goes rigid beside me, and I take his hand, staying on the edge of the room.

"Denny?" Remy's mom gasps, and I swear Colt flinches.

"What happened?" Remy asks as she turns to Roman, who winces before dropping Archer on the floor like the sack of shit he is.

"I guess Caleb's guy didn't get all of the Angel glass. That asshole still had a blade of it. I'm guessing that's all there was of it though because he fought pretty hard not to lose it. Unfortunately for him, it doesn't fuck me up. Your dad was with him when we caught up to him. They were arguing, but fuck knows what about. Denny charged Archer after we arrived, and then this happened. We subdued the fuckface as quickly as we could then hauled ass back here," Roman tells her, and my heart breaks for her.

"Angel glass?" Her mom's gasp makes my heart sink further. "Oh Fates, no. Please, no."

Colt barely moves. In fact, barely breathing. He's watching everything play out, silent as his hand tightens to a near painful level around my own.

"How are you here? Am I dead already?" Denny asks his wife, his voice hoarse.

"No, you're not dead." Her voice shakes as she moves over to his side, her hands trembling. She takes her hand in his, and it's like Denny transforms. He relaxes and smiles. I haven't seen him smile like that… Well, since she died.

"Then how?" His voice croaks, and she shakes her head.

"Later, we'll talk later, you stubborn fool." She looks up to Maddie who shakes her head.

He's not going to make it.

Bauer turns and leaves the room as Colt sinks to the floor beside me, letting go of my hand.

Their family line is officially broken. They'll only have

each other left. Angel glass isn't something a Hunter can come back from. And since their mom is here, that means she's not coming back either. She chose the true death and went to Avalon, the realm of Angels.

Shit.

This changes so fucking much. The Bennett line is over. I mean, Colt and Bauer will come back, but they won't be Bennetts anymore since both of their parents' souls are no longer cycling. The Hunter Curse is really fucked up, and it doesn't make much sense, but it is what it is.

It's as confusing as it is heartbreaking.

"Don't leave me." Their dad's voice is barely more than a whisper, and their mom grips his hand tighter.

"I'm not going anywhere," she says, but her face betrays her.

"This is bullshit," Colt fumes, standing back up. "You don't get to die, not with everything still unresolved. You don't get to act like a giant fucking asshole, and then die before we get everything sorted out."

"Colt," his mom scolds, but he's too angry. He's pacing, and when he's like this, nothing can slow him down.

"No, Mom, you weren't here. You haven't been here." Her flinch at his words is like a knife to the gut, but he doesn't seem to care. He's too far gone. "He doesn't get to treat Remy the way he has, and then look at her like he couldn't give a shit that he's dying. It's such a fucking cop out. He doesn't deserve the easy way out of this bullshit."

"Believe me, Colt. Your father and I have things I'd really quite like to discuss. Including his father's hand in having me fucking killed, but it doesn't look like this is the time."

"Fucking what?!" Colt rages and punches the wall. Plaster dust flies from the impact site.

"Fallon," Mama says quietly and waves me to join her out in the hall. "We should give the Bennetts some space. This is only the beginning of it all."

"What did you see, Mama?" I ask, though I know she won't answer.

"You know I can't tell you, baby. Just trust me. We've done all we can for the people here. Let's give them some space. Being close to the Bennetts right now isn't what's best for you." She takes my hand when I nod and portals us home. I know better than to argue with Mama when she gets like this. Especially after a vision. I want to stay back with Remy and Colt, but I know I'm not who either of them need right now. I can't help them when I can barely help myself.

So I vow to get my shit together because I've never been the girl who leaves my friends to deal with their shit alone.

TWENTY ONE

Once we're home, I let Mama shower first so I can send off a quick message to Colt, Remy, and Creek to let them know we're gone but that I'm thinking of them. I never knew my dad, so I've never had anyone to miss, but after everything the Bennetts have been through these last few months, losing him will be monumental. I need to be there for them both.

I can't even imagine how Bauer must feel right now. He was closest with their dad out of them all, and he helped Archer. Now his dad is gone.

I shake my head and drop onto the couch. Mama might have used a flick of her hand to clean me off magically, but I still feel filthy. It feels like I'll never get the blood out from under my nails. I don't even want to close my eyes because all I can see is blood and bullet wounds.

Fuck knows how I'm going to sleep tonight.

Feeling restless, despite being exhausted, I patter around in the kitchen, finishing the tidying Mama was obviously doing before I called her away earlier. I grab a pack of popcorn and throw it in the microwave, trying not to flinch while it pops as I clean. Apparently, popcorn was a bad idea, but I'm hungry and I'm a lousy cook for the most part.

Mama appears once I've finished cleaning and as I'm pouring the popcorn into a bowl.

"Ooooo, popcorn!" She grabs a handful with a grin before dropping down onto the sofa. "Film after you shower?"

"Sure thing. I might call Colt first, though," I tell her, biting my lip. I'm still not sure if it's a good idea, but I feel like an asshole disappearing with only a text.

"You should give him some space, he just lost his dad," she says, frowning.

"But, Mama, what if he needs a friend? Someone who isn't a guy that he can be with without having to be so on ?"

"Fallon, I know you like that boy. I love him like he's my own child, but you and him, it's not a good idea."

"And why not?" I ask, trying and failing to not sound like a petulant toddler. I'm not even sure a relationship with Colt is something I still want, but I'll be damned if I'm going to let her dictate my life to me. I only just got my freedom back. I'm not giving a damn ounce of it away, even to my mama.

"His life is dangerous. You saw as much earlier today. You could have died because you were there with him!"

"Mama, I could have died getting in the car and going to the store."

"Fallon Laveau, don't you sass me. You know exactly what I mean. The life of a Hunter is dangerous, and with everything else coming down on that family… He's an Elder now, which puts him at even greater risk. I don't like it."

"You don't need to like it!" I argue. "I had my freedom, my entire life, taken from me, Mama. I gave up because I thought I'd never get to come back here or live my life. But Remy and her guys saved me. I'm back because of that family!"

"You wouldn't have been taken if it wasn't for that family!" she shouts, and I swear the damn walls shake.

"Mama, it wasn't their fault. You're the one who keeps saying that!"

"Maybe it was, maybe it wasn't, but I only just got you back. I don't want to lose you again. Can't you see that?"

"That isn't fair. You can't ask me not to live my life because you're afraid. I'm afraid too, Mama! Do you really think I'm not? I'm scared every second of every goddamn day. But I keep moving, I keep going, and Colt is a part of the reason why. I'm not going to give that up!"

"You're a fool, Fallon. Why can't you see…" she sighs as she trails off and shakes her head.

"I can see perfectly clear, Mama. If you'll excuse me, I'm going to shower but then I think I'm too tired for a movie. I'll see you tomorrow."

I walk away from her, my hands shaking with my anger. Her words niggle in my mind about Remy being responsible for everything, but I try not to let that seed plant in my mind. I do get afraid—I wasn't lying when I told her I'm afraid all of the time. I live life feeling dirty, broken, and fucking terrified all the time. But I finally got my power back, the power of making my own decisions, and I'll be damned if I'm going to let anyone take that away from me.

It's been two days since the bloodbath at Colt's house, but when he texted me this morning asking me to go over, I couldn't say no. Even with Mama's words ringing in my ears. It's hard to dismiss her concerns, especially when I don't know if they're because she's my mama, or if it's because she's seen something. Either way, being around

Colt makes me happy, so I get up and head out without saying anything.

I step out of the portal, and it's clear to me that a shit ton of cleanup has happened here. It's almost as if nothing actually went down. Colt must've been working like crazy to sort this place out.

I head up the porch steps and let myself in the house. I stagger backward at the sight that meets my eyes. The inside of the house is a different story entirely to the outside. It's been cleaned up, but there's plastic sheets hanging everywhere, and the smell of dust and paint permeates the air.

"Colt?" I call out, heading toward the kitchen since that's usually where I'd find him.

"Hey," he says as he meets me in the doorway. "How are you doing?"

His gaze runs up and down my body, and I get a chill from the intensity of it. "I'm okay, more importantly, how are you doing?"

"I'm fine, it's been crazy around here, but that's my life these days, I guess. I'm better now that you're here. Come on, I just finished cooking." He takes my hand and leads me into the kitchen, which at least looks good as new. Or well, good as old because everything looks like it did before the attack. "Kain had some of his Dracul come and help with the work. Turns out vamp speed and the whole not needing to sleep thing means shit gets done real quick."

I smile as he pulls out a chair at the table for me and tucks me under. My smile only grows as he drops a mountainous pile of French toast and bacon on the table in front of us. I blink, a little shocked at how good it all looks. I'd ask if he took a cooking class, but this doesn't feel like the time.

"Colt, you know you can talk to me, right?" He sits beside me and piles food onto my plate before fixing his own. I wait for him to talk the entire time.

"Fal, I know. But I honestly don't want to talk about it. Not about my dad being dead. Not about my granddad having my mom murdered. Or about the fact that my mom is a fucking Angel. I don't even want to think about it. I have enough on my plate dealing with the Hunters Guild I'm overseeing, all of Archer's bullshit, and worrying so hard about Remy. I swear if I could get an ulcer, I'd have a couple hundred. I want to be here with you, in this moment, and not think about anything beyond the simple joy of it."

I look into his piercing blue eyes, and sincerity shines back at me. There's some hurt there too, but I don't mention it. I take his hand, running my fingers over his knuckles as I offer him a small smile. "Okay, I won't push. Goddess knows I know all about not talking. But I'm here if you need me." He squeezes my hand, and I smile before tucking into the plate before me.

I groan as the taste comes alive on my tongue. I close my eyes, savoring it. Food hasn't tasted so good since I've been back from the Shadow Realm. When I open my eyes, I see him staring at me with a cheeky smirk on his face.

"I always loved making you moan like that," he chuckles, and I swipe at him from across the table.

"Colt!" I laugh as a blush creeps up my neck.

"What? It's true. You were the one who talked about talking." I laugh at his ridiculousness before we settle into an easy conversation about nothing as we finish eating. I help him clean up, despite his protests, and then we head toward his room.

"The sitting room is still a mess," he tells me as he heads up the stairs, and I roll my eyes.

"Of course it is."

"We don't have to go up there if it makes you uncomfortable," he says, stopping his ascent.

"Don't be silly. I'm fine," I tell him, despite the trickle of sweat running down my spine. I know he won't touch me if I don't want him to. Except, I'm not sure that I don't want him to. After what my body went through in the Shadow Realm… There are still some scars, even with the Queen's magic touch. They make me feel dirty. Used. Broken. And the thought of him seeing me like that? Touching me like that? Nope.

Just no.

But I take a step up the stairs anyway because I know Colt. He's a safe place for me. He won't push me too far. He'll let me be if I ask him to. Besides, we're just supposed to be watching a movie anyway. Really, my biggest worry is falling asleep and drooling on him. He's always so warm, so falling asleep on him is a genuine hazard.

We reach his room and he kicks off his shoes before dropping onto the bed. I laugh as he grabs the remote and turns on Netflix. "What do you fancy?" he asks, wagging his eyebrows and making me laugh harder. I move and stand in the doorway, biting my lip.

Hello love, did you miss me?

No.

No.

This can't be happening.

I stumble as panic overwhelms me and manage to catch myself on the doorjamb.

"Fallon, what's wrong?" Colt scrambles off the bed until he's standing in front of me, less than an arm's length away. I step back as he reaches out for me.

This looks very cozy, pet.

No, no, no!

"I'm… I'm sorry," I stutter and run down the stairs and out the front door.

He can't be back.

He just can't be.

I crash into my room and fall onto the bed sobbing. This cannot be happening. He was gone. Morgan healed me, taking that part of crazy away. It just doesn't make sense. Because if he's still in my head, that means either I'm broken beyond repair, or he really did bind our souls together.

I don't relish the thought of either option being true.

What's wrong, pet? Don't cry. I didn't mean to make you cry.

"Why are you back?" I screech, glad that no one else is home to witness my breakdown.

I never went anywhere, sweetheart. I was always here. As for why I'm 'back' now, I told you once before, you're mine. You were about to cross a line.

I scream into my pillow, trying to release the building frustration. He doesn't get to do this to me! He's already taken so much.

You know I didn't want to hurt you, love. I wouldn't have had it been my choice. Rock and a hard place, remember. Plus, I heard you scream when that dick took my head. You didn't want me to be gone.

I try to ignore his mumblings, but since it's in my head, it's hard as fuck. He's not completely wrong. He did show me another side of him once we created the bond.

"Why don't you tell me exactly why you hurt me? Can't you help us? If you really wanted to protect me, if you wanted me to be yours, you'd keep me safe."

Things are never that easy, love. I'm bound, just as much as you were. Even though my body is gone, my soul is still here. My soul still holds that binding. I'd tell you if I could, but there's more than just you that I'm protecting.

I scoff at his reasoning. It sounds like poor excuses to me.

I take a deep breath, making the decision that I'm not going to let him fuck with me. I can shut things out, so maybe I can shut him away. Maybe I can build a wall around the part of my mind where his voice stems from.

If only it was so simple.

"Shut the fuck up!" I shout and then shake my head. My hands are trembling, and my heart races. I'm still not ready to use my magic properly, so I need to meditate. I desperately need to clear my mind and cleanse myself of him.

We're bound, love. You can't cleanse me away with some deep breathing. I told you, you're mine. You think I'd make it that easy for you to escape me? We didn't have enough time to explore what this could have been. Your friends saw to that. And I kept my word, didn't I? I was going to leave your friends alone even though I knew they were running around in the realm. I didn't attack until they did.

I shake my head, trying to shake away his words. He's right, he did keep his promises, and there's no reason for him to lie to me now.

Unless of course this is some PTSD manifestation of my own craziness. In which case, I'm officially losing my mind, and it could all be one big delusion.

I'm not a figment of your imagination, pet. I'm here. And I'm not going anywhere.

"We'll see about that."

It's been a week since Azriel's voice reappeared in my head in Colt's room, and I've suffered through a week of non-stop fucking chatter. I'm trying to pretend he isn't there, but sometimes it's so loud I want to scream.

Mama keeps looking at me like I've lost my mind because I keep having to ask her to repeat stuff when he talks over her. At this point, I've decided the voice is a figment of my imagination, and I've just officially lost my goddamn mind. I can work on PTSD and crazy voices, though, right? I tried to do a magical cleanse and nothing happened, which basically convinced me that I'm losing my mind to trauma. If his soul is actually tethered to mine,

I have absofuckinglutey no idea how the hell I'm going to untether it, so it has to be the manifestation of my trauma.

This way, it isn't another problem I have to share with my friends or with Mama. This is something I can handle myself. Which might seem really stupid, but I'm hearing voices, so my judgement might not be exactly sound right now.

I head to the store for my evening shift, taking over for Misty. I'm hoping for a quiet night. I already worked at the restaurant all day, so I'm dead on my feet. But our rent went up because our landlord is an asshole, and Mama won't let me wipe his memory or glamour him into thinking we're paid up, so I need to do more to help out. It doesn't matter how tired I am, shit needs to get done.

It also gives me the perfect excuse to avoid Remy and Colt. They can't know about the crazy in my head, and they both watch me too closely when they're around. They know me too well. They'll work out that something's wrong, and I really don't want to have to deal with that.

Why not convince the landlord that he sold you the house? Take what you need. That's what's best for your family. They come first. You need to protect what is yours.

"Because that would be wrong," I grumble quietly, and he snorts in my head. My phone buzzes on the counter. I glance down. It's Colt. Again. I let it ring out. I can't deal with that stuff right now. If it's urgent, he'll call back or show up.

I need some space to deal with this before I can think about anything else.

You don't need him, pet. You've got me. As soon as I work out how to get my body back, I'll show you how much you're mine.

I don't bother responding, there's no point. The bell above the door rings, and I look up and smile at the Dracul who enters the store. "Can I help you?"

"I'm good, just looking for some dead man's blood," she says, her eyes sparkling. I don't even want to know what she wants with that.

"We keep it behind the counter. How much do you want?"

"Three vials should be enough."

"Awesome, that's two-fifty," I tell her and she pulls a stack of notes from her bra, peeling off the couple hundred dollars and handing it over.

"Thanks so much."

"Anytime," I say with a smile and she grins back, fangs and all.

"You're very pretty," she smiles.

Yes, you are. And she can fuck right off.

"Thank you," I blush, ignoring the voice in my head.

"Do you ever donate?" she asks, and I blush even harder.

No, no you fucking don't.

"No, I've never donated. Not outside of sex anyway," I tell her, trying to stay casual.

"Well, there's an avenue to explore. I bet you taste delicious. You smell fucking amazing," she says, and I get flustered.

"Uhm, thanks? I think?" She laughs at me and shakes her head.

"Don't worry, little Witch, I won't bite without consent, but think about my offer. I bet I could give you an excellent escape if you wanted it." She raps her knuckles on the counter and tucks the rest of the notes back in her bra. "I'll see you around. My name's Emille."

"Fallon," I tell her with a smile.

"Pretty name too." She smiles again and then she leaves with her vials. The bell rings as the door closes behind her, and I let out a breath.

That is so not what I expected from tonight. It's flattering, but I think I have more than enough to deal with without adding some hot as fuck Dracul to my plate. I've never been with a woman, but something about her was different.

Different or not, love, you're mine.

"So you keep saying," I say, brushing off the voice and going back to sorting out the herbs and candles that I have in boxes behind the counter. Thank the Goddess for that monotony to pass the time.

"Fallon, are you ready?" Mama yells from the kitchen as I slide on my necklaces—my talisman and my sigil. One exists to help boost my power, and the other's there to help protect me.

"Yes, Mama," I call out as I head toward the kitchen.

Tonight marks the first coven meeting I've been to since the one that Remy came with us to. The one where we revealed the portals we create and brought her into the fold. This was way before everything happened, and while it hasn't been that long, and I only missed one meeting, the thought of everyone staring at me, the questions, the looks of pity. It makes my stomach churn.

I don't want their pity.

I don't need it.

I want to move past it.

There's no moving past me, sweetheart.

I don't even bother responding. Mama will officially lock me up and try to work out what's wrong if she catches even a hint of what's happening with me. She's already suspicious, and she's watching me more closely these days. So far, I think I've managed to convince her that I'm fine, just a little scatterbrained. I don't even want to think about what she'd do if I told her the whole-ass truth.

"Okay, Rebel is at her friend's house for the night, so if you have plans with Colt or Remy after, that's fine."

"I don't," I tell her with a smile, trying to keep it casual. I put my hands in the pockets of my jeans so she doesn't notice the slight tremble to them.

Of course you don't. You don't need them anymore, you have me.

I roll my head on my shoulders as Mama opens a portal, she looks back at me, her concern obvious on her face. I smile at her, trying to make it as bright and breezy as I can, and follow her through.

I step out and into the clearing we keep hidden from the humans. Mama follows me seconds later.

"Fallon," she starts, and I spin to find her staring at me, curiosity etched over her features.

My hands shake, and I clench the inside of my pockets harder. I offer her that same breezy smile from moments before before asking, "Yes, Mama?"

"Nothing. Let's get started."

As always, Mama moves ahead of me, setting the wards and the ring of protection before we call the other covens to meet. I join her, helping her set the circle and drawing each coven's sigil in blood at an even distance around the circle in their respective places.

"Are you ready?" she asks, and I nod, taking her hand.

Our blood combines and pools to the ground at our feet.

"Vocamus matri et sorori vestrae Misericordiam adducere nos ut et in hac lunae iungere nobis. Inhabitare facit unius moris in unum sicut et nos venit. Sit dea."

I follow Mama's chant, drawing the covens here. One by one, the covens appear, adding their power to the call.

"Welcome, sisters, we wish you well," Mama says, as is custom, and the others repeat the phrase. The entire Witches' Council is here, except for Lizzie. I look at Mama who watches the empty space for a second but doesn't show beyond that simple glance that their absence bothers her.

"We have much to discuss. First, as you can see, my heir has been returned to us, safe and well."

"Welcome back, sister," the others murmur, and I paste a smile on my face.

Well, isn't this all a little pretentious. The voice sniggers in my mind, and I fight the urge to roll my eyes since everyone is watching me.

"Thank you. I'm well, as you can see, and glad to be back here with you all," I say, putting as much pep as I can muster into the words.

Mama launches into an explanation of my disappearance and subsequent return. The heirs all look shocked enough, so I guess Mama only told the coven leaders about why I missed the last meeting. The secrets this council keeps are ridiculous. I swear, if I become High Priestess, I'm going to change that shit. It isn't right.

You won't need to become High Priestess, love. You'll be with me. We'll be far from this place. You'll never have to worry about anything ever again. I'll look after you. I look after what is mine.

I ignore the voice and try to focus on what Mama's saying, but I don't want to relive what I went through, so I try to clear my mind until she starts talking about the changes happening now that the Hunters' leadership has changed so drastically. The others look excited at the prospect of the new changes. I guess it hasn't changed much with me being gone. I know everyone's been more than a little preoccupied with Archer and his bullshit, so it isn't surprising that not much has started to change yet.

"Our role within the factions will change," Mama tells everyone. "I've been speaking not only with the Hunter Council, but also with the King of the Dracul and the Alpha of Alphas. Unity is coming, but we need to get over this last hurdle first. I have shown you all my vision of what is coming. Prepare yourselves for war. It's coming, whether we want it or not."

The Witches all nod, the weight of Mama's words hitting them hard.

You don't need to go to war. I can keep you safe. We simply need to find a way to get my body back. I could settle for a new one, I'm not fussy.

I look at the ground as I clench my teeth. I really need to get rid of this fucking voice in my head.

I'm not going anywhere, love. I keep telling you that.

TWENTY TWO

I pace back and forth in front of the huge door to the manor. This house is fucking ridiculous, but not as ridiculous as how nervous I feel right now. I shouldn't be nervous. Remy is my best friend. She has been for my entire life. I know that nothing that happened to me is her fault. I know that on both a fundamental and logical level.

But on an irrational and emotional level, some part of me knows that everything that happened to me only happened because I'm her friend.

I've been blaming it on her. Not that she knows it, but I've avoided her for the three weeks since the explosion. I've thrown myself into looking after Rebel, working at the shop, the restaurant, doing stuff for the coven, and pretending that Azriel's voice isn't back.

Because, obviously, that's the rational thing to do.

I've avoided them all for the last three weeks. Hell, I wouldn't be here if it wasn't for Mama. I've even been avoiding Colt.

I can't be around him with this voice in my head. I can't do it. It isn't fair to him, not after he's been so amazing about everything.

Pull up your big girl pants and ring the fucking doorbell, Fallon, I tell myself. At least Azriel's voice is quiet right now. I couldn't cope with being here if it wasn't. I think I'm getting some sort of control over it, but maybe I'm just kidding myself.

The thought of any of them knowing, especially after everything that's happened.

I'm a fucking mess.

I take a deep breath and push the doorbell before I can talk myself out of it. I wait for what seems like forever, but is probably no more than thirty seconds, before the door swings open and I come face to face with my best friend.

"Fallon?" she blinks, looking shocked to find me standing here. I guess it's to be expected, all things considered.

"Hey, girl. It's been a minute," I say with an awkward wave. She stares at me, a little bit like she thinks she's seeing things, and guilt crashes over me in a wave. She shakes her head and then offers me a small smile. I paste one on my own face and force myself to breathe. I need to be okay. Fake it till you make it, right?

"It has. Come in," she says as she takes a step back from the door. I don't miss the scrutinizing way she takes in my appearance. "Are you okay?"

"I'm fine," I say, walking through the door like I haven't been avoiding her for weeks. I'm just being my usual easy breezy self. Easy-peasy. "I missed my best friend, and dealing with trauma alone sucks. Trying to get back to what life was before this shit show is almost fucking impossible. So I needed a little piece of normal. What's more normal than brunch and mimosas with my bestie? Plus, Mama asked me to come and set some new wards on the place. We drink first."

I'm really going to need that drink to get through being here. Especially if the voice in my head starts up.

" I'm so down." She grins at me and hugs me tightly. I stiffen, I can't help it, but then I chant back the whole fake it till you make it thing in my head and loosen up. What happened is not Remy's fault. I'm safe here. I have to remember that.

"Let's head to the kitchen, yeah ?" I say waving to the grocery bags I bought with me that are still sitting by the door. I brought all of the good stuff.

"Sure." She smiles and grabs a few of the bags. I pick up the rest and head toward the kitchen. I can't help but feel a little weird. This is awkward as fuck, and it's mostly my fault, but she's being weird too.

"This feels weird," I say as I drop the bags onto the counter. "It shouldn't be weird."

"It does," she agrees and moves to get the champagne glasses. "But mimosas will help."

"I'm sorry I'm making it weird. This is what my entire life feels like right now. Like everyone around me hasn't changed, and then there's me. It's like I don't fit here anymore, like I left a part of myself in the Shadow Realm. It's almost like I miss it," I tell her quietly. I didn't plan on blurting that all out, but there I go, spewing out the truth. Well, some of it anyway.

"We've all changed, Fallon. But you went through a lot down there, and maybe you did leave a piece of yourself there. I mean, Deacon came to Morgan to save you. You guys were bonded, even if it was adopted from Azriel."

"Sometimes I find myself missing him. Like I'm sad that he's gone," I murmur, unable to meet her eyes. I don't know why I'm telling her this. I swore to myself I wouldn't, but I've always sucked at keeping my shit from her. She's my person, she's always been my person, and she always will be my person. I hope she doesn't judge me because I *need* to tell someone. Maybe not all of it, but at least some of it.

"Deacon?" I shake my head at his name, and her eyes

go wide. Shit. I take a minute trying to find the right words to help her understand my own brand of fucking insane.

"Well yes, him too, but I mean Azriel. I know, it's the worst. He was awful. But there was more to him than that. I saw glimpses of it. The man beneath the mask. And his art… Remy, the depth of emotion he put on canvas… I just. It's terrible, I know, and maybe it's just a lingering effect from the bond between us. But sometimes, I miss him and the talks we'd have. I hated him, but I hated him so fiercely that I think the line blurred a little. It's the same with Deacon. He helped me even though he still bowed down to Az, but in the end, he fought for me. No one has ever fought for me like that. And then I see Colt, and I know he would've fought for me if he could. But he didn't, and I struggle to rationalize the fact that I *know* he was fighting here. I feel fucking broken."

"Oh, Fal." She stands and hugs me, and I sink into her. I'm terrified of what she's going to say, but I know deep down she won't judge me. I think it's why Mama pushed me to come here today. "You feel whatever you need to feel. I'm not going to think any differently of you, no matter where your heart leads you."

"Thank you, Remy." I sigh as I pull back, trying to compose myself. "Now, about those mimosas..."

"Mama, I'm home!" I call out as I walk in the house, only a little tipsy. I'm pretty sure Mama has a spare tonic around here to cure that anyway. I portalled here since my magic is slowly seeming less daunting. While I hate Archer with a passion, the attack on Colt's home definitely was like a baptism of fire to make me try to use my power again.

"How was it?" she asks with a smile as I enter the kitchen, finding her at the stove. "I'm making gumbo, by the way."

"Mmmmm, you know I love me some gumbo. And it was good. You were right, I needed to talk to Remy. I also reset the wards around the manor. Man, that place is so big." Okay, maybe I'm a bit more tipsy than I thought because I cannot stop rambling. I drop into the stool at the island and grab a spoon to steal a taste of the gumbo. I swear Mama's recipe is her best kept secret. She'll tell me coven secrets before she'll give me that recipe.

"Fallon Laveau, you know better than to taste before it's ready." She slaps my hand, and I laugh as I pull my hand back from the pot. "I'm glad you feel better. I knew you would."

"Of course you did." I laugh, and she smiles at me.

"You must've had champagne. You always bring out the sass when you have the bubbles. There's a tonic in the cupboard. I suggest you take it."

"Yes, Mama." I climb down and grab it out of the cupboard. I try not to smell the tonic as I uncork it. This shit is vile, but I chuck it back like a shot of tequila and swallow anyway.

Goddamn that shit is awful. My eyes water, but almost instantly, I feel more like myself again.

"Now, come sit and tell me how they're all doing," she insists, so I take my seat again and fill her in on everything Remy told me about what they've been up to. About how everyone is coping, or not, since Denny died.

"I should talk to Colt," I say quietly, and Mama watches me intently. "He deserves to know what's going on, and I feel better after opening up to Remy. I think I'll feel even better if I let him in too."

"I don't know if that's such a good idea," she says softly as she puts the spoon down. "Getting wrapped up with a Hunter… It's not our way, Fallon."

Great, I guess we're back on this buillshit. "You sound like Denny Bennett, Mama. Love is love, remember?" I tell her, firmly enough that she knows I'm not playing, but not enough that she gets weird about it.

"Love is love, I know. But Fallon, I worry about you. Hunters get hurt. Their lives are dangerous."

"Mama, all of our lives are dangerous. I'm not a Hunter, and look at what happened to me. Maybe it was because I was friends with a Hunter, or maybe it's because Witches are seen as easy pickings compared to everyone else. He makes me feel stronger, Mama. He makes me want to fight past everything else."

A look of sadness crosses her face at my words, but she smiles anyway."You know I'd never stop you from doing anything that makes you happy. I worry for you, that's all. I don't want you getting hurt."

"If you know something, Mama, you should tell me."

"I don't know anything," she says, picking her spoon back up and stirring the pot. "Even if I did, I couldn't say a thing. You know that better than anyone. Now go get your sister, dinner is ready."

I leave the room, glancing back over my shoulder at her as I do. She looks lost in space, and that scares me. But after arguing about this once already, I know this is the last time I need to tell her. I might not be ready to dive all the way in with Colt yet, hell, I might never get over some of my shit and ever be ready, but that will be my choice and mine alone.

It's been five days since I was last here, but when Mama said we needed to see Remy, I knew she'd see us almost instantly. The minute we arrived, a crazy Dracul woman pounced on us, but once we found out she was Luc's—

Kain's second—gran, Mama and I both relaxed a little. Her love of Remy and Kain was obvious, and Mama has warmed to her quicker than I've seen her warm to anyone. Nonnie even let Mama help her with dinner, which I understand from Luc is unheard of, and maybe the highest of compliments. So I've simply sat here with Remy, both of us nursing a glass of Johnnie Black. It isn't my usual drink, but after my Demon reappeared in my mind a few weeks ago, I haven't exactly been drinking *less*.

Kain and the guys are all around the dining table, shooting the shit, when I realize that Creek's gone. I've been so wrapped up in myself that I forgot that he went back to the Shadow Realm, but I can practically feel Remy's sadness that he's missing from this scene.

"You miss him?" I ask before emptying my glass, and she laughs. "It's all over your face when you look at them all over there. You might have an epic poker face, Remy, but those of us who know you, well... We know you. You don't let many people in past your walls, but those of us that you do, we burrow in deep. So I know when you're missing Creek. You had a similar look when he disappeared after his twenty-first birthday."

"Well, shit." She laughs and takes another sip of her drink. "I do miss him, but we're not talking about me. We were talking about you." I raise an eyebrow at her, and she rolls her eyes.

"I'm sick of talking about my bullshit. All I've done is try to talk about it, and it hasn't helped." She pours herself another glass and shoots it back before pouring yet another. "I'm broken. I thought I wasn't. I thought I was shiny and new after Morgan fixed my soul. I thought I could come back and pick up where I left off, but that isn't what's happening. There's more important shit to talk about than me and my feelings anyway."

"The reason you texted me earlier?" she asks, and I nod, knowing that the grim look on my face isn't missed.

"Yeah, Mama has been trying to get ahold of Lizzie for weeks, since we got back pretty much. Her coven has gone completely dark. Until we started hearing chatter this morning that they've been attacking other factions across the UK, which is their base. Looking at your guys, I'm going to say that it's either a lie or word just hasn't reached them yet. That, or it was the Hunters they were attacking, which would explain why I haven't heard back from Colt." I try not to take it personally. I mean, I have kinda been ghosting him, but I can't help but worry about him. Especially with all this going on.

"Yeah, I texted him earlier, and he hasn't responded to me either," she tells me, and her worry is obvious.

"Hey," she calls over to the guys at the table. Heads swivel toward her, as she bites her lip. She seems nervous, which is insane, but it still… "Have any of you heard from any of your clans or packs in the UK?"

Luc and Kain shake their heads, while Roman pulls his phone from his pocket and shakes his head too before frowning.

"Nothing," Roman confirms, and my heart rate picks up. Colt had better be okay.

"The coven based in the UK has been dark for weeks… Ever since you returned from the Shadow Realm," Mama tells them, her forehead creased. "We got word of some chatter this morning that they've been attacking faction groups in their territory."

Kain looks to Luc who pulls his phone from his pocket and leaves the room. Roman taps his screen a few times and lifts his phone to his ear. He growls as the call rings out, and then leaves the room too, trying the call again.

"Has anyone spoken to the Hunters, to Colt?" Levi asks, looking around the room.

"I tried to reach out to him, but nothing," I tell him, trying to keep the wobble from my voice.

I'm sure he's fine, love.

I ignore the voice in my mind because worrying about that isn't gonna help right now.

"Same," Remy adds, and my stomach churns. Something doesn't feel right. At all.

"You should try and call him again, Remy." His eyes stare into hers like there's nothing else on this Earth for him. I want that. One day. But first, I have to deal with Colt.

Remy does as Levi suggests, worrying her lip as she presses her phone against her ear. "It's ringing out before going to voicemail," she tells us all, and an alarm sounds in my mind.

"I don't have any reports," Luc says as he re-enters the room. "All quiet for us."

He sits back beside Kain, and the niggling worry in my mind screams.

"Has your vision come to pass yet?" Remy asks Mama, and I feel the frown on my face. Mama told her one vision because it wasn't set in stone, but we can't say anything more than that. We don't mess with the Fates. It isn't our way. Magic has a cost, and talking about more than that would cost more than any of us is willing to pay.

"You know I can't tell you anything about it, Remy," Mama says softly, and Nonnie tuts.

"Nonsense, if there is danger, of course you tell her!" She flings the tea towel on the counter and crosses her arms. "You want more people to die because of some Witch superstition. Pfft."

"It is not superstition," Mama argues. "Telling her what I've seen could change it, and then I can't help when needed."

"Ha! If you can change it, maybe that would be better,"

Nonnie counters, and Remy sighs.

"Stop, please. I know you both mean well, but arguing amongst ourselves isn't going to help anyone." Roman stomps back in the room as she finishes speaking, his face thunderous.

"My Alpha isn't picking up his fucking phone. Theron is on it now," he grunts, as he flings himself back down at the table.

"Everyone should sit and eat, then you can go and save the world," Nonnie says, ushering us over to the table.

She brings over dishes of potatoes, cooked meats, and vegetables. Everyone digs in, but the whole room is tense. We eat in near silence, and I don't manage much because my stomach is churning at the thought of Colt being hurt. If I hadn't ignored him all this time, maybe I'd know where he is or what he's been up to.

I beat myself up as I try to eat, but it's pointless. Remy pulls her phone out again and looks around the table. "I'm going to head over to Colt's to see if I can find out what's going on."

"I'll come with you," Levi says, standing with her

"You don—" she starts, but he cuts her off with a shake of his head.

"I'm coming. Something doesn't feel right."

"Is this in your Witchy vision?" Nonnie snickers, and Mama rolls her eyes.

"Nonnie!" Luc groans.

"It's fine," Mama says, standing. "We should be going too."

"Let us know as soon as you find something out?" Kain asks Remy, and Roman grunts his agreement at the request.

"I will. Love you guys." Remy smiles as she turns to leave, but I just make out that it falls before she turns away fully.

"If we hear anything, we'll be in touch," Mama says, and I smile at the guys.

"Sorry we didn't come with better news," I tell them.

Kain tilts his head in my direction before saying, "It is better that we know so we can do something about it. Thank you for bringing it to our attention. If we hear anything, we'll let you know too."

"Thank you," I tell him, and he walks us to the front door.

"She loves you, you know. She's bad at showing it at the minute, but she worries about you. If there is anything wrong… We know the scars that come from the sorts of things you went through. I was in a similar situation once long ago..." He trails off, his eyes going glassy, before he focuses on me again. "What I mean is that we all have scars. They show that we're survivors. Talk helps, Fallon. If there's anything more that you need… You're family, and we look after our family."

TWENTY THREE

It's taken a little while, but I'm finally starting to feel more like myself despite the voice in my head. Granted, it's starting to get quieter, so maybe I'm finally healing and my trauma isn't manifesting anymore. I finally caved and spoke to Selena, the healer in our coven. We all heal, but she specializes in it. She said it was most likely a form of PTSD, a voice in my mind, and because I hadn't faced my trauma, it had the voice of my captor.

Talking to her made me feel better. I realized that a lot of the hang-ups I've had are part of the trauma. She put me in a deep sleep so I could relive some bits and realize the realities of it. It's helped me realize that I was blaming Remy for a lot of stuff that she had no control over. Which is the other reason it was so easy to shut myself away from my friends, when really, I probably needed them most.

That said, I'd still like to talk to the Queen of the Shadow Realm if I can. I want her to check that the bond is definitely gone. It's not that I don't trust my healer, it's more that we've never dealt with anything like this before.

But for now, I'm going to try and be more positive and look at the upside of things. Which is why I've spent the morning at the restaurant, working the breakfast shift and earning some nice tips to go to the spa fund for me and Mama. Another bright spot on the day? I'm going to have a long soak in a bubble bath. There is nothing more healing for the soul than a bubble bath.

I can think of something.

I sigh at the appearance of the voice. This stupid trauma is making me crazy. "The only thing you can do to help me heal is go away." I say it out loud, despite talking to myself. No one else is here, so there's no one around to witness my madness.

I start the hot water and place my crystals around the bathroom to enhance healing and calming feelings. I pour in a nice amount of bubble bath before lighting some candles. Every girl deserves some candles with a long soak.

Lifting my hair up into a messy bun, I undress and step into the hot water. The mixture of lavender, jasmine, chamomile, and rose in the steam instantly calms me as I lie back in the water.

You can't ignore me.

Watch me, I think, smiling to myself because I've booked another appointment with the healer to do therapy of sorts, to try to keep working through the trauma. And in turn, hopefully the voice will disappear as I heal.

My phone buzzes on the counter, and I groan. I don't want to deal with the outside world right now, dammit. I ignore it, opting for relaxing even further into the hot water.

A few quiet moments pass before I hear Mama's voice calling out through the house. "Fallon baby, are you home?"

"I'm in the tub, Mama."

"Okay, just wanted to let you know I'm home. I'm going to go out to the herb garden and start collecting some things for a few more tonics for the store."

"Okay, Mama," I call back to her with a smile. A real smile. Maybe my first real smile since I came back from the Shadow Realm.

You smiled in the Shadow Realm with me. You started to like it there. You started to like me.

I reach for my phone, opening my music app and playing Kelsea Ballerini in hopes of drowning out the voice. I sink further beneath the bubbles. My phone buzzes again, and I sigh when I pick it up to see Remy's name. One day of peace is all I want. Is that too much to ask?

But I know better than to think like that. Especially with how much chaos is going on in our lives at the minute. Until Archer is dead, chaos will reign.

Remy: Can you and your mom come to the Manor? We need your special brand of help.

Fallon: Sure thing, girl. Let me sort my life out and I'll be there. I'll ask Mama if she can come too, but she's busy so she might not be able to.

Remy: Okay, thanks. Even if just you can come, as long as you're up to it. Are you feeling better?

Fallon: I feel much more like myself, thanks. I went to see Selena. My mind is feeling much clearer after.

Remy: Awesome, well you know where I am if you want to talk. I'll see you in an hour?

Fallon: Won't take me that long, see you soon.

I put my phone down and lay back down. Hunters. Can't live with 'em, can't live without 'em.

You could definitely live without them.

I pull the plug on the bath and start up the shower.

Knowing Remy and the help she'll need, I'm going to need to be awake, which means getting these oils off my skin.

Colt picked me up since Remy called on him too. I hadn't even realised he was back, and I don't know how to ask the questions running through my mind about his trip. Thankfully, his friends were already in the car, so I didn't have to talk much, beyond Colt bringing me up to speed on what was going on. They found Archer's journals, and there's fucking tons of them. To speed things up, they want everyone's help to see if we can find any clues about what the fuck he has planned.

Once we arrive at the manor, I hightail it inside, trying to escape because things are still awkward as fuck with Colt after our last encounter.

"Fallon, wait up," Colt calls out, and I hear his footsteps gaining on me. "We should talk."

"We need to find out why Remy needs us. There's no way she called us all here if shit isn't blowing up."

"Fine," he sighs. "But we're going to talk soon."

We enter to find Remy, her guys, and Nonnie all in here, with towers of books on the table in front of them. Creek's absence is glaring. The whole dynamic feels off, but I'm not going to say anything. Remy is obviously hurting already. But I get it, he needed to go back to the Shadow Realm. He needs help dealing with his new Demon side. They're the best ones to help him, and it's better that he spends the time away learning than risking him accidentally hurting the people he loves.

"I guess we better dive in." Kain sighs as we step into the kitchen.

"Oh good, we arrived in time for the fun stuff," Colt says, rolling his eyes. "I caught Fal and the guys up on the way here. Anything new we need to know?"

"Not yet, we were about to dive into the journals," Remy tells us all, waving at the books in front of her.

"I will start getting dinner together for everyone," Nonnie announces gleefully, and everyone shifts at the dining table to make space for us all.

Roman passes the journals down so everyone has one each. "Let's descend into this madness, shall we? "

I read until my eyes feel like they're crossing. It's useless. It definitely feels like there isn't anything that's going to help us with what we're looking for anyway.

"Uhm, you guys... " I look up from the journal I'm no longer seeing and glance over at Remy, who sounds beyond creeped out. "I think I found something. It doesn't make much sense, but maybe it might to one of you."

She reads the passage aloud, and her guys all curse around the table. Roman curses the loudest when she mentions the Lycans.

“Who the fuck is the Archiver?” Colt asks, and Levi looks alarmed momentarily. The flash in his eyes is gone almost as quickly as it appeared.

My phone rings, breaking the silence. I wince at the noise, but then I look down and see who’s ringing, and I know I can’t ignore it. “Sorry guys, it’s Mama.”

I lift the phone to my ear to hear screams and shouts. “Fallon, we need you.”

“Where are you?” I ask her, my heart in my throat. I feel like I can’t breathe as panic tears through me. Nothing can happen to her.

“We’re at the crossing. Come, quickly,” she says before the line goes dead.

“I need to go,” I say as I stand, my hands shaking. I have no idea what the fuck could be going on, but I’ve never heard my mama sound that afraid. I don’t even know why she’d be there rather than home.

“I’ll come with you,” Remy says without hesitation, and I nod. I’m not about to turn down help. I have a feeling we’re going to need it.

“Okay,” I say quietly and open a portal.

“What the fuck is going on?” Roman shouts.

“You cannot rush into whatever is happening without a plan,” Kain says to Remy behind me, and I hear her words as I step through to my mama.

"She's family."

I step out of the portal and into absolute fucking chaos. The clearing, which is usually an open green field, runs red with blood. There are Witches and Lycans everywhere, fighting with both blades and magic. I don't think twice before heading into the fray to try and find Mama. I see Remy in my peripheral pulling a blade out of seemingly thin fucking air and following me. I look back as I hear cursing behind me and watch as everyone who was in Remy's kitchen appears through the portal before it closes.

"What the actual fuck!" Roman roars, and a ton of the Lycans still, hearing their Alpha's voice. I turn back toward the fray in time to see a bolt of magic hit Mama, and she falls to the ground. I scream and run toward her.

"Fallon!" Colt yells, but I can't look anywhere but at Mama. There're too many people in the fucking way. A roar sounds behind us, and I spare a look over my shoulder to see Roman's midnight wolf tearing through Witches and Lycans alike.

I finally reach Mama and fall to my knees, sobbing when I realize she's completely still and not breathing. I think she's dead.

She can't be dead.

"Fallon, let me see her," Colt says softly. I shake him off as a wave of calm comes over me.

We've got this, love. Let me help you.

Light shoots from my hands. Brighter than any I've ever seen. I put my hands on Mama's chest, pushing the magic into her. She moans, but I keep going; her eyes open, but they're still glassy, so I push harder. She can't die. I only just got back. I push the magic into her until I feel like there's no more space in her, and she passes out again.

"Fallon," Remy says softly. I look up at her, but she doesn't look right. The power I felt in my hands starts to spread as I stand up. I feel incredible, maybe this is the emergence. Maybe this is my power. But it doesn't feel like mine. Not even a little bit. It feels good though. It saved Mama.

"I will kill her," I tell them as I look around the mass of people, and my gaze locks onto the coven traitor. Lizzie. I move toward her, the power inside of me growing. It feels like I'm floating across the earth.

"Fallon," Remy calls after me, but it's like I'm underwater, and I can't hear her properly. I know her and Colt will look after Mama, so I don't look back. I head toward Lizzie, instead, looking forward to the moment that I make her realize what an epic fucking mistake she made.

I notice absently as Kain and Roman tear through

people as they try to attack. Levi hovers above us, wings out, and the beat of them almost matches the furious beat of my heart.

Everyone tries to leave the field as Remy takes Levi's hand, and I know that they're about to change the game. I lock my gaze with Remy and nod, then push the magic inside of me outward, to protect those in my coven against this baseless attack. Bubbles of gold glowing light form around my coven members, like the glow that came from my hands earlier. I might want my vengeance, but I'm not stupid. If Remy and Levi can clear the field a little, it will be easier to hunt my prey.

Thunder cracks through the sky and lightning scorches the ground as Remy and Levi do their thing. The Witches and Lycans who aren't protected start to scramble, so I move toward Lizzie. Portals start to open, but the lightning stops some of them before they can reach their escape hatch. More disappear than don't, but there are more than a few scorched bodies scattered on the ground beneath us.

I smile because Lizzie doesn't have a portal near her. I move in her direction, and with a flick of my wrist, she falls to her knees.

"You will pay for what you did here today." I place my glowing hands on the coven leader's head, her screams sound tortured, and I revel in them. I never thought I'd like screams, but hers make me want to smile as I fill her mind with the blinding light.

I release her, and the Witch falls to the ground, screaming as she writhes on the grass. Remy drops to my side, where I stand above Lizzie.

"Fallon, you don't want to kill her. Killing her will leave a stain on your soul that you won't be able to clean," she says softly as the power within me starts to withdraw. It feels I 've used up most of my reserves and I'm running out of gas. Levi drops to the ground beside Remy, but he doesn't say a word. My sight begins to clear, and I see them both properly.

"She tried to kill Mama. She deserves to die," I hiss, the rage inside of me unlike any I've ever felt before. It feels good, like I should let it free.

"She does, but your mom is okay. Colt has her. You should let your mom decide her fate, since it was her life she tried to take," Remy tries to reason, but I shake my head. This bitch deserves to die. My mama would be dead if I hadn't saved her.

"Fallon," Kain says softly, and I jump as he approaches from behind. "Your mother is asking for you."

My shoulders sag as his words sober me, and the rage washes away, along with the last few traces of the power I felt.

"Go to your mom. We'll deal with the Witch," Remy says softly, and I nod.

"She's not a Witch anymore," I mumble. I don't know how I know that, or even how I did it, but I know it's true. I leave with Kain, knowing Remy will secure Lizzie to be dealt with properly by the covens, and go to check on my mama.

The coven leaders come back with us to the manor, opening enough portals to get everyone back through. Once we managed to reassure them that Mama would be okay, they left, but only after Remy promised no further harm would come to Lizzie without Mama's say so. The looks they gave me were scathing, but I honestly couldn't care less. My thoughts are with my mama.

I think I might still be in shock about what I did, but I don't regret it.

Not really.

Even if I have no idea what actually happened out there.

Remy takes Mama and I to her room, and we tuck Mama in. She plies me with chamomile tea and tries to tell me everything will be okay, but I can't talk. I climb up beside Mama, instead, determined to close my eyes for a minute, to regain my strength.

But then I fall into what feels like a never-ending darkness.

It's been four days since what happened at the clearing, and Mama's only woken once. She ate a little and then fell right back asleep. My aunt promised to take care of Rebel for a few days until Mama is healed, so I don't have to worry about her. I'm not too worried about Mama. She was basically dead, and the healing, the cost of using magic, takes a toll. She's healing fully, which requires a lot of sleep.

The voice in my head has been absent since the day in the clearing, so maybe my emergence fixed me. I don't know. I'm honestly not even convinced anymore that was my emergence, but if it wasn't, I have no idea what else it could've been.

The covens haven't said a word about what happened, so I don't have too much information about what's going on with them. Colt has been in touch, letting me know that the Hunters were sent out to try and track the missing Witches, so the Hunters and covens have been working together. So far, there hasn't been much luck. Lizzie's coven has scattered to the winds, and with access to portals, they can literally jump to anywhere.

Colt's been amazing these last few days. We've talked. A lot. Probably not about the things we should be talking about, but knowing that he's taking so much time to check in with me, and keep me company when the whole Hunter

Elder thing has to be keeping him more than busy makes me feel loved. It reminded me of before this shitstorm started. Back when he was gone and we would FaceTime every day. I feel like we're getting closer again, but it terrifies me. I can't lose anyone else. There is still so much we don't know, including who's leading this bunch of misfits and rogues. We don't know what extra protections they have in place, which is likely why no one can find the missing Witches.

According to Remy, what we do know is that whoever it is, must be getting desperate. They have lost their foothold with the Hunters, Witches, and Shadow Realm, and potentially the Lycans, depending on who it was they turned, their forces must be dwindling. Her biggest worry with that is desperate people make desperate, unpredictable decisions.

Me? I still don't really feel anything.

"Fallon," Mama croaks, and I rush to her side, grabbing a cup of water for her on the way.

"Take it easy, Mama. You've been out cold for a while," I tell her softly as I tip the cup to her lips and let her sip on the water gently.

"What happened?" she asks, and I pause, trying to think of what to say. I can't stop myself from letting everything spill from my lips. She doesn't judge. She doesn't even scold me. She just pats my hand.

"It's all going to be okay, baby. We need to get home so we can deal with this ourselves."

"Okay, Mama, I'll let Remy and the guys know you're awake, and then I'll cast a portal so we can get home. You should lie back down and rest some more until I get back."

"Okay, baby," she smiles at me, but I can still tell she's worried. "Don't take too long, there's a lot we need to be doing."

TWENTY FOUR

Since Mama has been feeling better, I've spent a few nights with Colt. Nothing has happened except for a lot of talking and spooning, but it's been everything I needed from him. The voice has stayed quiet, so I'm feeling more and more confident that Selena was right. It was just a trauma response. Now that I'm moving on and learning how to live my life again, it's gone dormant.

"Fal, you want some lunch?" Colt calls up from the kitchen, and I smile. He's been taking really good care of me. I stand from where I'm sitting in the third floor library of his house and practically skip down the stairs. He catches me as I jump into his waiting arms at the bottom. I wrap my legs around his waist and my arms around his neck while he holds me up, chuckling. "You're feeling better, I see."

"I'm feeling much more like myself. Thank you for everything," I say, almost breathless from the way he looks at me.

"You don't have to thank me for anything," he says, turning so my back is against the wall before leaning in. His mouth hovers so close to mine we share breath in the moment before he speaks. "I'm going to kiss you now."

His lips brush against mine, and they're as soft as I remember. He kisses me gently, like he's scared to break me. I love that he's being so considerate, but I think I'm ready for more than a gentle kiss, so I thread my fingers in his hair and pull him closer to me.

He groans as I grind against him before pulling his lips from mine, resting his forehead against mine. "Are you sure you want this, Fal? I don't want to rush you."

He pants as I take one of my hands and place it over his heart. "Yes, I'm sure."

His grin makes my heart race, and he kisses me again. I get lost in the feel of him.

"Shit!"

He keeps hold of me as we stride into the kitchen. "Now, where were we?"

A knock sounds at the door, and I groan. His eyes go wide as we hear the door opening, so he puts me down with a quick kiss and heads out of the room.

"Oh hey, what are you doing here?" I hear him say, and I laugh softly. He sounds like a kid who got caught stealing chocolate from the pantry.

"Good to see you too, big brother. Do you have a minute?" I hear Remy answer him, and my eyes go wide. Oh, shit. I start sorting myself out, straightening up my top and hair. I hear her laugh as she enters the room.

"Oh, hey, Fal. Fancy seeing you here." She wags her eyebrows at me, so I flip her the bird as Colt groans behind her.

"Hmmmmm, I was coming to see you later anyway, so this will save me a trip," I tell her and run another hand through my hair.

"So is this like a thing?" she asks, practically vibrating with glee, and I roll my eyes. It's just like her to completely ignore my attempt to gloss right over what's happening here.

"Shut up, Remy," Colt begs, and she turns to grin at him.

"Okay, for now, I'll zip it. I mean, this totally makes me doubly sorry for coming to see you, though." She strolls to the fridge and grabs a can of soda before sitting at the table. "You should probably sit."

My stomach churns at her tone. Something's wrong. Fuck. Why does everything have to fuck up when I think things are going to turn around? And why the hell did she have to rib us if something is actually the fucking matter?

"What's going on?" Colt asks unsteadily.

"I found something out this morning, and I wanted you to hear it from me. We're still looking into stuff, but I wanted you to be aware. That being said, what I'm about to tell you can't leave this room until we confirm it," she says, eying the doorways. "Is Bauer here?"

"No, we're alone," Colt says, and pulls up an app on his phone. "And now, if anyone was trying to listen, they can't anyway. I installed a jammer on here."

"What's going on, Remy?" I ask, preparing myself for the havoc she's almost certainly about to unleash upon our lives.

"So, I don't know how much you remember about the day Levi saved me, Colt. Do you remember when he busted in on the council and saved me, that he mentioned something about me being the balance? "

"Yeah, I remember," he says, nodding as he leans back in the chair.

"Well, I'd completely spaced, but I remembered it in a dream a few nights ago, and this morning I asked Levi about it." She takes a deep breath and blows it out, looking up to the ceiling as if searching for the right words. "Essentially, the reason he saved me from the true death was because the Hunter cycle was linked to my mortal life span. It was the balance created by the forces around us. Because my immortal soul was saved, the curse of the Hunters was born and so all hunters would be reborn—we wouldn't know a finite lifetime.

"That even in death we would continue on, either being reborn, or in Avalon alongside our ancestors. The Hunters were only meant to be a one or two generational thing. It was never meant to be a long-term race. But then Levi saved me."

"I don't understand what this has to do with me?" Colt says, his brow furrowed.

"Oh shit," I gasp as the realization hits me. The Hunter Curse was linked to Remy. No, this can't be fucking happening.

"I'm not a mortal anymore, Colt. It means that we don't know if the curse is broken. We have no idea if Hunters will continue to cycle now that I'm not a Hunter. It means that if the curse is broken, Hunters will still be Nephilim, but they will only have one life."

"What the actual fuck?" Colt shouts and flicks his tongue bar around his lips. He grips the edge of the table so tight his knuckles go white. "So, everyone we've lost since you became an Angel…"

"We don't know," she says, hanging her head. "I'm sorry, Colt. We're trying to get answers, but I couldn't keep this from you."

"I need to tell the Elders." He pushes his chair back,

but she puts a hand on his and shakes her head. I can't even imagine what is going through his head right now, but my heart is breaking for him. This changes everything. For him. For his people. For us.

"You can't, Colt. Imagine the panic. What if it isn't true? We need to wait until we actually have answers."

"And how fucking long is that going to take?" He shakes her hand off of his and paces the kitchen.

"We've asked for an audience with Michael to get some answers," she tells him softly, and my eyes go wide. *Micheal? Surely not.*

"Isn't he like, out for your blood though, Remy?" I ask, and Colt stills.

"That's the theory. But this is more important than one person. This is the fate of an entire faction. Our way of life is at risk. That is worth more than the risk of Michael finding out about me and trying to kill me." She closes her eyes and takes another deep breath.

"Remy, no," I argue, and Colt growls. I try to not flinch at the sound, but my heart is racing, and panic is starting to take over. This can't be happening.

"We need to know what the fuck is going on," Colt says as he continues to pace the kitchen. He paused near the island, hanging his head with a heavy sigh. He glances over his shoulder and says, "I don't like this, though. Is there no other way?"

"If there was, then I'd have tried that way first," she tells us, and Colt starts pacing again, murmuring to himself as if trying to weigh everything up. He stops and hits Remy with his stare, a grimace on his face.

"Then into the lion's den we go."

"Thank you, Colt. As soon as I have details, I'll let you know." She smiles at him before turning to me. "But before that, Fallon, I was wondering if you and Marie could help me?"

I've spent the last half hour moving all of the furniture in my sitting room to the edges. Before this insanity mission, Remy asked Mama for some help in trying to access the memories that are still blocked from her, despite the fact that becoming an Angel unlocked everything else.

Mama draws out a salt circle on the floor while I grab the bright orange tonic she prepared for Remy. I wince at the thought of how it tastes. I still don't think this is a good idea, but changing Remy's mind is like stopping a bull after you wave a red flag.

Painful and probably impossible.

"Are you sure you want to do this?" Mama asks again. At this point, I've lost count of how many times she's asked, but Remy just smiles at her again.

"Not all of your memories will be good. Sometimes our body makes them inaccessible for a reason. Not all things should be dug up," I tell her, handing her the tonic.

"I'll be fine, I'm a big girl. If I see something I don't like, that's on me." See, absolutely impossible. She rolls her eyes at Mama, and so Mama motions to the bottle in her hand.

"Fine, well you'll need to drink this. It won't smell or taste great, but you need to drink all of it. It's going to help you access your memories."

Remy pops the cork off the vial and wrinkles her nose at the smell. I do the same because *holy shit.* Won't smell great was downplaying it a lot. It smells like something straight up died. Remy drinks the tonic down, and I can't help but laugh at her as her lips pucker up and her eyes narrow. "Oh, girl, your face."

She flips me the bird, but I can't help but keep laughing at her. Goddess, that must've tasted bad.

"Let's do this, shall we?" Marie says, scolding us both. "Remy, you'll want to lie down and stretch your arms and legs out so you take up most of the circle. Just try to remember that no matter what you see, it's all memories. Nothing can hurt you, at least in the physical sense."

She lies back and stretches out like Mama told her. Her eyes go glassy, and I know the tonic is starting to take effect.

“Close your eyes, Remy girl,” Mama murmurs before starting a chant. It’s so low that I can barely make out what she’s saying. Remy goes rigid, and then her whole body starts shaking.

“Mama, is that supposed to happen?” I ask, trying to stay calm, but she doesn’t respond. She’s still chanting.

This can’t be right. I’ve never seen a spell go like this.

She goes still again, and Mama finally looks up. “She’s there.”

“Is she going to be okay?” I ask, and Mama smiles sadly up at me.

“Only time will tell, baby.” I move into the circle once the spell is complete and kneel by Remy’s head, ready to keep her still if she starts seizing again.

Remy is under for what feels like forever, but the clock on the wall tells me it’s only been fifteen minutes before she starts screaming. Blood curling, fucking heart stopping, terrifying screaming.

“Mama!” I shout, “we need to stop this!”

Mama watches Remy closely and shakes her head. “She’s okay. Just facing something.”

“Mama, this can’t be right!” I hiss, and she glares at me.

“She asked for this, Fallon. Unless she’s in actual danger, I’m not pulling her out.”

I huff and go and grab a glass of water because the

screams are going to leave her hoarse. She's gonna need it when she wakes up.

We continue to wait, but then I notice the blood trickling from her eyes and nose. "Mama?"

"I see it. I'm pulling her out." She chants the spell, and Remy starts to seize again. My heart can't fucking take this shit.

Remy gasps and opens her eyes, and I finally start breathing again. I help her sit up as she blinks so quickly her eyes start to water.

"Thank fuck you're back. You scared the fucking shit out of us."

"Why am I back?" she asks, her voice is little more than a croak. "I barely started looking."

Mama hands her the glass of water, which she sips, but she winces as she does. Mama hands her a washcloth next, and she looks at us both confused. "You're bleeding, Remy. It's why we had to pull you out. Eyes, ears, and nose."

She looks so fucking shook, but lifts a hand to her face and pulls it away. Her fingers are tacky with blood. She pales and uses the washcloth to wipe her face clean before finishing the glass of water.

"What did you see?" I ask. It had to be nuts because that was fucked up.

"It was like I was falling, but then when I opened my

eyes, I wasn't here anymore. I was in the front drive of a house I didn't recognize. There was so much fog and howling wind. It was creepy as shit, but the house was surrounded by trees as far as I could make out.

"I went into the house, and it was rotten, so I moved as quickly as I could. The door closed behind me, and then I was somewhere else. Harsh white walls and red doors lined either side of the never-ending hall. There was music, a song I recognized, but I don't know what it meant. Each door had a plaque on it. I walked the hall and found a sole black door, and the plaque was blank. Something told me that was the door I needed, so I opened it.

"I was enveloped by darkness. A never-ending darkness, but I wasn't in there alone. I tried to escape, but I couldn't find my way back out. Then I felt like I was falling again and woke up here."

She shrugs, like she didn't make the most ridiculous decision while exploring her lost memories.

"It should have worked, though of course you picked the one door that didn't look inviting. I'll do some research and see if I can work out what happened. Then we can try again," Mama reassures her, but I shake my head.

"Is that a good idea, Mama? I don't want Remy to end up hurt." My gaze bounces between them both,and my voice shakes. I don't want to lose her. I *can't* lose her.

"I'm not going to let anything happen to her," Mama

says softly before standing and taking the washcloth before leaving the room.

"Please don't do that again," I plead with her softly and she smiles at me, a faraway look in her eyes.

"You know I'm not going to make that promise."

"Fine," I sigh, standing. "I got you a gift."

I run to my room and grab the box before coming back into the sitting room. I help Remy stand, and we push the sofa back to where it belongs. She eyes the black box as I hand it to her. She opens it to see the five rings laid in velvet and looks at me like I've lost my mind.

"Fal, what are these? Please tell me they're not wedding rings," she laughs, and I join her, shaking my head.

"No, they're talismans for the Queen and her guys. They'll help contain their power so they can actually come here if they want to. If you want them to. I figured you all did so much for me, I wanted to try to say thank you somehow," I say with a small shrug, wringing out my hands.

"Really?" she gasps and hugs me so freaking tight. "Fallon, these are amazing, thank you!"

"It's okay, it didn't take too much time. I couldn't think of another way to thank them. Or to thank you. Everyone lost a lot because I got myself kidnapped."

"You stop that right the fuck now, okay? Nothing that happened was anyone's fault but Archer's. Maybe Azriel's, but mainly Archer's."

"Okay," I say with a smile. The guilt is still there, but a little less so after hearing her say it so bluntly.

"I better head back before the guys start to wonder where I am. I didn't mention this little detour to them."

"You're going to get told off," I laugh at her, and she joins in, winking at me.

"Yeah, but I really enjoy their punishments."

TWENTY FIVE

I put a small bag together. Remy messaged me yesterday once she got home about taking a trip to the Shadow Realm with her. As much as that thought terrifies me, it will be nice to finally try to get over the fear. It'd also be hella nice to know Remy's friends a little better. I told Colt the plan, and he insisted on coming with me, so he's on his way here to get me before we head to the manor.

"Fallon, Colt's here!" Mama yells, and I pop my head around the door frame, seeing her peering out the window. I zip up the bag and say a quick goodbye to her, telling her I won't be gone long, then run out to Colt's truck with a genuine smile on my face.

While I might be terrified about going to the Shadow Realm, I'm excited to see him again. Maybe we'll eventually be able to pick up where we left off yesterday when Remy interrupted us.

"Morning, beautiful, are you all ready to go?" he asks, that cheeky grin plastered on his face.

"I am," I say as I buckle myself in. I glance at him, and the look of glee on his face makes my heart beat a little faster in my chest. Everything's been so dark, twisted, and fucked up lately that it's a welcome change. "You look excited."

"I'm both excited, and pretty fucking terrified, about meeting these friends of Remy's but they helped bring you back to me," he says, threading his fingers through mine, "so I should at least give them a chance."

I kiss his cheek, and he puts the truck in drive. We talk about stupid nothingness on the drive over, enjoying each other's company. I'm quietly nervous about seeing Deacon again. Especially with Colt there. I have absolutely no idea how that's gonna go. Deacon and I were close, but then he was so fucking weird as we were breaking the bond. So I have no clue what'll happen.

But Colt's right, we should give Remy's friends a chance. They did help save my life.

We pull up at the manor, and Colt takes my bag as he grabs his own. I jump down, and we head into the house. Remy's gleeful voice greets us. "She'll be here any minute. Apparently Colt is with her."

"That boy is officially struck." Roman chuckles, and I laugh as we head into the kitchen.

"Like you assholes can say anything," Colt says as he sees them. Remy jumps in surprise at her brother's sudden, loud exclamation, which makes me laugh again.

"You decided you want to walk on the dark side?" Remy asks him, and I roll my eyes and head for the coffee machine. Their coffee is *life,* and I need that shit this morning.

"Hell yes. I have a new appreciation for life," he says, his gaze fixed on Remy as he refers to the bomb she dropped on him yesterday. "I figure I'm going to experience everything I can while the opportunity presents itself."

"Hundred bucks says the kid shits his pants when he meets the Horsemen," Roman says to Levi, who nods and shakes his hand. I burst out laughing along with Remy while Colt grunts his protest.

"Fucking immortal assholes."

Remy disappears for a minute before returning a moment later with necklaces full of her blood. When she hands one to Colt, he goes white as fuck, and I swallow my laugh. Poor boy has no idea what he's in store for. I take mine and put it around my neck as she pours a shot glass of blood.

"Uh, Remy, what the fuck is that?"

"It's blood. Specifically Morgan's," she tells him, and

he somehow manages to go even paler, clearing his throat as he puts the necklace on.

"That's the Queen, right?" he asks.

She nods with a smile while indicating to the blood. "You'll love them, I'm sure. This will take us directly to the throne room of the Shadow Palace."

"So fucking weird, and yet so fucking cool," Colt murmurs as Remy catches my eye and then rolls hers. He's such a kid sometimes. You'd think the amount of lives he's lived, he'd be okay with a little blood magic.

Roman and Kain walk through the portal first, and then Colt takes my hand and I try to not squirm under Remy's watchful eye. "You're going to feel like you're falling, just don't throw up," she tells Colt, and he rolls his eyes at her.

"I have this, little bit," he says before stepping through the portal, and I laugh as I follow him. That cockiness is going to get him in a real shitload of trouble one day.

We step through, and Colt falters as he takes in the throne room. "Woah."

"I know," I whisper to him as we move out of the way of the portal so Remy and Levi can get through.

"Mara!" Caleb rushes to Remy and picks her up off the ground. He spins her around, and she squeals until he puts her down. "Wondered how long it would be until you came to get your boy."

"I missed you too, ya big crazy."

"Who is that?" Colt leans down to whisper to me, watching the guy spinning his sister. If anything, I think he looks a little jealous at how much they obviously care for her.

"That's Caleb. Conquest. One of the Four Horsemen and one of the Queen's lovers? Husbands? I don't know what they are to each other, actually," I tell him quietly, and he goes quiet, taking it all in.

"You need to learn to share better, Caleb." Remy pulls free from Caleb's arms at the sound of Creek's voice and runs toward him. He catches her as she jumps into his arms and kisses him like she can't survive without him.

I can't help but smile. I love how much she's loved. She deserves it.

I twist my hands as I take in the rest of the room. It's only Creek and Caleb in here, and there's gym equipment all over the place.

"You brought new friends, Mara?" Caleb asks as Morgan, Killian, Bryce, and Malik appear. Their power fills the room, and I'd clearly forgotten what it felt like being around the five of them. The power is almost suffocating.

"Guys, this is my brother, Colt," Remy says, "Colt, meet Caleb, Killian, Bryce, and Malik, the Four Horsemen, and my friend Morgan, the Queen of the Shadow Realm."

Colt pales and kind of looks like he's going to be sick. He swallows visibly before getting a hold of himself.

Some of his color returns. "Hey. They're not as scary as you made out." He grins, and I laugh quietly to myself. He's such a bullshitter.

"Sure we're not, kid," Bryce says, grinning at Colt with enough malice that I startle. What the fuck is that about?

"Bryce, stop it. He's our guest. Any friend of Mara's is a friend of ours, right?" Morgan says, patting his shoulder before hugging Remy.

"It's good to see you again."

"Who is Mara?" Colt asks, and Kain chuckles.

"Mara is your sister," Killian tells him with a wicked grin, and Colt looks confused.

"We've known her since she was Amantara," Morgan tells him. With a wave of her arm, the room transforms and the long banquet table reappears, as full of food as ever. There's no sign of any of the gym equipment. "Breakfast anyone?"

"Holy shit," Colt whispers.

"I like this one." Caleb laughs and puts his arm around Colt's shoulders, leading him to the table.

I follow them, using Colt as my safety blanket. Because right now, my hands are trembling, and I need him. I hate admitting it, even to myself, but it is what it is. I don't want the others to see how close we're growing just yet, but I need the support.

"Tell everyone what?" Morgan asks Remy as they all

join us at the table, bringing us in to their conversation halfway through, and I'm confused for a second until Remy pulls the box I gave her from her bag and hands it to Morgan.

"I wasn't going to jump straight in with this, but since we're all here, why not? Fallon has come up with a way for you guys to be able to come to Earth without causing literal chaos. Obviously, you don't have to use them, but I was thinking that this way, we get to see each other more, and you guys get to come and see us without issue. Plus, if we get into deep shit, it would be awesome if you could come and save our asses," she jokes as Bryce and Caleb chuckle.

"The Four Horsemen save the world. There's a plot twist," Colt says, and the entire table laughs with him. He's handling this considerably well considering how badly he reacted the first time he met Levi, Kain, and Roman. I guess he's getting used to it. That or they haven't done anything yet to show him why he should probably still be pretty fucking afraid.

"Yup, the kid can stay." Caleb grins, messing with Colt's hair. I don't know that the world could survive those two being friends. It could be the most epic bromance in the universe, but Fates save us all with the utter anarchy and chaos they would cause together.

"How did you forge them?" Malik asks me, his stare

intense, and I gulp. I forgot what it was like being here with them. They're all friendly enough, but they're still a lot to handle all at once.

"I adapted a spell from Antoine's grimoire for binding a Demon's powers. I made it so that your powers aren't bound, just muted unless you want to use them. I bound it to the rings, rather than spelling you because a stone holds a spell for an infinite amount of time unlike a spell bound to a person," I tell him, and he nods, taking it all in.

"They should work, but we should test it," Killian agrees. "Bryce should probably be the guinea pig. He'll do the least damage if anything goes wrong."

"Oh, thanks." Bryce rolls his eyes and Caleb grins.

"Don't cause too much damage, please." Morgan groans, taking a sip of the mimosa that appears in her hand.

Remy laughs as Creek nudges her with his shoulder. "How have things been down here since we left?"

Morgan groans and downs the rest of her glass. "It's been interesting. The power shift on level six has been a real pain in my ass. Caleb has been down there a lot trying to help Deacon with the transition while Bryce has been working with Creek, but it's been a headache." She sighs, and Colt stiffens at the mention of Deacon. Awesome. I was kind of hoping that we'd be able to avoid him altogether. "Other than that, it's been reasonably okay. Not too different to normal, if you don't count the influx of Fae down here all of a sudden from Avaenör."

"Avaenör?" Colt asks, eyes wide. I stay quiet, the pit in the bottom of my stomach making me feel like I'm gonna be sick. "Aren't Fae just Demons?"

"Oh, I forget how limited the knowledge pool is for you guys sometimes. Fae aren't Demons. They're like distant cousins, but they have their own realm. Avaenör."

"Did you guys know about this?" Remy looks at her guys who shake their head, except for Levi who nods. Of course the Angel knows.

"Well, every day is a school day and all that," Colt says with a shrug before digging into the mountain of food on his plate. I have no idea how he can eat right now. My stomach is doing fucking somersaults. But then, I have a bigger issue with this place than he does, I guess.

"Well, since you're all here, fancy helping us round up some bolshy Droken on the third level? Callie is having a fucking nightmare. I do love me a good hunt." Caleb grins, looking at the others. I grimace, hearing about Remy's run in with the ugly-ass Demons was enough, thank you.

"I need to talk to Morgan about some stuff, but you guys feel free." Remy smiles sweetly, and the guys all nod their heads.

"Sure, man. Shouldn't take long," Levi tells him, while Colt looks like a kid in a candy store. Except, he's about to go Demon hunting instead.

"Awesome. Well, if you guys are done with their food, we'll gear up in the armory and then head that way?" Bryce asks, and they all nod their agreement.

"I'll stay here with you guys." I smile at Remy, hoping it's okay that I sit the hunt out. She smiles back at me, and I let out a breath of relief. Thank Goddess. Exploring down here is so not on my want-to-do list.

"Sounds good to me. Then tonight, we're celebrating." Morgan grins, and her guys groan.

"What's up?" Remy asks, and Malik looks toward her. I laugh at the annoyed look on his face.

"Morgan celebrating means karaoke," he says, and I gulp. Oh Goddess, no. Not karaoke.

"Hell yes!" Remy says, and Morgan giggles. "Where is Mireya? I want to say hi to her while I'm here."

"She's with her tutors," Caleb answers her, as he pushes back from the table. "I'll let her know you're here. I've no doubt she'll want to come and say hello."

"Good. I love her."

"Who is Mireya?" Colt asks me while the others talk.

"Their daughter. Shit." I turn to Morgan and gulp.

"I didn't make her a ring," I whisper, but Morgan smiles at me warmly, calming my racing heart.

"I wouldn't take her to Earth just yet even if you did. Her powers are too unstable. Even if the ring kept her in check, all it would take is one tantrum, and civilizations would fall." Morgan chuckles warmly as she refers to the hellion that is her little girl.

"Whaaaa?" Colt asks, and Roman clasps his shoulder.

"We'll fill you in later. You have to see their armory. It's enough to make a guy jizz in his pants."

The guys head out, and Morgan whispers us up to her private rooms above the palace. There is already a bottle of bubbly in a bucket of ice and three glasses waiting for us when we arrive.

"So, what did you want to ask me?" Morgan asks as she strides to the open space at the edge of the room. Logically, you would think windows would be there, but instead there's a free fall to the ground way, way below us. I move over to the leather couch and sink into it. I feel like such a third wheel right now, but it's still better than Demon hunting. Remy settles in beside me and smiles at me, but it isn't her usual smile. She almost looks sorry.

What the fuck?

"A few things, but I'll start with one that's simple enough. My memories, they were meant to unlock when I became an Angel. They have for the most part, but some stuff still seems to be locked away from my reach for some reason. We even tried a spell to try and retrieve them, and well… It could've gone better."

"Memories are a strange thing." Morgan sighs, sitting in the chair on the other side of the room from Remy and I. "If you did something in the life they belong to, to stop you accessing them for whatever reason, without reversing what you did, you won't be able to access them. But you won't know what you did because you locked away the memory."

"Well fuck me, that's complicated. Of course past me is screwing with current me. That is literally the story of my life this year." Remy groans and pinches the bridge of her nose. "At least that's some semblance of an idea as to why the fuck it's going wrong."

She takes a deep breath and leans further back into the sofa, and then glances at me again, looking guilty as fuck before she opens her mouth.

"So this question isn't from me but from Marie Laveau."

What the hell? What the fuck have they been discussing behind my back? Why not talk to me? It stings knowing that they've been talking about me, but I turn to Morgan as Remy keeps talking.

"When we were home, there was an attack from some Witches, and Fallon's power seems to have changed. Marie wanted to know if you altered Fallon's powers when you healed her soul, as the power she was using wasn't drawn from the earth but from within herself."

"I'm fine," I insist with an annoyed sigh. I can't believe Mama would go this far. "But she's right, the power was different. I don't think it was Morgan, though."

"Oh?" Morgan asks, tilting her head. "I didn't give you anything that you didn't already have inside of you."

"I think it was Azriel." I sigh, admitting a small piece of what I've feared. I've been mulling this over a lot, but it's the only thing that makes sense. "He promised me power if I stood by him. I noticed something inside of me when I was down here, after he said it, but I didn't think anything of it. I assumed it was part of being down here. Then when he died the feeling disappeared, so I assumed that whatever it was died with him. But when we got home, I felt it again."

"Why didn't you say something?" Remy asks, and I shrug.

"I had a lot to process. We all did. I figured I'd either deal with it or find a way to come back here to fix it. It's part of why I agreed to come here today," I tell them, leaving out the bit about hearing his voice since it's finally gone. No muss, no fuss.

"Okay, well, I can have a look at your power tomorrow before you go. If it's causing issues, we can try to remove whatever it is, but that doesn't always go so well. If it is something from here, I'm sure we can work with you to help you learn to control it properly," Morgan says softly, smiling at me. I nod, wringing out my hands. "Was there anything else?"

"Yep, though I feel like a total skeeve coming here and asking you for a ton of shit," Remy says, squirming in her seat. I can't even feel sorry for her right now.

Morgan laughs and waves her hands at us. "Mara, we've been friends for a long time, you can ask pretty much anything of me. Just ask, it's fine."

"I wondered if you'd look at my power again. I've worked some stuff out, not much, but some, with Levi. But it's like there's a bottomless well inside of me, and I don't really want to drop into it, without some idea of what's waiting for me down there."

"That makes sense, but of course I will. I've been offering since you woke up as an Angel. I don't know what had you all twisted in knots." Morgan laughs.

"She hates asking for help," I snort, not that I'm any better, and Morgan nods her head.

"She's always been the same. You have no idea how long she tried to seal the realm on her own before she asked for my help." Morgan rolls her eyes, and I can't help but laugh. Maybe the Queen isn't as scary as she initially seemed.

"Now then, I had plans for a relaxing spa day type thing today, you ladies want to join me?" Morgan asks, grinning widely.

"Hell yes, girl. I haven't had a spa day in far too long," I say, excited at the prospect, especially if it takes their focus away from us.

"Why the fuck not? We all deserve some down time. Let's maybe not tell the guys since they're chasing Droken, though," Remy says with a shiver.

"Colt will have an experience, that's for sure," Morgan giggles, and I snort out a laugh. I hope he's okay, but really, I know I have nothing to worry about. Well not with him anyway. Remy laughs at Morgan like she's picturing it in her head.

"That's the understatement of the century."

After a day of massages, facials, and utter relaxation, Morgan, Remy, and I started the party a little early. Morgan busted out the nectar, pouring some for all of us, though Remy already warned me about its potency. I'm sipping it in between glasses of soda, but it's still affecting me way more than I thought it would. I feel like I'm freaking floating.

The guys popped back about half an hour ago, covered in goop, complaining about their day versus ours, but they all looked like they had an awesome day nonetheless. They all disappeared to shower, and and so far, only Malik has made it back to the throne room.

Morgan is on the karaoke machine, blasting *Toxic* by Britney Spears, and I can't help but smile at her enthusiasm. Who knew Demons had access to Earth's pop stars?

The others start to filter in slowly, grabbing food from the spread on the table and pouring themselves whiskey. Roman braves a glass of nectar while Levi laughs at him. Levi's right, no one should touch this stuff. My head is damn near spinning.

"Your turn," Morgan coos, as she drops onto the sofa next to Remy. My traitor of a best friend shakes her head and points to me.

"Nope, it's Fallon's turn. I went before you." What an asshole. I don't want to sing, and she fucking knows it. This bitch knows I freaking despise karaoke.

"Yes!" Morgan shouts. "I get to pick your song. I pick everyone's first song!" She jumps to her feet and scrambles over to the karaoke machine, waving for me to come with her. I groan and follow her, glaring at Remy as I go.

"I have the perfect song for you!"

"Really, I don't sing. It'll be really bad. You should do the song, you're so good," I lie, trying like hell to get out of this. Especially when I see the title for *Girls Just Want To Have Fun* come up on the screen.

Noooooo.

Morgan thrusts the microphone at me, and the music starts to play. She claps her hands giddily as I start to reluctantly sing along. I get through the song, glaring at the others while they laugh, flipping the bird at Remy because this is definitely all her fault.

Morgan cheers me on from the makeshift stage she created by the karaoke machine. The dim lights and flashing lights make it look like a bad elementary school dance from the 90s where the boys stand on one side awkwardly while the girls dance together on the other.

The song finishes, and I rush from the stage as quickly as I can to where Colt is standing pouring another drink.

"Roman!" Morgan squeals from across the room, and I burst out laughing. If she gets him up there, I'll be absolutely stunned.

So when he struts forward, and she claps her hands, my jaw drops. She whispers in his ear, and he shakes his head, making her pout. He says something back to her, and her joy is back in a nanosecond.

"No fucking way." Colt laughs as *Livin' on a Prayer* starts playing, and my jaw drops again as Roman's gravelly voice nails the first verse.

"Did you enjoy the hunt today?" I ask Colt over the music, the sing-a-long having sobered me up nicely. Fucking karaoke.

"It was fun. The Horsemen are fucking wild. You

should see them when they work together—I've never seen anything like it. And the Droken are ugly motherfuckers. Green scaled skin, red eyes with matching horns, and holy shit their teeth. Fal, their fangs, both sets, were so long, they protruded from their mouths. It was fucking gross. They bleed green too. So disgusting. But the armory here nearly made me come, I swear to the Fates."

I can't help but laugh at him. He really is fitting in better here than I ever could've expected. I'm almost jealous of how casual he is about all of it.

Morgan has Caleb dancing terribly on the makeshift dance floor with her while the other Horsemen sit at the table she set up.

Roman finishes his song and Remy lets out a woop as Morgan rushes back to the stage and takes the mic from him. He bows, and Colt belts out a laugh beside me.

"Are you ready to ditch this party?" he asks, holding his hand out to me. I let out a sigh of relief.

"I thought you'd never ask."

I thought it might be weird since Morgan put Colt and I in a room together, but it was surprisingly easy. We both slept in the bed, but it felt okay. We slept, nothing more, nothing less.

There's a knock on the door, and Colt dashes to it while I finish getting dressed.

"Remy and the guys are going down for breakfast. Do we wanna join them?" he calls over his shoulder.

"Sure, I'm ready now," I smile at him as I walk out of the bathroom. We leave the room to find Remy and Creek standing with Bryce and Caleb.

"Where's Morgan?" Remy asks as Caleb hugs her.

"She's a little worse for wear. She apologized, but she said she probably isn't making it down for breakfast. I'm surprised you guys look so fresh."

"I didn't drink that much," Remy answers, looking over at me, and I blush. I didn't drink that much either.

"That's not what I meant," he says, winking at her, and she elbows him in the ribs. He picks her up, starting to tickle her.

"Caleb, put me down, you big asshole. Stop it!" she squeals and I can't help but laugh. The mighty Remington felled by something so feeble and insignificant as being tickled, but it's like her kryptonite.

"What's their deal?" Colt asks before Caleb whispers us to the throne room.

"Please stop," Remy pleads and he stops, but only because he's laughing so hard he's struggling to keep hold of her. She runs across the room and hides behind Levi and Roman while Caleb tries to pick himself up from his laughing fit. Colt and I laugh. It feels weird to be laughing so freely here, like it should be illegal to enjoy myself in a place that sets me so on edge.

"Seriously? How are they so chill?" Colt asks again, and Bryce clasps his shoulder.

"So, you know we've known Mara since her first time round as an Angel, which is well before we were the Horsemen. Back before Morgan was Queen, when there was a war down here. Mara was our friend, even back then. I'm not even sure that Levi knows that," he says as we all sit down at the table, starting to pile our plates high.

"Well, Mara didn't exactly fight in the war, but she definitely helped us. Anyway, Caleb was separated from the rest of us. Captured by Morgan's dad. He was injured, fatally, and Morgan's dad left him in the dungeons to bleed out. But our precious little Mara broke in, not giving a flying fuck about the King of the Shadow Realm and his very well-known wrath. She gave Caleb her blood to help heal him—good old Shadow Walker blood. She didn't know if it would work, but she risked it anyway, and then got him back to us. The blood transfer bonded them. Ever since they've been like brother and sister, always fucking about, always tearing into each other, but that bond has never broken. It's why if she bleeds on the ground here, we know where she is. When we powered up as it were, and became the Horsemen, we did a blood transfer, which means her blood is in each of us."

"Holy shit. My sister is a badass," Colt says, leaning back in his chair, and she throws a biscuit at him.

"As if you ever doubted it."

"Yeah, but I mean, Remy, that is badass. Like without you saving him, the Four Horsemen of the fucking Apocalypse wouldn't exist."

I blink because holy crap. I always try to not feel inferior next to my friend, but yeah... She literally helped create this world.

Mind blown.

"Yup, our Mara is literally my savior." Caleb winks at Remy with a smile. "Luckily for all parties, our bond never went beyond annoying little sister."

"Hey!" she throws a biscuit at him too. He catches it and takes a bite, and I laugh at their antics. They're kind of adorable, though Colt looks a little left out.

"You know I love you, really." Caleb grins around his mouthful. "But yeah, now you know. Mara was saving worlds long before she started saving yours. This place wouldn't be what it is if we hadn't had her help back then."

"Can we like, talk about something other than how awesome I am, please?" Remy groans. "Ready for your trip to Earth, Bryce?"

I sit quietly and start to eat, even though I still feel a little sick about being here.

"I haven't really thought about it to be honest. It's been so long since I was there, it'll be strange for sure, even if I'm only there for a few minutes," Bryce says before taking a bite of the French toast on the plate in front of him.

The room goes quiet as we focus on our food and the upcoming experimental trip. It isn't long before a childish squeal fills the room. "Remy!"

This miniature version of Morgan must be Mireya. She runs toward Remy who crouches down to hug the little girl.

"Hey, sweet girl. How are you doing? Causing chaos for your mom and dads?" She nods eagerly at the question, and I chuckle. She looks over Remy's shoulder noticing the rest of us, but her gaze stops on Colt.

"I know you," she says, and everyone freezes. The noise level at the table goes from a level below deafening to absolutely silent as she walks toward him. Colt looks beyond fucking terrified.

"Mireya, this is Colt. My brother. He's never been here before," Remy tells her softly.

"But I know him," she insists, and Colt pales even further. "I saw him in my dreams."

"Mireya. What do you mean?" Caleb asks cautiously.

"I saw him in my dreams," she states again, as if his question is ridiculous.

"What dream, baby girl?" Bryce asks, and she stomps

her feet.

"I don't remember, but I know I saw him," she screams before she starts to cry.

"It's okay, sweet girl," Remy says, pulling her back into her arms and hugging her.

"Come on, Mireya, let's get you to your tutor," Caleb says, standing and moving toward us. "I'll catch you guys soon hopefully."

He looks suspiciously at Colt, and it pisses me off. Colt didn't do anything, and whatever she's talking about was only a fucking dream. Bryce looks at Remy, wiping his mouth with the napkin on the table and furrows his brow.

"I guess we should get to trying out this ring."

I gulp at the thought, momentarily distracted from the situation with the little girl.

This had better not end in disaster. I don't want to be Enemy Number One on Morgan's list.

We get back, and the world doesn't shrivel up and die when Bryce steps through the portal. Remy declares the test a success and makes Bryce promise that they'll come here for Thanksgiving.

What a fucking weird morning. Though I'm a little gutted that with everything that went on this morning,

Morgan didn't get a chance to check my magic. It's not like it's long until they'll be coming here, but it will probably feel weird to ask when she's here for a celebration.

"You have no idea why that girl recognized you?" Levi grills Colt, and I gulp. This could be really bad.

"I don't have a fucking clue."

I think about saying something when Remy starts to talk.

"It could be anything," Remy sighs. "Colt's involved in a lot of what we do. He's been on our side the entire time; let's take a breath shall we, before we start turning on each other."

Levi glares at her, which pisses me off. Colt might have wobbled when he first found out about everything, but he's been here for her every step of the way since then. And the girl, Mireya, didn't even remember her dream. It could literally be anything, dreams are wild like that.

"I was thinking of going and seeing my folks today," Creek says as he sits down next to Remy on the sofa. "Want to come with me?"

"I'd love that." She smiles at him before turning back to Colt and I. "Are you guys heading out straight away?"

"Yeah, I should get back to Mama and make sure she's okay." I smile sadly, she was okay before we left, and I know we've been gone less than a day here on Earth, but still. Shit's been real weird around here lately

“I should make sure Bauer’s not trashed the house again looking for Archer’s journals too,” Colt tells her, and she nods. She stands to hug us both before walking us out.

“Look after each other, okay?” she asks as I climb in the truck. Colt grins at her easily. “Don’t worry, little bit. We’re good.”

TWENTY SIX

It's been a week since we got back from the Shadow Realm, and it's finally Thanksgiving. We're all heading to Remy's for dinner along with the rest of the people we consider family, and I can't wait to see everyone. I haven't felt this excited in a long time. It seems so silly to be excited over something so trivial, but it's like a little slice of normal amongst all the insanity, and I've been craving normalcy for longer than I care to think about.

This week has been quiet. I've kept my head down and focused on what life should be: helping Mama, looking after Rebel, being at the store way more than I should be, and texting back and forth with Colt.

Life is finally getting back on track. I'm beside myself over it all.

We get to the manor, and it looks like fall threw up all over the house. I can't help but laugh at how overboard Remy has gone in here. Though, fall has always been our favorite season... Who doesn't love hoodies, spiced apple cider, and hot chocolate?

Maddie and Nate arrive soon after us, with Colt and Bauer in tow. Bauer looks at me, staring blankly like his eyes are dead. It sends a shiver down my spine, but in the next instance, he's all smiles and the look is gone. Maybe I was imagining it. It wouldn't be the first thing I've imagined since I've been back here.

"Hey you," Colt says, taking my hand and pulling me away from the masses of people as Remy makes the rounds of introducing everyone to Nonnie and the other Dracul here, Roman's Lycans, as well as Morgan and her guys. As funny as that's going to be, I'm happy hiding away with Colt. "How you doing?" he asks as he tucks a strand of hair behind my ear.

"I'm good," I say softly as he wraps his arms around me. I burrow into his chest and enjoy the warmth of his embrace. He truly is my safe space.

"Good, I was thinking you should come over to my place tomorrow. We can have our own fun with some possibly naked celebrations," he says, and I laugh softly against his chest.

"You're terrible," I say, and I feel the shake of his chest

as he laughs too.

"Maybe, or maybe I'm just extremely creative. Is that a yes?" he asks, and I pull back to look up into those icy blue eyes of his.

"It's a yes," I say, and he kisses me softly.

"Good, let's head outside. The smell of all this food is giving me life. I might die if I don't eat soon." His grin is contagious, and I let him take my hand and pull me in the direction of the others to prepare for dinner.

I look around the table, at the mishmash of people here and the happiness in this room, and my heart swells. This entire room is full of so much love, and I'm so blessed that I get to be a part of it. This year, I'm definitely thankful for my extended family and the love we have for one another.

Nate clears his throat and stands, raising his glass. "This year has been one of the most turbulent ones I've experienced in all of my lifetimes. I'm happy and grateful that we can be here together as a family, celebrating this day. I know there are faces that are missing from the table, but I like to think that they're still with us. Here's to family and a quieter year next year."

Everyone raises their glasses in toast and takes a nice, long drink. Nonnie hands the carving knife to Nate, who somehow ended up at the other end of the table from me and has been designated as the official speech giver and turkey carver.

Usually it would be Denny's job, but he's noticeably absent this year. Bauer looks uncomfortable as fuck, but I guess since he's basically betrayed every person at this table at one point or another, it's to be expected.

I put some food on my plate, but Colt scoffs and adds more to it.

"That's a good boy," Mama says smiling. "She's not been eating enough lately."

"Mama," I groan, but I don't object. I start to eat once the plate is back in front of me and enjoy the laughter and conversation that makes this room feel more like home than anywhere else.

I groan as I take my first bite. Goddess, Nonnie can fucking cook. I don't know that I've ever tasted food quite this good, but I'll be damned if I'm going to say that out loud. Not with Mama around.

"Nonnie, you truly outdid yourself," Remy says from further down the table, patting her stomach, and there's a chorus of agreement.

"I hope you saved space. I made cheesecake." I laugh as Remy's eyes go with excitement. I swear, Remy would eat cheesecake even if she was mortally wounded.

"There is always room for cheesecake." She grins and

the room laughs.

"You and cheesecake. I've never seen anything like it," Maddie chuckles.

"What can I say? I'm one of a kind."

"You can say that again." Caleb grins, and laughter rounds the table.

"Shall we take this outside?" Colt suggests, standing with his hand on the back of my chair.

"Yes, let's get this party really started," Caleb says, standing too.

"I'll start getting cleared up," Remy says, smiling at the others.

"Do you want some help?" Kain asks her, but she shakes her head.

"I've got it. You guys all go have fun. It won't take me long," she says loudly enough for everyone to hear. Nonnie scoffs, but Kain and Luc make her come with the rest of us out to the gazebo. I notice Maddie hangs back and starts helping clear the table. I catch Remy's gaze, but she shakes her head, so I leave them to it and head off to the gazebo with the others.

"Let's get this party started!" Caleb cheers, and Colt whoops.

"I challenge you, brother of my sister, to a dance off!" Colt declares and I can't help but laugh at him. Mama takes a seat with Rebel and Nate, so I grab a drink but stay planted at the bar. I've been sitting down for too long.

How they pulled this off, I don't know. There's a whole-ass dance floor, DJ booth, flashing lights, and fully stocked bar. It looks like a fucking wedding reception out here.

I lose track of time, but I do notice when Remy rejoins the party. Creek catches her as Colt takes my hand.

"Dance with me, pretty girl?" he asks with a cheesy grin.

"How could a girl decline such an eloquent invitation?" I smile and laugh when he bows before leading me onto the dance floor. A terrible dance song is playing, so naturally every single person is dancing, and the drink is flowing. This has been the best day I can remember having in a really long time.

Colt catches my hands and spins me around before pulling me back toward him. His hand lands on my hip and we dance, letting the beat carry us away.

After a night of dancing, drinking, and laughter, I'm a happy, hot mess. Some people have started heading to bed, but I'm happy exactly where I am. I'm slow dancing with Colt even though the beat is fast. Morgan and her guys dance up a storm while Creek, Kain, and Luc arm wrestle.

From my periphery, I can just make out Bauer sitting down beside Remy and talking before they head outside.

"Should we be worried about Bauer?" I ask Colt, and he stiffens a little.

"Probably, but Remy wanted him here. She's a big girl, and as much as I argued with her about it, especially considering who everyone here is, she's right. Everyone deserves a chance. He's family, but I'm watching him."

"Any idea why he led Remy outside?"

"Not a clue."

"Something doesn't feel right, Colt."

"You're right. Let's follow them," he says, and we watch as Levi slips from the gazebo too. We're not far behind him.

We catch up as Bauer starts talking to her.

"No, Remy, it was all you from the very beginning. You set everything in motion all those lifetimes ago, and it brought us right here to this moment. It was all you. And I'm sorry." His arm lifts, and I see the glint off of the glass in his hand. I scream as he slams the blade into Remy's shoulder. A strangled scream gurgles from her throat and then Levi is there, with his hand on the back of Bauer's neck. Colt puts his arm around my waist and holds me back as Levi literally rips Bauer's spine from his body. The crunching sound makes me gag, and Colt curses behind me as Bauer's body drops to the ground.

Levi kneels next to Remy and bubbles them both inside a dome of electricity.

"Remy!" Colt yells, but I doubt they're paying attention. Lightning weaves around the bubble, lighting up the space spectacularly.

"She has to be okay, Fal," he says, clutching my hand as the rest of the party joins us. I think everyone is shocked still because there's a weird calm before the storm feeling that permeates the air.

"Remy." The anguish in Levi's voice hurts my very soul. "I can't touch it—it's Angel glass."

He lowers the bubble and lets Caleb walk forward, who approaches with his hands raised. "I have her, big guy."

Caleb leans down and wraps his hand around the hilt of the blade, and I put my arms around Colt to try and keep him still. He looks so broken right now, and I wish I could fix it all for him. "I'm sorry, Mara. This is going to hurt." He pulls the blade from Remy's shoulder, and she screams so loudly that I practically feel Colt blanch in my embrace. Levi picks her up off of the ground, gently like she might break if he moves too suddenly, and turns toward us.

"Fallon," Levi growls, my name nothing more than a command as he walks back toward the house, Caleb at their side. Colt and I turn to follow them when the sky lights up so brightly I can barely see. Colt spins us around when he sees the guy behind us, and we move to stand with the others. Levi passes Remy to Caleb, and he stands in front of us all as if to protect us from whoever this new person is.

"Move aside, General," the low voice calls out. "I will not harm her."

"Michael," Levi growls, and enough people around me gasp, knowing who that is. Holy fucking shit. This is so not what we need right now. Caleb grasps Remy tighter as Bryce, Morgan, Killian, and Malik surround us, with her guys stepping up beside them. If Levi gives so much as even a slight signal, they're going to fucking disappear from here. I can feel their power building, stealing the oxygen around us.

"Why are you here?" Levi asks as the light dims a little.

"I'm here to help," Michael answers him, and the light moves toward us.

"Then turn down the light, asshole," Caleb growls. The light must be affecting him too. The light dims and Levi moves aside. The man before us has huge, white feathered wings. His blond hair practically glows too.

"That's Micheal?" Colt asks no one in particular with a scoff. I get it. He's such a pretty boy. No one that pretty should be as deadly as we know he is.

"Give her to me," Michael tells Caleb, who looks to Levi. I've never seen him look so torn.

"It's okay, Caleb," Remy says, and it feels like the

world is holding its breath along with the rest of us.

"Do it," Levi grinds out.

"What the fuck is going on?" Colt shouts.

"Shush!" I scold him, scared for him. This is not the time to get all protective. Remy has enough protectors right now, and Michael could reduce him to ash with a look.

Caleb transfers Remy to Michael's arms, and she sags in relief.

"Hello, little bird. I tried to warn you in my letter to not trust anyone." He smiles down at her, and it's so warm and full of love that I feel a little sick.

I know I told Colt to shush, but he has a point. What the fuck is going on?

"I think it's about time you came home."

A blinding light swallows them, and I can't see through it. I blink, trying to get my eyes to work, but then the light disappears, leaving us in complete darkness.

"What the actual fuck just happened?" Colt yells, taking a step toward Levi as he turns back to face us. I'm pretty goddamn sure a riot is about to break out. Levi glares at Colt, and Caleb places a hand on his shoulder, holding him in place. I'm sure it's more for Colt's safety than anything, and I'm glad because I really don't want Levi to smash Colt like a bug. For my sake and Remy's.

"Why the hell did you let him take her?" Creek grinds out, his eyes are black and his fists clench as he struggles to keep a tight leash on the Demon inside of him. I watch, barely able to move as Levi takes a deep breath and clenches his own fists before releasing them.

"First of all, I didn't let him do a damn thing. Stopping Michael is about as simple and easy as stopping a goddamn hurricane." He massages his temples, closing his eyes for a second before looking back at everyone.

I'm not sure exactly who the biggest threat is here right now, but Morgan looks like she wants his head. Between her and her Horsemen, I'm pretty sure they could probably take it too. "But much as I hate to admit it, she's safe with him. Probably safer than she is here right now."

Shouts start up all over again, and I try to stay calm. This can't be happening. Remy nearly died. Bauer is literally dead on the ground behind Levi. It's too fucking much, and I think I might be sick.

"Why, pray tell, is she safe with him?" Kain asks. His sarcasm overrides his anger, but it's still there, flashing in his eyes and in his descended fangs.

"Because he's in love with her." The words leave Levi's mouth and silence descends.

Holy fucking shit.

"Of course he fucking is," Caleb mutters.

I blink in disbelief as Levi flies backward through the air. I didn't even see who hit him. I watch in horror as he smashes through the trees, felling them, before crashing to the ground with a groan. This is so bad.

"We need to stop this," I say, and Caleb snorts beside us.

"He can hold his own, they need to get this out."

Levi climbs to his feet as Creek, Kain, and Roman barrel toward him. I wince as Roman reaches him and tackles him to the ground before fists start flying.

"They're going to kill one another." I sigh.

"Nah, they're made of tougher stuff than that." Bryce chuckles lowly, while Colt stands there silently, looking between the fight and his brother's body.

Levi throws Roman off and jumps to his feet as Creek and Kain attack him together. It continues for a few seconds more before Morgan puts her fingers in her mouth and lets out a piercing whistle. When that doesn't make a difference, she claps her hands, but it's so loud it sounds like the earth broke in two beneath our feet.

"As much fun as this is, boys," Morgan drawls, "this isn't going to bring her back, and I'm pretty sure she'll be pissed as fuck if you break each other."

She pauses for a minute, levelling each of them with a look that I'm very fucking glad isn't pointed in my direction. She turns to face Levi and glares again. "You fix it, or I will. We both know which will cause less bloodshed."

"And you wondered why we were the protective ones," Bryce mutters, looking toward Colt, who rolls his eyes. Levi hangs back as the other three move toward us and then follows slowly behind them.

"We should leave this to them, Fallon. This might be out of our depths," Mama says, coming up beside me and I can feel the power and anger rushing through my veins. It's almost like it doesn't belong to me, with a mind of its own, and I'm not sure I can control it. "You need to calm down."

"Mama, I'm not going to leave them to it. Remy is my friend and means as much to me as she does to any of them."

"Fallon, you're glowing again." She sighs, and I look down at my hands. Shit. I take a deep breath, trying to calm down. I hadn't even recognized the storm building to a fever pitch inside of me. Colt comes back toward me, taking my hand.

"You are in control," he says softly, never looking away from me. "You can do this."

I close my eyes, and take another deep breath before I feel the power subside. This shit is insane.

Nonnie breaks through the crowd, heading toward

Levi with a wooden spoon in hand, waving it at him like she's going to use it to break him in two. Kain intercepts her with the help of Luc, who is also glaring at Levi. Pretty much everyone here is pissed, though some are quieter about it than others.

"Stupid Angel boy, letting my Remy get taken. Go and get her. Right now," Nonnie insists, but he shakes his head. "I said right now! Stupid boy."

"It's not that simple," Levi sighs, and I turn to face him again, while only barely keeping a handle on my temper. This isn't the time to go postal, though I do feel half an inch away from it.

"What the fuck does that mean?" Malik asks, and Levi flinches at the venom in his voice. He and Killian might be the quieter two of that quartet, but that doesn't mean they're not just as dangerous, if not more so than the others. Never underestimate a Horseman. Too many people have died doing exactly that. There's a reason they became legends, even in the human realm.

Levi runs a hand through his hair, as if to gain himself some time to gather his thoughts before speaking. "It means that I'm still banished from Avalon. I can't walk in there and carry her away."

"The fuck you can't!" Roman growls.

"I really can't, not without declaring war. And unless any of you have secret wings, you aren't getting in either.

Plus, like I said before, she's probably safer there right now." He waves to the bloody remains of Bauer to prove his point. "Until we know exactly who the fuck is behind all of this, Avalon might be a safe haven for her. No factions can get there. And if she's with Michael, well… He's the head of the Archangels for a reason. Though we can't take too long deciding what the fuck we're going to do because like the Shadow Realm, time moves quicker in Avalon than it does here."

"And he loves her?" Roman growls, his eyes flashing silver.

"Yeah. He has for a long time." Levi sighs.

"Then she's not fucking safe with him," Creek adds. "If he lays a hand on her…"

"He won't," Levi explains, barely.

"I don't understand," Kain mutters. "You said he loved her."

"Safe haven or not, you need to get into Avalon and make sure she's okay." Morgan looks at Levi, her tone brooking no argument. I'm fully Team Morgan right now. We need to go get our girl. Leaving her with someone who, until this very moment, we thought wanted to kill her? Yeah, not okay. Not with that wound.

"And I will. I'll head there tomorrow. I think, for tonight, we should let her rest. Michael will have been able to heal her, Angel glass or not. She'll still need time to recover from that."

"He can heal damage by Angel glass?" Morgan asks, her eyes wide. I gasp as Levi nods.

"He's a Shadow Walker. Same as Remy. Their healing powers are like no other. They can't heal that sort of damage to themselves. Nature's balancing act. He doesn't advertise it, and he doesn't tell many people because so many people fear the true power of a Walker. Plus, he has other powers too, so it's never really been questioned. I only know because Amantara knew. Like I said, he loves her." Levi's face turns sour, as if admitting that cost him something dear to him.

Colt moves back near the Horsemen and stares at what's left of his brother. His death wasn't pretty, but he didn't deserve anything less. I knew something wasn't right with him tonight. I should've said something sooner.

My heart breaks for Colt when I realize that he's pretty much alone now. He's the last living mortal of his family, and with the Hunter Curse broken, he's the last living Bennett altogether. Levi moves toward him, clasping his shoulder.

"Shall we head back inside?" Levi asks, pulling Colt's attention away from his brother's corpse. Muttering ensues, but everyone eventually heads back into the house.

I hang back and wait for Colt. "You want to talk about it?"

"No, I want to sleep. Remy's okay, but Bauer betrayed us all again. I'm fucking exhausted, Fal. Will you stay with me tonight?"

"Of course I will."

TWENTY SEVEN

After Remy was taken and Bauer's death, Colt and I have been practically non-stop scouring the Hunter's library located on the third floor of his house. He burned Bauer's remains at the manor and scattered them in the creek. There wasn't a Hunter's Memorial. After everything Bauer did to them, Colt didn't think it would be right, and my heart breaks for him. We came back to his house this morning after the cremation.

It's strange to feel happy with everything else going on, but being here with him finally feels right. It isn't like the past is all gone, but slowly and surely over the last few weeks, he's been helping me heal. He said he would, that he wasn't going anywhere, and that he meant what he said about proving to me that he'd changed.

I mean, I already knew he'd changed, but while I was gone… Remy was right. He changed. Don't get me wrong, he's still cocky and pigheaded sometimes, but that's part of his boyish charm. He really has grown up a lot. He has a whole new aura to him. Being thrust into the position of leading the Hunters because he's Remy's brother? Dealing with the constant threat level, which has most definitely ramped up in this life? It's all just made him stronger. Quieter. For the first time I can remember, I can see in his eyes the memories of his past lives haunting him now that he knows what he does.

It can't be easy for him. Colt was a badass Hunter in his own right. To have his belief system shredded the way it has been and then to be made an Elder on the Hunter Council? It's a lot.

Yet, even with all of it, he's been here for me. Every day that I've let him, he's been at my side. Reminding me why it's okay to come back to myself. Telling me that the fact that I'm different is okay because we're all different now.

Maybe, just maybe, what we had before was the start of something impossible. Maybe our broken edges fit together now, giving us what we never had before.

I watch as he tugs at his hair. We've been sitting in here for hours, looking for some way to get Remy back from Avalon. It doesn't matter that Levi says she's safe with Michael; the jackass took her, and I think Colt might finally be at the end of his tether. This has been a wild few months for us all. Between the Queen and her Horsemen, the Archangel Michael, and everything else, I think he might feel a little powerless. I hate the shadows in his eyes, even if they match my own.

"What were you talking to Morgan about? When you pulled her aside and you thought no one was watching?" I ask, trying to not be *that* girl, but after Mama and Remy talked about me with her behind my back, I'm a little insecure.

"I was talking to her about Remy," he says with a small smile. "I wanted to make sure that she was willing to follow through on her word of getting her back if Levi can't do it for whatever reason."

"Oh, okay," I say, looking down at the book in front of me.

"Why?" he asks, looking concerned.

"Because Remy and Mama… You know what, it's nothing. I'm being weird."

I stand and head over to the book stacks, searching for another book that might have some more information on Avalon in it when I feel his heat radiating against my back. I close my eyes and lean against him as his fingers skim across my stomach before he rests his hands on my hips.

"Tell me to stop," his quiet words send a shiver down

my spine as his lips brush against my ear. But I don't speak, I've missed him too much. I've missed the feeling of his skin on mine. I've been too afraid to let him this close since I returned. Things have changed, though.

I tilt my head to the side, and his lips graze on the skin there as his grip tightens around my hips. I close my eyes and gasp at the warmth and softness of his lips. "Yes, Colt. More."

His chest rumbles in response to my words, and I lift my arm and grasp his hair. I want him to erase their touch on me. I need him to eradicate the horror of what was done. I want to lose myself in him. In us.

"Fal, I need you to understand something." His breath puffs over my hair in a warm wave, and I feel him all the way down my spine and in my pussy. I shiver and arch my back into him—it feels like he's already touching me.

"Anything."

"You're mine. All of you is mine. *Mine*. I'm going to own every single piece of you while I touch you. Do you understand? Nothing and no one comes between us, not even your memories. Especially not your memories."

Every muscle in my body tightens at his words. It's hard because the thought of being touched brings back the memories of the pain I endured, but I need to move past this if I want to actually live. No more of this just surviving shit. I want to live. I want this with him.

" I'm all yours, Colt."

I take his growl as a sign that he's happy with my response. When he sinks his teeth into the lobe of my ear, I almost come from that single act of possession.

"Colt?"

"Yeah, baby?"

"I want to own you too."

"I know."

It isn't until he speaks that I realize I'm holding my breath, but his words release the tight ball of stress that has been building up inside my chest. It evaporates into nothingness. At least, for now.

"Turn around." I'm too slow with my movements as a second thought about doing this does a drive-by through my mind, but I push it away. I want this.

"Don't think," he tells me, his hand buried in my hair, his delicious mouth at my ear. "Just do as I say. You don't have to worry about a single thing, Fal. I'll make it all feel good."

I turn around, tilting my head back to accommodate the difference in our height, and I'm hit with the force of his piercing blue eyes. In this moment, he's real, and he's raw. Gone is the laid-back, carefree man that I've always known. In his place is a man ready to take charge. A dominating force of nature. Power drips from his lips as he curves them at the corners, giving me a barely there glimpse of the boy I used to know.

Slowly, reverently even, he slides my blazer off, discarding it at our feet. He glides his fingers down my sides, and goosebumps follow his burning touch. The motion is agonizingly slow as he teases me, hooking his fingers under the hem of my shirt and lifting it, but only just so. With practiced grace, he pulls the thin cotton material over my body until I'm free of its constraints. I'm left in my lacy bra and pants, and Colt hisses a breath through his teeth as he steps back.

"You're so fucking beautiful, it's blinding." His gaze leaves a burning trail of lust over every inch of my skin. I'm surprised I can stand it, but I'm certain it's because of him. Only he can make me feel beautiful when all I've felt recently is dirty.

"Colt." I don't have any other words to give, but all of my wants, my needs, and my desires are trapped in those four letters.

"I know, baby. I know. I'll make you feel good. Trust me?"

"Always," I gasp as he takes my wrists in one hand, lifting them above my head and pressing my fingers against the shelf at my back.

"Keep your hands up right there and don't move." I do as he demands with zero hesitation. The anticipation makes me wet between my trembling legs. Every single one of my nerve endings is on high alert in response to his soft yet commanding touches.

His fingers circle my wrists for a beat then glide down my forearms. Slowly, he follows up to my shoulders until he reaches the straps of my bra. He teases me with a light touch down my chest to the front fastening on my bra. Practiced movements make quick work of the clasp, leaving me bared to him. My heavy breasts spill from the lacy cups, and the way Colt licks his lips causes my nipples to ache with need.

I want to bury my hands in his hair, but I don't.

I don't move because that's what he demands. And the fact that I don't need to think about any of it, just follow his instructions, is the most free I've felt in a long time. Maybe ever. He lifts the bra up over my arms, lifting my fingers from the lip of the shelf before placing them back, and lets it drop at my feet.

With his hands resting on my ribcage, his thumbs barely graze the peaks of my nipples. The rush of heat that I feel is immediately aimed at my clit. How does he do that? Like there's a direct link from wherever he touches me to my pussy? I didn't know if I'd be able to feel this again. If I could stand any other hands on my skin, but now I know that all I needed was him.

From beneath the long black strands of his lashes, he looks up at me with a strange mixture of roguishness and downright filthiness. I want it all. I want everything he has to offer. I try to be discreet as I rub my thighs together, hoping to alleviate the ache growing between them, but the move immediately catches his attention. The grin that follows tells me that he knows exactly what he's doing to me. I should've known better. Colt always seemed to know my body better than I did.

He's making me crazy with desire and loving every second of it.

Bracing himself against the shelves on either side of my head, he bends his head and slides his lips against mine. It's a barely there brush of flesh-on-flesh that ignites a fire within me. A fire I was sure was dead. It's not. It's very much alive, scorching me from the inside with every tender touch he offers me.

"Colt," my whimper is barely audible. "Kiss me. Please."

I feel his conquering smile against my mouth in the moments before his tongue licks a path across the seam of my lips and plunges unapologetically inside my mouth. I feel cold metal against my warm tongue, remembering his tongue bar in an instant. I groan, the feeling decadent and wild. Our kiss turns into a battle of wills, ruled by a dominating intimacy that makes me feel wanted beyond my expectations. When his clothed body rubs against my nearly naked one, I moan into his mouth. He swallows my needy offering without hesitation.

And then he's gone, leaving me panting like I've run a marathon.

The fact that he's equally breathless gives me a sense of pride that I hold close to tuck away for another time. This is his show, and I'm happy to let it be.

Flicking his gaze to my hands, verifying that I'm being an obedient girl, he takes my bottom lip between his teeth before releasing me just as quickly.

"I want to taste the rest of you."

Yes, please.

His first stop is one of my nipples, his tongue alternating between furious flicks and deep sucks. Just when I think I can't take any more of the delicious abuse, he releases me with a pop of his lips and gives the same lavish attention to my other nipple. I'm squirming, and the sounds coming from my throat are more animalistic than human, which only serves to urge him on.

"Colt, I can't."

Abandoning his ministrations, he pins me with his demanding blue gaze and says, "You can, and you will. You will take what I give you. I need you to trust that I know exactly what your body craves."

Nodding, I bite my lower lip to keep myself from saying something sassy that'll earn me more trouble than it's worth. Though, a small part of me exists that craves that too.

“Baby, that sassy mouth of yours will get you spanked and then fucked until you can’t catch your breath.”

I want to be afraid, but all I feel is a level of lust I didn’t think was possible.

Colt returns to undressing me, finding himself on his knees before me like a servant to his queen. In one swift motion, my pants are off and my legs spread wide enough for him to place his head at the apex of my thighs.

My breath catches as he deeply inhales my scent and moans like he’s found his buffet nothing short of mouthwatering. I squirm under his gaze, which earns me a swift smack to my ass. Even with my panties still on, the sting is real. It’s heady, and it makes my pussy clamp down onto nothingness. Gods, I want his cock inside me so badly, I’m practically panting.

“I’m so fucking hard for you right now, Fal. You have no idea the amount of control it’s taking to keep from coming in my fucking jeans.”

“How about you forget your control and fuck me like you mean it?”

When I look down, his gaze is pure ice. The contrast with his usually carefree gaze is almost frightening. Almost.

I should be afraid, but all I feel is overwhelming lust. Maybe there’s something more there, but I’m not ready to name it just yet. For now, I want him more than I've ever wanted anything else before.

"That sassy mouth has earned you a long wait for your orgasm."

I whimper at his words. I want him, and I want my release. I swear one swipe of his tongue against my clit would push me over the edge at this point.

"Colt, please. I'm sorry."

His response is quick and comes in the form of my shredded panties falling to the floor in wisps. I'm completely bare to him, and the fact that he's completely clothed amps my desire to insurmountable levels.

"Now, whatever should I do with this perfect little pussy? Should I fuck you with my tongue? Taste every inch of you, feast on your cum as you lose your mind from what I'm doing to you?"

With a long, languid, lap of his tongue, he sends me spinning into space. I feel the warm wetness in contrast to the cold metal of his piercing gliding from near the pucker of my ass to my engorged clit that's waiting to be stimulated. But he barely pays attention to it, denying me any kind of lasting satisfaction.

"Or," he continues, his breath teasing my opening as he speaks, "maybe I should fuck you with my fingers? Getting you nice and ready for bigger and better things?" His cocky tone makes me groan, and I grip the shelf behind me tighter to stop myself from pushing my pussy against his face.

In an instant, he has two fingers inside me, and I can't help but cry out. My fingers dig into the wood above my head, and my chest heaves with the incredible sensation that he's causing inside me. Rubbing my walls, he groans at how responsive I am to his touch.

But then he's gone. Standing, he runs his nose along the side of my face until his mouth is back at my ear. His breath tickles my skin and his low, commanding voice brings me to the very edge of pleasure.

"Or maybe I should drop my jeans and bury my dick so deep inside you, your body memorizes me. Memorizes the feel of me pounding that pretty little pussy to within an inch of its life. You'll feel me for days. Weeks. Is that what you want, Fallon?"

I'm deadass panting now. My entire body feels on the verge of exploding without even being touched.

"Whatever you want, Colt. I want it all. I want you."

"Good answer, baby."

The sound of his zipper is like music to my ears. My eyes are closed because I can't trust myself to look at him. He's so fucking gorgeous that I might come from the sight of him alone.

"Look at me, Fal. Don't hide from this. Never hide from me, do you understand? I'm about to own you, and you need to look in my eyes while I do it."

When he uses that deep, rumbling tone of voice, all I can do is obey. I open my eyes, and the relief and pride I see reflected in his depths is humbling. There's a vulnerability to his tough exterior that draws me even closer to him. I realize that no matter the façade he uses, Colt is constantly on guard. He keeps permanent armor in place at all times. Being carefree gives him his unthreatening aura, which is far from the truth of what he really is. But this domineering side he's showing me is also a way of protecting the soft spot inside of him that so few get to see. The fact that I see it gives me all the push I need to let myself go. Let myself trust him. Let myself absorb the pleasure he's so intent on offering me.

"Own me, then, Colt. I'm yours."

Suddenly, his t-shirt is over his head and flying through the air, revealing his colorful chest to me. I swear I groan at the sight of his abs and the V that seems to make girls stupid. It gets me good, and he grins at me, like he knows just what he does to me.

He moves back toward me, almost too slowly. I tremble with anticipation as he reaches for my thighs, spreading me wide and lifting me high enough for me to wrap my legs around his waist. The rock-hard planes of his chest and the bars through his nipples are flush against my softer curves. I hear his jeans hit the floor, and his weight shifts from one foot to the other while he holds me up. I look down, my eyes drawn to the monster cock that rests against his stomach, hard, velvety, and angry with lust. But that's not what catches my eye.

I mean, it does because holy fuck how did that thing fit in my pussy before? No, what has me gasping is the twin rows of silver studs, sizes varying as they move up his shaft, drawing a path all the way to his bulbous head. That's sure as fuck new.

"Colt?"

He chuckles, angling his hips and rubbing himself against my wetness.

"It's called a Jacob's Ladder. Don't worry, baby. You're so wet, it'll feel amazing rubbing against the walls of your pussy."

He doesn't impale me, but rather slides his monster cock along my soaked lips. I ride him, practically begging for him to thrust inside me. The determination on his face tells me a million different things. He's making sure I'm desperate for him before he gives it to me. Making sure I'm wet enough to take him without hurting me. Making sure he keeps his promise of delayed gratification.

Colt has always been a man of his word.

"Please, Colt. Please, fuck me."

His lips curl into a damn near predatory grin. He balances me against the bookshelf and lines his cock up before sliding into me, stilling as my body adjusts to his size. It takes a minute for my mind to come back to me. He's so goddamn big, so thick and hard that I can feel every ridge of his huge, pierced dick.

"Yes, yes, yes." I chant the words but don't really know if I'm saying them in my head or out loud.

But when Colt begins moving inside me, I suck in a breath, almost choking on the perfection of the moment. Holding me against the shelves, his hands on my ass, like I weigh nearly nothing at all, he fucks me with sure, rough thrusts. The breath is beaten from my lungs every time he pounds back inside me. The feeling is so raw, so complete, that I almost forget where I am, and why I'm here in the first place. I damn near forget who I am and live in this moment alone with him.

"You feel so ridiculously good, Fal. So fucking good that I don't ever want to stop. Let go of the shelf. Now."

I do as he tells me and within a second, we're moving. Colt walks and fucks me at the same time. It's inconceivable that he could have that much rhythm. Every once in a while, he slams me against a flat surface and pumps his cock inside me a couple of times before we're on the move again. By the time we reach the stairs, I'm practically screaming with ecstasy, my orgasm possessing my very soul and making my voice burst through the open spaces of the house.

Still, Colt keeps on fucking me like an animal. He's sweating, and the sheen covering his skin makes his piercings glimmer in the light.

He pulls out of me, still hard, for the minute it takes for him to carry me downstairs, but then he's back inside me, his mouth owning my mouth. His fingers dig into the flesh of my ass. He's fucking me everywhere, taking the breath right out of my body and soul.

By the time we reach his bedroom, I'm coming again, my clit raw from his pelvis rubbing up against me every time he walks, every time he slams into me.

We fall on to his bed, and he pulls out of me once more. I don't know how he's controlling himself like this. I've come twice already, and he's pounding me like he has all fucking day.

"One more, baby. Give it to me."

That's when his tongue plunges back inside me, the barbell caressing me. He devours me like a beast that hasn't eaten in weeks. He licks, bites, and sucks every inch of me. He laps at my lips, drinking in my orgasms before sucking on my clit and building me up yet again. When he adds two fingers to the mix, I lose my goddamn mind. My back arches, my fists gather the sheets between my fingers, and my scream probably wakes up the Shadow Realm and beyond.

I lose my fucking mind.

And then, before I'm even half through with my orgasm, he impales me and fucks himself to orgasm while my pussy squeezes down on his cock.

I open my eyes in time to watch him lose control.

Colt throwing his head back, his eyes closed with pleasure, his mouth open on a silent cry is a beautiful sight. His chest heaves with his climax, sweat dripping from his skin, and he leans down to kiss me like he needs it more than he needs air. He pulls out of me, rolling off the bed and disappearing from the room. I'm too boneless to protest… or move. He comes back after a short moment and uses a warm cloth to clean me up before climbing into the bed beside me and pulling me onto his chest.

I snuggle into him, feeling safer than I have in a long time while he strokes my hair. "Sleep, Fal. I've got you."

TWENTY EIGHT

It's been two days since Remy was taken. Colt is still holed up in his library, avoiding his grief, but I needed some time to check on Mama and Rebel, so he dropped me off at home this morning. I've spent most of the day playing with Rebel, but she's off to dance class now, and I'm finally alone.

I'm exhausted.

You'd think that I'd be used to it by now, but our lives are getting more and more insane with each day that passes. Who would've thought a year ago that this is where we'd be? With Angels in our lives and the factions coming together. Fucking Archangels keep kidnapping my best friend.

It's all beyond frustrating. If Michael can save Remy's

life, awesome. But he needs to give her the fuck back. I know Levi is working on it, but Morgan's threat was real, at least according to Colt.

A knock at the back door makes me jump, so I put my head around the frame of my bedroom door and nearly swallow my tongue when I see who's standing there.

Deacon.

I take a deep breath and lean back against the wall. Why the fuck is he here?

You don't have to answer the door, pet. Ignore him, he'll go away.

No, this can't be happening. Deacon is here, and the fucking voice is back. Fucking no.

"I know you're in there, Fallon, I saw you," Deacon calls out, and I curse. Of course he fucking did. I take another deep breath and head to the back door, wrenching it open and coming face-to-face with him. His hair is longer, and he looks tired, but he also looks struck.

"Hi," I say awkwardly. What else does a girl say to a Demon who turns up on her doorstep?

"Hey," he answers with an awkward wave.

"What are you doing here?" I lean against the doorjamb while he scratches the back of his neck.

"Can we sit?" he asks, motioning to the chairs we have on the back porch.

"Sure," I say, closing the door firmly behind me and

padding over to one of the chairs. I curl up in it, my knees pressing against my chest as I wrap my arms around them. I'd like to say I'm not trying to protect myself, but I'd be lying. I know Deacon helped me, but there's a small part of me that can't forget what he did to me before that. Even though I know he had no choice.

"I heard you were in the Realm, and I missed you. So I thought I'd come and talk to you here, but I couldn't come till Morgan and the others were back. Then I heard there were some fireworks over here, and I wanted to give you some space; but honestly, I couldn't wait any longer." He pauses, watching me closely, and I get this feeling, like everything is about to change.

"Fallon, I know we've been through so much, but I miss you. I needed to know that you were okay. I needed to see it with my own eyes. I haven't been able to get anything done because I can't stop thinking about you." My eyes go wide at his words, and my stupid-ass heart races in my chest. "Let me help you heal. I know we have shit to overcome, but I don't see a future that doesn't have you in it."

"I—" I start, but he shakes his head.

"I know, it's a lot. It's why I've stayed away. I know you have a life here, but I couldn't keep away. I couldn't not tell you."

"Deacon, I need space. Time. Things have happened

since I came back."

"I know. The Hunter. I know all about him. But that's not enough for me to give up. I'll give you space, and I'll give you time, but I'm not going anywhere. I'm not giving up. I've never felt like this. Not in my entire existence. I know I need to earn your forgiveness and pay my penance, and I swear I will. To you, for the rest of our lives. The way I feel, it isn't going to go away. I tried to ignore it, and yet, here I am."

Of course he's here now. Declaring his undying love. He wants what he knows is mine, pet. Ignore this wanker.

"Shut up," I mumble, and Deacon's smile falls from his face. "No, I wasn't talking to you," I tell him, blushing.

"What?" he asks, and I sigh. At least I can make him go away. He's seen me at my worst, so he can't think I'm any more crazy.

"I have a voice in my head. I've had it since I came back. It sounds like Az." He pales at my words but doesn't interrupt me. "I think it's a trauma manifestation. It went away and has been gone until now."

"Have you spoken to Morgan about this?" he asks, a tremor in his voice.

"No, I haven't told anyone else."

He stands and holds out his hand. "You need to come with me."

He takes me through a portal to the Shadow Realm, and we arrive at the Shadow Palace. I guess Morgan knew he was coming to see me because she and Remy sealed these portals. How else would he get through? He strides through the palace, his hand still wrapped around mine, and bursts into the throne room.

Morgan and the Horsemen are sitting with Mireya around a small dining table, and I immediately want the ground to swallow me up. This isn't exactly what I had in mind when I mentioned my crazy-ass trauma-voice to him.

"Sorry to interrupt, but we need to talk to you," Deacon says, his gaze never leaving Morgan.

"Come on, sweetness. Let's go see if we can find some ice cream," Malik says to Mireya, taking her hand. They disappear from sight before the little girl has a chance to say a word in protest.

"Nice to see you again, Fallon," Morgan says with a tight smile. "Which of you wants to explain why you burst in on one of the few dinners I've managed to have with my daughter in a while?"

"Tell her what you told me." Deacon demands, urging me forward.

"Is this about your power? I know we didn't get a chance to check you with everything that's been going on, but it shouldn't be a major problem," she says, and Caleb frowns beside her. Bryce and Killian glare at us. I want to shrivel up and fucking die right now. I'm so mortified.

"No, not quite," I manage, my mouth as dry as the goddamn Sahara. This is not what I wanted to do today. Fuck my life. Without Remy here, these guys are kind of terrifying. "I have a voice in my mind. That no one else can hear," I start, and Morgan frowns even harder. "It sounds like Azriel, but like I told Deacon, I think it's a manifestation of the trauma from everything I went through. The voice went away until Deacon appeared at my house today."

"The voice was there as soon as you left here? But not before?" Bryce asks, and I nod.

"On its own, I wouldn't worry. Same with the strange extra power, but together it's definitely worrisome. Can you hear the voice now?" Morgan asks, and I gulp.

"Not right now, no."

"If he bound his soul to hers, she won't hear it here. She's altered here. It would explain why the power and the voice only appeared back on Earth," Deacon says, and Killian nods.

"He's right. It makes sense, but I thought you broke the bond."

"I did," Deacon tells him before looking back to Morgan. "You severed the last ties, but you know as well as I do, without knowing the exact binding he did, he could've done this and it might've been missed."

"Wait, you're trying to tell me his soul is attached to mine?" I ask, trying to not freak the fuck out.

"It's possible. I need to check you out, but at least you're safe here because he won't be able to reach you. That being said, I'm going to need to check you back on Earth to be certain. It's a good thing we decided to keep these rings of yours on." She sighs, and Caleb takes her hand.

"I'll come with you. I'm not letting you leave here alone." He looks at her, like his world starts and stops with her. Considering everything I've seen and heard, it's probably his truth.

"You know I don't need a guard, but you can come if you want to. We can get an update on Remy from Levi too. Okay, let's do this, I guess. Bryce, Killian, please say goodnight to Mireya for me. Hopefully I'll be back before she wakes up tomorrow."

"Of course," Bryce says, standing and kissing her gently. Killian does the same and then they both disappear from the room.

Morgan moves toward us, Caleb at her side, and Deacon grips my hand tighter as she looks me over. "Let's get to it."

We arrive back at my house, and I've never been more glad that Mama is so distracted with Coven business. I'm pretty sure she'd have a conniption about Demons stomping all over her house.

Oh love, why did you have to get them involved? I'm not going anywhere.

"He's back," I whisper, trying to stop my hands from shaking. This is fucking insane. I mean, I knew it was a possibility, but I'd really hoped it really was just the trauma. That's how fucked up my life is. I'd earnestly hoped for a trauma response. Fuck my life.

"Hmmmm," Morgan sighs and takes both of my hands. I feel as her power creeps over my skin. It's like little zaps of electricity as it makes its way over my entire body. She frowns, her eyes closed, but then her power pulls back and she looks to Caleb. I can't tell exactly what their shared look says, but it doesn't look good.

"Deacon was right," she says softly, "a part of Azriel's soul is attached to yours."

"Can we get rid of it?" I ask, trying to not sound as hysterical as I feel.

"I'm not sure, but definitely not without damaging you more than you already are. There are holes, and I'm not sure how to fix them right now. My biggest worry, though, is the power in you. It's definitely not yours, but he seems to be feeding on it. Every time you use the power he gifted you, it gives him a stronger foothold."

"Holy shit." I fall back into one of the chairs on the porch, trying not to lose my shit. This can't be happening.

"I'm going to look into this, Fallon. We will do everything we can to help you. But you need to be careful."

"I don't even know when I'm using that power though. I barely feel it. I've only realized once others have told me I'm doing it."

"I can help you learn some control," Deacon offers. "I can stay here for a while, or you can come back with us."

"I can't go back there. I have too much going on here. I can't leave everything behind," I tell him, and his face falls. But I have Mama and Rebel here. Plus, there's everything that's going on with Remy. Not to mention what I have with Colt. I can't abandon all of that.

"I'm sure your friends would understand considering the circumstances," Deacon sighs. "But I won't push."

"Fallon, if you don't come back with us, I have to stress how careful you must be," Morgan says, watching me closely. "Because if you're not careful, and you use that magic too much, he'll grow stronger."

"What does that even mean?" I ask, trying to not freak out. I'm failing epically.

Morgan moves to sit beside me and takes my hand. Her

voice is gentle as she explains, “It means that he’ll grow strong enough to take control and take you over. Fallon, if that happens, then you’ll completely lose yourself forever. There’s no coming back from that.”

ABOUT THE AUTHOR

Sloane Murphy is the author of the international bestselling series, The Immortal Chronicles, as well as a range of other paranormal and contemporary romance. Sloane lives in Peterborough, England, with her husband & fur baby and over the years, she has developed an unhealthy appreciation for cheesy YA Films, cupcakes and bad pop music. She adores fairy tales, ballet and all things supernatural, drinks far too much coffee, and watches an ungodly amount of Netflix. When she's not busy writing, she can be found exploring the world with her husband and chocolate Labrador.

If you would like to send Sloane an email, you can reach her at sloane@authorsloanemurphy.com

Want to sign up for her mailing list? You can sign up HERE

Or come join her reader group on Facebook, Sloanes Little Monsters

facebook.com/sloanemurphybooks

twitter.com/SloaneMurphyBks

instagram.com/sloanemurphybooks

bookbub.com/authors/sloane-murphy

ALSO BY SLOANE MURPHY

THE SEVEN REALMS SAGA

The Shadow Walkers Saga

(Reverse Harem Paranormal Romance)

A Crown of Blood and Bone

A Crown of Smoke and Ash

A Crown of Shadows and Secrets

A Crown of Thorns and Lies

A Crown of Fire and Wrath

A Crown of Pride and Ruin

The Shadow Weaver Series

(Menage Paranormal Romance)

Witch's Curse

Hunter's Heart

Demon's Blessing

The Shadow Queen Series

(Reverse Harem Paranormal Romance)

The Shadow Queen

The Shadow Legacies Series

(Rejected Mates Romance)

Luna Rising

THE IMMORTAL CHRONICLES SERIES

(YA Paranormal Romance. Complete Series)

Descent

Crash

Soar

Rapture

BLACK WATER ACADEMY SERIES

(Upper YA/NA Paranormal Romance. Reverse Harem)

Marked

Chosen

Hunted

DARK FAE DUET

(Paranormal Romance. Dark Fantasy)

Summer Princess

Winter King

OTHER AUTHORS AT HUDSON INDIE INK

Paranormal Romance/Urban Fantasy

Stephanie Hudson

Xen Randell

C. L. Monaghan

Sorcha Dawn

Sci-fi/Fantasy

Devin Hanson

Crime/Action

Blake Hudson

Mike Gomes

Contemporary Romance

Gemma Weir

Elodie Colt

Ann B. Harrison

Printed in Great Britain
by Amazon

79419831R00301